Little Eden

Book Three

A Magic Book opens the heart & expands the mind...

For Dad

KT King lives in England & has suffered with Myalgic Encephalomyelitis for over 25 years. A healer, psychic and ascension coach she has put her life experiences into fiction & created Little Eden as an escape place for the kind hearted & curious!

ISBN: 978-1-9164296-5-9
Little Eden – Haunted or Not

KT KING

Little Eden

Book Three

Haunted or Not

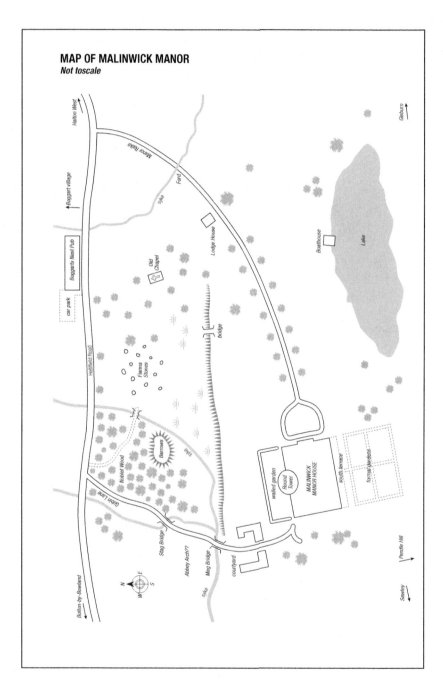

MAP OF MALINWICK MANOR
Not to scale

Halton West

Manor Road

Boggart village

Boggart's Nest Pub

car park

Hallfield Road

Bolton-by-Bowland

Syke

Ford

Lodge House

Old Chapel

Fianna Stones

Noblet Wood

Barrows

Gobin Lane

Stag Bridge

Abbey Arch??

Meg Bridge

Syke

bridge

Syke

courtyard

walled garden

Round Tower

MALINWICK MANOR HOUSE

south terrace

formal gardens

Boathouse

Lake

Gisburn

Pendle Hill

Sawley

N
W E
S

The story so far...

~ * ~

In the town of Little Eden, an ancient walled hamlet in the heart of London, a group of friends and residents are trying to raise enough money to save their beloved homes from sale and demolition. Owned by the Bartlett-Hart family for nearly 1,000 years, the sanctuary of Little Eden is facing its end-times.

When Lilly D'Or dies, leaving her beloved No.1 Daisy Place Café-Bookshop to her nieces, she also leaves a vacant position on the Little Eden Trust, which had kept the town safe for hundreds of years. Taking advantage of being down to three trustees, Jennifer Bartlett-Hart persuades her younger son, Collins, and great nephew, Lucas, to sell the town (worth over eight billion pounds in real estate) but her eldest son, Robert, is determined to save his ancestral home and protect the dragon portal which lies beneath the Abbey.

The dragon portals around the world are now open for business and the 2012 ascension of the planet and mankind is underway. The current guardians of the Earth, the Atlanteans, have to hand over control of human incarnation to the Pleiades Council. The transition can go smoothly or it can lead to Armageddon; no-one yet knows which it will be.

After some hard ball negotiations (or blackmail depending on how you look at it) Roberts', on and off, girlfriend, Shilty Cunningham, persuades Collins and Lucas to accept less money but on the understanding that they only have to wait two years to be paid. The money still has to be raised quickly - somehow.

Robert and his friends have managed to raise some of the money and to upgrade the Little Eden dragon portal, creating new keys of consciousness which can be grounded into the London lay lines so that the Pleiades can begin the mass incarnation of their Star Children. Patriarchal Egyptian spells have been cleared away and Mother Mary consciousness has been re-awakened but there is still much to do and more adventures, mysteries and mayhem yet to come.

Chapter 1
~ * ~

Shrouded by white mist and ever-changing clouds, Pendle Hill loomed out of the dark grey sky like a gigantic humpback whale eternally gliding through a sea of emerald-green fields.

It had not stopped raining for three days.

The meandering roads carved jet black channels through the rolling fells where high banks of sodden grass and dripping brush sheltered scatterings of bleating sheep, trapped by tumultuous rushing streams which threatened to engulf the twisting lanes. From within the shadow-filled valleys the undulating highways rose up and out onto fog laden moorland, where lonely barns, hardly visible through the swirling clouds, nestled in the ancient glacial crevices, their whitewashed walls flickering into view then disappearing just as quickly. High screens of tall trees hid small hamlets where grey stone cottages clung to the roadside, their weather beaten roofs and tiny windows smothered by exhaust fumes and mud giving them a sombre, dour aspect to the passer-by.

Robert, Lancelot and Jack had been driving for several days through the flooded Lakeland and were still cooped up in their Land Rover, listening to the radio and battling with the steamed up windows whilst navigating the narrow, twisting byways of the Forest of Bowland. The unrelenting rain crashed against the windscreen in such violent waves that the wipers, even at full speed, were unable to clear the deluge.

"Turn that radio off," Robert yelled over the din of the pounding rain, the crazy wipers and the raging music of Stone Sour, 'Say you'll Haunt Me'. "I can't concentrate. It's like driving through Niagara Falls. I can't see a bloody thing!"

Suddenly he caught site of the layby they had been looking for and only just made the turn in time. Slamming on the brakes he pulled up amongst the deep muddy furrows and skidded, nearly hitting a wooden sign which read:

Public Footpath Pendle Hill

The three of them wiped the condensation from the windows and peered out, but saw very little except water, and to be honest - more water.

"I don't think it's worth going up there today," Robert sighed.

"This whole trip's been a washout," Lancelot admitted from the back seat.

"By heck but it's grim up North!" Jack laughed.

"Lucy did warn us," Robert moaned. "She said it always rains in Lancashire. We might as well head straight for Malinwick Manor. We'll never get the tents up in this, even if we did find somewhere to pitch them."

"Come on, old chap," Jack said. "Give it a chance. It can't keep on like this forever. There'll be a gap in the clouds soon enough. Let's just sit here and wait for a bit."

"I've always wanted to visit Pendle Hill," Lancelot admitted. "It'd be a shame to come all this way and miss it."

The boys had left Little Eden a few days earlier with the idea of taking a short hiking holiday through the Lake District before descending into Lancashire to visit the mysterious Malinwick Manor which Robert had just inherited from his cousin, Roger Montgomery. A bit of wild camping and some hiking had been their plan, but so far they had spent most of the time playing darts and pool in local pubs and sleeping in B&Bs. The journey had become almost impossible at times with whole villages being flooded out along the way. Their forced detours had already taken them into unexpected territory. They hadn't even made it to the Lake District proper.

"I'd like to at least get some fresh air today if we can," Lancelot said, feeling cabin fever taking hold of him. He was starting to get the jitters.

Putting the radio back on they waited.

And they waited.

And they waited.

And finally, the rain began to slow.

A few minutes later, the heavy clouds parted, revealing blinding rays of bright sunshine which illuminated the sky for miles around with spectacular shafts of light, cascading down onto the surrounding untamed highlands and stone-walled fells. The drenched landscape shimmered into life as if sprinkled with a million tiny diamonds.

"There, you see!" Jack said, putting on his sunglasses. "Let's go quickly before it starts again."

The boys marched along the public footpath at a brisk pace. The imposing bulk of Pendle Hill was now bathed in the midsummer heat, and they took off their outer layers, wrapping their windbreakers around their waists to begin their ascent.

The summit was masked by low cloud but as they slowly climbed up the rocky path the panoramic view was breath taking. Overflowing streams and sykes glistened like silver ribbons wending their way through the craggy valleys. The green hills were gently stroked by racing cloud shadows rolling over the outcrops which were scattered with trees and burnished umber grasses.

Steam rose from their clothes as the raindrops began to evaporate. They paused for a few moments to breathe in the invigorating freshness of wet earth and sweet heather which filled the air. The path was uneven; the ground sodden, slippery and treacherous; it was slow going.

Finally, they reached the summit where a singular white, stone marker, in the shape of a monolith and encircled by blocks of stone, awaited every traveller. They stood for a while, admiring the expansive vista laid out before them. Deep black reservoirs lay amongst rolling fields, and long dark hills merged with the storm clouds on the far horizon which seemed to mark the edge of the world.

Alone on the hill, they felt an eerie, desolate sensation, and it wasn't long before the return of the storm could be seen rumbling towards them from the West.

"It feels like we've stepped into another world," Lancelot mused.

"It certainly does," Robert agreed. "It's as if we have entered an alternate dimension up here."

Even Jack had to admit the atmosphere was other-worldly amongst the clouds - spookily still and strangely secluded - there wasn't another soul to be seen.

The black sky tsunami, which had been heading their way, reached the hill sooner than they expected, suddenly enveloping them in a black wall of water.

Shrouded by sheets of rain they lost sight of each other and, as Jack called out to locate them, something narrowly missed hitting him in the face. He wasn't sure if it had been a bird or even a small rock.

Jack's disembodied voice drifted through the cloudburst, "Robert! Lancelot! Where are you? Walk towards my voice."

No one answered through the swirling din.

Uneasy, Jack called out again, and to his relief, he saw Robert and Lancelot appearing out of the hurricane of water towards him.

"We should try to make our way down," he yelled, but they couldn't really hear each other over the roar of the rain which bounced off the rocks so violently it hit them in their faces like shards of glass.

Gesturing to each other, they pressed on, carefully picking their way down the stone path but only a few yards further on they all stopped abruptly.

"What the f**k was that?" Robert exclaimed.

Over the din of the rain he had heard a sharp piercing sound.

"It sounds like metal scraping on metal," Jack shouted.

"There it is again!" Robert said.

The high-pitched noise cut through them all and set their teeth on edge.

Lancelot pointed up into the clouds. He thought it sounded as if it was coming from directly above them, but in the midst of the storm it was impossible to tell where anything was.

The strange, shrill noise became fainter as if moving away from them.

Blinded and deafened by rushing water, the mysterious noise had unnerved them, and they were all anxious to be on safer ground.

As they continued to descend, they often lost sight of each other, so kept calling out to make sure they were all still close by; then about halfway down, Lancelot suddenly slipped...

...he gashed his hand on a jagged rock trying to save himself from falling down the steep side of the hill...

..."F*ck! F*ck! F*ck!" he cried out to mask the pain searing through his right ankle and his hand. He came to rest against a large boulder, and feeling a little foolish, he attempted to get up. But his foothold wasn't steady, and he stumbled again - this time skidding further down the sheer slope, slamming against some jagged stones and falling amongst a large wet tuft of russet-coloured grass.

Realising he needed help, he shouted out to the others, only to find that his voice didn't carry on the stormy airwaves.

The pain in his ankle was starting to make him feel sick and dizzy.

He lay back against the mud and stones - unable to move.

As he gazed up at the blanket of grey, from which rain drops showered down upon him like millions of sharp pins, he almost passed out with pain. He began to feel as if he was slipping in and out of time. He couldn't believe his eyes when out of the amorphous sky appeared seven small silver balls of light, floating in a V formation, hovering above his head as if they were looking directly at him. The unidentified flying objects shimmered for a few moments and as he held them in focus, realising he could actually see them and he wasn't dreaming, they mysteriously melted, like liquid mercury, and slid downwards, merging with the shards of water. He covered his eyes, afraid the strange liquid might blind him, but when he looked through the crook of his arm, he saw the ethereal matter miraculously sloop back into perfect spheres and spin together in a disk before suddenly disappearing completely from view.

He felt something spinning on the top of his head.

He forgot where he was for a few moments.

A blinding white light seared through his eyes.

He passed out.

Robert and Jack shouting for him brought him back to consciousness, and he became aware of the hardness of the rocks and sliminess of the grass again. The smell of the land filled his senses, and he knew he was back in his own body.

"F**k!" Lancelot muttered again, as he tried, unsuccessfully, to push himself up. "Here," he answered as loudly as he could. "Over here."

Robert nearly slipped on the same muddy patch as Lancelot, but Jack managed to grab his arm to stop him sliding away. They helped each other down the perilous slope and finally found Lance.

Poor Lance's face was as white as a sheet, and they could see he was in terrible pain.

Alarmed, they helped him to his feet, but it was obvious that he couldn't put any weight on his ankle.

"Can you make it down?" Jack shouted. "It could be broken." He looked at his watch. "It's nearly five o'clock. I think we should get you down rather than go for help. You'll get pneumonia if we leave you here too long."

Robert agreed and helped Lancelot sit up on a boulder whilst Jack acted quickly and with purpose. He swiftly pulled out one of the poles, which were stiffening his rucksack, and cut off the straps to make a splint. Then he deftly strapped up Lance's ankle and bandaged his hand.

Only able to see about a foot in front of them at any one time, Robert and Jack supported their friend between them and then, very slowly and with great care, they descended through the maelstrom until, well over an hour later, they finally reached the layby and the shelter of the car.

Chapter 2
~ * ~

The wind-chimes tinkled like fairy bells as Lucy opened the door to the Daisy Place Health Food Shop. Thunder and lightning crashed and rumbled outside and she shook the raindrops off her pink umbrella and stamped the worst of the rain from her wellies. She was glad to be out of the storm, which was flooding the square and leaving ankle-deep puddles in the gutters.

The Health Food Shop always gave her a little thrill as if she was entering a magical shrine to Nature. She let herself float upon a wave of peace and tranquillity amongst the heady scents of dried herbs and exotic spices. Feeling an invisible cloak of relaxation draping itself over her, she took another deep breath and inhaled the restorative fragrances.

As she surveyed the brimming shop which, although at this moment was empty of customers, could never be considered void of stock, she was aware of a low humming sound coming from the air purifier which glowed with all the colours of the rainbow in turn. Soothing oriental meditation-music wafted gently through the mellow space, and she felt as if she was being healed just by being there.

As children, the Health Food Shop had always been such a fascinating and other-worldly place to her and her sister. They had imagined that the owner, Hector Livewell, (younger and full of vigour back then) was a wizard, and that his elderly mother was a white witch, selling potions and mystical elixirs.

The shop itself, having been a pharmacy since 1870, still boasted its grand mahogany medicine cabinets with tiny square drawers, each individually labelled, and a large, glass fronted counter which now overflowed with baskets of garlic, root-ginger and ripe avocados. Dried fruits, nuts, seeds and cereals were displayed in glass dispensers, from which you could scoop as much as you liked into a paper bag; and in the open fridge were sprouting greens, vegan cheeses and cartons of various milks. Hundreds of bottles of vitamins and minerals adorned the shelves, and if what you wanted wasn't there, Hector would order it for you.

Lucy was intrigued by a tester-jar of the latest face cream containing snail mucin; and trying a little on her hand, she sniffed it hoping it didn't smell of snails - which it didn't. Suddenly a flash of lightening jolted her out of her reverie, and she jumped with fright, thinking she had seen the face of Hector's mother looking at her through the internal window which gave onto the storeroom and office. Her heart stopped for a moment as she caught her breath and told herself it couldn't possibly have been Mrs Livewell as she had been dead nigh on twenty years.

She was relieved to see Hector, who wandered out from the back and greeted Lucy with his usual cheery smile. He offered her a bowl of dandelion-and-burdock boiled sweets. "I made them yesterday," he said with pride. "Took me sixteen goes to get them right, but here, try one, let me know what you think. I think I've got them just about perfect now."

Lucy gladly took one and popped it in her mouth. After a few moments she involuntarily screwed up her face in disgust and she couldn't help spitting it out into her hand.

Hector looked in the bowl as if some foreign body might have contaminated his delectable treats, but they were just his own, rather dreary looking, brown bonbons.

"I'm so sorry," Lucy said, embarrassed. "It was just...well...what's the word? ...Err..." she tried to think of way to put it without offending Hector..."Earthy! Yes, they are a little too earthy for me."

Hector took one and sucked hard, keeping it moving around his mouth, clacking it against his teeth as if he was tasting a fine wine. "Tastes jolly good to me," he said after a few moments.

Lucy tried to find somewhere to put her sticky sweet but couldn't see a bin, so reluctantly ended up putting it in her raincoat pocket. "Perhaps I'm used to much sweeter sweets, if you know what I mean?" she tried to explain, whilst also trying to get rid of the unwelcome, lingering taste from her tongue - it tasted like horse manure!

Hector nodded. "I think you must be right," he replied. "I haven't eaten sugar in over thirty years. At my cousins wedding, last year, I felt obliged to try a little piece of their cake and goodness me if it didn't taste absolutely rancid! But everyone else seemed to like it." He sighed. "We are conditioned from childhood to want sugar. If only there was rationing, as there was during the war and the ten years after, we'd all be a lot healthier and happier."

Lucy knew Hector wasn't actually old enough to remember the war but didn't like to argue. She had to admit to herself that she would be healthier if she didn't eat so many sugary cakes and biscuits, chocolates and sweets, and wished she had his will power.

Hector continued to suck on his very unsweet sweet and seemed so preoccupied with analysing the taste that he started to wander off into the back room as if Lucy was going to leave without buying anything. He was startled out of his trance by another bright flash of lightening, which was followed, almost instantly, by a deafening clap of thunder which made them both gasp.

"It sounds as if it's right above us," he said. "You're not afraid of storms, are you?" Lucy shook her head.

"My second cousin was hit by lightning three times," Hector told her.

"I thought lightening never struck the same place twice," Lucy replied, thinking once was unlucky never mind three times. "Was your cousin hurt?"

"Nearly died the first two times," Hector said, "Did die the third time."

"Oh, how awful, I'm so sorry," Lucy said, and they both looked up at the ceiling again as if half expecting a fork of lightening to hit the counter at any moment. They were both taken aback by the next great flash outside the window.

"I came for some things for Sophie," Lucy explained. "She rang you the other day to order some bits and you said they'd be here Wednesday?"

"Ah, yes," Hector replied, but he didn't look as if he knew where the order was. "She did, yes, she did, ah yes, she did," he muttered, whilst rapidly crunching the last of his dandelion and burdock. "Now, where did I put them? I know I had them, they came this morning, and I put everything in one bag." He looked under the counter and in various drawers, cupboards and baskets. "Don't worry, they are here somewhere," he assured her and then disappeared out the back after all.

Lucy wished he would hurry up; all this talk of storms had dispelled the relaxing atmosphere in the shop and she felt nervous instead.

Hector soon reappeared carrying - well, nothing!

Lucy was disappointed to see that he hadn't found the items. "Is that it?" she asked Hector, pointing to a bag which was sitting on the top of a pile of health magazines.

Hector looked at it, "Ah, yes," he exclaimed. "That must be it! I knew I had them here somewhere." He looked inside and reeled off the contents; "We have the usual Q10 and Magnesium for the migraines, Kelp for the thyroid, Spiralina for the gut. I suggested she try Turmeric for the pain and a multi-vitamin plus Echinacea for immunity. There's Arnica for the muscle aches, and as she told me she's been diagnosed with Fibromyalgia so I've put a free sample of Emu Oil in there for her too. It is such a shame no one understands Myalgic Encephalomelitis yet," he pondered. "I don't really know what to suggest for that except an exclusion diet and lots of rest."

Lucy was amazed he knew how to pronounce it. She just always called it ME or Chronic Fatigue.

"I've done research on it myself but it's a mystery," Hector admitted, shaking his head. "It seems to be a post-viral syndrome which either alters the brain chemistry or damages the nervous system, or perhaps both, creating constant symptoms of having a virus."

"It's like she has the flu or glandular fever all the time," Lucy nodded. "Some days are worse than others but it's always there. It's as if her body thinks it's fighting a virus all the time."

Hector nodded. "I tell everyone with any illness to give up sugar, wheat and related grains, dairy and red meat, poultry and eggs, caffeine and all acidic foods, as well as all deadly nightshade foods, processed carbohydrates and saturated fats. I believe a vegan diet is the only way to get well, whatever is wrong with you. Although if someone has digestive problems, they are best avoiding nuts, seeds, yeast based foods, legumes and citrus fruits as well."

Lucy couldn't really think of any foods which were left that one could eat! "Sophie has tried all sorts of exclusion diets and taken so many supplements I think she's tried most of them in her time," Lucy told him. She couldn't help thinking that a life without cake wouldn't really be worth living. "I think a little of what you fancy does you good from time to time," she laughed, but then stopped when she saw Hector was not amused.

Hector frowned. "Food is fuel and medicine for the body and the mind. Eating should not be used as an emotional crutch. Comfort eating is not good for you."

"You're right of course," Lucy admitted, "But Sophie has such a restrictive, isolated and boring life it doesn't seem fair to take away all her pleasures," she added. "Being almost housebound and in bed most of the time with chronic pain and exhaustion isn't fun."

Hector nodded. "I have a few customers with ME and chronic fatigue. I'm afraid one of them committed suicide the other month. They'd just had enough."

Lucy's heart skipped a beat at the thought of losing Sophie to suicide, and she made up her mind to ask Mrs B to make Sophie's favourite chocolate cake as soon as she got back to the cafe.

Hector looked at the bill and told her how much it had all come to.

"Being ill isn't cheap either," Lucy commented, shocked at how much it had cost.

She nearly jumped out of her skin again as a rumble of thunder shook the shop.

Hector didn't seem bothered about the price of his goods saying, "You can't put a price on health," and slipped a leaflet into the bag. "I'm giving a lecture on healthy eating this Friday at the Quaker House, you and Sophie should come along."

Lucy was relieved to be able to give him a genuine excuse, "I'm afraid we can't, we're going away this weekend," she told him.

"That's a shame. Are you going anywhere nice?" Hector asked her as he handed her the bag and she picked up her umbrella.

"I'm not sure yet," Lucy smiled.

"You're not sure where you are going?" Hector asked surprised, holding the door open for her.

"Oh, we know where we're going," Lucy told him, opening her umbrella out the door to shield herself before braving the storm. "We just don't know whether it'll be nice or not 'til we get there!"

Chapter 3
~ * ~

After having helped Lancelot back to the Land Rover, Jack ascertained that his ankle wasn't broken. "It's only a sprain, old chap," he told him. "It'll be fine in a day or two. Just stay off it and keep it elevated. We'll have to see if we can find you some crutches from somewhere. We'll ask at that pub, what's it called again?"

"The Boggarts Nest," Robert replied.

"Odd name," Jack commented, "What the hell is a boggart when it's at home?"

"Mr T told me it's some kind of creature from local mythology," Lancelot explained, and reaching over for his bag, he found the folder, full of information about the Manor and the surrounding area, which Mr T had put together for him. He looked through the many papers which included some illustrations of boggarts (they all differed from each other, so it was hard to tell which one was an accurate likeness). Talking distracted him from the pain so he carried on, saying, "It says here that a boggart is akin to a troll or a gnome only it is slimier and thinner. They are made out of mud and live in bogs; hence the name I suppose, and in some fairy stories they have sharp teeth and eat children. Mr T suggests we stay on the right side of them, or they may curse us."

"They sound a bundle of laughs - good job they're not real," Jack said, laughing at the idea whilst he typed the postcode of the public house into the Sat Nav. "This damned thing's not working," he said, exasperated.

"What do you mean it's not working?" Robert asked. "It was fine before."

"I mean it's not working," Jack replied, pushing all the buttons. "No signal by the looks of things."

"Great!" Robert said, also exasperated, "That's all we need."

"Didn't you bring a map?" Jack asked him.

"I thought the Sat Nav would be enough," Robert admitted, now wishing he hadn't put all his faith in modern technology.

Jack pulled out his phone, but he had no reception. "You'd think we'd been up Kathmandu not a paltry little hill in Lancashire," he said. "We're in the flipping twilight zone, what with strange noises and bloody boggarts." He had been cut off from civilisation in worse places than this, but he had felt uneasy since being on top of the hill. He couldn't put his finger on it - something just didn't feel right. The fog-laden hills and valleys seemed so ephemeral and eerie they inspired in him the oddest sensation that he was in a dream and that he might wake up at any moment to find himself in bed and not out in the wilderness of the Forest of Bowland after all.

"Mr T put some local maps in here," Lancelot said, "Although, he did say that the Manor doesn't appear on all maps," he added. As he unfolded them, some were old and ripped at the creases, some were more modern and in colour, and there was even a World War II military map which was one of the few denoting the existence of Malinwick Manor. "According to this map we need to head for Downham then Sawley until we reach Bolton by Bowland, then head north-east towards Halton West," he explained. "The pub should be outside the village of Boggart by Noblet with Malinwick just off Hellifield Road."

"That's a mouth full," Jack said. "What's the village called? Boggart or Noblet?"

Lancelot laughed. "There's the village of Boggart and the one next to it is called Noblet, and according to this map there was a medieval village called Malinwick, which isn't there now. Around here they seem to combine village names together quite a bit. According to these maps neither village is more than a small hamlet, although Boggart does have a church. Noblet looks as if it is mainly woodland. There seem to be a few farms dotted around the edges of Malinwick Manor, but no village to speak of anymore."

"Let's hope we can find this pub and the Manor," Robert said. As he carefully pulled away from the layby, the rain continued to lash against the windows making visibility almost zero. The roads were like rivers, and he couldn't even make out the hedgerows, ditches or dry stone walls on either side of him.

All of a sudden, a sharp bend came upon him, and something ran out across the road!

Robert swerved and scraped the side of the Land Rover along a barbed wire fence, coming to a stop and just narrowly missing a tree.

"What was that?" Lancelot called from the back seat.

"A sheep, no doubt," Jack suggested. "This place is teaming with the blighters."

"I don't know what it was," Robert admitted. It had looked more like a big cat. He agreed with Jack however that it was much more likely to be a sheep than a lynx, although he wasn't sure sheep could move that fast. "I bet the bodywork's ruined," he moaned, but didn't want to get out in the downpour to check. "I'll be glad to get to that damned pub or any civilisation," he muttered. Robert could feel the tension in his arms from holding onto the wheel so tightly, and he was getting a headache from squinting and concentrating so hard.

"It says here, in Mr T's notes, that there are often sightings of unidentified creatures in this area," Lancelot told them. "There have been sightings of big cats, aliens, ghosts and even a Yeti."

"Sheep, goats, cows, deer," Jack replied, "They must be all over the place. People just like a mystery, and out here, in this weather, I should think tourists 'see' all sorts of crazy things if they expect and want to."

A few miles on they came to a roadblock. Orange plastic barriers had been erected and they could just make out the blurry, flashing, blue lights of police cars and fire engines. Robert wound down the window and a policeman, wearing a long rain mac, peered in to talk to him. "You can't get through here," he told them. "Flooding! Where you headed?"

Robert explained about the Manor and The Boggarts Nest.

The policeman looked surprised. "You'll have get there via Gisburn," he explained. "Follow the A59 a few miles up an' it'll be on your left. Mind you, by the time you get there, they may 'ave closed it up there too if this deluge keeps up. You might want to head back towards Clithero. You'll like as not get cut off by tomorrow where you're going."

Robert thanked him and wound the window back up. "What do you think?" he asked the others. "Should we risk it?"

"Might as well," Jack suggested. "We've come this far. It'd be a shame not to make it to the Manor now. The rain can't keep up too much longer like this surely?"

They continued to drive through the walls of water and finally saw the signpost for Gisburn. The village was still passable, but once off the main road it felt as if they were in the middle of nowhere again. Along the one track country lanes it was hard to make out the signposts and they began to wish they had turned back after all.

Then suddenly, out of the sheeting rain, flashed the ugly grey face of a slimy boggart.

Robert slammed on the brakes.

The public house sign of The Boggarts Nest rattled and swung in the raging wind making the image of its gnarled and hideous face seem even more grotesque. They had missed the entrance to the carpark, so Robert did a U-turn and pulled up alongside the old stone building.

They all breathed a sigh of relief to see signs of human life.

Helping Lancelot hobble along, they headed towards the solid, two story building which had been first built as a coaching inn, but since the 19th Century had been clad in an austere, rather gloomy, Gothic Revival style facade. It squatted alone, tight up against the side of Hellifield Road. Longer than it was wide, it had several doorways along its front and many mournful, narrow windows set deeply into heavy, recessed, stone frames. A dreary grey slate, chimney-packed roof ran with rivers of water, and the lads were glad to shelter in the gable porch.

They were about to say hello to the stranger who was lurking by the door, when they were taken aback with fright - the person was not a person at all but a witch!

A very life like mannequin greeted them with an evil smile.

"What kind of place is this?" Jack asked, as they went through the double swing doors and were greeted by a warm blast of air. They shook the rain off their outdoor clothes and hung them up amongst the many other wet coats and cagoules which lined the damp-smelling vestibule. On a dimly lit table, overflowing with tourist leaflets, maps and local advertisements, a stuffed fox eyeballed them as if watching their every move. On the door into the bar an advertising poster caught their eye:

Psychic Nights
Every Thursday 8pm

They looked at each other with raised eyebrows. Walking through into the main room where they were hit by a cacophony of noise and overwhelmed by the potent odour of stagnant beer and centuries of stale tobacco. A motley crew of goths, wiccans, new age druids and a scattering of hippies filled the pub. The crowds seemed to ooze in and out of the thick stone walls, reappearing and disappearing into the shadows, as they came and went to the bar for more drinks. The laughing, talking, shouting and general merriment was deafening, backed by the 'Ballad for Dead Friends' blaring out from the speakers. The flagstone floor, worn into smooth dips in places, was sticky underfoot, and the heat from the log burner evaporated the damp off the customers clothing causing many of them to give off the faint whiff of wet dog. The low beamed ceiling, yellowed by smoke, was hung with hundreds of horseshoes and every beer mat ever produced. On shelves and half dressers were collections of old bottles, hideous Toby jugs and dented pewter tankards, all covered in layers of dust and cobwebs. The lights were few and dim, and the dark wooden bar stools, tartan covered chairs, and worn leather banquettes all seemed to blend into one amorphous mess.

The boys looked at each other, wondering whether it was safe to stay in such an alternative place. It wasn't their usual type of drinking establishment and they felt like intruders in a strange land.

Chapter 4
~ * ~

India and Minnie tucked into a healthy dinner of salmon stir fry in Lucy's kitchen. "I felt guilty after what Hector said to me today about food," Lucy admitted, "I thought I'd better try not to eat so much of..." she paused for a moment..."Well, so much of everything really."

Minnie frowned. "You mean there's no dessert?" she said, a little alarmed. Minnie ate dessert only when she was dining with Lucy and looked forward to her weekly treat.

Every Tuesday for years, Minnie, India and Lucy (and more recently Sophie - if she felt up to it) had had a mid-week meal together, taking it in turns to cook. Linnet used to come too but things were still emotionally strained between her and Minnie after their break-up and, whilst she was welcome, she had decided to stay away a while longer.

No.1 Daisy Place apartment above the Café-Bookshop is really the most delightful place to be and it is rare for there to be an evening without someone popping by for a chat and a cuppa (and of course a piece of cake). The beautiful living area and inviting kitchen are one big room with a delightful Victorian conservatory at the far end making the whole space light and bright even on the dullest days. Decorated in a cosy combination of shabby chic in the French and English country style, the friendly white painted furniture and snuggly sofas, which are scattered with big soft cushions and cosy hand-knitted throws, give the whole atmosphere such a welcoming and comfortable vibe it is like walking into a big hug. Once you are cuddled up on one of the big armchairs, your feet up on a velvet buttoned poof, a hot cup of tea in your hand, surrounded by the warming scent of the log burner and fresh flowers, there isn't a more agreeable or more enchanting place you would rather be.

"There's fruit salad," Lucy replied, as she produced a large, decorative glass bowl filled with strawberries, blueberries, melon, peaches and grapes.

"It looks delicious," India said.

"There is cream though isn't there?" Minnie asked hopefully.

Lucy laughed, "There's always cream here, you know that! What would you like? I've got whipped, squirty, single, clotted, double or ice-cream. Downstairs there's soya cream, coconut, almond or tofu too. Most of them come in low-fat versions as well."

"Single, normal, full-fat cream is just fine with me," Minnie giggled.

"There's no harm in cutting back a bit on the naughty stuff," India said, as Lucy produced a pretty, little jug of cream.

"That's rich coming from you," Minnie teased India.

"What?" India replied, and then realised she had a large glass of Chardonnay in her hand. She laughed. "It's not naughty if it's medicinal," she smiled.

"I think its red wine that's medicinal," Minnie grinned, "And in much smaller quantities."

"I comfort eat too much," Lucy admitted, as she poured a good helping of cream onto her fruit. "Since Aunt Lil' left, what with Linnet's problems, Joshua's death, Sophie getting worse and Little Eden being under threat, I'll be the first to admit I might have been a bit of a greedy guts lately." She sighed. "I think that's why Jimmy had that affair. I got too fat for him."

"Don't even go there!" Minnie exclaimed. "He'd have had an affair even if he was married to a supermodel. It was not your fault!"

India chimed in with her support, "He's just that type and you know it," she said. "He'd never be satisfied with whoever he had - like those men who cheat on beautiful women and no one else can understand why."

"Talking of men who don't know a good thing when they have it," Minnie said, "Is Sophie okay? I've not seen her for days. She's still coming with us at the weekend isn't she?"

Lucy shook her head. "Tobias ghosting her last week, after she finally told him about her having ME, has set her back emotionally. She tries so hard to stay positive but we are all struggling, and poor Sophie even more so. I can't imagine how it must feel to have no future and no hope of a cure. I sometimes think she'd rather have a terminal illness than something which steals your life yet doesn't kill you. It must be a bit like being under house arrest without hope of reprieve. I suppose I can't blame Tobi for pulling out, she could hardly ever go out on a date with him, and a day out just made her relapse for weeks afterwards, but he could have been more honest about it and not just stopped calling her."

"He seemed to like her so much," India said sadly, "You could see it in his eyes - he really liked her."

"I thought he was the one she'd been waiting for too," Minnie agreed. "He was handsome, intelligent, a snappy dresser…"

…"An idiot," India added.

They all laughed but Lucy was genuinely concerned about her sister. "I'm worried about her," she said, "She's really struggling to cope with the pain and the constant exhaustion. She says it's like having a hangover all the time, all day long, every day, and her whole body feels like one big bruise." Lucy almost burst into tears at the thought of her sister's life going to waste right before her eyes and she was powerless to stop it. Going to the fridge she brought out some left over chocolate cheesecake from the day before. "Sod it," she said. "Life's too short," and she gave each of them a large slice with cream on too!

"All the more reason why she should come with us this weekend," India said.

"I don't think I'm coming either," Lucy replied. "Sophie says she won't manage a whole weekend away, what with the travelling and the socialising. She'll be back in bed for a month at least when she gets back. I don't think I should leave her alone here and go without her."

"But you were so looking forward to it, "Minnie exclaimed. "You said yourself it's the first holiday you've had in years."

"Since what happened with Joshua, I'm really not happy about leaving Tambo and Alice either," Lucy said decidedly.

"Nothing bad is going to happen," India reassured her.

"A lot of bad things have happened here since Aunt Lilly passed away," Lucy replied. "You can't deny it."

They couldn't deny it.

"I thought the kids were going to stay with Elijah and Iris?" India said.

"If there's anyone you can trust to keep them safe it's Iris," Minnie added.

"I know, I know," Lucy admitted. "It's just…"

"Do you actually want to go?" Minnie quizzed her.

"Of course," Lucy replied.

"Then you should still come," India said, and Minnie nodded in agreement. "We just need to find a solution which works for everyone - a compromise."

Lucy sighed. "When did life become so complicated?" she mused. "If only Aunt Lil' was here." She looked at the empty plate of cheesecake and felt sick. She wished she hadn't eaten it after all.

"Have Tambo or Sophie said they don't want you to go?" India asked.

"No, they both want me to go," Lucy admitted. "Tambo is looking forward to it. Iris is going to take them on the London Eye and to the Tower of London, and Sophie thinks it'll do me good to get away for a few days."

"Well, then," India replied, "You have to come, and we won't take no for an answer; will we Minnie?"

Minnie shook her head. "I want us all to go," she added. "If we can just find a way to persuade Sophie to come with us," she pondered. "If only we had one of those camper vans she could sleep the whole way there and back."

India thought for a few moments. "I have an idea! Wait here, I'll be back in moment." Without explaining she went out onto the roof terrace to make a phone call.

Lucy put the kettle on and Minnie flopped down into her favourite armchair. "What with me, and you, and now Sophie, it's like we're the broken hearts club or something," Minnie said. "All of us are single, and I for one do not feel ready to mingle."

"I want a break from relationships too," Lucy admitted, "And I think Sophie has given up hope altogether of ever finding someone to love." She was just pouring the tea into delicate china teacups when India came back into the room with a big smile on her face.

"Guess what I've just arranged?" she said triumphantly.

"What?" they both asked her at the same time.

"The perfect transport so we can take Sophie in comfort and style," India replied.

Minnie clapped her hands together in glee, "You've got us a campervan? How exciting! I hope it's a proper old Volkswagen?"

"Not exactly," India smiled.

"Oh," Minnie said, a little disappointed.

"But I did get Bob Tackle to lend us a car," India explained.

"We're going in a wedding car?" Minnie giggled.

"No way!" Lucy exclaimed, "Which one?"

"Your favourite," India said to Minnie.

"Not the white, vintage, London taxicab?" Minnie grinned.

"The very one!" India replied.

"Bob pimped it big style - it's like a motorised palace in there!" Minnie explained. "It's got two bench seats in the back, all quilted in white leather, so Sophie can lie down and sleep all the way if she needs to!"

"Exactly!" India agreed. "She'll feel like a queen being chauffeur driven all the way by yours truly."

"I still think such a long day on the road would be too much for her," Lucy said. "It's about eight hours drive isn't it?"

"Already ahead of you there," India said. "I thought, why don't we set off tomorrow evening, and stop halfway at a spa hotel for the night? We can lounge around in the morning and still get to the Manor for late afternoon as planned! The boys are having a holiday out of this, why not us too?"

"I don't want to be the gloom in the room again but how do we afford a spa hotel?" Lucy asked, as she handed them both their cups of tea and, as she was starting to feel stressed and excited at the same time, she opened a box of Devlin's chocolate truffles.

"Not a problem," India said happily. "I have vouchers! I won them at the WI raffle at Christmas. They can be used at all sorts of places. They run out next month. I don't know why I didn't think of it before!"

"Brilliant!" Minnie said. "This is getting more and more exciting by the moment. I can hardly wait!"

"Do you think Sophie will say yes?" India asked Lucy.

Suddenly, they all jumped with fright and nearly spilt their tea in their laps.

From the shadows in the doorway, Sophie appeared, looking like death warmed up in her dishevelled pyjamas and winter slippers (which she had to wear even in the middle of summer).

"Good god! You made me jump!" Lucy said to her sister.

"Sorry," Sophie replied, and came to sit on the sofa. "I wanted to be sociable," she explained, yawning and closing her eyes with exhaustion. "Keep talking, I'll just listen if that's okay."

Lucy made her a cup of tea and looking at the empty cheesecake plate. She felt a bit guilty that she hadn't saved some for Sophie; but it didn't matter as Sophie was too tired to eat anyway.

India told Sophie of the plan.

In her mind, Sophie really, really, wanted to go, but her physical body would never do what she wanted it to do. "It's so kind of you to go to so much trouble and cost to include me," she told them, "But you'll have a much better time without having to look after me."

"The way I see it is, we all get an unexpected stay at a spa hotel and get to ride in the plushest car in the world. So you've done us a favour really!" Minnie told her.

"We don't want to go without you," India said.

"Thank you," Sophie replied, with tears in her eyes. She felt so lucky to have such amazing friends and knew that not many people in her situation were so fortunate.

"So you'll come?" Lucy asked her.

"Sounds like the best weekend away ever!" Sophie replied, sipping her tea - half excited about it and half dreading it at the same time.

Chapter 5
~ * ~

In The Boggarts Nest, a girl of about twenty years old, with long blue hair and an outlandish number of body piercings, lurched over to the boys through the throng (I say lurched because she was wearing such oversized, studded, knee high, black leather boots that she had trouble picking her feet up). "You 'ere for tha solstice?" she asked them, having to shout over the din in the overcrowded room.

"The solstice?" Jack asked her.

She nodded over to a flyer on the wall:

Happy Litha
Annual Solstice Celebrations
The Fianna Stones, Malinwick Manor
Alban Hefin Bonfire Ceremony led by Druid Master Grainne
Birchwhistle
Rendezvous 21st June Midsummers Day 4am at The Boggarts Nest,
Hellifield Road
Camping and refreshments available
Advance booking advised

"No," Robert told her in a raised voice, "We're actually here to visit Malinwick Manor."

The girl looked taken aback, as if she was suddenly afraid of them. Before they could ask her anything else she vanished.

Baffled by her sudden disappearance, they prised their way through the mob to the bar and tried to catch the attention of the barwoman who seemed unable to keep up with the demand. She kept yelling to someone in the back to come and help her, but no one ever appeared.

Whilst they waited, a woman, dressed in long flowing gown with tinkling bells dangling from her waist, shimmied her way between the masses and leant over the end of the bar. Seemingly unaware of her invasion of personal space she shoved her craggy face a little too close to Lancelot's. Her unruly, shaggy mane draped itself over his arm and her eyes pierced his with a searing feline-like gaze.

Lancelot pulled away from her - so close was she that he thought she might try to kiss him, or worse, spit on him. He recoiled even further when, opening her dry, bright orange lips, her breath nearly knocked him out with its rancid combination of cigarette smoke and red wine.

"You've come to take back the stones," she whispered loudly, almost touching his cheek with hers as she did so.

"I beg your pardon?" Lancelot replied.

"The Fianna Stones," she hissed.

Suspiciously, and slightly sensually, she eyed up the three boys making them feel a little violated.

"The… what?" Lancelot asked - he couldn't quite hear her over the deafening background noise.

"The sacred stone circle. The dragon portal," she replied.

"Oh, you mean the stone circle at Malinwick Manor?" he said, and turning to Jack he explained, "She thinks we have come to see the stone circle in the grounds of the Manor."

"I didn't know there was one," Jack replied.

"We are the new owners of the Manor," Lancelot told the woman, whilst still trying to avoid actually touching her.

Suddenly, she pointed an accusing finger at them saying, "You think you will take back the ring site, but you are mistaken. You have no power here. The witches will never give up the lay lines, not even to you."

Lancelot looked at her in amazement and wonder - he didn't know what to think!

What they didn't realise was that the woman was psychic, and she wasn't seeing them merely as they appeared to be to everyone else. She had the gift of second sight and could see their spirits. She saw their astral bodies, which were dressed in dark robes from head to toe, their eyes shining blue-white from within the blackness of their billowing hoods, and a glowing golden cross flashed across their pupils. She knew they were working with King Arthur and the Holy Spirit.

"I don't know who you are madam," Lancelot said, as politely as he could, "But we are simply here to have some supper and see the Manor, so if you don't mind…"

But she interrupted him…

…"You bring the new energy. The galactic energies - the energies of the Star Children." She almost spat the words out as if they were poisonous. Then she laughed at them as if she thought very little of the new matrix. "The Siriens won't let you take control of this planet," she added with

26

authority, "Nor will the old guard, not without a fight."

Then she stopped laughing…

…Astrally, the boys had stood up, thrown off their cloaks and revealed their shining armour beneath. Lancelot had drawn his spiritual sword which shimmered with the new matrix light. He held the sharp tip against her throat and then, with one quick swipe, he cut through the glamour which had made her look like a woman. Uncloaked, she shrank to the size of a small child and squatted on the floor with grey, frog like skin and bulging eyes.

She was a boggart.

Realising they were far more powerful than her, she scurried away in fear.

Not knowing consciously what he had done, Lancelot was just relieved she had gone.

The boys looked at each other, thinking that this was the weirdest place they had ever been in.

If it hadn't been the only place for miles around and blowing a gale outside, they'd have left as fast as they could.

Luckily help arrived. A barman came over with a big smile, which matched his big bald head, and apologised for keeping them waiting. He could see they had nothing to do with the pending pagan celebrations and suggested they come into the snug where it was much quieter, and where some locals were supping their ale in peace.

"Don't pays too much attention to our Meg," the barman told them. "She's our resident psychic - sees things others can't. I've told 'er afore not to bother the customers with 'er shining but she gets things into 'er head and blurts 'em out."

"Are there always this many people for the solstice?" Robert enquired, still shouting a little loudly as they went into the snug - the residents looked up - it was quiet now and he had no need to raise his voice.

The snug had a large open fireplace at one end where a fire was burning brightly. Although it was cosy, it was also gloomy - the few lights seemed thickly coated in layers of sticky dust. Elderly men, sitting on wooden chairs and a couple of high backed pews in front of scruffy tables of different sizes, were dressed for working in the fields, and they sat in silence; some playing dominos, some taking the occasional sip of their ale, and some just sitting together in quiet contemplation.

"Ay," the barman replied, as he pulled pints of Red Ram and Scraggy

Neck. "There's maybe more 'ere than usual. This year's special. Some believes this solstice is a day of reckoning."

"What does that mean?" Jack asked. He could see the handful of men looking up from their drinks - they knew what the barman meant - but without commenting they resumed their absent-minded drinking.

"Armageddon for witches," the barman replied, handing them their drinks. "Meg's been on about it for weeks, sayin' white knights and aliens a' coming to take back the stones."

"She sounds like she's lost her marbles," Jack said.

The barman shrugged. "When you lives 'round 'er you comes to understand tha' be more goes on than meets the eye," he said. "I seen things. We all seen things. Some doesn't like to talks about it," he laughed and then added, "An' some does nowt but talk about it!"

Robert couldn't help noticing the barman's tattoo sleeves. On one of them was a red and white rose entwined above a golden chalice with two silver crossed swords flanking a large crown. Perched inside the top of the crown was a white dove with an olive branch in its mouth. Robert knew those images - he had seen them in a stained glass window in Little Eden Abbey. He had a strange feeling that the people here were old souls, steeped in the karma of the old order, and fiercely protective of their spiritual culture.

"Tha'll be wanting rooms and some'at to eat?" the barman asked. "I ain't got no rooms tonight mind you. Tha's can have a pitch in back field if tha's got a tent. There's some hotpot left if you'd like some - homemade by the missis."

The boys were glad to get some hot food, although they didn't relish putting up their tents outside in the howling weather.

"Do you have a phone I could use?" Lancelot asked. "We don't seem to be able to get any signal around here."

The barman laughed along with three men who were sitting on the table nearby who had overheard the conversation. They looked as if they had just walked off their farm, still wearing their woollen waist coats and heavy boots, their large and rough hands stained with mud.

"Tha's no signal for miles," the barman replied. "I've a public phone on t'wall near back door."

"Dunt work," one of burly men piped up. He looked about seventy years old and had an uncanny resemblance to the other two chaps who were drinking with him. Lancelot deduced they were likely three generations of the same family.

"What's that Trev'?" the barman asked him.

"I tried phoning her indoors," (by which he meant his wife) Trevor explained. "Likely the lines a' down due t' storm," he looked at Robert and added, "We's not had rain like this since 1980's. Reckon we'll be cut off by mornin'." Trevor suddenly stood up and downed the last of his beer. "Sup it up," he told the other two, "Burra be geddin' back."

"Tha' be reet," the middle aged man agreed.

"Do you know a lady by the name of Mrs Ada Mould?" Lancelot asked them.

As the three men put on their heavy wax coats, which, being damp, stank strongly of horse manure. The middle-aged man asked, "You ghost tourists?"

"Actually, I have just taken possession of Malinwick Manor," Robert told them.

This time everyone overheard and they looked up in surprise.

Trevor chuckled.

"What's funny about that?" Lancelot asked them.

"Tha'll needs the luck of the Irish with that awd place," he replied.

"And wi' Ada Mould too," the youngest man added with a grin.

"We are expected at the Manor tomorrow," Lancelot explained. "Do you know how we can get in touch with Mrs Mould to see if we can go there tonight instead?"

"Ada'll be at th' Lodge," the barman told them. "I wouldn't advise yous staying there 'specially not on a night like this," he added. "No one stays tha' after dark on account of the haunting. All come scurrying back here." He laughed. "We has sweep stakes on how long the tourists'll stay, don't wes lads?"

"Ay," Trevor smiled.

"Bet on it, Father?" the younger man asked his dad, and slapped a five pound note down on the table. "I bets eleven," he said.

"Eleven twenty an' 'eres a tenner," Trevor said, producing a ten pound note from his inside pocket.

"Eleven fourty-five," the middle aged man laughed and waved his money in the air.

"What's tha' takin'?" the younger man asked the barman.

"I'll give 'em 'til twenty past twelve," he replied, and wrote the times down by their initials on the blackboard next to the bar. The others in the snug started shouting out times and laid down their money too. No one picked any later than half past midnight.

A little shocked and embarrassed, Lancelot asked how they could get to the Manor anyway.

"Tha'll not git t' Lodge bys Manor Raike nows," Trevor told them. "Tha's like as not ha' take Gobin Lane but tha' knows tha' cannit drive o'er Meg Bridge."

"What's wrong with Meg Bridge?" Jack asked.

"Not been safe to drive o'er fur years," the middle man replied. "Wood's rotten. Park under awd Abbey arch and walks it from theres, but like as not it'll be flooded an' all."

"Why not pitch up 'ere tonight," the barman said. "Go in't morning?"

"I'd not go near that place if tha paid me," the younger man said.

"A few ghost stories won't hurt us," Jack said, a little exasperated at the superstitious locals.

"Burra believe me," Trevor said, "Tha's rather camp out in't hurricane than stays tha night in that place."

Whilst they waited for their hotpots to arrive, Robert headed down a long, fusty corridor towards the men's room. He dodged the occasional goth and biker as it was a squash for more than two people to walk side by side and, standing against the wall to let a couple of druids go by, he noticed some black and white photographs all mounted in the same black frames. One maudlin image in-particular caught his eye. It was a portrait of a small, plump woman wearing a long, black, mourning dress and strange cape-like headdress. Behind her stood the faint but discernible figure of a man who seemed to have his hands on her shoulders. On closer inspection it was clear that his hands were incorporeal and were those of a spirit not a living person. The gentleman standing behind her was a ghost.

Robert was so transfixed by the disturbing image that he almost jumped out of his skin a moment later!

"Good god man!" Robert exclaimed, as Jack put a hand on his shoulder. "You scared me half to death." His heart began racing, which happened a lot lately, and he was still afraid he might have a heart attack even though the doctor had assured him his heart was fine. He regained his composure and nodding towards the strange photograph, he asked Jack, "Who does that man remind you of?"

"That's Abraham Lincoln," Jack laughed.

"Or the spectre of him," Robert replied.

They both looked more closely at some of the other ghoulish images.

Robert shuddered involuntarily when he realised that amongst the grandly dressed family gatherings, some of the people were actually corpses, made to look as if still alive, propped up in her best dress or his best suit. All the macabre photographs had something in common. "They're either of spirits or corpses in all of them," he said.

Jack laughed, then said, in a spooky childlike voice and rolling his eyes for dramatic effect, "I see dead people."

Robert was spooked and the hairs stood up on the back of his neck. "I think I'd rather take my chances at the Manor than stay in this place. It gives me the creeps," he admitted. He couldn't help feeling uneasy. There was something about this place that was out of balance and sinister. He knew he wasn't going to get much sleep tonight wherever they stayed.

~ * ~

<Van_Ike@hauntedornottv.com>

Dear Mr Bartlett-Hart

Due to our recent successful business venture 'Finding Frith' I take the liberty of contacting you regarding Malinwick Manor which I believe has recently come into your possession.

Malinwick Manor is of great interest to the international paranormal investigative community and I would consider it a great favour if you would allow myself and my team an opportunity to film there.

We have planned to film at the Manor several times but have not yet been able to co-ordinate dates which were suitable for everyone concerned. I have heard that you intend to visit the Manor yourself the weekend of the summer solstice, which would be a perfect opportunity to make a special Haunted or Not episode about your visit. The Network is interested in the idea and is offering substantial royalties which I am sure would benefit your Little Eden Fund.

If you are interested in this project please contact me as soon as possible.

Yours sincerely,
D Van Ike

<LBHsec@littleeden.co.uk>
to Van Ike

Dear Mr Van Ike

Further to our correspondence regarding the Manlinwick Manor project, I am returning the contract you kindly sent via registered post today. I draw your attention to some minor alterations which are annotated for your convenience. Please note that Mr Robert Bartlett-Hart requires full consultation and final decision on the final cut and will in no way sanction the use of any false historical information or defamatory content which may in anyway damage the Bartlett-Hart family, the Montgomery family or any of their associates.

I invite you to accompany Mr Robert Bartlett-Hart on a visit to Malinwick Manor from Friday 22nd June to Sunday 24th June. You may arrive after 2pm and will have limited access to the buildings and the grounds. We request however that Mr James Pratt also known as James Hollywood is not included in your team due to the attendance of Miss Lucy Lawrence.

I am informed that dinner, breakfast and lunch can be provided by the caretakers on site although the accommodation may not be to a high standard. Please inform us immediately as to the number in your team (we can accommodate up to five of your people).

I enclose a map and directions. I am reliably informed that the nearest accommodation, telephone, internet access and catering is in the public house, The Boggarts Nest in the nearby village of Boggart by Noblet with Malinwick.

Yours sincerely,
Birgitta Jensen
Secretary to Mr Lancelot Bartlett-Hart

<Van_Ike@hauntedornottv.com>

Dear Mr Bartlett-Hart

I and a party of two regular team members and one guest will rendezvous with you and Mr Robert Bartlett-Hart at 2pm Friday 22nd June at Malinwick Manor and gladly accept your offer of accommodation and meals.

As to your email this morning, I can assure you that James Hollywood will not be one of the party attending and understand your wish for him to remain absent due to the presence of Miss Lucy Lawrence in your own party.

The members of the team are as listed below:
Director and Producer/Presenter - Derek Van Ike
Researcher/Camera - Carrie Seeker
Camera/Sound and Professor of Parapsychology - Dr Zac Wolfman
Guest Psychic Investigator - Kaya Ashburner
I look forward to the event with much anticipation.

Yours sincerely,
D Van Ike

<Van_Ike@hauntedornottv.com>
to Carrie

Carrie
We're on for the solstice weekend at Malinwick. Cancel everything else and get Wolf on to it. I'll give you details nearer the time but you have to be there for 2pm on 22nd June. Accoms' and food included. Kaya Ashburner is joining us. I told Lancelot that Jimmy won't be part of it because his ex doesn't want him there so I'm coming instead.

V

<Carrie@hauntedornot.com>
to Van Ike

On it. Send directions. Better arrange alternative accommodation in case we can't stick it all night at the Manor. I hear no one ever makes it past midnight.

Carrie

<Van_Ike@hauntedornottv.com>
to Carrie

We'll all stick it out from dusk 'til dawn or there'll be hell to pay. Our reputations are all on the line.

V

<LBHsec@littleeden.co.uk>
to Dootson

Dear Mrs Mould and Mr Dootson
Further to our telephone conversation, I can now confirm that there will be 11 people needing accommodation and catering.

We require the house to be comfortable and clean for all guests. Dinner, bed and breakfast, lunch and afternoon tea will be required over the three days.

The fee re the agreed payment terms for the extra work you are undertaking on our behalf will be paid by bank transfer on Monday 18th June.

As to your enquiries regarding the future plans for the estate, Mr Bartlett-Hart is yet to make any decisions but will let you know as soon as possible as regards your positions.

Yours sincerely,
Birgitta Jensen
Secretary to Lancelot Bartlett-Hart

<Dootsonguidedtours@hotmail.com>
to LBHsec

Dear Mr Bartlett-Hart
We will prepare the house but best you book rooms at the Boggarts Nest, in Boggart village.

No one stays all night at the Manor because of the paranormal activity.

We has been caretakers for the Manor since 1968 and the Lodge House is our home. We was promised by Mr Montgomery that we can stay here for the rest of our lives. We hope Mr Bartlett-Hart will stick to this arrangement.

Arthur Dootson and Ada Mould

Chapter 6
~ * ~

At the spa hotel, halfway up the motorway, the girls had had a relaxing evening and a very delicious buffet breakfast. Feeling as light as a feather and as clean as a whistle, they packed up their things ready for the rest of the journey further up North.

"Still no answer from Jack," Lucy said fretfully, as she checked her phone for the millionth time. "I hope they're alright."

She packed the rest of her suitcase and zipped it up.

"Maybe they don't have a signal," India suggested. "I get the impression from Mr T that the area around the Manor is a bit remote."

"Perhaps," Lucy said anxiously, "I hope nothing awful has happened to them."

She txted Tambo again to check he and Alice were safely with Iris, and then txted Iris to double check.

"Tambo won't thank you for txting him every twenty minutes. Everyone is going to be fine," India told her.

Lucy was about to txt Iris again when India took the phone off her saying, "Stop it! You'll drive us all crazy."

Lucy laughed and taking the phone back, she put it in her pocket. "Alright!" she said, putting her hands in the air to show she had no phone.

Wheeling their suitcases behind them, Minnie, India, Lucy and Sophie headed down in the hotel lift. Lucy snook a quick look at her phone again then realised India could see her in the mirror and quickly put it away.

At Reception, as India paid, Lucy's phone pinged. "Tambo and Alice are having fun," Lucy told the others. "They're having brunch at the Juice Bar before heading off into the city. I'll just txt Tonbee and see if the café is okay."

India reached over and took Lucy's phone from her again. "The café will be just the same as it was half an hour ago and half an hour ago before that," she said exasperated. "If they need you, they'll txt you. Now, for goodness sake, try to chill out and enjoy yourself."

"Sorry," Lucy said. "I'll try."

"I didn't realise you were such a control freak," Minnie said to Lucy.

"I'm not a control freak! I just worry about people, that's all," she replied.

"Well, let's worry about the people we are with," India suggested, and glanced over at Sophie who was looking pale and as if she was

35

about to pass out.

They helped Sophie with her bag as they headed back to the car. "Thanks to your superb planning and the comfiness of the car I'll be okay," Sophie replied, pretending to not be fighting for every thought, breath and movement. "And thanks to Minnie's extra pillows and cushions - it's like a gypsy caravan rather than a London cab!" She didn't mention that she had a brain fog, nausea and was struggling to walk. She had drugged herself up to her eyeballs with pain killers and was determined to enjoy herself as much as was humanely possible. This trip was a rare treat and she wanted to make the most of every second.

Minnie giggled as she tucked Sophie into the quilts and blankets she had put in the car for her. "I wanted you to feel as if you were floating to the Manor on a cloud."

"I certainly am," Sophie smiled, and was glad to lie down again.

Handing Lucy a leaflet she had found in the tourist advertising rack at reception, India got into the driver's seat, and they all strapped themselves in. The leaflet was promoting ghost tours of the Manor. The horrific image on the front, of a blood stained hand about to strangle a beautiful lady, made Lucy think of the Hammer House of Horror films. She began to read the leaflet out loud to the others - it went like this:

Dare you spend a night in the most haunted house in the World? The terrifying, bone chilling, horrifying, spine tingling Malinwick Manor awaits your pleasure and your fear!

Secretly situated in the mysterious Forest of Bowland, famous for witches, unexplained phenomena and UFO's, Malinwick Manor is said to be the most frightening location on Earth. Nowhere else has been witness to so many ghastly, hideous and terrible supernatural events.

No one has ever dared stay after the stroke of midnight in this haunted house..."

"…Hold on," Sophie interrupted. "I don't think we should read too much about the Manor before we get there."

"Why not?" India asked.

"Because it'll make us afraid and suggestible," Sophie explained. "The less we know about what we might encounter the better, don't you think? Otherwise, our imaginations will run wild based on what we expect to see. I mean, we all knew it had a reputation for being haunted, but best not work ourselves up into a tizzy before we even get there."

"What do you mean? Is there really something horrible there?" Minnie asked, a little alarmed, whilst looking at the leaflet which Lucy had passed her through the glass partition. "I thought all that was just make-believe to attract the tourists."

"I'm sure it's all made up," Sophie reassured her. "But if you think you're going to see the ghost of Roger Montgomery walking headless in the hallway, then with every shadow you see, every crack or creek you hear, every door that bangs or curtain that moves, you'll imagine it might be him come back from the dead to frighten you."

"Oh, don't say that," Minnie pleaded - she was beginning to feel very uneasy.

"It's all hype," India called from the front of the cab. "I bet every haunted house claims to be the most haunted house in the world just to pull in the visitors. Lancelot said the Manor makes quite a tidy profit from ghost tours. It helps pay for the caretakers' salaries, but it's all just hype for the visitors, like the Little Eden Ghost Tour."

"That's what I thought," Minnie said, a little relieved, but she couldn't shake off the eerie feeling she had that there might be something to be afraid of at this spooky Manor.

The girls settled into their cosy cab, playing their favourite songs on the stereo. When 'I will Survive' by Gloria Gaynor came on they all sang along thinking of all the men (and women) who had done them wrong!

As they reached the Lancashire border, they were enveloped in the torrential rain which had been flooding the area for days now. Their journey slowed down somewhat as India tried to navigate the traffic. She was only able to see the end of the bonnet most of the time as the rain crashed onto it then splashed up onto the windscreen, as if buckets of water were being thrown at the car. When they overtook lorries, it was if they were driving through a deafening waterfall. "If this keeps up, we'll never make it by mid-afternoon," India said, shouting over the noise of the rain and the windscreen wipers which were going full pelt.

Three hours later, they pulled over at a motorway service station to re-fuel and go for a wee. It was just a garage and a small, outdated café - more like a truck stop.

"Shall we have a cuppa and cake here?" Lucy suggested. "If we're behind schedule, who knows when we'll find that pub the 'whatsit nest' and meet up with the boys. There's still no answer from any of them. They really can't have any signal."

Braving the downpour, they ran to the café entrance and were greeted by a waitress, wearing a black uniform and white apron, who seated them at a small, round table adorned with a wipe-clean, red gingham cloth and a small vase of plastic flowers. Lucy wasn't keen on the place. It smelt of a combination of dust, stale chip fat and cabbage. The cloth might have been wipe-clean, but it didn't look as if it was wiped very often, and there was half an inch of grime on the fake flowers. There were no other customers, and looking around, they realised that the café was partly an antique shop. The naïve pictures, old fashioned vases, various knickknacks and curios on the dressers and shelves were all for sale.

The waitress, as she brought their order, overheard India mentioning how, according to the map, they would find The Boggarts Nest on Hellifield Road outside of Sawley. "You'll not get close to there this weekend," she told them. "Radio says flash floods. Not passable there now an' maybe not for several days."

The girls were horrified.

"Is there another way there?" India asked the waitress. "We've come all the way from London."

The waitress shrugged. "I don't know that area real well," she admitted. "That pub, The Boggarts Nest, it's famous for witches an' we gets a lot of wiccans an' druids through here on their way up for midsummer. We was rushed off our feet yesterday. You might get there if you come at it from Halton West. Radio says A59's still open going East."

"Thank you," India said. "We'll try going to…Halton West or East…did you say? I'll put it in the Sat Nav. We'll find it."

"Ay, Halton West," the waitress said again. "Your Sat Nav'll not work up there," she added. "Phone and t'internet signal is rubbish up there too."

"No phone signal?" Lucy said in alarm.

"Around Pendle and alike, it's patchy at best," the waitress explained. "I gets customers complaining about it all the time. Some say its 'cause of all the restless spirits an' aliens messing with the signal."

"No signal?" Lucy muttered under her breath again and began to fidget with anxiety. "How'll I get hold of Tambo?" she said fretfully.

"If you wants to make a call I'd do it from here," the waitress suggested. "Like as not you'll not be able to once you gets up there. An' if you wants a map they's on the counter."

"Ring Tambo and Iris now and tell them you might be incommunicado over the weekend," Sophie suggested to Lucy.

"But what if he needs me?" Lucy replied, with a look of sheer panic on her face. "What if something happens? We'd better go back."

"There was a time before mobile phones," Sophie reminded her sister. "We didn't have them when we were kids, and we were okay. We walked home from school, we played in the street, we didn't wear bike helmets and we went out in the morning and didn't come back 'til we were hungry."

"Ah, those were the days!" Minnie sighed. "I remember we'd go into the woods to climb trees, swing off ropes, play in the fountain in the park, roller-skate around the World Peace Centre…we'd stay out all day with some sandwiches and a can of ginger beer. Kids don't seem to have that kind of freedom anymore, do they?"

"You travelled through Africa without a phone, and Aunt Lil' and I didn't think something terrible had happened every day whilst you were gone," Sophie reminded Lucy. "Tambo and Alice will be as safe as houses with Elijah and Iris, and a little independence is good for them - it teaches self-reliance and self-confidence. You don't want them growing up thinking they are not capable of looking after themselves, do you?"

"I suppose," Lucy agreed, but she wasn't too happy about it. Going out into the car park, she sheltered under an overhang, to phone home whilst she still could.

"Did you hear what that waitress said about witches and UFO's?" Minnie said as she stirred her mug of tea. "It sounds too spooky for my liking up there." She looked around the café and thought that it was rather spooky in there too. A painting of a little boy, with tears rolling down his cheek, gave her the willies. "Maybe we should just go back to the hotel and then go back home tomorrow after all?"

"We can't just not turn up at the pub," India said. "The boys are expecting us, and we have no way of contacting them. We'll be at least two hours late as it is. They'll be worried about us already. We'll be fine. We're nearly there now. Once we get to the Manor, we'll be cosy and warm, and even if there is a bit of stormy weather it won't matter. The house sounds big enough to keep us occupied inside the whole weekend. Jack wants to see if there's anything of value we can sell and we can explore the whole place from top to bottom."

"It'll be like visiting a stately home only we get to go into all the secret places and through all the doors that the public are never allowed to," Sophie said. "There might even be some secret passages!"

Minnie didn't think the idea of secret passages was so exciting - she thought it sounded more frightening.

Lucy returned from her phone call. "Iris says its fine with her if I can't get in touch with them over the weekend. I just hope this Manor is worth it."

"I don't know about actually staying at the Manor," Minnie said, as they ran back to the car. "Like that leaflet said, no one stays after midnight. Where will we sleep if we can't bear to stay there?"

"You are a funny old thing," India said to Minnie as she shut the doors and turned on the fan heater to try to clear the fogged up windows. "You're not scared of anyone in real life, yet you're frightened of ghosts."

"You can't hit a ghost," Minnie explained.

"That's true," India agreed, "But on the other hand, they can't hit you either!

Chapter 7
~ * ~

Back at The Boggarts Nest, the boys were trying to sleep in the Land Rover which felt like being on a trawler, in the mid-Atlantic, during a hurricane. The rain was thunderous and bounced off the roof like thousands of nails were showering down. None of them were able to manage much more than the odd forty winks here and there. Just before dawn the rain had ceased; and they had finally dozed off only to be awoken again, not by the rain, but by the deep roaring of Harley Davison motorbikes drawing into the car park. Peering through the steamed up windows they could just make out crowds of people carrying flashlights.

"What are they all doing?" Jack asked.

"I presume they're going to the standing stones to watch the sunrise," Robert replied. "It's midsummer's day remember?"

"Bunch of crazies," Jack muttered, and hunkered down again to try to get some more shut eye.

"I think I might go with them," Robert said.

"Are you mad?" Jack asked him.

"I'd like to know what they get up to on my property," Robert explained. "I'm not sure I like the idea of them casting spells and doing god knows what kind of rituals on my land."

Lancelot had to agree but couldn't really offer to go with him due to his ankle. "According to some of the maps, there is a public right of way through Noblet Woods to the Fianna Stones, but once at the circle they are technically trespassing and have been all these years."

"I don't fancy trying to tell them that right now," Jack laughed, as a particularly burly biker crossed in front of the car.

"I just want to see what they do," Robert said. "I don't mind people visiting the stones, but modern day witchcraft gives me the creeps as much as old fashioned witchcraft does."

"They can't really cast spells," Jack said. "That's just superstitious nonsense."

"Don't you believe it," Robert exclaimed as he got out of the car. "There are evil and satanic rituals going on to this day, sometimes in the most unlikely locations, and I want to make sure they are not happening on my watch."

Robert hid himself behind a low wall at the back of the car park and sheltered in the shadows so as not to be seen by the devotees who were milling about waiting to be led to the stones.

In the dark, the head druid, dressed in a white, floor length robe, tied at the waist by a string belt, gathered her group of about sixteen others, all dressed as she was and wearing headdresses of green mistletoe and oak. They prepared to lead the procession, some holding fire torches and others carrying long wooden staffs decorated with ribbons, crystals and charms in the shape of sacred symbols. Two of them bore long strands of fennel and green birch. A man, dressed like a scarecrow, began to quietly, rhythmically, steadily and repeatedly beat a large Bodhran drum, and as the hundred or so marchers followed in line, they began to solemnly promenade along Hellifield Road. It was quite the spectacle. The long white robes of the druids flowed out behind them, luminous and ethereal, as the golden flames of their torches reflected pools of fire in the shining black tarmac, which, wet from the rains, shone like an obsidian mirror.

The clack of their wooden staffs on the hard ground and the slow beat of the marching drum echoed through the valley, and Robert, keeping well hidden, observed their sacred pilgrimage. Some of the goths carried musical instruments or large crosses; some of the wiccans were adorned with garlands of flowers and held woven corn pentagrams and dollies in their hands. Robert thought it all looked innocent enough until some men, dressed in black leathers, raised a huge crucifix, woven from willow and wheat, whilst another man, using one of the fire torches, set it ablaze. The burning wicker cross flared and flashed against the dark sky shedding sparks of burning grass which dissolved into nothingness as they hit the wet ground.

Robert continued to trail behind them the few hundred yards to the Public Footpath at the edge of Noblet Wood. Silently, one by one, the flock of worshippers climbed over the wooden stile, and leaving the main road behind them, dropped down onto the muddy bridle path which cut through the trees towards the stones. Through the forest the fire torches danced up and down, illuminating the narrow, uneven path and the pale pink of dog roses and white sparkles of enchanter's nightshade. The eerie silence, in the last vestiges of night, was palpable, and Robert felt as if he had stepped into another dimension. This was an ancient, magical fairyland and the rest of the world seemed to fall away leaving only the sweet scent of bracken and the crackling sound of dried twigs.

Robert kept well behind the trespassers. He wasn't sure if it was just his imagination running wild, but he felt as if the trees were whispering to each other as if warning each other of coming evil. The sensation he felt was one of unease, trepidation and anxiety. Fear was ignited in every tree, every leaf and every drop of dew. He mused on the idea of an 'ill wind' and realised this must be what people spoke of - he could feel the presence of the Devil in the chill morning breeze.

Suddenly, his attention was caught by a ghostly light hovering amongst the undergrowth. Intrigued, he paused for a few moments, bewitched by the luminescent green, dancing flame. He finally realised he was witnessing a will-o-the-wisp which was rising like a spectre from the boggy land beneath. He was sure the land was trying to tell him something, something important, but he didn't know what.

The congregation was far ahead of him now and he felt isolation enveloping him with a malevolent presence. He started to walk on, hurriedly now, afraid that if he lingered too long, he might lose himself in this enchanted wood.

Stepping out into the open field where the Fianna Stones lay, he was greeted by the ripples of the midsummer dawn. The dark clouds were lit by the first drop of golden light which shattered the deathly silence of night by sparking the loud chirrups and tweets, high pitched twills and repetitious natters of the dawn chorus. All around him the leaves, the grass, the wildflowers, seemed filled with a ripeness, lushness, bloom and bounty he had never noticed before. The early morning smelt damp and fresh, and as the grey bands of clouds were broken by a river of buttermilk-yellow, he felt as if the whole world was beginning anew. He had the strange sensation that he had never known this Earth before - this sky had never been seen by a living soul before - and looking up at the moon, still visible over the dark silhouetted trees, he felt as if this moon was witness to a new dawn in more ways than one.

In the clearing, the long grass came to life, caressed by the burnished gold of the midsummer sunrise. The watchers meditated and prayed amongst the ancient menhirs as the roughly hewn, grey stones, scattered with flower bursts of white lichen, began to glow; and as the sky-river widened, the dew-laden ground was covered with a blanket of pale sunlight. The wet scent of grass and swollen leaves filled the air as the earth began to rustle and shimmer. Waiting for the first breath of the sun's rays to burst forth over the central stone, the head druid held her staff skywards to greet the rising sun and welcome in the spirit of The Holly King.

A dancing mist seemed to weave its way through the stone circles, shrouding the worshippers in veils of white.

Robert crept closer - hiding behind one of the larger outer-ring stones.

He wondered what the head druid was handing out from a large picnic basket. He hoped it wasn't drugs, but he need not have worried as it was simply honey cake and elderflower champagne, given as a traditional blessing to those who had joined their solstice ceremony. The musicians struck up, playing tambourines and guitars, flutes and drums, and it wasn't long before many of the worshippers were holding hands, dancing in circles or to their own tune. Some stayed seated on their chosen stone, quietly meditating on the wonders and blessings of Mother Nature.

Now that the giant wicker cross had burnt away, a fire pit was lit, over which men and women began to jump to cheers and encouragement. Some revellers seemed to enter into trance-like states, becoming lost in the whirling, ecstatic energy; whilst some sat in groups of two or three drinking beer and smoking roll ups, which smelt, suspiciously, a little too herbal.

Some of the wiccans made elaborate crystal grids on the grass and then lay down with their foreheads upon the wet earth, their arms outstretched as they soaked up the chi from the dragon lines. Some sprinkled water on the stones, with little wooden spoons, saying mantras as they did so, and some even crawled through the hole in the 'fertility stone', hoping to gain abundance in all aspects of their lives. Robert recognised 'Salute to the Sun' being practised by a group of yoga enthusiasts, and another small group were performing what looked like Tai Chi.

Robert couldn't see any evidence of actual satanic rituals and he was relieved no one was sacrificing animals, or worse, each other. He had a strong feeling that he mustn't be seen though he wasn't sure why. He retreated back to the trees, and as he leant against one of the larger oaks, he felt the familiar spirit of King Arthur manifesting behind him, and his heart began to race as if too much energy was flowing through his nervous system. His feet began to buzz, and his blood began to freeze. Looking down at his feet he knew he was wearing his astral suit of armour and, as he had before, he could feel the hilt of a heavy etheric sword in his hand.

"What is it you're trying to tell me?" he whispered to King Arthur. "I don't understand."

Feeling dizzy, he sat down upon a moss covered, rotten tree trunk and knew his thoughts were no longer his own - he had given his mind over to his spirit guides. His request for information was answered. Amazed, he could see faces in the bark of the trees; men and women seemed to peer out at him; and although he felt unnerved, he also felt protected; he tried to relax into the vision, and, asking three times in the 'name of the true source of all that is good' if it was safe to receive the communication, he felt a strong 'yes' each time. A grand oak tree shuddered as if drawing his attention and he looked intently at the bark. To his astonishment a clear face appeared - that of a woman; her features were gnarled and ridged but her eyes were bright like those of an owl in the night. He could feel her words running through him, rather than hear her speaking, and this, dear readers, is what she told him:

"We live only in the trees. We are the ancient ones. We watch, we guide, we weep. Karma has bound the souls of mankind to their own destruction, and in turn, they destroy the planet which gives them life. They destroy us - their very breath. As they destroy us, they destroy themselves."

Robert had a sudden flash of decimated forests across Europe and felled rainforests across Asia. In a tsunami of images, he witnessed lush landscapes burning into deserts and ancient habitats being destroyed to make way for houses and roads. He felt an overwhelming sadness - the sadness of the whole world weighed heavy in his heart, and he too felt like weeping.

The tree spirit continued to explain to him, "The stones mark the dragon portal. Here lies one of the most powerful dragons on Earth, but see how it is abused, raped, corrupted and polluted by those who do not understand its power. Every wish, every prayer, every thought they leave here remains in the dragon lines and the stones. Millions of spells of greed, fear, control and desire, weave together to make a collective cloud of consciousness recorded in the earth for eternity. Their fear flows into the springs and the streams, into the soil and lingers in the air. Evil begins to grow where love and life once reigned. When evil flows through everything and when the darkness consumes the sacred places, all humans will drown in despair."

Robert shuddered.

"What do you want me to do about it?" he asked the oak spirit.

"You must take back the stones," was her reply.

He instantly recalled the strange lady in The Boggarts Nest - she had accused them of 'coming to take back the stones.' *She wasn't wrong*, he thought, and now felt that this visit to Malinwick Manor might have been orchestrated by spirit and not just, as he first thought, a jolly away from home to see how much the house and its contents might be worth.

"How do I do that - take back the stones?" he asked. "I mean, take them back from whom? And how?"

But as always with spirit communication, his vision was short lived, vague and cryptic; and the answer to his last question remained unanswered as the faces faded and he felt himself back in the land of the living again. *That's just great*, he thought to himself. *Just as I was starting to get the hang of these visions I go and lose it. I wish Sophie was here, she'd know what to do.*

With that, a strong gust of wind shook the oak leaves above him, sending a shower of cold rain water over his head. Now wet and cold, he quickly made his way back through Noblet Wood to the roadside and arrived back at the Land Rover just as the storm clouds suddenly let loose and the rain hit the ground in a thunderous wall of water.

Chapter 8
~ * ~

The boys were glad to find that even at that time of the morning the bar in The Boggarts Nest was already open and they ordered a full English breakfast. Waiting for the girls to arrive, they spent the rest of the morning playing darts, pool, dominoes, cards and even Scrabble. Robert told them a little of what had happened during his experience at the stones but he didn't tell them about the trees talking to him as he thought it might make him sound like a total nut-case.

As the morning wore on, the news on the television informed them that the flooding was escalating all over the region. They could hear a helicopter flying almost constantly overhead and the sirens of fire engines and police cars along with the rumble of tractors up and down Hellifield Road - all braving the storm to rescue stranded locals and take them to safety.

With still no phone signal, the lads began to worry about the girls when they didn't arrive at the agreed time. They listened to the local weather reports, hoping the roads were still passable. Around two o'clock, a couple of very tired looking police officers arrived to inform everyone that the road out to Pendle Hill and most of the A59 were now completely flooded, and that before long the village of Boggart would be totally cut off. They advised all visitors to leave the area as soon possible and to look for accommodation outside the flood zone.

The pub was soon deserted.

"You'ds best get t' Manor afore you can't," the barman suggested to Robert. "Either that or goes somewhere else."

"I think we should wait here," Robert replied. "I'd hate the girls to arrive and find we're not here. If we're going to be stuck here, we should at least all be stuck together."

Lancelot and Jack concurred. Looking out the window at the sodden landscape, they hoped the storm would blow itself out, once and for all, as soon as possible.

To their relief, around four o'clock, Minnie, India, Lucy and Sophie arrived safe and sound.

"I'm starving," Lucy said as she sat down on one of the banquettes near the fire. "I hope the food here is better than the ambience," she said, unnerved by the stuffed animals and sci-fi movie posters on the walls.

Jack laughed. "It's a strange old place but the food's good."

"Thank goodness for that," Lucy replied, happy to see the boys and to have finally arrived.

As they tucked into toasted sandwiches and chips, a news bulletin, updating the public on the flooding, came on. Their hearts went out to locals whose houses were now, at best, two feet under water. Some houses had been almost swallowed whole by the flood waters, only their roofs and chimneys remaining above the water line.

"I don't know if we'll get to the Manor after all," Robert explained to the girls. "We've been told the usual road to the house is already flooded and the other one might be too now."

"The taxi won't make it that's for sure," Lancelot said. "According to the map, Gobin Lane, which goes through Noblet Wood to the back of the Manor, isn't much more than a dirt track."

"We could all squeeze into the Land Rover," Minnie suggested.

"You've changed your tune," India laughed. "I thought you didn't want to go to the Manor in case the ghosts got you!"

Minnie shivered at the thought, but she didn't like the dingy, dirty, and to be brutally honest, downright smelly pub and hoped the Manor would be more welcoming. She'd seen the macabre photographs, on the way to the loo, and they had spooked her. She'd also been accosted by Old Meg, who had frightened the life out her when, pointing a bony finger in Minnie's face, she had accused of her of being a witch. She didn't relish going to the Manor but thought it couldn't be any worse than this god-forsaken place.

"I can't get hold of Ada Mould or her brother so I'm just hoping they are still expecting us," Lancelot said, "But if we're going to go we'd better go now. Minnie's right, if we all squeeze into the Land Rover we could try to get down that lane. It takes us through the old Abbey arch, and we can park here"…he showed them on an old map that Mr T had given him. "There's a humpback bridge halfway down called Stag Bridge, and then a wooden bridge near the back of the house, called Meg Bridge, which we're told we can't drive across, but we could walk over and carry the bags - it's only a few hundred yards from the house according to this map."

As the friends rose to leave, the three men who had been in the snug the night before, walked in and lifted their caps in greeting. "How do," old man Trevor said and smiled a toothless smile at the girls. "Tha'still wanting to git t' Manor?" he asked them.

They all nodded.

"Tha' can still git down by Gobin Lane if tha' goes now," he told them. "Just bin up there me sein. You'll be reet if tha's quick about it."

"Ay but tha'll have to stays at the Manor all night," the younger man chuckled.

"Or swim back afore midnight," his father added with a low snigger.

Minnie looked scared. "Is it true that no one stays after midnight?" she asked them.

The men laughed again but didn't reply. Their silence freaked her out even more.

"Come on," Jack said. "Let's get your bags on the roof rack and get going."

The four girls squeezed onto the back seat of the Land Rover and the three boys into the front. The heat from their breath and bodies soon steamed up the windows as the rain lashed down upon the bags and roof. As they made their way down Hellifield Road, Lance said, "Everyone look out for a gate on the left about half a mile along." They wiped the windows to try to see out but it didn't make much difference - they could hardly even see the verges.

They all kept an eye out, the best they could, then India called out, "There! Stop! There I saw a gate between those trees."

Backing up, they found the entrance to Gobin Lane, through Noblet Wood. Jack jumped out to open the gate, getting soaked to the skin and covered in mud as the Land Rover gouged out deep furrows in the soggy ground.

Noblet Wood wasn't large, but once they started driving through it, it could have been the largest forest in the world for how overgrown and unmanaged it was. Dead, fallen trees and large, rotting branches lay lifeless by the side of the narrow lane, and dark green patches of weather-beaten nettles feasted off the dank earth. The overhanging trees blocked out the sun, even when it was shining, and the perpetual, purple-tinged darkness enveloped them in an eerie chill which sent the temperature in the car down by several degrees. At least the tree tunnel provided some shelter from the pouring rain enabling them to see a little further around them, but it felt as if they were driving into no-mans-land and a frisson of fear rippled through the car as they headed into the unknown. As they slowly navigated the rough track, the trees seemed to devour it behind them, and the lane became narrower and narrower until it was nothing more than two muddy furrows with long wet grass growing between. The black-blue tangled branches of downy birch trees twisted through each other in wide canopies, whilst deeper into the woods the light disappeared altogether amongst the taller alders, their dark, fissured bark coated with leaching white lichen. Fluffs of luminous white wool draped themselves over the goat willows whose roots buried themselves amongst the bogs and peaty hollows. Drooping bracken fronds fanned together creating a deep carpet of bronzed-green. Occasionally, along the edges of the road, little purple and white stars of red campion and lesser stitchwort were illuminated in the dark-light, and where there had once been strong, dry stone walls, there now lay piles of fallen boulders smothered in grey creeping moss.

Suddenly, Lucy let out a piercing scream!

A low hanging branch had scraped the windscreen like a giant finger trying to smash its way in.

It had scared the life out of her.

Minnie shivered. "I don't like these woods," she muttered. Usually, Minnie loved a good woodland walk and adored being amongst the trees in Little Eden where she always felt closer to the fairies, but here, in this ancient, tangled copse, she felt as if she had never been in such a depressing and oppressive forest in all her life.

"It feels as if the trees are crying," Sophie sighed, as she pressed her nose to the car window and gazed upwards into the dense canopy. Dotted amongst the lush, leaf-laden trees there would be, inexplicably, the occasional dead one, its decaying fingers poking sharply out towards them in an almost accusatory manner. "I can't work out if they want us here or not."

"I think they want us here," Robert told her, recalling his conversation with them earlier that morning. "I think they were expecting us. In fact I know they are."

Everyone felt his words resonate deep inside them and a melancholy hush came upon them.

India laughed to break her nervousness. "Even I think there is something spooky about this place," she admitted. "I almost expect to see a sign that says, 'Turn Back' or 'Do Not Enter'"

Lucy agreed. "You know what it feels like to me? As if we've entered a past-life. Once we left the road we entered another time-zone and no-one else knows we are here but us."

"Yes," Sophie agreed. "As if our real bodies are still in the pub and only our spirits are entering these woods."

Suddenly Minnie yelped in fright and shouted to Robert to stop!

Robert slammed on the brakes in alarm - mud splattering up the windscreen and the windows.

"What the hell?" he exclaimed and turned to look at Minnie.

"Sorry," Minnie apologised. "It's just..." she paused and pointed out of the window..."Look!"

They wound down the windows to get a better view and all saw what Minnie had been so frightened by. A group of ancient oak trees formed a ring which the road sliced in half. All the trees were long since dead, and dangling ominously from one of the low, crippled branches was a hideous garland of animal skulls; some still fresh, some half decomposed, some bone dry - stripped of all life. Suspended from another branch were the decapitated corpses of crows, mice and rabbits, flapping in the wind, their skin hanging off in wasted strips - maggots feasting on their rotting flesh.

"Oh my god," Lucy exclaimed and put her hand over her eyes, wishing she could unsee it.

"It's probably the gamekeeper keeping the vermin at bay," Jack reassured them.

"It's disgusting," Minnie replied, her skin crawling with horror at such a macabre display of death.

"It's pretty yucky," India agreed and turned her head away.

"I'm not sure what's worse," Minnie said, "That awful pub or this ghastly place."

"Don't worry," Robert told them. "I can see we'll be coming out of the woods just up there. We'll be at the Manor soon." They had caught glimpses of the house, which now and again came into view, and they could make out parts of the roof and the many chimneys, as well as a round tower with windows which looked like empty eyes staring menacingly over the grounds.

The last part of the track was even more slow-going than the first. As the last tree fell away they could see flooded, open fields appearing on either side of them. Reaching Stag Bridge, which was hardly wide enough for them to pass over, the water from the syke was close to breaching it and from then on the lane was running like a river making the rest of the ride rough and jerky.

Robert felt his hands going numb from gripping the wheel to keep the Land Rover from completely getting stuck in the squelching mud. He tried his best to keep going, afraid they might not make it all the way to the house, but to his relief, as they rounded the bend, they finally reached the huge 12th Century stone arch which had once been part of the old Abbey. The wind beaten carvings had almost vanished and the medieval stained glass windows were long gone. It was a strange sensation to be driving beneath what had once been the entrance to the north transept.

Sophie shuddered as she felt the energy field shift - the arch was a portal and there was evil behind it.

They suddenly felt a rumble beneath them and Minnie squeaked with alarm.

"Must be a cattle grid," Robert said to reassure her, unable to see anything beneath the rising waters.

"Stop!!!" Lancelot shouted.

Just as Robert stopped the car they all heard a loud cracking sound followed by the stomach-churning feeling of the car sinking.

"Christ!" Robert muttered and tried to back up but the wheels just span round in the mud.

"That must have been Meg Bridge," Lancelot said.

Jack jumped out of the car to take a look. The bridge was barely visible beneath the water but he could see some of the old wooden planks were crushed and broken. "That was damned close!" Jack said as he poked his head back into the car. "We'll have to walk from here," he told them, although looking around there wasn't a dry piece of ground on which to stand.

Thankfully, the rain had eased a little and, as if it knew they needed to get to shelter, the sun poked its head out from between the dark clouds, creating delicate strips of golden light beneath each one.

Jack went ahead to test the ground. The water was only a couple of inches deep near the car and a little further on the ground was higher - obviously the beginning of a pathway to the back of the Manor. He returned, offering to carry each of the girls one by one. He and Robert took them over, placing them down on the dry patch of gravel which was surrounded by overgrown, glossy-green rhododendrons and the bright, nodding pompoms of heavily laden hydrangeas. The actual house was still out of sight but its invisible presence seemed to loom down upon them and they knew it was not far now.

Robert helped Lancelot limp across, and Jack put Lucy down onto the gravel. As he did so she cockled over on her ankle and he only just caught her in time to stop her falling.

"What was that?" Lucy asked.

As she looked down at the ground she got the fright of her life!

Chapter 9
~ * ~

❝What is it?" Jack exclaimed, as Lucy clung to him - she was almost paralysed with fear. As he looked down to see what had scared Lucy out of her wits he saw a broken human skull staring up at him. Its lower jaw bone was hanging off and several teeth were missing, giving it a gruesome expression; from one of its empty eye-sockets jumped a fat, swollen, grey-green toad.

Then Minnie screamed...followed by Sophie...

Something was crunching beneath their feet and it wasn't just gravel.

Soon enough they all realised they were surrounded by decapitated, dismembered and mutilated human bodies.

"Good grief!" Lancelot cried out, as he scanned the driveway. "There are bones everywhere - look!"

Minnie didn't want to look and screwed her eyes tight shut, stood stock still and wouldn't move a muscle. She was too afraid she might step on someone else. "I knew I shouldn't have come," she muttered under her breath. "It's a friggin' nightmare."

Lucy jumped up onto a large tree stump to get away from the bones. She shuddered with disgust, and once the initial shock had worn off, she began to feel a wave of overwhelming sadness, wondering who all the poor, lost souls could be and why they were there - unearthed for all to see.

"There are more over here too, bones of all kinds," Jack said, as he looked back over the rushing syke. Sticking out of the water's edge were thigh and arm bones, jaws and teeth, small pieces of toes and fingers and bits of scattered vertebrae.

"There are dozens of them," Robert said astonished, as another skull floated passed.

Collapsed skeletons were being tossed about in the flood waters, colliding and smashing into each other as they flowed down stream. Some had been taken up by the rising water onto the gravel path and were scattered throughout the bankside.

Minnie and Sophie joined Lucy on the tree stump, and they linked arms, giving themselves the illusion of some kind of protection. "Where are they coming from?" Lucy asked. "I don't like this. I don't like this at all." She wanted to pick up her feet and hug her knees to get away from the disturbing and macabre sight.

Suddenly, Sophie had a flash of psychic information, and she knew exactly where they were all coming from. "Ancient burial sites," she said.

They all looked at her, not understanding what she meant.

"Stone and Bronze Age burial sites," Sophie explained. "I just had a flash from the past of funeral rites and the graves of the people who lived here long ago. Are there any barrows recorded on the maps of the Manor grounds?" she asked Lancelot.

"Yes, there were some marked on the Ordinance Survey Map, if I remember rightly," he replied, "They are to the West of the standing stones next to the lane we've just come down."

"The rising of the water table must have dislodged the underground tombs and they've floated up here," Jack said.

Minnie, who was terrified to her own bones, now pleaded with the others, "Let's go back to the pub whilst we still can," she begged. "This place is as creepy as everyone says it is."

"Come on," Jack said, offering to give her a piggyback so he could carry her across the worst of it. "We're here now and we're staying. They're just remains of the ancestors, old girl. They can't harm you."

"Let's not get spooked before we've even gone inside," Robert said kindly. "It's just the floods. It's nothing supernatural."

"We should go and get the bags before that bridge disintegrates completely," Jack suggested. He pointed over to Meg Bridge and they all watched as a couple of the planks floated to the surface and rushed off with the raging waters.

As Jack and Robert waded back to the car, the rest of them tentatively picked their way through the dead bodies, and thankfully, after a few yards, the ground seemed clear. The shabby path opened out into a well-worn, cobbled courtyard, which was surrounded by single storey out-houses. Some had been stables, some coal houses, some garden sheds and stores. Many of the seasoned, faded green, wooden doors were hanging off their hinges and the crumbling roofs were falling in. Grey slates lay shattered amongst piles of brown rotten leaves, overgrown teasels and rampant mugwort. Creeping ivy had taken over long ago. The small, cracked windows were cloaked in dirt - their frames rotten or devoured by wasps. A dankness oozed up from the undergrowth and enveloped the yard in a shroud of eerie stillness. The dereliction and abandonment which had let Nature reclaim the once cultivated grounds made them feel like trespassers in a forbidden land.

To their dismay, the heavens opened again, sending giant, heavy drops of rain splashing down upon them, and they ran, and Lancelot hobbled, into the nearest open doorway to take shelter. Going further inside one of the gloomy, dilapidated farm buildings, they found everything covered in sawdust, which, disturbed by their presence, danced in the tiny shafts of light poking through the holes in the roof. Much to Lucy's dismay, large spiders' webs, strewn with the long dead corpses of half-eaten flies, winked at her from between the beams. The shed smelt of wood and soil and was scattered about with vintage gardening and farming implements, from scythes to spades, hand drills to double ended saws. Piled up on the rotting wooden benches were balls of mouldy string, a multitude of mostly broken, terracotta plant pots and rusting metal watering cans. It was as if the gardener had just walked out one day, a hundred years ago, and never come back.

Jack and Robert joined them with a few of the bags and Jack was glad to spot an antique handcart, which luckily had not rusted up completely, and whose wheels still worked. "We can use this to bring the rest of bags from the car," he suggested. He rooted around to see if he could find a tarpaulin to cover it with, and from beneath a pile of wood he pulled out a canvas sheet, sending a dust storm into the air and making everyone cough.

Whilst Jack and Robert braved the rain and the rising waters again, the others waited, in what felt like the 19th Century, sitting on dry grain sacks.

Sophie raised Lance's ankle onto a three legged milking stool which was so worn away with years of use that is sagged forwards and slightly sideways too.

"Does it hurt a lot?" Sophie asked him.

Lance shook his head. "No it just aches," he told her. "It'll be alright tomorrow if I rest it."

He looked rather forlorn as he leaned back against the sacks.

Sophie knew he was still pining for Adela - he was nursing a broken heart as well as a sprained ankle. She knew how emotional pain makes physical pain even harder to bear and how bad luck can follow bad luck like a row of ants eating your strength little by little. She couldn't help but think about Tobi, but she thought it best to take both their minds off their emotions rather than dwell on them right now. "Some of these implements look deadly," she commented, pointing at some plough blades which were stacked in the corner. "It's sad to think no one uses them now. I bet this was a hive of activity once upon a time."

Lancelot sighed. "I always feel life must have been harder but simpler back then."

They all sat in silence pondering the romance of the past for a few moments.

"This place reminds me of Little Eden," India said.

"How?" Lucy asked, a little surprised.

"Well, it's sort of separate from the surrounding area isn't it? It's a place by itself, if you know what I mean, and there's an old Abbey and standing stones…"

…Minnie interrupted her… "We don't have corpses strewn all over the pavements in Little Eden," she said, shuddering again at the thought of all those bones snapping and cracking beneath their feet.

"I suppose you'd call it a sacred site though, just like Little Eden?" Lucy said.

"There's a dragon portal under those stones no doubt," Sophie replied. "There always is a sacred portal leading to the other dimensions where there are stones or a church. A circle of stones usually marks where lots of lay lines intersect - like a hub of electromagnetic energy and where you can access keys of consciousness."

"We are at the geographical centre of the British Isles here," Lancelot told them. "I suppose if there is an epicentre of lay lines for the whole of the U.K it might very well be here."

They fell silent again, wondering if there was a connection between the Manor and Little Eden that went beyond just Robert's family inheritance, and suspecting that they may have been drawn here, not by their own curiosity, but by forces much stronger than their own free will.

Suddenly, they nearly jumped out of their skins, as a bundle of long handled brooms went crashing to the floor.

"What the f**k?" India exclaimed.

A frisson of ice-cold fear raced through their blood - stopping their hearts for a moment.

For a few seconds they hardly dared breathe.

The door had blown shut, causing a slat of wood to snap off the frame with a loud crack, and as it flew to the ground, it took the brushes with it.

Sophie laughed nervously. "It's started already," she said.

"What has?" India asked in a half whisper.

"The imagining," she replied.

"The what?" Minnie said, feeling afraid something wicked was coming their way.

"Our expectation is that there are ghosts and spirits everywhere, just waiting to do us harm," Sophie explained, "Every bang becomes the hand of death approaching. Every shadow becomes a serial killer. Every coincidence becomes a sign."

"Sophie's right," Lancelot agreed. "We need to keep our heads whilst we're here. Otherwise, we'll not last five minutes, never mind forty eight hours!"

"I'm not going to last eight minutes at this rate," Minnie admitted.

"The back of the house should only be a few hundred yards away," Lancelot told them. "Let's try to get there. It sounds as if the rain has eased off again now."

They came out into the courtyard and were not sure it made them feel any safer being outside rather than inside. The rain was now that fine (the kind that soaks you through) and they hurried as much as they could, towards a large, classical-style archway which marked the way to the house. Beyond some half-broken, wooden gates, the path, which had once been gravelled though there was now little left of it, was a weed-filled track, flanked by green-black yew trees hanging low on either side, creating dry patches of lifeless earth beneath their sprawling branches. Lucy gasped as she spotted some tiny grave stones poking up out of the wasted ground. Her first thought was that they were the graves of little children, then she realised, to her relief, that they must be those of family pets. She gave them a wide birth all the same.

As they came around a bend, the dark side of the ancient manor house loomed down like a spectre upon them.

Immediately they gasped, wanting to turn back!

Chapter 10
~ * ~

"It's not a very pretty house, is it?" Lucy sighed, as she gazed up at the dark facade. She thought of the picture she had seen on the internet, and although she had known it was going to be less Pemberley and more The House of Usher, now, actually being there, she was overwhelmed by the macabre aura it gave off; it was even gloomier and more spooky than she could ever have imagined.

It was as if the walls were seeped in sadness, and as they drew closer, melancholy and misery seemed to fall on them like a heavy cloak which they couldn't shake off.

"It is the back and north facing," Lancelot said. "It's bound to be less appealing from this aspect."

He wasn't wrong about it being unappealing. Designed in the Queen Anne style with pointed gables seemed too heavy for the grey stone walls, which were marred by green and white lichen. Small paned, leaded windows with heavy stone sills looked at them like suspicious and hostile eyes. Low balustrades hid the fall-aways to the basement windows and a doorway, on the ground floor, which looked as if it had once been part of the old Abbey, had clearly not been used in a very long time.

"It's not very friendly," Minnie remarked.

"How can a house be friendly," India teased her.

"Minnie's right," Sophie said. "Houses have an energy signature - an emotional imprint. They're not just bricks and mortar. They take on the energy of the inhabitants like a sponge, soaking up emotions. The older the house is, the more emotions it holds. Some houses feel welcoming, some just feel empty, but this one, well, it feels downright depressing."

"It hasn't been lived in for a hundred years," Lancelot said, half laughing. "What did you expect?"

India stood on tiptoe and peered through a window, but it was so grimy she couldn't see through it. "Let's see if we can get inside," she suggested. "According to Mr T there's been restoration to some of the rooms. There was an attempt to make it into a hotel in the 1990's so it might feel much better inside than out."

"Why didn't they finish it?" Minnie asked.

"It became too expensive I suppose," India replied.

"Probably because of the ghosts more like," Minnie whispered to Lucy, and her words sent a chill up both their spines.

Down to the left was a set of stone stairs leading to the cellars. Piles of brown, crunchy leaves had been brushed aside to leave a central walkway and India figured someone had been using it as an entrance fairly recently, so she ventured down the well-worn steps into a dark, sheltered stairwell, but was disappointed when she found the old door was locked. "We'll have to try round the front," she shouted back up to the others.

"Why don't you girls go and see if you can get in around the front, if you can, then come and open the back," Lancelot suggested. "I'll wait here for Robbie and Jack."

"You stay here with Lancelot," Lucy said to Sophie. "Why don't you shelter down there?" She pointed to the over-hang which shielded the cellar entrance. "We'll let you in as soon as we can."

Sophie and Lancelot picked their way down the steps and sat down on a stone seat under the covered doorway, waiting for the others to return. Sophie leaned against Lance's shoulder and took the opportunity to rest a while. Lancelot's thoughts wandered back to his fall on Pendle Hill and the silver balls which had floated so mysteriously above him. "Can I tell you something," Lancelot asked her, "In confidence?"

"Of course," Sophie said, keeping her eyes closed but she was listening.

"On Pendle Hill, when I fell, I thought I saw something, something supernatural," he told her.

Sophie murmured to let him know to carry on speaking.

"I suppose you might call it a UFO, but not in the flying saucer sense. It was a V shape with silver balls which lit up and hovered above me for a few seconds, then it just disappeared. What do you think it might have been?"

Sophie sighed. She was too tired to speak anymore and really needed a cup of tea, but she forced herself to reply, "Probably a weather phenomenon. You said the clouds were so low that you were walking through them, didn't you?"

"Yes," Lancelot replied. "It could have been a natural phenomenon, but I did wonder if it was a sign of some kind?" He was a little disappointed that Sophie wasn't more interested. "I thought of all people you might think it was supernatural."

Sophie was interested and tried her hardest to speak, but the exhaustion of ME had taken hold of her in the last few minutes and brain fog made it seem as if there was a satellite delay between her thoughts and her speech. "I'm a sceptic, you know that," she managed to say. "I look for a rational explanation first."

"All I thought was..." Lancelot began to say, but then paused, as if he felt a little silly suggesting such a thing…"Well, you know the founder of the Quaker movement, George Fox? He had his vision to start the new religious order whilst on Pendle Hill."

Sophie forced her mind and mouth to sync so that she could get the words out to reply, "In that case, you being from a Quaker family, I would say it may have been a spirit communication. Did you feel anything or hear anything else?"

"Only a sharp metallic sound," Lancelot said. "If it did have a message for me, I have no idea what that message was."

"The best thing to do is ask your spirit guides to download the information into your conscious mind in a way that you'll understand," Sophie told him.

"How do I do that?" he asked.

"Just ask," she replied.

Lance closed his eyes and asked, just like Sophie had suggested, but no message came to him. He listened to the drips of water tip-tapping around them and he could hear his own, and Sophie's, heart beats, but his mind remained totally blank.

"No, I'm not getting anything," he told her after a few minutes.

"You're most likely to download the information form a higher consciousness when you least expect it," Sophie said. "I often get information downloading when I'm on the loo."

"On the toilet?" Lancelot laughed.

"When our minds are not pre-occupied with other things, and we are alone, we can sometimes get a vision or an inner knowing," Sophie said, almost losing her last few words in sheer fatigue.

"You're getting past it aren't you?" Lance asked her.

She nodded, still resting her head on his shoulder.

"I hope they find Ada Mould or her brother round the front and let us in quickly," he said, putting his arm around Sophie who was starting to fall asleep.

Lance sat quietly for a while letting Sophie rest when suddenly, they were both startled by the arrival of a huge, black crow which landed only a few yards away from them. It squawked so loudly it frightened them both and the way it looked directly at them made them shiver.

They both knew a visit from a crow could be a warning that evil was not far away.

"Do you think the Manor really is haunted?" Lancelot asked. His voice was little shaky - he found himself surprisingly unnerved by the place and was even more unnerved when Sophie replied, "It could be, it very well could be."

Chapter 11
~ * ~

Attached to the side of the time-worn house was a high, brick arch which led the girls into an overgrown walled garden. Trapped between the creeping tentacles of rambling roses, thorny brambles and yellow ragwort, they hesitantly made their way along the uneven herringbone path which ran alongside the imposing manor house.

The windows, with their great, lumbering, stone sills, were too high to see inside and the large base of a round tower curved outwards, forcing them to walk around it. Raising their eyes upwards towards a high balcony covered in creeping ivy, they could see the tower was capped by a witch's-hat turret. They did their best to avoid the heavy drops of rainwater which dripped down on them from the gutters through short, stubby lead pipes which were guarded by the hideous stone faces of monstrous gargoyles. The girls felt they were being watched by the beady eyes of the Green Man, a crazed imp and an ugly boggart.

They felt like trespassers in another time zone and began to walk a little faster.

"I don't like the look of those faces," Minnie said, trying to dodge the fat drops of water but finding there wasn't much room to manoeuvre.

"They're supposed to ward off witches," Lucy told her. "They're protecting us."

"I don't know about that," Minnie replied. "They look like they're the nasty ones."

She particularly didn't like the largest one which stuck out of the corner of the building. A long bodied, stone dragon protruded outwards, pointing in the direction of the Fianna Stones, and silhouetted against the grey, cloud-filled sky it seemed to have a cruel smile on its lips.

"Shhh," Minnie suddenly whispered. "What was that?"

They all stopped in their tracks and held their breath for a few moments, listening.

"Over there," Minnie said in hushed tones.

They waited again.

The complete silence was eerie, and they realised that there was a total absence of bird song.

"I don't see anything," India said at last. "Come on, keep walking, it's going to pour down again any minute."

They carried on a little further, but before they had gone more than a few steps, Minnie shushed them again, "Didn't you hear it?" she murmured.

The hairs on the back of her neck began to bristle and she felt a cold chill run through her veins.

They paused to listen again - their hearts in their mouths.

"Someone's watching us," Minnie said under her breath.

They waited in terrible anticipation...

...until...suddenly, from beneath a drooping elderflower bush, a low flying blackbird shot out almost hitting Minnie in the face with its flapping wings before swooping upwards into the dark sky.

"It was just a bird," Lucy sighed with relief, wondering if everyone's heart was racing as fast as hers. "We're all so on edge," she said. "I'll be glad when we find the caretakers and can have a nice cup of tea and a piece of cake."

They were thankful to reach the end wall and the rusty, wrought-iron gate which opened out onto an expansive driveway from which they had panoramic views of the parkland. Towards the South, the rolling countryside seemed to go on forever, dotted here and there with beech, oak and sycamore trees, all flat bottomed from deer nibbling at their lower leaves. Beyond a large, inky lake, stood the white crumbling pillars of a Grecian folly, and a red tiled boat house was just visible at the near-side.

To the North, a wide barred, iron fence, so common to English stately homes, ran along a ridge which sloped down towards a Ha-Ha. A small ornamental bridge crossed the ditch, leading into a long stretch of land, beyond which the Fianna Stones were clearly visible in the distance.

They paused for a moment to take in the grand vista, including a dark avenue of copper beeches, at the end of which the girls could just catch a glimpse of the high, brick chimneys of a Victorian lodge house.

The openness was a happy relief from the enclosed dankness of the back and side of the house, but as they turned to look at the front facade of the building their happiness faded, as the oppressiveness of austere window frames, frowning over leaded windows, gave the house a forlorn and unwelcoming aspect. An array of steep pitched gables, large dormas and overly ornate chimneys made for a ramshackle effect which was both confusing and uncomfortable on the eye. Long windows flanking both sides of the entrance, let in a great deal of light but from the outside they appeared bleak and sombre.

As the girls stood hesitating, wondering if it was safe to go inside, the wind whipped up, causing a sudden chill to whisper through the air. Then the heavens opened and huge hail stones, the size of golf balls, began to hit them hard on the head and in the faces and their fear of the house took a back seat to the painful shower as they ran to take shelter under the spacious porch.

India tried one of the double doors.

It was unlocked.

Cautiously they ventured in…

The wooden floor creaked and groaned beneath their feet as they walked into the grand entrance hall where a sweeping staircase filled the central space, leaving dark narrow cloisters on either side. A top heavy, canopied fireplace, carved with heraldic images, was cold and bare; the whole place smelt of wood polish mixed with soot, giving it a musty, smoky odour. Dark, fielded, oak panelling added to the morbid atmosphere, as did the macabre, stuffed stag heads, ornate and very sharp swords arranged in circles, and a collection of drab looking portraits of proud ancestors who were dressed in elaborate costumes and long curly wigs.

"Mrs Mould," India called out, and was a little taken aback by how her own voice echoed all-around.

There was no answer - just silence.

"Mr Dootson," India called out again.

Silence.

"Is anybody there?" India shouted, as loudly as she could.

Still silence.

Suddenly, they all jumped!

The front door had slammed shut with a loud bang! A sharp gust of wind had cut through the hall.

Lucy shivered.

She couldn't quite place the sensation she felt wash over her. She was convinced that whilst the place seemed deserted, they were not alone and that someone, invisible to the eye, had just entered through the open door.

She wanted everyone together again - feeling there might be safety in numbers. "This place'll be the death of me," she said, "Let's try to find our way to the back and let the others in."

"Good idea," Minnie agreed.

They looked around and then at each other.

There were doors leading out on all four sides of the hall.

"Which way?" India asked.

"I think it's this way," Minnie told them with an unexpected and strange confidence. "Yes, this way," she continued to say as she headed towards one of the tall mahogany doors on the right hand-side of the stairs. It led into a small, panelled vestibule with a corner fireplace - its shelves laden with blue and white porcelain. Minnie tried the brass handled door at the other end, and as they went through that doorway, they found themselves at the top of some simple, rather shabby looking, service stairs. "It's down there," Minnie said, then hesitated.

The stone staircase seemed to go down into an abyss of shadows.

She didn't fancy going down there.

India decided to be brave and led the way. She held tightly onto the rope handrail as the steps were steep and uneven; worn down by the footsteps of thousands of servants over the centuries. As the air became colder and damper the further down they went it made them cough and as they stepped into the basement they were overwhelmed by the claustrophobic oppressiveness. They all felt the impulse to run back up the stairs but instead they reluctantly made their way down a murky, long, thin corridor hung with paintings and black and white photographs of previous maids, housekeepers, gardeners and grooms. Rows of bells, which connected to the rooms above stairs, had handwritten tickets beneath them saying things like; Library, Second Drawing Room and Master Bedroom. The grim passageway led towards the only natural light that was faintly peering through the bars of the dirty window at the end.

"Where now?" Lucy asked Minnie.

"Halfway down to the right," she replied without hesitation.

"How the heck do you know that?" India said and laughed a little nervously. "You've never been here before."

"I don't know," Minnie replied. "To be honest it's freaking me out that I know. It feels so familiar it's giving me the creeps."

"You've clearly been here before," Lucy told her.

"I've never even been to Lancashire in my life and certainly not here," Minnie replied.

"I mean in a past life," Lucy explained. "Perhaps you were a maid here or even the mistress or master."

"Ooo, don't say that," Minnie said, uneasy with that idea - although she couldn't help feeling that Lucy might be right. She felt afraid of the Manor and yet now that she was inside the house she felt as if she belonged there. It was a strange mixture of emotions which she didn't really understand.

Minnie opened a door which led into a large, rather gloomy, fusty-smelling kitchen, with peeling, mushroom coloured paint on its walls and a red quarry-tile floor. A blackened range sat next to a massive, open-grate fireplace that still retained its old metal spit, wound by a handle and chains. Copper pans and jelly moulds were arranged on big Welsh dressers and a long wooden table, with an eclectic mix of ramshackle chairs around it, ran down the centre of the room. If it had not been for an electric kettle, toaster and rather battered looking refrigerator one might have thought it was exactly as it had been in 1912 when the family had left for the last time.

India looked around for the light-switch but when she tried it, nothing happened.

Lucy went to the fridge, but it was empty, and the light didn't come on, "It's not working either," she said.

Minnie flicked the kettle switch on and off a few times, but it too wasn't working.

"The phone doesn't work either," Lucy said, having found a 1960's phone on the wall. "No dial tone."

"Maybe the electricity hasn't been turned on," India suggested. "We need to find that back door to let the others in." Going over to the corner she found a small porch in which logs and coal were piled up against the wall. Some outdoor clothes were hanging on big coat hooks, and a metal umbrella stand had a few forlorn looking brollies stuffed into it - it led to the back door.

Luckily the key was in the lock, and on opening it, she found Sophie and Lance still sitting under the over-hang waiting for them.

Robert, who was looking down from above, holding an old piece of tarpaulin over his head to shield him from the hail, called down that they would bring in the cases.

Sophie and Lance came into the kitchen, and like everyone else, they felt a sense of disappointment and regret that they had come. The house was already having a depressing effect on them. Sophie, whose body temperature was always lower than normal, was feeling the cold crawling through her skin and into her bones, and she looked longingly at the open fire wishing it was lit. She plonked herself on the wooden bench next to the empty hearth and sighed with exhaustion and sadness.

"We'd better go back to the pub," Minnie suggested. She was feeling very uneasy. The kitchen had a strange aura about it, and she wasn't sure what century she was in from one moment to the next. When she had entered the room, she thought she had seen two women, dressed in black with white aprons and cotton caps, preparing food at the long oak table, but as she blinked, they had disappeared into thin air, and she wondered whether she really had seen them or whether it was just her imagination. "This place is creepy," she said, and seeing Sophie looking as pale as a ghost didn't improve her confidence.

"We can't stay here without light or even a kettle to make a cup of tea with," Lucy agreed.

"If Ada Mould and her brother are not here, maybe they're stuck in the floods somewhere or didn't think we would be coming after all," Lancelot suggested.

"I hate to admit defeat, but I think it's best if we head back," India said.

"Sorry, old girl, not possible," Jack told her as he came through the back door carrying several cumbersome bags and cases. "As we came back over that wooden bridge it totally collapsed. The water has covered more of the path now too, so unless you want to swim over to the Land Rover, we'll have to wait until the water subsides."

"Oh no!" Minnie exclaimed and sat down on one of the wheel-back chairs in despair. "Can't we tell the Police, or Search and Rescue? They might be able to help us?"

"There's no signal," Jack said, as he shook the water out of his hair. "I've already tried my phone god knows how many times. We'll have to make the best of it. I thought you'd have the kettle on by now," he teased Lucy as he took off his wet t-shirt and jeans and rummaged about in his bags to find some dry clothes to put on.

"I would have but there's no electricity and no food," Lucy told him. As she sat down next to Minnie a wave of hopelessness washed over her too.

Robert came in with more bags. "These hampers Mrs B sent are so heavy there must be enough food in them to feed an army," he said.

Lucy perked up - she'd forgotten about the hampers.

Robert was also soaked to the skin and opening his suit bag he took out a neatly pressed shirt. Then, with a little more modesty than Jack, he changed too.

"Do you have any matches or a lighter?" Lucy asked Jack. "If we can light a fire, I could boil some water for tea, and we could hang your clothes up to dry."

"I've got the First Aid Kit here somewhere," Jack said, and he fished out a flint. India screwed up some old newspapers whilst Robert carried in some wood from the porch, and they set about lighting a fire in the range and the open grate.

Lancelot sat in a rocking chair by the fire, and Minnie made a little bed for Sophie on a high backed, wooden bench using dressing gowns and jumpers from their luggage.

Looking through the cupboards, Lucy had managed to root out some tins of fruit, corned beef and baked beans along with some old Rooibos teabags - nothing that would make anyone's mouth water. When she opened up the hampers though, everyone felt things were not so bad after all. Mrs B had done wonders for them, providing the most delicious looking picnic. There were pork pies and sausage rolls, Cornish pasties, cheese scones, cold chicken, ham and tongue, wild-mushroom pate along with crackers, bread sticks and various homemade dips. Mrs B had made them tea-loaf, custard tarts, flapjacks, banana bread and even popped in some of her gingersnap cookies, gooey brownies and carrot muffins.

Lucy got cracking and did what she did best - preparing afternoon tea for them all - but much to Jack's dismay she was quite strict about rationing.

"This little lot might have to last us all weekend," she told him.

"Let's go and see if there's a generator in one of those sheds," he suggested to Robert, thinking the kettle was taking far too long to boil on the old stove.

But as the boys put on one of the raincoats that they found hanging near the back door, they paused...

...They heard footsteps on the gravel above...

...Falling silent, they waited to see who was approaching...

...The footsteps stopped...

...Then started again...

...Someone was coming down the stone steps to the cellar...

Chapter 12
~ * ~

Jimmy Pratt's stupid face suddenly appeared in front of them. He was drenched from head to toe looking like a wet dog.

"Those hail stones are something else," Jimmy said, and then grinned inanely, thrilled by their obvious surprise. "Aren't you going to let me in?"

"Oh my god," Lucy gasped. She recognised his voice even before she clapped eyes on him. She felt sick to the pit of her stomach and the blood drained from her face.

"What the f**k are you doing here?" Jack exclaimed angrily.

"Didn't expect to see me, did you?" Jimmy laughed as he pushed past them and threw off his soaking wet, tweed jacket onto one of the dining chairs.

"No we f**king didn't," Jack replied, looking at Lancelot as if he might be able to explain.

Lancelot was just as confused. "You weren't supposed to be here," he told Jimmy. "That was the deal with Van Ike. What are you doing here?"

Jimmy shrugged and greedily looked at all the food laid out on the table. "Change of plan," he replied, helping himself to a mini pork pie. "Get me a towel, babe," he said to Lucy as he pulled off his water filled Espadrilles. "They'll be p**sing ruined," he moaned as he examined them, unsuccessfully trying to rub mud off the string soles.

Lucy was still in such a state of shock that she automatically reached for a tea towel and handed it to him.

Everyone in the room wanted to punch Jimmy's lights out but Robert diffused the situation the best he could.

"Where are the others?" he asked Jimmy.

"Upstairs," he replied, and reached for another pie. Minnie pulled the plate away but she was too late to stop him grabbing another and in doing so she knocked his elbow, sending the pie out of his grasp and hurtling across the room where it splatted into pieces against the wall.

Everyone looked at the pie and then at Jimmy who just pretended it hadn't happened. "We nearly didn't make it," he explained. "We got stuck halfway here. That weird old couple from the Lodge towed the van the rest of the way with their tractor. The ford was so high we thought we'd have to turn back, but here we are! We couldn't find any of you in the front of the house, so I came round the back."

Everyone, except Lancelot (because of his ankle) and Sophie (because she was too tired), hurried up to the hall to find out who else had arrived.

Milling about in the entrance were the rest of the Haunted or Not team. They were bringing in equipment from a mud splattered, white van, all looking harassed and drenched expect for Carrie who, as always, looked immaculate. She was folding up a large golfing umbrella whilst trying to contact Van Ike, without success, on her mobile. She climbed up onto one of the window seats, holding the phone as high as she could to try to find a signal and whilst up there, she spotted the Little Eden friends coming up from the basement. "Hiya," she called to them. "Is there no signal around here? Sorry we're a day early, but we thought we'd better come now due to the flooding, otherwise we'd never have made it."

Carrie took one look at Jack and smiled. Holding out her hand she encouraged him to help her down. Jack gently brought her to the floor - his strong arms and muscular torso didn't go unnoticed by her - just as her shapely figure didn't go unnoticed by him!

There was something captivating about Carrie and she knew it. Her face was caked in contour make-up and her eyebrows were twice their normal size, as were her lashes, which gave her the supernatural look of a human-cyborg. Even women couldn't take their eyes off her, wondering if she was real or not. When she spoke, a perfect set of fluorescent-white teeth shone out from beneath her impossibly shiny, swollen lips. From her wrists hung heavy silver jewellery which jangled when she moved - unlike her augmented boobs which remained stationery at all times, floating, motionless, like two basketballs in front of her tiny, elongated waist. To top it all off she had legs like Shirley Maclaine, which she'd wrapped tightly in an expensive pair of patent leather jeans, and her wedge sneakers made her even taller than her natural 5ft 10inches. She constantly flicked her extended peroxide hair over her shoulder and her insanely long, fake nails looked as if they could be deadly weapons. Unfortunately, they also meant that she held everything, including her phone, in an odd looking way as she could never pick anything up without turning her hands sideways.

Minnie couldn't work out if she was beautiful or grotesque and had an urge to poke her to see if she was flesh and blood.

Lucy tried not to judge a book by its cover, although she couldn't help feeling inadequate in her presence, especially now that Jimmy was there.

She wished she'd not eaten quite so much cake since they'd split up and pulled her cardigan tightly around her, hoping to hide her bouncier bits.

Carrie made the introductions…"This is Dr Zac Wolf our cameraman," she said with a smile that gave everyone the impression that she was either very proud to have Dr Wolf on the team or that she was sleeping with him - no one was quite sure which.

Dr Wolf shook their hands in turn and in an alluring Canadian accent said, "Just call me Wolf." When he shook hands with India, he lingered a little longer saying, (with a twinkle in his eye) "Any problems you come to me. We're going to have some fun." India wasn't sure if he meant just with her or in general and nearly blushed. As he shook hands vigorously with Robert he added, "I've been looking forward to seeing this place for years. I've read about it, heard about it, but never been in it until now. You have some amazing places in England. Everywhere is so old and quaint."

"You should see Little Eden where we're from," India blurted out and then realised she'd maybe said it a little too eagerly.

Wolf smiled at her replying, "I'd like to see all of Little Eden if you'll be the one to show me around."

India was a little baffled by her immediate and visceral attraction to him - he wasn't her usual type at all. His dark, spiked hair was shaven at the sides into curved lines which accentuated his short anchor beard and gave him an unusual but very intriguing look. No one could help noticing the many tattoos which covered his sturdy hands, arms and neck. His charcoal, knee length shorts revealed more tattoos on his legs which depicted coiled snakes and the Tree of Life. He had a rugged, throw-on-whatever-is-to-hand, appearance and yet it was a deliberate style, well thought out and planned for effect and practicality. His Caterpillar boots meant his feet were not the slightest bit wet and his weather-beater coat had protected his 'Misfits Wolf Blood' t-shirt from the elements.

India felt as if he was buzzing with an electrical charge that was coming off him in waves. She wondered if she was just imagining it, but seeing the look on Minnie and Lucy's faces it was obvious they thought there were sparks flying between the two of them. She blushed fully this time and, feeling out of her depth, went to stand behind some camera cases out of his reach.

Carrie then introduced the other team member, Kaya Ashburner. "Kaya's local to the area and our guest Psychic Investigator on this shoot," Carrie explained. "She knows more about this house and the surrounding area than anyone else. We're lucky to have her onboard."

Kaya was quite the opposite of Carrie. She was short and tubby, shy and reserved, with bird like eyes which were framed with heavy eye liner. Her black lipstick, along with her ruby coloured hair, accentuated her pallid complexion (of which she was secretly very proud). From under long, flowing, velvet sleeves she offered Robert a pearlescent-white hand which was adorned with at least a dozen silver rings and finished with chipped, black painted fingernails. "I have been researching your family tree," she told him in a disguised Lancashire accent (which she sometimes forgot to cover up). "You're only a distant cousin of the Montgomery's so I was surprised to find you'd inherited the place. Still, I suppose no-one else wanted it. You may not want it either after you've met the spirits."

"Kaya knows where all the most haunted parts of the house and grounds are," Carrie explained.

"So it is haunted then?" Minnie asked, linking arms with Lucy for safety.

"Of course," Kaya replied, astonished that anyone would doubt it. "It's the most haunted house in the world." She handed Minnie a leaflet (just like the one India had found in the roadside café). "I've been here several times with different psychic investigations. No-one ever stays long after dark which is very disappointing. I'm hoping we can stay two full nights this time."

Minnie shivered. When they had come up from the cellar into the hall, she could have sworn she had seen a woman walking behind some of the pillars and had presumed it was Ada Mould, but when she had looked again, the woman had vanished. She realised that there wasn't a rug on the hall floor as she had first thought either. The house now felt so familiar to her that it was spooking her almost out of her wits. She found it difficult not to notice the things around her: like a chair by the large fireplace, a table near the front door, even a small dog running through one of the doorways, all of which were there one moment and gone the next. It was making her feel a bit wobbly and more than a little anxious. She felt a chill wafting around her from time to time and her 1960's, vintage sundress didn't feel protective against the elements.

Taking Carrie aside, Robert asked her why Jimmy Pratt had been allowed to come after all.

She apologised for his presence, explaining that Van Ike had had to change his plans at the last minute and that Jimmy was the only one who could fill his shoes. "If it makes you feel any better, I didn't want him here either," she told him.

Being far too polite to get angry with her, Robert said it was okay, but he knew it really wasn't okay at all and he felt uneasy for poor Lucy. He was also worried about what Jack might do if Jimmy annoyed him too much. They had often nearly come to blows over the last two years and Jimmy, being in his own environment, was in a particularly arrogant mood.

Just as Lucy invited them all down to the kitchen for a cuppa, out of the shadows appeared an elderly, rather skinny, slightly scruffy-looking couple. When they moved it was as if they were tied together by an invisible string.

Minnie held her breath for a moment unsure whether they were real of not but then was relieved that everyone else could see them as well.

"You must be Mrs Mould and Mr Dootson," Robert addressed them. When they didn't answer he added, "We were expecting you to have prepared the place for our stay."

He waited for an apology, but none came.

The strange couple just stared at him with unflinching eyes.

They were so obviously brother and sister, possibly twins, as their features were identical in every way except that Ada had her long, grey hair tied into a loose, scruffy bun and Arthur had his long, grey hair tied into a scraggy ponytail which clung to his damp, slightly whiffy, donkey jacket. Arthur's green wellington boots had obviously been patched quite a few times and Ada's plastic clogs were so worn down at the back she slopped around in them when she walked, making her gait seem like a drunken shuffle.

The curious couple reminded Robert of Bertie and Margie Flowerdew - the husband and wife who ran the allotments in Little Eden - they always had soil under their fingernails and bits of greenery in their hair. Robert had always suspected that their souls were visiting the human world from the land of the trolls and gnomes and imagined that one day they would disappear back into soil and become at one with Nature again.

Robert went to shake hands with Ada and Arthur, but they didn't seem to want to reciprocate (which he was rather glad of as their hands were stained yellow with tobacco and looked as if they hadn't been washed in a very long time). After an awkward moment he stepped away - they smelt of old socks and stale cigarettes. "Can you prepare the rooms and turn on the electricity?" he asked them.

Again, they didn't reply.

"And find us some food for dinner?" Lucy interjected.

No reply.

Minnie was starting to wonder if they were a hallucination after all.

"Can you take us back to the village in your tractor?" India asked hopefully.

Still no reply from either of them.

Everyone just stared at the odd couple, unsure how to break their steely gaze and their stony silence.

It was Kaya to whom they seemed to respond, and only to her. She nodded to them as if they had been waiting for her permission to speak.

Ada, began to explain that due to the floods they hadn't expected anyone to arrive at all. Due to years of chain smoking, her voice was cracked and barely audible and her accent was virtually incomprehensible but they got the gist that even the old tractor wouldn't get back through the ford over Manor Raike and back to the pub now.

"No one ever stays overnight," Arthur said suddenly, in such a booming voice it shocked them all as they had been listening so intently, trying to understand Ada. "We prepares the rooms then folks don't stay," he added.

Ada laughed which sent her into a coughing fit. Arthur hit her on the back, and she hacked up some phlegm which she wiped on her faded, and already stained, fleece sleeve. "No one ever stays," she hissed in agreement. Her eyes flashed as if she was turned on by the idea of visitors being so afraid that they couldn't bear to stay more than a few hours.

"Well, we are staying," Robert assured her. "It doesn't seem as if we have much choice in the matter anyway. We'd like the rooms preparing and we'd like the food we paid for to be brought to the kitchen."

"No food," Ada grunted.

"I'm sorry?" Robert asked, not understanding what she meant.

"Cut off by floods," Arthur added. "No supplies."

"Why didn't you get the provisions a few days ago?" Lucy asked - she was feeling anxious about the food situation again.

Neither of them offered an explanation so Kaya tried her best to encourage Arthur to take Jack to find the generator and Ada to prepare the bedrooms.

Before heading down to the kitchen, the Little Eden lot helped the Haunted or Not crew bring in the rest of their equipment. India picked up a very heavy bag which Wolf quickly took from her before she dropped it; their hands inadvertently touched. They smiled at each other both very aware of the frisson which passed between them.

"I don't suppose you brought any food in those bags, did you?" Lucy asked Wolf.

Wolf laughed, "Ghost hunting can give you the munchies, especially after midnight. I always bring some supplies." He opened the hold-all to reveal about twenty different chocolate bars, packets of crisps and some bottles of Budweiser as well as a couple of bottles of Jim Beam whisky. "Of course, if anyone wants any help getting the munchies, I've got some of that too."

India frowned. She disapproved of drugs. He really wasn't her type at all…but as she walked down the stairs she couldn't help feeling the heat rising through her body at even just the thought of him.

Chapter 13
~ * ~

Down in the kitchen, Lucy tried to work out how to make the food stretch between them all. She cut up the cakes and picnic food into even smaller pieces and arranged them decoratively on a large platter she had found in the cupboard.

Normally she found cooking, baking and serving others took her mind off things and she especially wanted to get Jimmy out of her head. This time though, with him there, flouncing about and constantly trying to be the centre of attention, it was impossible to ignore him. She wanted to hate him for cheating on her, but found, as usual, she was unable to hate anyone for very long, and wondered if, perhaps, he had come to the Manor deliberately to see her - to win her back.

"Don't you have anything healthier?" Carrie asked when she saw what was on offer.

"This all looks amazing," Wolf remarked, as he tucked into one of Mrs B's homemade sausage rolls.

"There's a full day's calories in that alone," Carrie pointed out. "I'll stick to what I brought, thank you," she told Lucy as she pushed away a plate of flapjacks. She fished about in her handbag for a cereal bar and an energy drink." She looked at Lucy and added, "I suppose you don't need to worry about what you look like as I do. Being in the public eye I have to watch my figure."

India knew that Carrie had meant to offend Lucy and weighed in to defend her friend, "I suppose if you did, heaven forbid, eat a piece of cake or a sausage roll, you could always have liposuction when you go for your next Botox injection."

Carrie grimaced but didn't reply. She'd had both of those treatments so she couldn't argue.

"I'm a vegan," Kaya said, "Is there anything I can eat?"

Lucy looked through the hampers and found some humus, mushroom pate and breadsticks. "These are about the only things that are vegan I'm afraid," she told Kaya.

"I believe being vegan helps with my psychic abilities," Kaya explained. "Meat is a low vibration. The fear the animal feels at the time of slaughter stays in the muscle memory, so you are essentially eating fear."

"But if you communicate with the dead for a living," India said, "Death and fear must be your bread and butter."

Kaya gave India a look that could have killed her - if looks could kill - and went off upstairs under the pretext of helping Ada prepare the bedrooms.

Jack and Robert came back from the outhouses, with Arthur in tow, having succeeded in getting the electricity working. Jack had investigated Arthur's vintage tractor, hoping he could take them all back to the pub, but Ada had not been lying when she said the tractor wouldn't get them very far now. It would crush what was left of Meg Bridge and end up in the syke and, as Arthur had explained, the ford crossing Manor Raike was now over 4ft deep.

When Jack told everyone that they were trapped at the Manor until the flood subsided, arguments ensued about whether to try to get across the fields on foot. The atmosphere in the kitchen became quite fraught and heated. Being stranded in such a gloomy, melancholy house seemed to be having a negative effect on everyone!

Arthur warned them that the bogginess of the land between there and the village was treacherous, "The bogs a' claimed many a life over t' years," Arthur told them. "Last 'ear a bairn were lost t' bog in Noblet Woods, yonder. You'll not sees the bogs 'til youse in 'em," he explained.

Robert remembered the will-o-the-wisp he had seen, hovering ominously over just such a quagmire in the woods. The wooden bridge he'd crossed to reach the stones had almost been breached by the swollen stream beneath it hours ago. He assumed it would be lost by now.

"What did he say?" Minnie whispered to Lucy, unable to fathom Arthur's strong accent.

"He says people have died in the bogs here and last year a child died in Noblet Woods," Lucy translated.

"But if tha' wants to takes tha's chances wit bogs be better than stayin' 'ere tha night," Arthur said with a half-smile. "Wait 'til dark and tha's had it either way. We ain't got room for yous at Lodge. Be sleeping under tha' trees tha' will."

Lucy was about to translate again but Minnie had understood this time and was torn between risking the bogs, sleeping outside in the storm, or being trapped inside the house with ghouls and spooks for the night.

The Haunted or Not team voted to stay, thrilled by the idea that the house was truly inhabited by the restless spirits of the Montgomery family. They were sure to get evidence on camera and amaze their viewers with all the supernatural phenomena they would witness.

Jimmy was particularly excited by the prospect of communing with countless ghosts.

It seemed as if no-one had any choice but to stay anyway. With no phone lines and no signal, they couldn't contact the local police - they were cut off until the floods drained away whether they liked it or not.

"Does as tha' chooses," Arthur said, and gladly took a custard tart which Lucy offered him. With that he left via the back door. As Robert went to shut it after him, he realised that Arthur had disappeared, up the steps and out of sight, quicker than was humanly possible. Puzzled, he climbed halfway up the steps to try to see which way Arthur had gone but he couldn't figure it out. *There must be a path through those bushes*, Robert thought. *Very strange.*

"I don't like him," Lucy said, when Arthur had gone, "He gives me the creeps."

"He just needs a wash, old girl," Jack chuckled.

"Both of them seem very peculiar," India agreed.

"You're out in wild North country now," Lancelot teased her. "We're not in Little Eden anymore."

"I think this whole Manor is one scary place," Minnie said quietly, afraid the ghosts might hear her.

Lucy decided a distraction was needed. She was starting to feel more and more uneasy too. She also wanted to get Sophie somewhere she could really rest. The general arguments and shouting hadn't done Sophie any good (being super sensitive to noise was unfortunately one of the symptoms of her condition). Lucy suggested they go and see if Ada and Kaya had prepared the bedrooms yet.

India, Minnie, Lucy, and Sophie made their way to the entrance hall together. They felt safe when they were with each other, although Minnie, even when not alone, was chilled to the bone by an ethereal creepiness which seemed to pervade every dark corner and lurk behind every door.

The grand staircase had the aura of a by-gone era with invisible ripples of stale energy emanating from the woodwork. Old clocks and occasional tables, which had been left untouched for nearly a hundred years, all seemed to hum with the presence of the ancestors. As they climbed the stairs, the shallow, wide, smooth oak steps creaked and groaned, and the portraits of the Montgomery family seemed to be observing their ascent - Lucy could swear their eyes were following her.

Due to the lack of carpets and soft furnishings, every footstep, every word, echoed around. The house felt barren, and Sophie couldn't help thinking that any happiness the rooms had once enjoyed had died long ago. Desolation and sadness seemed to have seeped into the very fabric of the building and loneliness sulked in the shadows.

Sophie stopped suddenly in her tracks...

...A cute King Charles spaniel came running down the stairs and danced around her feet. She looked at the others but it was clear that only she could see it. Not wanting to alarm them, she ignored it with her real-self whilst her astral-self secretly bent down to pet it. "What's your name then?" her astral-self asked the gorgeous little dog whose tail was wagging almost to the point of frenzy. She intuitively knew his name - it was Humphrey. "If you're the only ghost it'll all be alright," she told him as she picked him up to cuddle him. The real Sophie could feel invisible warmth in her arms and smiled to herself. She was glad of his company in such a hostile, dispiriting place.

Reaching the landing, they could turn either left or right; guided by the faint sound of Kaya's voice, they turned left into the south wing, which had been renovated in the late 1990's, and where the decor and energy were lighter and a great deal more pleasant.

Kaya came out of one of the rooms carrying some clean towels. "Ada has put you in the best rooms," she told them. "There are two renovated drawing rooms downstairs where the Haunted or Not team can bed down if they want to take a break from filming. There are only three fully renovated rooms up here. You'll have to share." She looked at them as if she wasn't sure they had ever shared anything in their whole lives (she thought they were spoilt southerners just there on a jolly).

Lucy assured her that sharing was what they would prefer as they didn't want to be left alone in such a place as this.

Kaya nodded over to some of the portraits saying, "There are plenty of previous residents still wandering the halls. This is an unquiet house, full of spirit visitations and lost souls." One of the portraits, a stately looking man in a long white wig and a black cassock, was the spitting image of Lancelot. "Some of them look like your friends, don't they?" she commented and pointed to another of a man wearing armour, sitting on a horse with a sword in his scabbard and carrying a flowing standard which was waving in the wind - he was a carbon copy of Robert. "The house has many secrets and mysteries within it," she continued to say rather dramatically. "I find it fascinating that these people used to live here, think and talk and play out their lives here. I feel them all around, don't you? It's as if they are still whispering - breathing - as if they are still alive." Kaya paused for a few moments. She seemed to pass into a dream-like state as if she had vanished into another world for a few moments. "Only their bodies are buried - their souls live on here. It is their house and always will be."

"It's Robert's house now," India pointed out.

"I suppose it is," Kaya admitted. "Although he isn't a direct descendent of the Montgomery family, is he?" She took them down the corridor a little to see a more modern portrait of a gentleman in military uniform. "The last Lord Roger Montgomery left the house in 1912." She drew their attention to the painting next to him of a beautiful young woman wearing a powder-blue silk gown and a wide-brimmed hat trimmed with white chiffon and fresh flowers; around her were three small children, each with pretty ringlets and adorable cherub-like faces, playing with a King Charles spaniel (which was clearly Humphrey). "That is Lady Edith his third wife. Beautiful, isn't she? She and her children died in mysterious circumstances."

"What circumstances?" Minnie asked, not entirely sure she wanted to know.

Kaya lowered her voice to a whisper, as if it was a secret, "Poor Lady Edith threw herself from the round tower after drowning her three small children in the lake."

"If that's the case, it's hardly mysterious," India said. "It's only mysterious if no-one knows what happened."

"No one knows why she did it," Kaya replied defensively. "They say one day she was as right as rain and the next...she'd gone mad, and they were all dead."

Minnie gasped at such a sudden and bewildering switch from sanity to total and violent insanity. She couldn't believe such a serene-looking lady could brutally murder her own children.

"His first two wives died young, they say it was from Tuberculosis and Smallpox, but I believe they were both murdered by..."

...Suddenly Ada stepped out of a doorway giving them all a fright...

"Don't go in't other rooms," Ada warned them, her eyes flashing with authority. "Only these three rooms is safe." Her cracked voice and piercing gaze made the girls afraid to venture anywhere else for fear of her disapproval, rather than fear of the supernatural. She looked at Minnie with her beady stare, "You've been 'ere afore," she said.

"No, I've never even been to Lancashire before," Minnie replied, but the hairs on the back of her neck were bristling and she shivered as goose bumps rose up on her arms.

"Hmmm," Ada replied. She hadn't meant in 'this life' but was in no mood to explain herself to the uninitiated and she shuffled off towards the stairs (or least they thought that's where she must have gone as she seemed to disappear rather quickly into nowhere).

"Does she mean it's not safe because of the ghosts?" Minnie asked Kaya.

Kaya shrugged, "She means that the floors and ceilings in most of the rooms are unstable. Some were never finished during the renovations or not even started." As she left to go downstairs, she turned and added, "As for ghosts - they're everywhere. Even in these rooms. If they don't want you here, they'll soon let you know."

Chapter 14

~ * ~

Minnie grabbed hold of Sophie's hand and shuddered. Kaya's words had frightened her.

"Don't worry," Sophie reassured her friend. "They're just trying to scare us like they do everyone who comes here. Even if there are some ghosts…"

…India interrupted…"Which there aren't…"

"…They probably can't see you," Sophie added and astrally patted Humphrey's cute little head.

Minnie wasn't convinced.

They all peered into the first bedroom.

"Is this room haunted?" Lucy asked her sister. "You can always sense if there's a presence in a room."

Sophie tried to walk through the doorway but felt across it the familiar, invisible force-field which she usually sensed when a room had an active spirit in it. She'd felt it since childhood and often wondered if it was her guides protecting her by stopping her entering haunted rooms, or whether it was the ghosts keeping her out. She didn't want to disturb whatever presence might be in the room, worried that connecting with one ghoulish manifestation might set off a chain of unstoppable supernatural events. She felt it best to keep her distance, keep quiet and keep hoping that it was all going to be alright.

She didn't want to scare Minnie, so she just said, "Let's look at the others first. I'm not sure I like the yellow wallpaper in this one."

"The boys can sleep in that one then," Lucy giggled.

Suddenly, Lucy screamed her head off, causing everyone else to scream too!!!!

"Thanks a lot, old girl," Jack had said in her ear as he'd come up behind her.

"Don't do that!" she exclaimed and slapped him on the arm.

Jack laughed. He'd brought up their bags for them. "I was just being gentlemanly," he grinned, "But I see all the thanks I get is to be put up in a room with a bunch of spooks."

"Oh, don't say that," Minnie said.

"Jack's teasing you," India told her. "He doesn't believe in ghosts any more than I do. There's nothing here that can harm us."

Jack pulled a face. "I don't know about that!" he said. "Jimmy Pratt needs to be afraid of me, that's for sure."

Lucy sighed. "I'm not happy about him being here either, but he's here now and we'll just have to get on with it. If I can be civil to him, everyone else can be too. I don't want any trouble. We might be stuck here all weekend. Don't start on him."

"I won't if he won't," Jack reassured her, "But one wrong word or move from him and he'll be…"

…India intervened as she could see that Lucy was getting upset and shooed Jack back downstairs before he could say anymore.

"Let's try this one," India suggested and opened another door.

Sophie hesitated, but feeling no astral barrier, she stepped inside. "This one is prettier," she said with a sigh of relief. The walls were lined with pale-pink silk and the opulent gold furniture gleamed in the early evening sunlight. "You can't get much grander than that bed, can you?" she said.

They all had to agree about the bed which was draped in gold damask with long magenta tassels dangling from a grand over-canopy. The mattress was covered with clean, white sheets a satin, feather-filled eiderdown. Amongst the many gilt mirrors hung paintings of gardens, billowing flowers and exotic birds, and above the fireplace, facing the bed, was a long portrait of a beautiful lady wearing a sumptuous gold and silver gown.

At first glance, Minnie had thought the room was decorated with wooden panelling and hung with a tapestry depicting the Garden of Eden, but that image passed away instantly and she too saw the luxurious silk. She wanted to say something to the others about the strange visions she was having but didn't know how to explain it to them.

"I like this one too, but let's check out the other one before we decide," Lucy suggested.

The final room was even more splendid than the other two, with Chinese-style wallpaper from floor to ceiling depicting cranes and pergolas, delicate bamboo forests and blossoming chrysanthemums. The twin, queen-sized, sleigh beds looked inviting, and a bejewelled cut-glass chandelier cast rainbows across the room.

"This is the nicest," Sophie reassured them. "It has a very calm feeling to it and the light refraction keeps it clear of stale energies." Humphrey seemed to like this one too and jumped out of Sophie's arms, settling himself on the end of one of the beds, curling into a fur ball and falling asleep.

82

Minnie was relieved to see that the room stayed as it was in the present except, she had thought, just for a second, that she'd seen a little dog curled up on the bed, though there was no dog to be seen in reality.

India opened a door at other end of the room to reveal an opulent marble Jack-and-Jill en-suite which was shared with the pink room. "Look!" She beckoned to the others to come and see. "They're connecting."

"If anyone feels scared, we can leave the doors open between us," Lucy suggested, "And worst case scenario we'll all have to bunk up together!"

Sophie's brain was lagging again, and she couldn't keep up with the conversation. All noises seemed sharpened as if everyone was shouting despite the fact that they were speaking quite normally. Her body emptied of energy like a popped balloon and her balance was becoming shaky - she knew it was time to give in. "I think I need to lie down now," she admitted. "I hate to ask, but will one of you stay with me?"

"Of course, I'll stay," Minnie said. "I feel safer with you because you can give me a heads up if any spirits start coming out of the woodwork." She looked around and prayed that they wouldn't. "Besides, I could do with a nana nap," she added.

Sophie climbed wearily onto the nearest bed and gladly let her aching back and head rest on the soft pillow. Closing her sore eyes, she mumbled, "I'll just rest here for a bit."

India and Lucy went to collect the bags from the landing and took them into the pink room.

As Lucy looked out the window she couldn't help saying, "I don't like being stuck here with the Haunted or Not team, do you?" What she really meant was with Jimmy.

"I don't like that Kaya," India replied, and then thinking of Wolf, she surprised herself by hoping he was a good kisser and, involuntarily, a little vision popped into her mind in which he pulled her into his strong arms for protection as a banshee flew out of the bathroom towards them both.

Her little daydream was cut short by Lucy asking, "Why don't you like Kaya?"

"Oh, I don't know," India replied. "She's got an attitude. She doesn't want us here. The way she talks about the Manor you'd think it was her house."

"Perhaps she's a bit shy," Lucy said. "She's new to their team and doesn't know any of us. I suppose she must feel a bit of the odd one out. You've been a bit curt with Carrie too since we got here," she added.

"Have I?" India asked. "Perhaps I have. I can't explain it, but I feel as if I want to run away. I feel trapped by the floods. I don't like feeling out of control of my surroundings. I'm not saying I would leave but I prefer to feel that I could leave if I wanted to."

"Don't let cabin fever get to you just yet," Lucy told her, "We might be stuck here for a few days."

Outside, on the lawn, they could see Carrie, Wolf and Jimmy were making the most of a short lull in the rain and the rare bursts of sunshine - they were setting up some establishing shots of the exterior. Jimmy was introducing the show, giving his usual hyperbolic and florid speech about ghosts, hauntings, unquiet spirits and dark, sinister goings on which only they, as professional paranormal investigators, could explain, and how the supernatural would play with their sanity and lead them into a dangerous world of the undead.

Lucy couldn't help wondering if Jimmy really wanted her back and how he might go about it if he did. Would she take him back? *Only if he begs me*, she thought to herself, *Gets down on bended knee and tells me I'm the love of his life and that he wants to marry me.*

"I wonder how you decide your profession is going to be ghost hunting," India pondered, thinking about Wolf again. "Do they really believe they can capture someone's spirit on camera?"

"Yes, or at least Jimmy does," Lucy replied. "I'm not sure consciousness is something you can film though. Perhaps thoughts and emotions do emit a sound or a light wave and one day someone will invent a device sensitive enough to read them. After all, emotions do have colours, don't they? You know, we say we're 'feeling blue' when we're sad or 'green with envy'.

"Or the 'red mist', when you are angry," India laughed, "Or red for passion," she added, looking at Wolf again and wondering why she was so overwhelmingly attracted to him. Her rational mind saw a liquor-drinking, joint-smoking, tattooed wild-child who was too interested in the macabre world of the dead; but her body fizzed with excitement at the thought of his touch and hummed with an electrical charge when he was near her.

Still watching the three outside, Lucy saw Jimmy stumble over some of the old Abbey foundation stones which were poking up out of the grass. He lost his balance and slipped on the wet grass falling flat on his back like an upturned turtle.

84

"I wonder what colour you go when you laugh?" Lucy pondered and couldn't help giggling as Wolf tried to pull Jimmy up but struggling to keep his own footing he fell right on top of his friend, hitting Jimmy in the nether regions with the sound boom.

"Yellow, maybe? Or orange?" India suggested as she began to laugh out loud too. "Dr G wears orange and he is always smiling and laughing."

"I hope they didn't hurt themselves," Lucy said, feeling a little bad for laughing at someone else's misfortune. She was sure Dr G would run to their rescue rather than find it hilarious. She suddenly shuddered as she felt a mysterious sense of foreboding wash over her along with a tinge of guilt. She didn't feel like laughing anymore.

Looking out towards the horizon, they could both see raging, grey storm clouds gathering over the trees, heavy and saturated with more torrential rain.

"If this place was a colour," Lucy sighed, "It would be black."

Chapter 15
~ * ~

India and Lucy were curious to see the other renovated rooms and went back downstairs to take a sneaky-peek. Lucy always had romantic ideas about stately homes and wondered what this one would look like if it were treated with love and care. The first drawing room off the hall, was spacious, welcoming, and full of light, (when it wasn't raining). The sun poured in through two magnificent, square, bay-windows which gave a fair prospect over the parkland and down to the lake. The walls were blood-red and the ornate furniture was upholstered in the same rich colour. The whole room felt regal, with ornate columns at the far end and an arching ceiling which was decorated with fine, delicate, white plasterwork. A marble fireplace took centre stage and a large hearth, surrounded by a brass club fender, was laid ready for a fire to be lit. The paintings in this room were copies of the valuable originals but they were still charming and of friendly subjects such as vases of flowers, fruit bowls, horses, dogs and scenes of Venice.

Going through to the second refurbished room they found it was much the same size as the first, but with French doors leading out onto a crooked paved terrace. Finely carved swags of flowers and fruit, by Grinling Gibbons, adorned the upper mantelpiece as well as the light wooden panels on the walls. The furniture was more modern than in the previous room. A velvet covered Chesterfield sofa and comfortable armchairs were arranged in a square near the fire and a grand piano stood by one of the windows. A green baize covered card table was laid out as if a game was just about to begin, but on closer inspection, the girls realised that instead of playing cards, they were divination cards, and in the centre of the table there was a large, heart shaped planchette, ready to be used, with a blank piece of paper underneath and pencil inserted into the hole.

"I don't like the look of that," Lucy remarked with a shiver. "It's a shame because the rest of the room is delightful. Everything looks so new, as if it's never been used." She plonked herself down on the sofa. "I would love this sofa in my flat. And these silk cushions are to die for." She immediately wished she hadn't used those words as the creeping feeling of doom, which had been haunting her on and off since entering the house, returned.

"I suppose most of this hasn't ever been used much," India said, as she played a little ditty on the piano (which was somewhat out of tune). "If only the original furnishings were still here, we could have raised millions towards saving Little Eden. Mr T says there used to be Chippendale chairs and original Greek statues."

"Perhaps the family didn't take everything of value out of the house?" Lucy hoped.

India sighed. "Roger sent us an inventory and it all seemed to be reproduction. "I don't expect we'll be finding any secret treasure in a wardrobe. As she looked around, she realised that the pelmets above the windows were not velvet, as the curtains were, but were made of wood. The trompe l'oeil was extraordinary and she was about to comment on how things are never quite what they seem when they heard voices coming from the next room.

The door was slightly ajar and intrepidly they both tiptoed towards it.

They couldn't quite shake the idea that it might be ghosts.

Even India was a little on edge and she didn't believe in them!

They peered through the gap to see Kaya and Robert sitting together under a highly decorative stained-glass window that depicted several family coats of arms, and through which the sun created coloured patterns on the table in front of them.

Kaya was giving Robert a lecture on the history of the house and showing him old lithographs of the Manor in a large, leather bound book.

Robert heard the door creak open - it startled him out of his concentration. He was relieved to see it was the living not the dead as he feared, and he hailed Lucy and India over to join them. "Come and look at these illustrations of the Manor," he urged them. "You can see how it's been changed and added to over the centuries."

As the girls entered the room proper, they could see it was a vast library, with glass-fronted shelves still packed full of books, except on the mezzanine floor where the mahogany bookcases now stood empty. It reminded Lucy of Daisy Place Bookshop and she suddenly felt homesick and anxious about Tambo. She checked her mobile phone in the vain hope that there might have a signal. There wasn't one of course.

The library had not been fully renovated and looked a little worse for wear; it also smelt oppressive with the odour of fusty paper and years of dust. Lucy felt sorry for the books, so neglected and unloved. To her books were living, breathing entities each with their own soul and consciousness, deserving of respect and care. She loved books.

"This is an etching of the Abbey," Robert said, pointing to one of the fine ink drawings. "At the Reformation it was demolished, and the stones were taken to build the first house as well as some of the surrounding farm cottages. It's a travesty that such beautiful architecture was destroyed," he sighed. "I feel ashamed it was my ancestors who did it."

"Don't be too hard on them," Kaya reassured him. "The Montgomery family were closet Catholics for at least three centuries after the Reformation and risked their lives to worship in the old way. If they hadn't taken the stones from the Abbey, their religious leanings would have been discovered and their land confiscated. I suppose, in a funny kind of way, they were preserving it by building this house with the stones. The arch you came under and several low walls around the house are all that remain of the Abbey above ground, but you can still get into the crypt from the basement - it was used as a wine cellar until 1912, when the family finally moved out and took all the wine with them."

Lucy couldn't help herself; she wanted to explore the room and see what the books were about. Some of the books were so huge it would have taken two people to lift them. The collection was like a 19th Century Wikipedia. "Some of these books might be worth a bit," she told Robert, but she could see there were gaps on the shelves and guessed that the most valuable ones had been removed long ago.

"Don't go over that side of the room," Kaya suddenly called out.

Lucy's heart skipped a beat and she stopped dead in her tracks.

"The ceiling isn't safe at that end," Kaya explained.

Lucy looked up at the discoloured plaster and, as if on cue, a chunk came crashing down, along with a big cloud of fine dust, and nearly hit her on the head. Coughing, she ran back to the window and stayed close to Robert.

"Unfortunately, the house is still in need of major repair," Kaya told Robert. "It was requisitioned during both world wars; during the First it was a hospital and during the Second it was a secret military headquarters. It's a long time since it was a family home."

Kaya showed them some black and white photographs in which rows of metal beds were lined up with neatly dressed nurses standing proudly beside their heroic patients. One image showed a picnic by the lake, but Lucy's heart broke when she saw that nearly every man had had one or both of his legs amputated.

"The Manor lay empty for decades until the 1990's when a member of the Montgomery family thought it might make a high class boutique hotel," Kaya continued to say.

"Ah yes, Cousin Caroline's daughter, Florence," Robert replied. "Roger told me she didn't like the weather over here - too cold and far too much rain - compared to Monaco."

India laughed, "Based on the weather here so far I can't blame her for wanting to go back to the sunny Mediterranean."

"That's not the reason," Kaya said emphatically, "And it doesn't always rain like this - this is unusual even for us. The real reason the renovations stopped was because no tradesmen would stay here for more than a few days before they quit. The builders and architects refused to come back due to the overwhelming paranormal activity."

"Is it really that bad here?" Lucy asked and shivered at the thought. "I know it feels a bit creepy, and it feels really sad - at least I keep feeling really sad - but we haven't seen or heard a ghost yet. Sophie would have mentioned it if it was really haunted." (Lucy had no idea that lying on the window seat beside her was Humphrey, the ghost dog, who had come to investigate the noises in the library).

"I think I know more about the spirit world than your sister does," Kaya said condescendingly (also totally unaware of Humphrey's presence). "You and your sister may be a little intuitive or empathic but I'm a professional psychic and medium. I have even done guided tours here on occasion. I know all the undead spirits who walk this house personally." Turning to Robert, and putting her hand on his, she added, "You're a little bit psychic. I can always tell when I meet another with the gift."

Robert was a bit taken aback. "I...er...well, yes sometimes. How did you know?" he asked her.

Kaya smiled and squeezed his hand. "All the women in my family, going back generations, have been psychics and healers. My mother read tea-leaves and palms. My grandmother was a highly respected medium. We can always tell another with the shining. I think we seek each other out, don't you? We are kindred spirits drawn together through time and space to meet again in other lifetimes. I believe we are reunited from long ago, don't you? I feel we are soul mates."

Robert slowly moved his hand from under Kaya's and continued to turn the pages of the book. He didn't feel 'reunited' with Kaya and actually felt a little uncomfortable with her over-friendly advances. "I'm not sure I would call it a gift," he said. "Sophie calls it a curse."

"Then Sophie doesn't understand it," Kaya replied angrily - frustrated that everyone seemed so obsessed with Sophie's opinions. "I feel the suffering of the ancestors. I sense their grief and their pain as if it were my own. I feel more akin to the dead than to the living. For now, I must be content with being their earthly medium, but I long for the time when I can join them fully in death. Don't you feel it?" She looked at Robert as if he should understand how she felt. "You must sense the spiritual union which calls out to us over the ether. Come home it says. Come, be your true self beyond the human world."

"That's a bit much!" India remarked.

"On the contrary," Kaya replied, a little less poetically. "Anyone who is enlightened knows that death is the reality and life is the illusion. To me, the afterlife is far more romantic than this mundane human life, don't you agree?" she asked Robert.

Robert didn't know what to say. He would rather be alive rather than dead - if he had the choice.

"I don't think there is anything romantic about death," Lucy said, thinking about poor Aunt Lilly and little Joshua with tears welling up in her eyes.

"That's because you don't comprehend the mysteries of the universe," Kaya told her. "Death is the ultimate adventure! The infinite journey of the soul continues long after we have 'shuffled off this mortal coil.'" Then, dramatically and wistfully, she began to recite a few lines of a poem...

"Death drags the hell hounds into Heaven with a warrior's cry.
Victorious over Life
Sounding
Resounding
The bell of Peace.
'The war is over' echoes in the air.
Death Invictus!"

As Kaya had spoken the words out loud they had given Lucy goose bumps and the library was starting to give her the heebie-jeebies. It was as if the poem had set the books chattering and whispering amongst themselves.

"If you are not interested in the supernatural and life-after-death, why have you all come here for the weekend?" Kaya asked them incredulously.

"We're not really interested in the ghosts," Robert explained. "We joked about whether it was haunted or not but really we came to see what value the house and land might be to us - to Little Eden."

Kaya frowned and was annoyed. "I hope you haven't got any ideas about selling it?" she said impertinently. "This is a historical landmark and an important research centre for the paranormal."

"Seeing as no one can stay in it after dark it doesn't seem much use as a research centre," India said. "It's not 'Miss Cackles Academy for Witches' for goodness sakes."

Kaya didn't find her remark the least bit amusing.

Suddenly, a book shot off the table and crashed to the floor, making them all jump out of their skins (even Humphrey darted off his cushion and ran off into the next room)!

Kaya went to pick it up. "That's psychokinesis," she told them, as if it was perfectly normal for inanimate objects to fly around the room. "It happens when there is an emotional charge. I'm so attuned to the astral vibrations that light bulbs, electrical items, watches… they often blow up when I'm around."

India wasn't sure if Kaya had just pushed the book to the floor with her elbow when they hadn't been looking and was highly doubtful about such things being possible.

Lucy was freaked out and clung to Robert's arm. "I don't want to stay here after dark," she said, "I don't like it."

"It's only those who are not professional who run away - scared of that which they can't explain," Kaya said. "I would have stayed overnight many times myself only I don't think it's safe to stay alone and no-one else has ever had the courage to stay with me. Dr Wolf and James Hollywood are famous for their professionalism - they won't be frightened away by anything. You go back to the village if you want to, but tonight, those of us who stay will witness the many supernatural phenomena which are reported to happen here, and you'll see - it really is the most haunted house in world."

Chapter 16
~ * ~

Upstairs in the Chinese bedroom Minnie awoke with a jolt. Her heart was racing.

She had no idea where she was, what time it was, or even what year it was.

She looked across and saw Sophie asleep in the adjoining bed and breathed a sigh of relief.

It was just a bad dream, she told herself.

She realised she was sweating and her palms were clammy.

She needed a drink of water.

The rain had started to thunder down again and the storm clouds shut out the evening sun. The house creaked like an old wooden ship in a storm, and she listened, with dread, to every tap and every moan. A sombre light in the room, and the relentless lashing of water against the windows made her feel uneasy - she didn't like moving about on her own. Gathering her courage, she walked quietly (so as not to wake Sophie) into the en-suite, where she found a glass and ran the cold water. Looking up into the mirror, she gazed at her face thinking she looked drawn and pale.

Suddenly she ran out screaming - flinging herself onto Sophie's bed!

"What the hell?" Sophie exclaimed, scared out of her wits by the unexpected drama.

Minnie couldn't speak she was so terrified. She just pointed towards the bathroom, trying to catch her breath.

"It's okay. It's okay," Sophie told her friend, although she had no idea if it really was okay. Sophie felt her heart racing and Minnie was visibly shaking. "What happened?" she asked.

Minnie still couldn't answer.

"Deep breaths - keep breathing," Sophie told her friend, to reassure herself as much as Minnie.

They both sat on the bed, encouraging each other to calm down, whilst still clinging to each other, petrified that there was something invisible and sinister in the room with them.

When Minnie managed to get the words out, she told Sophie…"It wasn't my face. I mean it was my face but then it wasn't my face. I swear it wasn't me. Oh my god it was hideous."

"Your face? Where?" Sophie asked, confused.

"In the mirror," Minnie explained, and pointed to the en-suite. "In the bathroom. I looked in the…" she shuddered at the memory of it and her toes curled with horror…"I looked in the mirror and it wasn't me. Someone else was looking back at me!"

"Do you know whose face it was?" Sophie asked.

"I don't know," Minnie cried. Then she realised something, "I think it was the lady from the portrait in the room next door."

"The one in the big gold dress?" Sophie asked.

Minnie nodded.

"Okay," Sophie said slowly, giving herself time to take in all the information. She closed her eyes and turned on her third-eye, scanning the room with her astral sight. There didn't seem to be any spirits present, or at least not that she could see. Praying to St Margaret for courage, and saying the Lord's Prayer to invoke white-light protection, she got out of bed. "I'll go and have a look," she offered, but her legs refused to move and she couldn't quite bring herself to go alone. "I think you'll have to come with me," she told Minnie.

Holding hands, they tentatively and very slowly, tried to walk into the bathroom, but with each step forward their feet seemed to want to take two steps back.

Finally, they peered through the door.

There was no sign of anyone in there.

Sophie took another big deep breath and made herself go to the mirror.

Minnie, still holding onto Sophie's hand, looked away.

Sophie stood in front of the mirror. She half closed her eyes in trepidation. She prayed that if she did see the strange and grotesque face instead of her own, that she'd be able to handle it. Gradually, opening her eyes fully, she stared into the glass, and to her profound relief, there was only her own countenance reflected back at her. *God my hair's a mess*, she couldn't help thinking, *And I really should wear make-up. I look like a ghost myself.*

"Is it still there?" Minnie asked fearfully, her eyes still firmly shut.

"There's nothing here. Maybe it was a trick of the light," Sophie suggested.

Sophie led a terror-stricken Minnie past the mirror and through the linking door into the pink bedroom to look at the portrait of the lady in gold. "Was it her?" she asked Minnie, wondering how such a beautiful woman could appear as a hideous monster.

Minnie nodded and then felt sick, remembering what she had seen. "She looked like her but then she turned into a vampire and nearly came out the mirror at me, like in one of those 3d movies. Oh god, it was awful."

"Did you have a nightmare before you went into the bathroom?" Sophie asked.

Minnie couldn't deny that she had.

"Tell me about the dream and it might dispel the fear," Sophie suggested. They sat on the big four-poster bed and wrapped the eiderdown around themselves, feeling that the quilt might somehow protect them - if there was something to be protected from. Sophie was relieved when Humphrey pootled into the room and jumped on the bed with them - his presence seemed reassuring and calming even though he was a ghost.

"I was dreaming about Little Eden and Buttons and Bows at first," Minnie explained. "Alice was asking me if she could sew a costume for the school play, which now I realise was that dress in the picture, but then I wasn't in the shop anymore but standing in the entrance hall here at the Manor. At first it looked like it does today, but as I climbed the stairs it was as if I was walking into the past, the furnishings changed, the pictures, everything was different. It became really vivid, like I was in a virtual reality game rather than a dream. It felt so real, more than real."

"You had what's called a lucid dream," Sophie explained. "The visuals and noises from the lucid dream can often carry on when we are awake too. You might have been sleep-walking to the bathroom but thought you were awake and only woke up fully when you screamed. I often wake up but can hear voices down in the café or in the yard, then when I get up to look there's no-one there. It's really disconcerting and disorientating - scary even. The voices always sound so genuine."

"You might be right," Minnie conceded. "I sometimes dream I've woken up but then realise I'm still asleep. I did used to sleep-walk as a child but I haven't done that in years."

"What happened in the rest of the dream?" Sophie asked.

"I woke in a four-poster bed in the yellow bedroom. Then suddenly the walls weren't yellow anymore but covered in dark, wooden panelling from floor to ceiling and it felt oppressive and gloomy. The furniture was different too - older, chunky, heavy looking. The bed wasn't very comfortable and I remember thinking I didn't like it in there when I felt something wet on my face. I put my hand up to feel it and it was blood. My head was bleeding. I remember thinking I had had a migraine and that's why I had gone to bed. Then I had the memory of a doctor cutting my head with a knife to let out bad spirits. All of a sudden, the door opened and there was candlelight coming from the landing, so I got up. I was wearing a full-length, white cotton nightdress, and I remember I felt cold and that my feet were bare on the wooden floor boards. I went out onto the landing where it was the same gloomy panelling, but there wasn't anybody there. I don't know who was holding the candle. Then the dream switched, you know how dreams do, and I was in this room, only it was blue not pink, and I was dressed in a fine, silk evening gown, looking in a dressing table for a necklace; and that's when I woke up. Or at least that was when I thought I'd woken up."

Sophie sighed. "That's a disturbing dream. I bet you thought you'd woken at that point but you didn't really wake up until you were in the bathroom - after you saw the face."

Sophie felt a little safer now that she had a rational explanation and bravely went over to look more closely at the painting to see if it had a name written underneath. A small plaque in the frame had some letters on it but they had faded to the point of being almost illegible. "I think it says 'Isabelle'?" she told Minnie. She noticed that Isabelle was standing with her hand lightly resting on an ornate dressing table, and her first-finger seemed to be pointing just under the mirror. "Did you say you were looking for something in here?"

Minnie nodded and came to inspect the painting too. "In a dressing table - in fact, that dressing table, that's the very one I saw."

Sophie looked around the room and noticed that the same dressing table was being used as a bedside table. The mirror was different to the one in the painting, but it was standing on a row of small drawers just like the original. Opening all of the drawers she was disappointed to find that they were empty.

She felt like Catherine Morland in 'Northanger Abbey' finding nothing exciting after all.

"I think there might be a secret compartment," Minnie told her. She pulled the right-hand drawer out fully, and putting her hand inside, she felt around and pushed against a little button; out from the side popped a secret drawer.

"How did you know there'd be a secret place?" Sophie asked in a hushed

95

voice. She wasn't sure why she was whispering but it felt the right thing to do when faced with a mysterious secret.

"I can't explain it," Minnie replied under her breath. "I kind of just knew what to do - as if I'd done it before."

"Is there anything in it?" Sophie asked hopefully.

Minnie put her fingers as far in as she could and pulled out a red velvet pouch.

They both gasped and couldn't wait to find out what was inside.

Opening it up, Minnie drew out a shimmering, glittering, diamond necklace with a deep-red ruby set inside a bow of emeralds.

"Bloody Nora!" Minnie exclaimed as she held it up.

Even in the dullness of the room it shone with an almost electric brilliance.

Sophie gazed at it in wonder, and even Humphrey lifted his head in curiosity.

"Wait a minute," Sophie exclaimed, "Look! The lady, Isabelle, in the picture, it's her necklace!"

Minnie turned to look at the portrait and Sophie was right. Isabelle was wearing the exact same necklace.

They were both really spooked.

They felt a chill crawl up their spines.

The hairs stood up on the back of their necks and they both felt their stomachs flip, causing a wave of nausea to ripple through them.

"She must have been communicating with you in your dream," Sophie said, "Passing you a secret message from beyond the grave. She must have been dream weaving from the other side to guide you to it."

They both fell silent; stunned and afraid; pondering the necklace and the idea that Isabelle's spirit might be haunting the house after all.

Unexpectedly, a gust of wind threw the rain at the window with such force it almost crashed right through the glass, causing them to jump nearly out of their skins!

Minnie dropped the necklace on the bed in fright. "I don't like this. I'm out of here!" she exclaimed, and ran out of the room and onto the landing.

Sophie picked up the necklace, and with Humphrey at her heels, she was only a few steps behind her friend as they both raced down the stairs, sacred out of their wits!

Chapter 17
~ * ~

As Minnie and Sophie came racing down the main staircase, they nearly collided with Wolf who was setting up an EMF meter halfway up.

"Woah!" he said as he caught Minnie in his arms, just in time to save them both from tumbling down the rest of the steps.

Sophie, who was so close behind (with Humphrey in hot pursuit) that she couldn't stop herself in time, ran into them both, nearly knocking them all flying - she managed to grab hold of the balustrade and Wolf's arm as her astral-self saved poor Humphrey from going head over heels.

"What's going on?" Wolf asked as he steadied them all.

"There's a face in the mirror," a breathless Minnie told him, "And a necklace and a ghost called Isabelle."

"Where?" he asked with excitement.

"In the pink bedroom," Sophie told him, "And in the bathroom mirror in the en-suite."

Wolf didn't need to hear any more, and without hesitation, he began to run up the stairs, two at a time, calling Carrie on the walkie-talkie to tell her and Jimmy to grab the cameras and meet him upstairs.

Sophie and Minnie hurried down until they reached the kitchen where, much to their relief, they found Lancelot talking to Jack by the fire. Robert, who had brought some of the books from the library for the others to see, was deep conversation with Kaya, whilst India was helping Lucy prepare a picnic supper.

"There you are!" Lucy said. "Did you have a good…?" She was about to ask them if they'd had a good nap then stopped short when she saw the look on their faces. "What's happened?"

Minnie explained, and Lucy quickly gave them both a cup of tea and made them sit down.

Sophie was calmed by Humphrey who came and sat on her lap; she wished she could tell Minnie about him but didn't want to spook her friend any more than she was already. They told everyone the story about the mirror, and then Kaya asked, "Which portrait was it again?"

"The one in the pink room, opposite the bed and above the fireplace," Sophie told her. "I think it says Isabelle underneath."

"Yes, that's Isabelle de Lacy," Kaya replied. "She's the most famous ghost here."

Minnie nearly choked on her tea. "What?"

"The ectoplasm of Isabelle has been seen by most people," Kaya told them in a matter of fact way. "She's been seen more times than any of the others, usually on the stairs. People often report a white mist about halfway up the main staircase and it's believed to be the manifestation of Isabelle's spirit."

Minnie's blood ran cold, and she felt sick. She sat closer to Lancelot and Jack for protection.

Kaya was happy to tell them all about Isabelle de Lacy and relished being centre of attention - the one with the knowledge. "Isabelle was married to Roger Montgomery - if memory serves - I believe they married in 1608. It is said that they were so in love they never spent more than a few minutes out of each other's company, and he doted on her - bought her jewels from the Far East and furs from Scandinavia, the latest fashions from Paris and even slaughtered all the songbirds on the Manor to feather her hats."

"Oh, the poor little birds," Lucy said, and cringed at the vision of hundreds of little innocent birds being slaughtered and plucked just to decorate a hat or two.

"Anyway," Kaya continued, a little annoyed at being interrupted, "All was going well until a new maid came to work here called Molly Liptrop. Molly was a local girl, very young and pretty, and within a few weeks Roger and her were apparently…well, you know…"

"Enamoured?" Robert suggested.

Kaya smiled and felt a frisson of excitement run through her, thinking Robert was using the word to hint about how he was feeling about her!

"Getting his end away I think she means, old boy," Jack laughed.

Kaya gave Jack a stern look for being totally devoid of romantic sentiment. "Roger and Molly were lovers, but I believe it was because Isabelle became ill. They say she was bedridden for years - too ill to leave her room."

"What was wrong with her?" Lucy asked.

"I don't know, no-one knows," Kaya replied.

"Probably migraines," Sophie interjected.

Minnie felt a stabbing pain in her left temple and took a sharp in-take of breath.

Kaya ignored Sophie and continued with her story; "Isabelle went mad with jealousy and accused Molly of witchcraft. Molly was tried, and found guilty of bewitching Roger and of trying to kill Isabelle with hexes, and she was hanged at Lancaster Castle as a witch."

"What, you mean there was a real witch trial?" Lucy asked.

"One of many," Kaya told her. "Haven't you heard of the Pendle Witch Trials of 1612?"

Everyone shook their heads.

"I can't believe you haven't heard of them - they were very famous witch trials," Kaya explained (she was a little put out that they knew so little about local history but pleased that they didn't at the same time). "In August 1612 several locals were arrested and tried for witchcraft. A young girl confessed to hexing a peddler, and then her family and neighbours began accusing each other of witchcraft. Some admitted that they had sold their souls to the devil in return for their powers. Some claimed their innocence, but several were found guilty and hung. As for Molly Liptrop, she was hung in 1610. I've written about her in my pamphlet, 'Haunted Lancashire'. She rifled through her bag and pulled out a thin booklet with the image of a graveyard, a full moon and a flying bat on the front. She flicked to the page about Molly Liptrop and read it out loud to the others.

This, dear readers, is what it said:

~ * ~

The Trial of Molly Liptrop

The famous witch trials at Lancaster Castle in 1612 are well known, but one story, which often goes untold, is that of Lady Isabelle De Lacy Montgomery and her maid, a local woman from The Forest of Bowland, Molly Liptrop.

Molly, aged only fifteen, was engaged within the Montgomery household at Malinwick Manor as an upstairs maid. Molly soon became a favourite of Lord Roger Montgomery. Isabelle, in a fit of wild jealously, publicly accused Molly of witchcraft, and the poor young woman was tried and found guilty; subsequently being sentenced to death to be hung by the neck until dead. Some of the original transcripts from the trial give us an insight into the psychic evidence and visionary accusations laid against Molly, which were believed by the judge and jury at the time:

Lady Isabelle: "*Molly did appear as a familiar, a white owl, who did sit upon my breast. I became lamed, not able to stir either hand or foote for many minutes together. By conjuring worde, herbe and stone she accursed me. With envie and with unlawful charms did shee deceave my husband with perswaisions to give her his soule. Thus inticed, shee did have the power to doe anything shee would.*"

The housekeeper Mrs Alice Dootson, claimed: "*Knowing the rites of herbes Molly did prepare a remedie of willow bark for my mistress these foure moons since. Old Liptop teacheth the dark arts to her familie.*"

Another member of the household, Mr Todd, told the court that he had seen Molly: "*Appear by the dairy in the spirite of a black dog with terrible fangs and foaming mouth.*"

Molly defended herself by stating that: "*I do not know the power of the devill. I go to church.*"

The evidence was enough to condemn her and her unborn child. The spirits of Molly and Isabelle are said to roam the Manor at Malinwick, trapped in limbo for eternity, unable to find peace.

~ * ~

"We had our share of women coming to Little Eden to find sanctuary after being accused of witchcraft," Robert said. "I'm now wondering if any of them were actually guilty. I always presumed they were being unfairly persecuted, but what if they actually had harmed others by practicing the dark arts?"

"Witchcraft is basically healing and psychic work," Sophie said. "Spells are made by transferring consciousness into a person's aura, a stone or a plant, or even an inanimate object like a shoe or a doll. Trouble starts when the healer uses their own ego or the Evil Spirit rather than using the intercession of the Holy Spirit. Anyone can astrally project - we all do it and don't even know we are. Some people just know how to do it more successfully than others. That's why we have to be careful what we think about. If we hate someone enough and send hateful thoughts to them it can actually start to have an effect on them."

"You mean you think witchcraft is actually possible?" India asked.

"When King James came to the throne in 1603, he genuinely believed that witches were real," Lancelot said. "He thought they trying to kill him, and he clamped down hard on them. Back then people genuinely believed witchcraft to be a real and physical threat."

100

Sophie nodded. "Thought forms are more powerful than people understand, or modern people believe them to be. I suppose these days, instead of calling it witchcraft, we say it's emotional and mental abuse, manipulation, brain-washing, gas lighting..."

"Many of those tried as witches in this country were Catholics who wouldn't renounce the Pope," Kaya interjected. "Others were female brewers, herbalists and midwives who were just trying to help people. They meant no harm. It was the patriarchal political and religious leaders who wanted to get rid of free-thinking, powerful women. A woman who could make her own living didn't need to rely on a man and in their eyes that made her dangerous."

"Many Protestants considered healing, herbalism, brewing and midwifery as the dark arts because it had been the work of Catholic monks and nuns before they were expelled or killed," Lancelot added. "In 1562 there was an act of parliament against witchcraft. It was after that that Little Eden started getting more 'so called witches' escaping death by fire, drowning or the noose."

"It wasn't until the 1950's that the earlier witchcraft acts were repealed," Kaya added.

"As late as the 1950's?" India said aghast. "I can't believe there was actually a law made about it in the first place."

"It's scary to think that witchcraft is no different from what Hector Livewell does," Lucy said, remembering her recent visit to the Little Eden Health Food Shop. "Selling herbal products for their healing properties seems so innocent, but he would have been hung or burnt as a witch back then, wouldn't he?"

"So would Peony with her perfumes and aromatherapy," Minnie sighed.

"Silvi Swan with her healing and reflexology would definitely have been considered a witch," Sophie said.

"Even us and our work with the Pleiades and the Star Children," Robert mused. "The Star Child Academy would never have been allowed. And all the dragon portal work we've been involved in - even though it is for the greater good - it would have been illegal not that long ago and considered the work of the devil."

"We would all have been tried as witches," Kaya said. "We would all be suspected of dancing with the devil just by being in this house tonight."

They all looked at each other, wondering if they were, indeed, all witches.

Chapter 18
~ * ~

Around nine o'clock, in the dusky evening light, Robert, Jack and Lucy set off along the front driveway, towards the Lodge House in search of Ada and Arthur, hoping to cadge some food for breakfast the next morning. Lucy hadn't wanted to go, but she didn't trust the boys to return with any relevant food, even if Ada and Arthur had any to spare. The gravel crunched beneath their feet giving Lucy an uneasy feeling as she couldn't help remembering the human bones they had encountered at the back of the house. Even though the water didn't flow next to this part of the park, she was still worried that she might suddenly step on more dead bodies washed up from the Iron and Stone Age barrows.

Luckily, they had caught the weather between showers, although the sky seemed ominous, ever-changing and constantly shifting. Beneath full, white clouds, billowing through the turquoise sky, thin, dappled grey ones scudded swiftly by, and in the distance loomed a deep, heavy blanket of blackness threatening to usher in the next downpour.

Lucy shivered.

Beneath the tree tunnel there was no lingering warmth - the deep-purple leaves of the copper beeches shuddered like dark crow feathers in the gusty wind, and she felt the uneasy, spooky sensation that the trees were alive - whispering to each other. The atmosphere was heavy and close, as if the warmer air had become a clear, almost tangible film which encompassed them in an otherworldly enclave that seemed to belong only to the Manor and its grounds.

"It feels like the middle of winter, not the middle of summer," she said as she took Jack's arm and huddled close into him to keep warm. She carried an old wicker basket that she'd found in the kitchen, and Jack carried a larger one, designed for logs; she felt like Little Red Riding Hood venturing out into the terrible woods. "Do you ever get the feeling you're being watched?" she muttered as she kept scanning the wet grass and tangled hedgerows on either side of the avenue, half expecting to see trolls and boggarts, peering at them from the undergrowth with their beady, evil eyes.

Robert strode ahead, using his umbrella as a walking stick. He was pensive and wanted some time alone to think about the house and its future. He wasn't as concerned about the weather or the atmosphere as he was about the safety of everyone and what to do about the Manor.

"Do you think Robert will sell this place? Lucy asked Jack.

Jack sighed. "I don't know old girl," he replied. "There's not much of value left as far as the contents go. The real antiques were removed a long time ago. The only thing of value seems to be that necklace, but technically it belongs to Roger not Robert. The house itself is only worth what someone is willing to pay for it, and all this superstition about ghosts seems to have put prospective buyers off over the years. The cost of maintaining a place like this means there are only ever going to be a handful of buyers in the market: film stars or oligarchs mainly, maybe a lottery winner or two. It's not the most attractive place either."

Lucy had to agree with that. "Even if it isn't haunted it looks as if it ought to be," she said.

"Plus, the land is protected due to the standing stones and the Abbey ruins," Jack continued to say, "And apparently there's an old chapel somewhere over there," he pointed into the trees, but they were too dense to see beyond. "Lance was saying it's got bats in the belfry, which are protected, so there'll be no building a housing estate in the grounds that's for sure."

"So, Cousin Roger hasn't done Robert or Little Eden such a big favour by giving him this house after all," Lucy sighed.

"I think old Roger was only too glad to pass the place on," Jack replied.

Lucy was pondering on how the house and grounds might end up costing Little Eden money rather than making it any when she was shocked out of her reverie by a rustling in the thicket, and she gasped with fright!

She clutched hold of Jack even more tightly. "What was that?" she whispered.

"I didn't hear anything," Jack replied. He looked around but could only see Robert, a few feet ahead of them, and no-one else.

"It sounded like there was someone behind those bushes," Lucy murmured.

"Probably a fox or a deer," Jack told her. He could tell by the look on her face that she was afraid. "It's not a ghost for goodness sakes."

"Don't be too sure about that," Lucy replied and shuddered.

As they rounded the bend, her attention was taken by the most ramshackle, Victorian-style Lodge House she could have ever imagined. Half of it seemed to have subsided and it sloped dangerously into the ground. Surrounded by overgrown shrubs, gnarled fruit trees and tangled ground cover, it felt as if it had been neglected for a century or more.

"It's in worse condition than the Manor," Lucy exclaimed. "How can anyone live in there?"

Robert wrenched open the rickety wooden gate and it nearly fell off its hinges. "I'm not happy about this," he muttered under his breath. "That couple have no respect."

They made their way along the cracked concrete path which was riddled with weeds and flanked on both sides by high grass. Behind a tumble-down fence, knotted brambles and wild nettles strangled each other as they fought for supremacy over the rest of the garden. A clack, clack, clack could be heard, and Lucy shivered with fright again until she realised it was the sound of a weathervane carved into the shape of a woodcutter, chopping at a log, his axe slashing down faster and faster as the wind grew stronger, rustling and rippling through the leaves.

"Listen," Jack said, "I can hear chickens."

They peered over to the far side of the house and could just make out a dilapidated chicken pen where several scrawny birds were pecking at the parched, bare earth - surrounded by their own faeces.

"They must have some eggs they could sell us at least," Lucy said hopefully.

Robert knocked loudly on the crooked front door but there was no reply. There was no sign of life.

Jack went round the back and called out to Ada and her brother, but still no reply.

Trying the back door Jack found it was unlocked.

"We can't just walk in," Lucy said as Jack opened the decrepit door and was about to enter.

"Robert owns the place now," Jack told her.

"That doesn't matter," Lucy replied. "Even Landlords have to give notice before they come round. It's still breaking and entering."

"To be fair, old girl," Jack said with a smile, "It's only entering. We didn't have to break anything."

Robert agreed they should go in. "It's already broken as much as it can be," he said, and pointed to a smashed window which was patched up with a warped piece of chipboard. "As their new landlord, I'm going to have words with them about how they've neglected this place. They get a pretty penny in wages and an allowance to keep this house in good repair. I'd like to know what they've been spending it on all these years because it's clearly not on maintenance."

Reluctantly, Lucy followed the boys into the gloomy kitchen where they called out again for Ada and Arthur, still receiving no answer.

Looking around, they were utterly disgusted by what they saw.

The room was absolutely filthy. Draped over the other casement window hung a torn hessian rag, used as a makeshift curtain, which blocked most of the light, although the window was so coated in cobwebs that it didn't make that much difference. The walls were soaked in decades of grease and the ceiling was a deep shade of tobacco. In the corners hung faded strips of flypaper, covered in long dead flies and general detritus. An old electric cooker, once gleaming-white, was encrusted with years of splattered food; and a tap, with a worn rubber tube on the end, dripped constantly - staining a cracked Belfast sink with yellow and green slime that clung to the encrusted limescale.

Lucy grimaced - even the air itself felt unclean. Although she wanted to take back some food for the others, she wasn't sure if there would be any safe food to be found amongst the mould and the damp.

On a discoloured Formica table, sitting next to rotting fruit and stale breadcrumbs, was a shot gun, and hanging from large hooks above were three dead pheasants. Jack reached up and could feel they were still warm to the touch. "They're fresh," he said, and took two of them down to put in his basket. "We'll take a couple of these for starters."

Lucy didn't feel comfortable stealing stuff, but Robert suggested they leave a note apologising. He put some ten pound notes on the table as payment which made her feel better about helping themselves.

The house suddenly creaked and groaned. Lucy grabbed hold of Jack in alarm as she was sure she'd felt the floor move.

"What was that?" she whispered. "It felt like an earthquake."

They held their breath, looking up as if there might be someone on the first floor, but no footsteps were heard.

"I think the house is slowly sinking," Robert said.

"See if you can find anything else to eat," Lucy told them - wanting to get out of there as quickly as she could. She felt physically sick when she saw some discoloured nail clippings amongst a pile of mouldy, used teabags on the dresser. Not wanting to look inside the cupboards, but knowing she must, she opened one of the doors. Sitting on the shelves she found jars of pickles and preserves. Reaching in, she found some of them were sticky to the touch, and after taking a couple for her basket she suddenly screamed out, dropping one of the jars which smashed loudly all over the cold, concrete floor.

Jack rushed over to help her and realised why she had let go of the one that she'd been holding - instead of onions or beetroot it was filled with pickled baby-birds. He glanced in the cupboard and saw newts and chicken feet.

"Oh my god," Lucy cried as she looked away.

"Don't worry, old girl," Jack told her. "You've only got ordinary pickles in your basket."

Robert came to look and was repulsed by what he saw.

"I'm not touching anything else," Lucy protested.

"They must be into witchcraft in the worst sense," Robert said.

"What's in this one?" Jack asked and opened it.

"Oh god," Lucy exclaimed. "Don't open them!"

The pale, gloopy, frothy liquid smelt familiar.

"It's yeast," Jack replied. "Look! Here's some bread flour. They must make their own. You could make some couldn't you?" he asked Lucy.

Lucy's lips pursed at the idea of using anything from this house now.

"I suppose so," she agreed. "See if there's any butter and milk too. That's not gone off that is," she added. Between them they found some dairy products which seemed to be in date, plus bacon and sausages, along with some tins of beans, tuna and fruit.

Robert had ventured out into the dingy hallway, deciding he wanted a look around the rest of the property - now that he owned it and was responsible for it.

He furtively opened the nearest door...

...then shut it again immediately!

He wasn't sure what to think or do about what he had just seen.

Then he jumped out of his skin! He'd not heard Jack come up behind him.

"You okay, old boy?" Jack asked him.

"Take a look," Robert said and stood aside to let Jack open the door.

"Bloody hell," Jack exclaimed as he peered into the room.

Lucy didn't want to be left alone in the kitchen, and whilst she would rather have gone outside rather than further into this revolting house, she followed Jack, "What is it?" she asked.

"If you don't like the kitchen, you'll not want to take a look in there, old girl," Jack laughed.

Lucy wrinkled her nose. "Don't tell me that!" she said. "Now I'll have to look!"

Jack opened the door wider to reveal a devilishly strange and macabre sight.

The sunless room felt as if a funereal vigil should be taking place inside, though there was no coffin and thankfully no dead body! However, on the mantelpiece, above the blackened fireplace, was a human skull, and above it hung a large, reverse pentagram made of twisted willow and a string of bird-skull bunting dangled just below. On the hearth, six, tall, black church candles, partly burnt down, were arranged amongst dried lavender and sage.

Lucy gasped in fright and refused to enter the wicked room.

Robert and Jack crept in for a closer look.

A crescent shaped occasional table was being used as some kind of occult altar, decorated with a crystal mandala and more human bones. In the centre of the room, another table, covered in a threadbare, purple, velvet cloth had a large crystal ball in the centre and a pack of Rider Waite tarot cards was laid out in a Celtic cross formation. As they were about the only items not covered in several layers of dust, it seemed as if fortune telling was a recent, if not common, occurrence in the eerie room.

Opposite the fireplace was a damaged piano, with yellowed keys and, where the sheet music should have been, was a price-list for clairvoyant readings, herbal remedies, crystals and charms. Due to the dust and cobwebs covering the baskets of corn dollies, amulets and bunches of tired looking herbs, it was clear that very few people ever bought any of them. On the wall was a faded print of Harry Houdini and several photographs which appeared to be of a magician and his assistant in the process of performing various well-worn magic tricks.

As Robert turned to leave, he gasped with fright!

A hideous looking ventriloquist's dummy was staring at him from behind the door. It sat bolt upright on an old, wicker, child-sized chair.

"Come on," Lucy called anxiously from the hallway. "They might come back at any moment and find you snooping." She was more afraid of Ada and Arthur than she was of ghosts right now.

The house shook and moaned again, and they hastily left - relieved to be back outside in the fresh, night air again.

Quickly Jack navigated his way through a tatty vegetable patch, scattered with a few carrot tops and runner beans, towards the chicken coop where he found a dozen fresh eggs and carefully laid them in his basket amongst the pheasant's wings to keep them safe. If he hadn't already got the game birds, he'd have snapped a couple of chickens' necks instead.

"I'm not happy with those two," Robert moaned as they headed towards the gate. "Not happy at all. They lied to us about not having any food to share."

"They're old," Jack reminded his friend. "Old people can get a bit paranoid."

"That doesn't excuse their attitude," Robert replied. "I don't like the idea of black magic being done anywhere, never mind on my property, and age is no excuse for practising satanic rituals."

The wind whipped up for a moment, sending the woodcutter into a chopping frenzy on his weathervane.

Lucy was chilled to the bone.

She felt as if it was a warning for them to leave.

"Let's just get out of here," she pleaded with the boys. "This place is evil."

Chapter 19

~ * ~

Lucy was glad to get back to the Manor kitchen which now seemed like a palace in comparison to the one at the Lodge.

They recounted to Lancelot, India, Minnie, Sophie and Kaya what they had found there and how dismayed they were to find out that black-magic was being practised.

"I don't consider Wicca, clairvoyance or fortune telling to be black-magic," Kaya said defensively. "You've been brainwashed by main-stream religions, which demonise the ancient pagan ways and healing arts. Ada and Arthur are famous around here for their psychic and healing abilities. We are light-workers and way-showers. We are the chosen ones."

"The difference between healing witchcraft and dark witchcraft is a fine line," Sophie said. "Just like good and evil - they are hard to define, things are not always black and white, and it's easy to get caught up in the darkness without constant self-awareness and humility."

"I don't see how someone can work with the Light and not even clean-up their house after themselves," Lucy commented. "You should have seen it! It was more a home for boggarts than for angels."

Jack laughed. "You mean cleanliness is next to godliness."

"Something like that," Lucy nodded, seriously. "Aunt Lilly always used to clean the café and the flat with music as well as soap and water. She used to say that sad or angry energy gets stuck in corners and dark places and can drag you down with it, 'Open the windows and let in the fresh air and the light,' she used to say to us, "Evil dwells in shady places and cluttered corners."

"Some really bad energy has got stuck around here," Robert agreed. "Perhaps it could be because of the boggy land? The energy in the lay lines probably doesn't flow away very well around here."

Lancelot agreed, "The atmosphere here is oppressive and dense. It feels as if it could suck you under - emotionally I mean. I've been sitting here for hours now, and I can feel a kind of despair and depression seeping into me."

"I agree," Minnie said, "After a few days living here, I think I'd go mad."

"The fear and sadness, anger and hate build up like cobwebs and dust," Sophie said. "It's a vicious circle. Once you get down, you don't want to open your curtains or clean the house anymore. You stop showering and changing your clothes. You even stop going outside, and hey presto, you're stuck in the web of fear and it gets harder and harder to break free. That's what is so hard when you've got a chronic illness because you have no chance to blow away the cobwebs, you don't have the energy to do those things, even if you'd really, really like to."

"I feel as if I want to give the entire manor place a good spring clean," Lucy said, "And take a shower. No wonder poor Lady Edith went mad - it was probably the house that done her in!"

"I feel as if I'm losing my mind," Minnie admitted. "I keep thinking it's not 2012 anymore but another century altogether. I don't know how to describe it exactly, but I do feel as if I've been in this house in a past-life and that I knew poor Isabelle." Minnie picked up the necklace and ran her fingers over it. "I think she's trying to tell me something else, but I don't know what."

They all felt a wave of sadness and melancholy washing through them; their worst fears rose to the surface, and whatever their hopes and dreams might have been, they suddenly felt hopeless and thwarted. They sat with glum faces for a few moments, lost in a mournful meditation.

"Oh, come on now," Jack finally said, breaking the spell. "You can't blame a house or someone else for your own state of mind."

"Don't you remember how Linnet was affected by Marcus?" Minnie asked him. "She said she could feel him, and his anger, around her even after he was dead. His evil didn't die with him."

"It is possible to affect someone else with your own consciousness," Sophie nodded. "When Lucy and I can feel Aunt Lilly around us we feel comforted, joyful, safe - just as we did when she was alive. She is projecting her love to us even from spirit. But imagine if someone was projecting hate instead of love?"

"I've always had a phobia about madness," Minnie admitted, starting to feel as if her skin was crawling with bugs. "I always fear I'll be taken away to the funny-farm by men in white coats and lose my mind, ending my life locked in an asylum with no-one to rescue me."

"There are no asylums like that anymore," Lancelot reassured her, and put his arm around her.

"Yeah, they just leave you to become homeless and die on the streets instead," Jack said, then realised that his comment didn't really help.

Minnie put her head on Lance's shoulder. "My mother lost her mind, and her mother before her. I hate feeling as if I don't have control over my thoughts or my emotions."

"Ghosts can mess with your mind," Kaya said, also without realising she was making Minnie feel worse. "They rarely physically hurt someone, usually they send them mad and drive them to commit suicide or murder, or you might die of fright."

Before Kaya could say anything more, they all gasped in fear!

A loud booming sound was coming from all around them. It sounded as if an angry giant was trying to break out of the walls.

"What the f**k," is that?" Jack said. His heart was racing, as was everyone else's.

The unexpected and strange sound came again, like a train travelling towards them from one end of the room then fading off towards the outside wall.

The third time the noise grew louder, this time more violent and more furious.

"It must be the heating or water pipes," Lucy suggested, trying to comfort herself with a rational explanation. "On dad's farm we used to hear it like that when the pipes were contracting or expanding. Old pipes do that."

"Yes, that must be it," Minnie agreed, but in her agitation, she sat even closer to Lancelot.

"I've heard this sound before in other haunted houses," Kaya said. "It's spirit activity in the walls. It's usually an enraged spirit."

The banging came again, and Minnie nearly leapt into Lancelot's lap. "Make it stop," she begged.

Kaya radioed to let the Haunted or Not team know there was something worth recording and they came, as fast as they could, rushing into the kitchen with their equipment.

Wolf pulled out an EMF meter and held it against the wall. The lights went nuts - flashing up and down like crazy. "There's a spirit in that wall. Hand me the camera," he told Carrie. He began to film, and Jimmy bounced into action telling the viewers about the scary, supernatural sounds emanating from the walls...

..."A malevolent spirit haunts this ancient and crumbling mansion," Jimmy said, then put his hand to his forehead as if focusing his third eye, and closing his eyes he added, "I can sense it. It wants to communicate with us. A male spirit - he's angry." He paused for a moment hoping the banging would come again but it didn't. He knocked on the wall saying, "Who are you? Bang again if you don't want us here."

They all waited anxiously but the sound didn't come again.

Jimmy knocked again. "Bang if you can hear me," he told the invisible spirit. "Did you die in this house?" When he didn't get a reply, he turned to the camera again, dramatically saying, "We will have to be careful here tonight, the spirits have already started to warn us to leave. I can feel this spirit, lost and imprisoned in the darkness; its soul trapped inside these walls for eternity."

Jack stuck his head in front of the camera and said, "Or, it could just be heating pipes."

The Haunted or Not team were not amused by Jack's interjection.

"Don't worry," Wolf told Jimmy, "We'll edit that bit out."

Carrie took Jack by the arm and led him just outside the kitchen door. "If you wouldn't mind staying away from the camera and remaining quiet whilst we are filming?" she asked him. She gently stoked his arm and pouted, gazing up at him and fluttering her long fake eye-lashes. "You can behave for me, can't you?" she added.

Jack smiled his irresistible smile. He knew she was flirting with him, so he flirted back. "I can't promise to behave where you're concerned but I promise I'll be a good boy when you're filming."

"That's good enough for me," she replied as she leaned in towards him anticipating their first kiss - which to her disappointment didn't come - they were rudely interrupted by Jimmy who suddenly poked his head through the doorway.

"The banging's stopped," he told Carrie. "Did you hear it out here?"

"No!" Carrie replied exasperated. "Nothing to see or hear out here," she added and under her breath muttered, "Worst luck!"

Chapter 20
~ * ~

E veryone was jumpy now.
      Even India and Jack felt a little anxious.

"It is more likely to be the pipes than a spirit," Sophie said.

"No, no!" Kaya insisted. "Knocking in the walls is a genuine paranormal phenomena recorded in several genuine hauntings. The Amityville case recorded multiple spirit sounds and poltergeist activity." She looked around and added, "The kitchen cupboard doors were reported to have opened and closed by themselves for example."

Everyone automatically stared at the pine cupboard doors in alarm and half expected them to start flying open of their own accord.

"You've been watching too many horror movies," Jack laughed.

"Whatever the banging is, it's not going to happen again whilst we are all standing around looking stupid, and you're scaring Minnie," India said. She looked at Wolf for support.

"It could be the pipes," Wolf reluctantly agreed. "As paranormal investigators we should always try to find a logical explanation before jumping to the conclusion that it's supernatural." He dug out a small hand-held camera from his bag and offered it to India. "Would you mind carrying this around with you?" he asked her. "If you see or hear anything and one of us isn't with you, can you record whatever it is?"

"Me?" India replied in astonishment, but she couldn't help feeling pleased that he trusted her with it. "I'm afraid I'm a non-believer," she told him.

"I like a good sceptic," Wolf smiled and stood behind her to show her how to use it. His stomach flipped as he felt her body-heat radiating between them, igniting his desire. He lost his breath for a moment as he leaned over her shoulder to turn on the camera. She smelt divine and he wished he could kiss the nape of her neck; swallowing the impulse, he tried to focus on the job in hand. "If you don't get scared easily you'll keep filming and won't drop it and run," he explained. "There's nothing more frustrating than people running away screaming just as it's getting interesting!"

India agreed to help him. She had been almost overwhelmed by the sexual tension between them. Feeling as if she could faint and fall backwards against his chest, she pretended she needed showing how to use the camera again (even though she knew perfectly well how to use it).

After a few more minutes, they all agreed that there didn't seem to be any more action coming from inside the walls.

"Let's get into our groups," Carrie suggested, looking at her watch. It was nearly eleven o'clock. "It'll be dark in a few minutes."

Wolf pulled out a map of the house and laid it on the table. "I've zoned the house according to where the apparitions and other activity have been reported in the past, and where it is safest to go due to the disrepair of parts of the building," he explained. "I'm suggesting that Kaya and I should go into Zone One - the hall - and see if we can get a glimpse of the white lady on the stairs; Carrie, you go with Jimmy into Zone Two - through the lower basement which leads into the old Abbey crypt - see if you can get anything from the monks down there."

"Minnie should come with us into the hall," Kaya suggested. "If the white lady is the spirit of Isabelle, she's been trying to communicate with her already; Minnie might draw her out."

Minnie flatly refused.

"Would you come too Robert?" Kaya asked him. "Isabelle might appear to you, being a family member - distant family anyway."

"I don't mind coming to the hall," Robert said. He was curious to find out whether they would see anything.

Kaya was happy that Robert was coming with her, but less happy when he invited Sophie.

Sophie declined the invitation. She was too exhausted - besides she didn't like shaking up spirits without good cause. She was wishing she'd never agreed to come. Her mind had wanted to be with her friends, on a jolly holiday, but her body had other ideas. She felt nauseous, foggy, and bruised all over. She just wanted to sleep.

"Why don't you come into the cellar with me, babe?" Jimmy asked Lucy.

"I don't think so," Lucy replied.

"Oh come on, babe," Jimmy said, trying to persuade her. "We can always do with a third person and you know how you can sense and smell spirit, you'd be invaluable."

Lucy's heart wanted to go with Jimmy. He'd never asked for her assistance with his job before and she always felt guilty about saying no to any request for help, no matter who it was from.

"I'll come if Jack can come too," she told Jimmy.

Jimmy pulled a face. Jack was the last person he wanted with him.

Carrie wasn't best pleased about Lucy joining her and Jimmy in the cellar, but if Jack was coming, that made up for it, and she helped persuade them both to come along.

"Come and get changed," Carrie suggested to Lucy.

"Changed?" Lucy asked.

"You know, hair, make-up, clothes - for the camera," Carrie explained. "You can't go on television looking like that. Let me fix your hair for you. Do you have any make-up with you?"

Carrie took a reluctant Lucy into the toilet, just down the corridor from the kitchen, and lent her some of her make-up. "I'll get you one of our official t-shirts to wear, you can tie it in a knot at the bottom, it'll look sexier that way," she told her.

"Hold on," Lucy said as Carrie headed for the door. "Don't leave me on my own! Where are you going?"

"To get a t-shirt from my bag," Carrie said. She could see the real fear on Lucy's face so reluctantly agreed to stay with her. "You and your friends are such scaredy cats," Carrie laughed, "Especially Minnie."

"I wouldn't say that to Minnie's face," Lucy warned her. "She's trained in martial arts and could have you on the floor in one move."

"Don't be silly," Carrie laughed, unable to believe that petite, terrified Minnie could possess such strength or courage.

Lucy shrugged. She knew Carrie didn't believe her.

"I don't know what all the men see in you," Carrie said as she put some false eye lashes on Lucy.

"What do you mean?" Lucy asked bewildered, and a little hurt by her comment.

"Jack, Jimmy...they can't keep their eyes off you," Carrie replied. "You hardly wear make-up, and your clothes are not exactly sexy and yet, I don't know why, you attract men like flies to honey."

"I'm not used to wearing much make-up," Lucy admitted. "I work full-time and am a single mother, plus I have to take care of my sister and the little girl next door most of the time too. I get about five minutes a day to myself."

"That's my point," Carrie said as she searched for some blusher. "None of you look as if you've ever owned a decent make-up set in your lives, or seen a hair straightener. Your sister looks terrible."

115

Lucy's anger rose for a moment and she defended her sister immediately, "Sophie is unwell and struggles to even take a shower never mind put on a full face of make-up. Besides, she's sensitive to most make-up, she can't stand harsh chemicals."

"What's wrong with your sister exactly?" Carrie asked. "She seems fine one minute then nearly dying the next."

"She has a chronic illness known as ME. It's like she has a battery inside her that only ever charges to 5%, and you know what it's like when your phone has a low battery, you can be halfway through a conversation and just get cut off. Some tasks take more battery than others. If you're on the internet, your phone battery goes down super quick doesn't it? Well, for Sophie, showering, walking, talking, listening, all of those things we take for granted, take some of her already nearly flat battery. It wouldn't matter if she charged her battery all night or all week or even all year, it would only ever charge to 5%. No-one knows the cause or cure."

"Sounds sh*t," Carrie replied. "She'd be better off dead if there's no cure."

Lucy wasn't shocked by Carrie's comment as Sophie often thought that herself. "She has to use her limited energy wisely," Lucy explained. "We try to help her as much as we can. I'd rather she was alive, even if I only get to see her for an hour a day, and I don't care what she looks like on the outside, she's my sister and I love her."

Carrie felt a wave of envy that Lucy loved her sister so much and that she had the confidence to face the world without lipstick. "I can't go out of my bedroom until I have a full-face on," she said. "I get up at 6am, wash my hair, style it and put on my face all before breakfast at 8am. I wouldn't let a man see me without make-up."

Lucy was shocked. "What? Even if you woke up next to him?"

"Certainly not!" Carrie replied, a little horrified at the notion. "I get up before them and take a shower and put my face on. Talking of men, what's with you and Jack?" she asked. "Are you an item or not?"

"Everyone gets the wrong idea about Jack and me," Lucy replied. "We're like brother and sister. You're welcome to him if you want him. But I warn you, he can't stay with a woman more than a few months, never could, never will."

Carrie wasn't sure if she believed Lucy or not. She was sure she would be able to keep hold of Jack once she had him. "You're welcome to Jimmy," she told Lucy.

Lucy wasn't quite sure why Carrie had said it like that. *Has Carrie had a fling with Jimmy?* she thought to herself.

"I don't want Jimmy back," Lucy told her.

"Well, he certainly wants you back," Carrie smiled. "You stick to Jimmy and I'll stick to Jack, deal?" She didn't wait for Lucy to reply and started taking selfies. "It's so frustrating having no phone signal," she moaned. "I want to upload to Insta' and I can't. I've got over a hundred thousand followers and they'll be wondering what's happened to me."

Lucy wasn't sure why so many people would want to see Carrie posing like a poodle every day.

"You have to build a brand if you want to get anywhere in this game," Carrie told her. "My brand is myself. I don't want to be working on this crappy TV show forever. I'm thinking I'm more suited to a travel show or a prime-time chat show." She took another selfie and said, "My USP is my looks."

Lucy wasn't sure that Carrie's unique-selling-point was her looks as she looked like everyone else who was trying to get famous but she didn't like to say so.

Jack looked out of the kitchen door wondering where they had got to and saw them returning. "Hurry up you two," he told them and looked at Lucy with a quizzical expression. "You look different," he told her as she walked past him.

"Good, different?" she asked. "Carrie put make-up on me for the camera. Do you like it?" She fluttered her fake lashes at him and pouted as if she was taking a selfie.

Jack smiled. "You look beautiful with or without make-up," he replied diplomatically.

"Come on," Jimmy said impatiently, not liking that Lucy seemed to be flirting with Jack. "Are we going down the cellar or not? It'll be light again before we get any footage at this rate."

Wolf tried again to persuade India to come with him to the hall, but she had agreed to stay with Minnie, Sophie and Lance in the kitchen, and her friends always came first with her, no matter how much she was tempted by her lust for Wolf.

"Now you film anything you hear or see, especially if the noise in the walls comes back," Wolf told her with a smile, "And call us on the radio if you get anything good," he added. Then, carrying his big tripod, he winked at her, and they all went off to their designated danger zones.

As India washed up the last of the supper plates, she looked out of the window up to the railings at the back of the house. The last golden ribbon of solstice sunlight faded from the sky and the Manor was plunged into night.

Huddled by the fire, they could hear torrential rain crashing down again, splashing along the gutters as the wind ripped through the trees and whistled in the eves, surrounding the house with a raging maelstrom. Sophie sighed and looked at her phone: it was 11.11 exactly. She hoped it was a sign that angels were amongst them. Humphrey came and sat by the fire with them and she smiled - his presence did feel like a good spirit watching over them, but she wasn't sure he'd be much protection against the madness and despair which seemed to whisper through the walls and knock on every door.

India sighed and closed the wooden shutters. "Let's put the kettle on and get comfortable," she suggested. "I've a feeling this is going to be a long and very strange night!"

Chapter 21
~ * ~

As Robert, Kaya and Wolf came into the entrance hall, a flash of lightening lit up the stairs, illuminating the grand, ancestral portraits; and for a moment the faces of the Montgomery family seemed animated - watching their every move. Then, as thunder rumbled towards the Manor, they each felt a cold shiver creeping slowly up their spines.

Suddenly, there was a deafening crash against the tall, leaded windows. A fierce gust of wind had rammed the rain so violently against the glass it sounded as if it might smash right through and shatter the panes to pieces.

"I can understand why no-one has ever stayed here after midnight," Robert shuddered. "If we weren't stranded here, I would take everyone back to the village right now. There's something unnerving about this place, storm or no storm. I can't put my finger on it but it's as if the aura of the house has become so sad it's become angry. Like a person or an animal that's been so badly treated and abused it lashes out even when you mean them no harm."

Kaya felt a frisson of deliciously, dangerous excitement ripple through her heart. "I've not stayed here after dark before, but I've always wanted to," she said. "This is an amazing opportunity to communicate with the spirit world. I hope to record enough supernatural phenomena to write a book about the Manor."

The lightening flashed again, followed by an alarming crack of thunder which sounded as if it was trying to get in through the front doors.

"I think we should be able to put together one of the best shows we've ever done," Wolf said. "Nothing scares me - I won't be running away because of a few bolts of lightning or because a few ghosts come out to play." He made sure the equipment was working and suggested they turn off their head-torches and switch the cameras to infra-red. "In the dark our senses are heightened," Wolf explained. "Light deprivation helps our psychic brain register higher and lower vibrational frequencies which sunlight and noises block out during the day. We have a greater range of awareness outside of our usual frame of reference if we remain calm, quiet and in the dark."

"I agree," Kaya nodded. "Our psychic awareness is much better when everything is dark and peaceful."

"Or our imaginations can start to run wild," Robert mused. "Even the most common noises, that we accept perfectly happily during the day, seem ominous in the middle of the night." He didn't like being in such a large space in the pitch dark. He realised he may have slight agoraphobia - the fact that he couldn't see the walls around him made him feel exposed. His heart was racing which it always seemed to do now when spiritual matters were afoot.

"Stay close to me," Kaya suggested and reached out to hold his hand.

Robert didn't really want to take her clammy hand in his but thought she must be frightened, so out of politeness he held it in his own.

"If you feel anything, see or sense anything, anything at all, say so out loud," Wolf told them. "Ham it up a bit if you can. Viewers like to see you're frightened, it makes them frightened too, that's the great thing about fear - it's contagious."

"What if we don't see anything?" Robert asked, looking at the empty stairs.

"It's up to Van Ike what he does with the final footage," Wolf told him. "If nothing shows up, the fact we are stranded here in the middle of a storm, in the most haunted house in the world, is enough to get people watching. We can edit it to make more of it if we need to. It'd be great if we could get something never before seen on film though. I'm hoping we might capture the white mist that some people say they've seen on the stairs, or even some major poltergeist activity."

They all stood in silence for a few minutes, listening to every creak, crack or tap which could be heard over the thrashing rain outside. The house seemed to groan and moan, whimper and whine, but they all knew these were just the natural sounds of an old house in a storm.

"Speak to Isabelle," Kaya suggested to Robert.

"What do you mean speak to her?" he asked.

"Call out to her spirit," Wolf prompted him. "Ask her to show herself to us." He made sure the camera was pointing at the staircase.

Robert called out to Isabelle and as he did so the EMF meter, which Wolf had placed halfway up the staircase, began to flash like mad. "There, look!" Wolf exclaimed. We've awoken the spirit energy. It's manifesting."

There was a very sudden, very loud, creak and they all involuntarily jumped. "Was that you moving?" Wolf asked Kaya and Robert.

"I haven't moved at all," Robert admitted, and Kaya said the same.

"Did you hear that?" Kaya said urgently. "Another creak, as if someone is walking about on the stairs."

"I heard it," Wolf responded in a loud whisper, "It's coming from the stairs."

"There it is again," Kaya added.

Robert heard it this time too.

"It's coming from near the EMF meter," Wolf said. "Let's go and stand on the stairs."

They cautiously went part-way up the staircase and stood just below the middle step, hoping to capture the ectoplasm of the materialising spirit.

"Oh my god, what was that!?" Kaya shrieked in a loud whisper, and she squeezed Robert's hand so hard he cringed in pain.

"What?" Wolf asked her, spinning the camera around to capture whatever it was.

"I felt someone behind me," Kaya whispered. "My arm is freezing cold."

"I can feel a cold spot," Robert admitted, "From the step. It's like a faint draft."

"We must be standing on top of a vortex or portal to the other side," Wolf said.

They all stood with bated breath, waiting for something else to happen, but the creak didn't occur again, although the freezing air was still circulating around them, chilling them to the bone.

Kaya called out again saying; "Show yourself if you are Lady Isabelle, the white lady. Make a noise to let us know you are here." She stood as close as she could to Robert as all three stood together on the same step. "Did you hear that?" she asked them.

"I did," Robert admitted and Wolf concurred.

"It was like a dreadful, woeful moan," Kaya whispered. "Make that noise again if you are Isabelle," she called into the ether.

"Can you feel the floor vibrating?" Robert asked.

"I can," Kaya replied. "The whole step is moving. I'm shaking - I can't stop shaking."

They looked down at the wooden tread and Wolf flashed his torch over it to see if it was moving. "What's that?" he asked, focusing the beam on a small dark patch.

"It looks like blood," Kaya exclaimed.

Robert didn't think for a minute it was blood and bent down, switching on his head torch, to take a closer look.

"It wasn't there earlier, I'd have seen it when I was setting up the EMF meter," Wolf said.

Robert gingerly put his finger into the sticky liquid. To his astonishment it was bright red - just like fresh human blood.

Suddenly, a tiny cloud of white smoke floated up from the side of the step and wound its way through the twisted banister rail before disappearing into thin air. Then there was another and another. Before they could really tell what it was, it evaporated.

"Did you get that on camera?" Kaya asked Wolf.

"Yes," Wolf said. "What the hell is it? Where's it coming from?"

"It must be the ectoplasm of the white lady," Kaya said. "This must be what other people have seen. This is amazing!"

"Woah," Wolf suddenly said. "The most enormous orb just floated across the screen."

"Where?" Kaya asked.

"Just above your heads, it floated over that way," he explained and hoped another one might appear.

"There's spirit energy here for sure," Kaya said. "I feel it's a female signature. It has to be the white lady. It has to be Isabelle!"

"Did you hear that?" Robert asked. He had distinctly heard the distant sound of shrill, hideous laughing.

"Oh my god yes," Kaya replied and took another opportunity to hang onto Robert. She was surprised how edgy she was feeling now that the spirits had started to become active, but she was strangely thrilled by it too.

They all heard the high-pitched phantom laugh again and then a distant creaking sound.

Abruptly, a door banged, so loudly they all jumped out of their skins and without thinking they found themselves running down the stairs.

Before they could compose themselves, they were nearly scared to death again by the unexpected cacophonous chiming of several clocks coming at them from every direction, surrounding them with piercing, clanging tones. The bells reverberated around the hall in a malevolent wall of sound.

They stood stock still, held their breath, and counted…twelve chimes. The ringing echoed and lingered for a few seconds more - then all they could hear was their hearts beating and their quickening breath.

Wolf looked at his watch. "It's not midnight," he said. "It's only eleven thirty."

Robert looked at the grandfather clock, which stood majestically next to the front doors, and was shocked to see that the hands said three o'clock. He opened the case to find that the pendulum was still and silent. The clock wasn't even working.

"We didn't hear any clocks chiming earlier today," he said and gathering his courage, he went to investigate the others which were dotted around the entrance hall. Shining his torch at the ornate mantel clock, it showed the time as one minute past one, and it wasn't ticking. A mounted wall-clock and barometer showed a different time again, and the grandmother clock near the door to the drawing room a different time also. "These clocks aren't even wound," he told the others.

"How can they strike midnight if they're not even working?" Kaya asked, now more than a little afraid. She didn't want to be scared but fear was like an invisible, unstoppable force which cut into her aura, and she had no defence against its icy grasp.

They all looked at each other, not knowing what to say, and all felt a rising and terrible sensation of absolute dread.

A flash of lightening lit up the whole floor for a few seconds followed by a deafening crash of thunder which was right over the top of them. The whole hall had taken on an overwhelmingly creepy and downright macabre atmosphere.

"Damn it," Wolf exclaimed. "The camera battery's stopped working. It's been drained."

"Drained?" Robert asked, just as his torch went out.

"The spirits can drain the electromagnetic energy from the equipment," Kaya explained to Robert. "They act like vampires and use the energy to manifest themselves."

"The radio isn't working either," Wolf told them as he flicked the switch on and off a few times, trying to contact India. "We'd better get back to the kitchen," he suggested. "We can get a new battery and I'll see if we've got anything on the EA recording. We need to come back and keep filming some more. I have a feeling this is just the beginning of an extraordinary haunting."

Chapter 22
~ * ~

Meanwhile, Lucy, Jack, Jimmy and Carrie had made their way down the corridor from the kitchen to the lower basement door. A short flight of wooden stairs led them down into the dank, low rooms where crumbling, white-washed walls, crawling with black mould and dripping with some unidentifiable sticky gloop, enveloped them in a cavernous dungeon.

With no electric light, only the narrow beams of their head-torches, the eerie shadows immediately began to play tricks on their minds, causing disorientation and dislocation of their senses.

Jimmy took Lucy's hand to help her navigate the narrow steps, whilst Jack made sure Carrie could find her footing.

The ground was covered in cracked quarry-tiles through which bare earth protruded like dirty fingers reaching up to grab at their feet.

The rotten stench of damp was almost suffocating.

Lucy put her hand to her nose in disgust. She was having second thoughts about agreeing to come.

She quivered with fear and cold.

The slightest noise made her jump.

"I know all basements are creepy but this one is the worst I've been in," Lucy said, grasping tighter onto Jimmy's hand.

Jimmy liked that fact that Lucy was scared - it made him feel like a hero. "Don't worry babe," he told her, "There's nothing down here but rats and spiders. The ghosts can't hurt you. I've set up equipment in the next room. I want to check it before we start filming. Wait here, I'll come back for you in a jiffy."

"Don't leave me," Lucy begged him, horrified that he was about to wander off and leave her standing there in the terrible darkness.

"I won't be long, babe," Jimmy said and to her surprise he kissed her before he let go of her hand.

Jack took hold of her hand instead and held her close to him. "It's okay, I've got you," he told her, "I won't let anything bad happen to you."

Carrie, annoyed by Jack's concern over Lucy, followed Jimmy through a doorway that led into a second unlit room. Hanging from the ceiling were half-clad water pipes from which most of the insulation had dropped off, attracting rodents who had used it to build their nests. The floor was scattered with yellow fluff and scraps of silver paper, filthy excrement and rotting rat carcasses.

The stench was putrid and sharp.

"This is the part I hate about this job," Carrie muttered as she checked the previous footage on the static camera. "Some places stink of death."

Jimmy, who seemed unbothered by the smell, replayed the EVP recorder to hear if anything of interest had been captured. Through the whirring, clicking and fuzzy, white-noise a distorted, disembodied voice was just about audible. "That sounds like, 'God help us', don't you think?" Jimmy said. He played the haunting tape again. "Listen again! There! 'God help us. God help us'. That'll be great when it's enhanced - really add to the spooky atmosphere. There's going to be plenty of spirit activity down here tonight. I can feel a ghostly presence already."

"We won't need to enhance the spookiness very much," Carrie replied. "It's so bad down here, I bet they'll feel the creepiness through the TV screen." She looked at the footage already recorded, "There are few orbs on this, look, there's a cluster."

"Fantastic," Jimmy said, "Let's hope we get plenty more of those."

Suddenly, Lucy screamed, and they all jumped.

A rat had run over her foot.

"Everything alright in there?" Carrie called through the doorway.

"Fine, just fine," Jack replied as he kicked the rat away.

"Can we come through now?" Lucy asked. She wanted to get on with it. The sooner they had something on film the sooner they could go upstairs again!

"In a minute, babe," Jimmy called back.

Carrie checked the camera batteries and grumbled under her breath, "Apart from Jack, that Little Eden lot are getting on my wick," she said.

"You were the one who organised this little weekend away," Jimmy laughed.

"It was Lancelot who insisted they were here as well," Carrie replied, "Otherwise it would just have been us."

"Didn't trust us with the family silver, eh?" Jimmy sneered.

"People are never really that nice to each other," she said. "I bet under all that nicey, nice stuff they all hate each other. The only one I can stand is Jack."

"You've made that obvious from the moment we arrived," Jimmy smiled.

"I don't know what you mean!" Carrie retorted. "I can't help it if he's been flirting with me."

"Jack'll flirt with anyone in a skirt," Jimmy said, rolling his eyes.

"Oh, and you don't?" Carrie said defensively. "I didn't want you to come on this shoot. I told Van Ike I'd never work with you again."

Jimmy laughed. "You can't get enough of me, and you know it," he replied, coming up close so that he could whisper in her ear, "You keep Jack occupied. I'm planning on winning Lucy back, and so far, it seems to be working." He looked over his shoulder to check he couldn't be overheard or seen and then kissed her gently on her ear.

"That fat cow won't take you back," Carrie said vindictively, and she pulled away from him. "She wants to get into Jack's pants even more than I do. She's all over him like a rash and he fawns over her like she's the..."

...Aroused by her jealousy, Jimmy suddenly spun her around and kissed her (although due to the size of her boobs it was hard to get too close to the rest of her).

"Get off me," Carrie whispered loudly and tried to shove him away.

Jimmy leant in to almost kiss her again but then held back just enough to tempt her - not to satisfy her.

Carrie narrowed her eyes as she tried to override the involuntary ache of desire she felt for him. Part of her wanted to kiss him and part of her wanted to slap him. "Stop it," she moaned under her breath, trying to extricate herself again from his embrace.

"You want me," Jimmy teased her, almost touching her lips with his again, but then he suddenly and flippantly let her go...

...as he did so she lost her footing!

Carrie grabbed hold of the camera tripod which, not being fixed to the floor, didn't save her, and she fell backwards into the rat droppings and half decomposed rodent skeletons.

"You're a total tosser!" she snapped, lying on her back in the pile of poo with the camera on top of her.

Jack and Lucy came rushing in to find out what was happening.

"You okay?" Jack asked Carrie as he helped her up.

Carrie dramatically flung herself into Jack's arms.

"Oh my god I must look a state!" she cried. "I can't go on camera looking a mess."

"What is it?" Jack asked concerned. "Did you hurt yourself?"

"One of my nails has come off!" she exclaimed but knew there was no point looking for it now.

Jack didn't want to tell her she looked like Einstein after an electric shock. "You look fine," he replied, brushing her down and picking yellow fluff from her t-shirt and bits of dried poop out of her hair.

"Is it safe in here?" Lucy asked, freaked out at the sight of Carrie covered in rat shit and bits of insulation.

"There's nothing to be scared of, babe," Jimmy reassured her. "I've told you before - ghosts can't hurt you."

"I meant is the building safe?" Lucy replied. She looked up at the low hanging pipes which didn't look as if they attached particularly well. "It's not going to collapse on us, is it?"

"It's all okay, babe," Jimmy told her. "Come this way, we need to get on this side of the camera and in front of that doorway into the crypt."

"Any sign of trouble and we get out," Carrie said, finding her composure again. "Van Ike takes Health and Safety very seriously. We've never had a situation we couldn't handle."

"Well apart from that time in Massachusetts when Aliester Fielding got possessed," Jimmy said.

"Apart from that time," Carrie agreed.

"And the time in the Tower of London when Wolf was thrown against the wall and…"

…"Yes, thank you, Jimmy," Carrie interrupted. "They were isolated incidents."

Lucy was really scared now. She didn't think there was much Health and Safety going on. The cellar seemed to shudder and chatter as if the bricks and mortar were alive. Whatever it was that was down there made the hairs on the back of her neck stand up and sent her into a cold sweat. "I'd like to go back to the kitchen," she admitted.

Jimmy took her hand in his. "Come on, babe, you always said you'd like to join me on one of my ghost adventures. Well, here we are. This is what I do. I commune with the dead. I've done it a thousand times. Trust me. I know what I'm doing."

With the infra-red camera running the viewers would be able see them but they couldn't see each other. Their eyes shone strangely like cats-eyes giving them all an other-worldly appearance. Carrie encouraged them to comment on every creak, bang, groan or scratch they heard so that the viewers could feel part of the action.

"Spirit is all around us," Jimmy said to camera. "There are many unhappy souls trapped down here in this accursed cellar. I can sense wandering, lost, angry spirits reaching out to us through the ether, desperate for our help."

They all gasped with fear as a loud and continuous knocking sound could be heard which then faded away as quickly as it had started.

"It's the pipes," Jack said. "It's the same sound we could hear in the kitchen."

They waited for a few minutes but nothing more happened. Carrie and Jimmy were disappointed. They wanted to find some real paranormal activity.

"Let's go down further into the old crypt area," Jimmy suggested after a few more uneventful minutes. "I'm told people have seen the spectres of monks floating in procession through the crypt then disappearing through the wall over there. There are bodies buried down here so there are bound to be restless spirits just waiting for us to communicate with them."

Jack couldn't help thinking that if he was buried down here, the last thing he would want would be an idiot like Jimmy shouting out to him, trying to get him to knock on a wall three times.

Lucy's fingers and toes were turning to blocks of ice and she had a headache coming on due to the intense odour of damp and putrefaction. "I don't like it," she said and pulled back against Jimmy's hand as he tried to go through the next doorway. "Let's go back, I'm scared."

Jimmy let go of her hand and ignored her. He began to squeeze his way down a narrow brick passageway. Carrie felt obliged to follow him with the EMF meter and she begged Jack to stay with her and carry the other camera.

Jack was torn between taking Lucy back to the surface and protecting Carrie from Jimmy's antics. He persuaded Lucy to stay a little longer, promising not to leave her side, and as they walked through the doorway, Lucy felt the temperature dropping even further.

A frisson of fear ran through her blood.

She began to feel nauseous, and her knees wanted to give way.

When the dingy corridor opened out into the ancient Abbey crypt, Lucy felt some of the oppressive fear she had been drowning in lift a little. The shadows cast by the vaulted ceiling were strangely beautiful, and the floor was neatly laid with small, square tiles, painted with naïve images of white doves, crosses and circles. She felt the symbols were in some way protective and positioned herself right on top of a dove, hoping the Holy Spirit would ward off any unholy spirits.

Some empty wine racks and dry whisky barrels, leaning up against the back wall, gave off an odour of sweet liquor, and Lucy could smell a powerful scent of invisible roses wafting through the freezing air. "I can feel more than one spirit presence in this area," Jimmy said. "It's more than just residual. There are active spirits..." he stopped short and whispered loudly, "Did you hear that? A low growl."

"Yes, I heard it," Carrie replied in hushed tones. "Did anyone else hear that?"

Lucy was about to say that she hadn't heard anything when all of a sudden, the growling noise came again, this time so much louder that everyone heard it, even Jack!

They all held their breath and waited to hear if it came again.

They waited.

"Stay quiet," Carrie whispered.

They waited...

Carrie and Lucy suddenly screamed as an unexpected projectile whizzed past them and hit Carrie on the shoulder.

"What was that?" Carrie cried out. "It hit me! It hit me! Something hit me!"

Looking around they couldn't see anything obvious on the floor.

"It felt like a stone, a small stone," Carrie insisted.

"OMG!" Lucy exclaimed, and nearly broke Jack's hand as she squeezed it tightly with hers. "There's another one. It almost hit me on the head."

They all looked up but there were no obvious loose stones above them.

Unexpectedly, Lucy's head torch went out. She tried tapping it, but it wouldn't re-light. "I think we should get out of here," she cried. She was visibly shaking with fear now and Jack wrapped his arms around her (much to Carrie's dismay).

"It's okay, babe I'm here," Jimmy reassured Lucy, whilst continuing to film her in her state of unadulterated terror.

"I don't like it," she said to Jack. She wanted to pick her feet up off the floor and run.

"It's okay..." Jimmy began to say again, but stopped when he too was hit from behind with, what felt like, a small sharp pebble. "Sh*t!" he yelled.

After he got over his initial surprise, he stood in front of the camera, his arms outstretched and his eyes scanning the crypt, calling out to the spirit world, "Throw another stone if you can hear or see us," he dared the spirits. "Let us know you're here. Communicate with us!"

In response, another stone came flying out of nowhere and landed just short of Jack's foot.

"One of the spirits is very strong," Jimmy said. "I'm sensing a male aspect. A man, an angry character, he doesn't want us here." He put his hands to his head. "I'm getting a mental picture; it's a man, dressed in a dark robe, he has been here a long time, a monk - a holy man."

"Throw another stone if you can hear or see us," Carrie called out.

"Don't ask them to throw things at us!" Lucy begged and clung desperately to Jack.

"Shhh," Carrie replied in a harsh whisper. "Did you hear that?"

Lucy wanted to cry. Her body seemed to have a mind of its own. She felt paralysed with dread.

"This holy man doesn't like women," Jimmy said, turning towards Carrie and Lucy. "He doesn't want you down here. Women are not allowed down here." Jimmy pointed his finger accusingly at them both. "Leave! Leave this place," he cried out in a voice that was not his own.

"Stop it," Lucy said. "Make it stop."

"Is that you crying?" Jack whispered to Lucy.

"I'm not crying," Lucy replied. "I want to but I'm not."

"That was weird," Jack said. "There! I just heard it again. Like a child crying - off in the distance."

Lucy's blood ran cold. She called out to Aunt Lilly and Mother Mary in her head, asking them to send angelic protection to them all.

"Let's take a bit of time and just be quiet," Carrie suggested, then after about thirty seconds she spoke out into the ether saying, "Show yourself! Throw something, touch someone - make a noise if you are there. Knock once for yes and twice for no. We mean you no harm. Communicate with us. Make a noise if you can." She paused for a few seconds, but nothing happened. "Are you there? Can you see us?"

"That's not exactly being quiet," Jack commented. "If I was a spirit who could hear or see us, I'd be thinking what the hell are these nut cases doing down here asking us to knock on walls and throw things at them. Lucy is really scared, we should go."

"You're okay, aren't you babe?" Jimmy asked Lucy but as he did so he doubled over in pain.

"What is it? Oh my god, what's happening?" Lucy screamed.

"Bad energy, demonic," Jimmy growled, holding his stomach as if he had been winded.

Suddenly his head flipped up and his eyes rolled back in his head.

"You shouldn't have come here," he shouted in a deep, grunting voice which was full of venom. He spat the words out of his contorted mouth - "Get out! Get out!"

Without warning, he was thrown backwards against the whisky barrels, and several bottles of wine fell on him, clonking him on the head and smashing his torch.

As he flailed about, he accidently hit Lucy in the face, then fell to the floor with a thud.

Lucy screamed again and burst into tears. She put her hand to her face, "My nose, it's bleeding," she cried.

Jack tried to find her something to soak up the blood, but he didn't have anything. He took off his t-shirt and gave it to her, then grabbing hold of Jimmy and pulling him up by his collar, he yelled at him to, "Get a f*cking grip!"

Jimmy felt like jelly and flopped back to the floor.

"That's enough theatrics - get up!" Jack told him with authority. He shone his torch right into Jimmy's face. "I said get up!"

"I'm out of here," Lucy cried and turning, she began to run back towards the stairs.

Jimmy seemed to come round a bit and Jack was finally able to pull him roughly to his feet. He pushed Jimmy back the way they had come, through the second room and into the first, where he dumped him at the bottom of the wooden steps.

"Idiot," Jack mumbled as he went up the stairs to open the door. "We're leaving."

To his horror - the door was locked.

Chapter 23

~ * ~

Jack banged on the cellar door and tried to force it with his shoulder.

"What is it?" Lucy cried, from the foot of the stairs, "What's happening?"

"The damn door's stuck, or locked," Jack told her.

"How?" Lucy exclaimed in horror. She began to feel a panic-attack coming on.

Carrie tried the walkie-talkie, but the battery had gone dead. Then, as if it was perfectly timed by some malevolent spirit, her head torch began to fail, flickering on and off, then fading away.

With only Jack's head torch still working, the darkness was all encompassing, and they felt as if they were being swallowed by an abyss.

Jack kept banging on the door and shouting, hoping Lancelot or India might hear them from the kitchen.

Unfortunately for them, in the kitchen, having come back from the entrance hall, Wolf was replaying some of the footage of the supernatural phenomena they had witnessed on the stairs and running some of the audio enhancements, so the distress signal, from the poor stranded souls in the cellar, went unheard.

After a few minutes, Lucy was becoming almost hysterical. Her nose had stopped bleeding but was now throbbing along with her cheek. She began to make her way up the steps so that she could be closer to Jack. Feeling her way upwards in the blackness, without warning, she suddenly lost her footing as one of the treads cracked beneath her foot and fell away.

Fortunately, she was able to pull herself up onto the tread above and, whilst screaming her head off, she clung to the wall in terror.

Jack rushed down to help her; as he put his weight on the step above, it too gave way and half of it tumbled down towards the cold flagstones beneath. His quick reactions saved them both from falling down the hole, and grabbing her around her waist, he hoisted them both up onto the top step.

In the light of his torch, it became apparent that, between them and Carrie and Jimmy, there was now a gaping gulf in the staircase and no safe way over it.

Lucy was having full-on hysterics. She had seen her life flash before her and wanted to get home to Tambo immediately. She was terrified that there was no way out of the cellar, never mind out of the house and grounds. Little Eden seemed a million miles away, even a whole other dimension away right now.

Jack tried to calm her down, "Don't be afraid, old girl," he reassured her.

"They'll come and find us - eventually."

Calling down to Carrie and Jimmy, he told them not to try and climb the stairs.

Suddenly, his head torch started to grow dim, then went out completely, plunging them all into pitch-black darkness.

They couldn't see each other or the stairs now.

Carrie wasn't easily scared, but being locked in a cellar with no way out and no light was too much even for her.

"Do you think there are evil spirits trying to harm us?" Carrie whispered to Jimmy as they sat on the bottom step. "It reminds me of that old prison in Portsmouth when the door got stuck and the Fire Brigade had to come and rescue us."

"It is bloody creepy here," Jimmy had to admit. "This old place is living up to its reputation. Van Ike is going to be psyched by this place. We should come back on Halloween and do a live special."

"Come back! Are you mad?" Carrie muttered. She could feel slow panic frosting her veins and the hairs on the back of her neck bristled as fear began to take hold.

"You want to be famous, don't you?" Jimmy asked her. "This place is going to send the ratings through the roof. We should be filming this bit. If the bloody torches were working, I'd go back and get the camera."

"I just want to get out of here," Carrie moaned, taking hold of Jimmy's hand for reassurance.

He didn't pull away.

I just wanted to be a TV presenter, be on prime-time; she thought to herself, *How did I get mixed up in all this horror?* Suddenly, she gasped with fright. "Can you hear that?" she asked, "It sounds like footsteps. Someone's coming."

They all listened intently. They wanted it to be someone coming to rescue them but couldn't help wondering if it was the sound of ghostly footsteps, rather than real ones. The sound, which seemed to be overhead, rather than outside the door, faded away, and they lost hope that it was India or Minnie come to let them out.

Jack began hollering and banging on the door again.

"I don't understand how it can be locked," Carrie said. "It was unlocked earlier, when we first came down here, and there wasn't even a key in the lock! Your friends wouldn't play a prank on us, would they?"

"Never," Lucy replied earnestly. "Would Wolf or Kaya?"

133

"Wolf would never do that to us," Carrie said. "We take Health and Safety very seriously."

"So you keep saying," Lucy sighed and wondered who had checked to see if the cellar steps were still safe to use.

"No one would have locked it," Jack said.

"No one human anyway," Jimmy added.

Lucy shivered. Then, she froze. She felt something breathing over her shoulder, then a horrible tickling sensation in her hair. She was afraid to move thinking it might be the ghostly hand of an undead monk come to push her down the stairs. She wanted to scream but no sound came out of her mouth. She couldn't move a muscle, she was so terrified. Then, she heard a squeak, felt a long tail dangling over her arm, and realising it was a rat, she began to scream her head off again.

"What the f*ck?" Jack exclaimed.

"A rat!" Lucy cried. "Get it off me! Get it off me!" She couldn't help squirming with disgust and terror.

Carrie and Jimmy quickly stood up in alarm and kicked the step and floor around them, unable to see if there were rats gathering around them too. Carrie shuddered with horror. "Check me!" she told Jimmy. "Check there aren't any on me," she begged him.

Jimmy didn't really want to come into contact with any rats himself, but he brushed her down, paying particular attention to certain areas of her body in the process.

"I bet there are hundreds of the critters down here," Carrie said, her legs going wobbly at the notion. "Hurry up," she shouted up to Jack, "And get us out of this hell hole!"

Jack tried to break down the door again, and although he could feel it loosening, it wouldn't fully give.

"Shh!" Jimmy suddenly told them all. "Did you hear that?"

Footsteps again...

"Didn't anyone else hear them? They sounded as if they were overhead," Jimmy said.

But apart from some occasional creaks and groans, the old house was as silent as the grave.

Lucy was finding it hard to keep her hysterics under wraps when it suddenly came into her mind to send a telepathic message to Sophie that they were in trouble. A wave of calm washed over her, and she felt the spirit of Aunt Lilly enveloping her. Instantly comforted, she involuntarily began to sing - under her breath to begin with - "Bring me Sunshine in your smile,"…and then a little louder… "Bring me laughter all the while…"

"What are you doing?" Carrie asked, shocked and a little disconcerted by Lucy's sudden break into song.

"I don't know why I didn't think of it before - my Aunt Lilly taught us to sing when we are afraid or sad," Lucy replied and continued…"In this world where we live there should be more happiness…"

Carrie had to admit that Lucy's singing was making her feel less scared and that the atmosphere in the cellar was becoming lighter, even if the actual darkness was still as black as coal.

Lucy had sung the whole song before, to their utter relief, they heard Robert's voice calling to them from behind the door.

The handle began to rattle, and then they heard Sophie calling to them, "Lucy? What's going on? Are you okay?"

"Oh, Sophie," Lucy cried out. "We're locked in."

"There's no key on this side," Robert shouted back.

"There never was a key," Carrie hollered from down below.

"Stand back," Robert yelled. "I'm going to try to break it down." Robert tried his shoulder against it but, as Jack had found, the lock was strong and wouldn't give.

"Get us out of here!" Carrie suddenly screamed. She could hear rats scratching and squeaking around her, "For god's sake get us out of here!"

"I'll have to find something to break it down with," Robert said to Wolf, who was standing with him in the corridor. "Help me find a makeshift battering ram."

Lucy had a sudden flash of inspiration. "Sophie! Sophie! Are you still there?" she shouted.

"I'm here," Sophie replied, putting her ear to the door.

"There were some keys in a drawer in the kitchen," Lucy told her. "Near the kettle, there were spoons and other cutlery in there too."

"I'll go and look," Sophie replied but India told her to stay with Lucy and she dashed off to the kitchen instead.

Sophie tried to send good vibes through the locked door to her sister. "We'll get you out one way or another," she reassured her.

"Hurry," Lucy begged her and shuddered with fright again. "There are rats! Or at least I think there are…"

…It suddenly occurred to Lucy that the rats might not be real after all but might be ghosts as well.

Chapter 24

~ * ~

"Help me look for some keys," India told Minnie and Lancelot as she raced into the kitchen.

"What's happening, what was all that noise about?" Lance asked.

India explained as they pulled out all the drawers and finally found a pile of keys. Luckily, they had paper labels tied to them with mucky-looking string. Unluckily, the words had nearly rubbed off over the years.

They tried to decipher them...

"I think that one says Lobby," Lancelot told India, "And, this one, it looks like Icehouse."

"This one is completely illegible," Minnie sighed. "This has a double 'll'. It could be cellar?"

"I think that's an F," Lancelot said, taking a closer look. "Could be Folly? Just take them all," he suggested and he followed them back to the cellar door, holding the wall and hobbling on his one good ankle.

India frantically tried the key she thought it might be but it wasn't the right one.

She tried another...

Then another...

Then...

...the fourth one fitted the lock!

Triumphantly, she opened the door.

Lucy and Jack were standing there looking rather worse for wear and covered in black dust. Lucy had streaks down her face from where she had been crying and dried blood around her nose and down her top.

Sophie hugged her sister and they both burst into tears of sheer relief.

"What happened?" Wolf asked as he and Robert came back, carrying a log they had found outside - which was now no longer needed to break down the door.

"Someone locked us in," Jack said angrily.

"It wasn't one of us," Lancelot reassured him.

"I didn't think it was but someone did," Jack replied.

"Or someone - not necessarily human - did," Kaya suggested.

"Where's Carrie and Jimmy?" Wolf asked.

"Down here," Carrie called up.

Wolf shone his torch down the steps. He was shocked to find that part of the staircase was missing and that they were stranded at the bottom.

"We need some rope," he said to Robert, "We'll have to haul them up."

Whilst Robert, Jack and Wolf went searching for rope to rescue Carrie and Jimmy, the others headed back to the kitchen.

Minnie put the kettle on and, at Lucy's request, Sophie checked her sisters hair to make sure she didn't have any rat droppings in it. She then began to clean Lucy's face.

"Did you get so scared you had a nosebleed?" Sophie asked her.

"Jimmy hit me," Lucy explained.

"Oh my god!" Sophie cried.

"I'll give him a bloody nose!" Minnie exclaimed.

"It was an accident," Lucy added, although she was upset that Jimmy had not yet apologised.

"We should leave him down in that cellar," India said angrily.

Eventually, Carrie and Jimmy were helped out of the darkness and joined the others, glad of a cup of tea and a piece of cake.

"I'm sorry about your shirt," Lucy told Jack, who was standing there still bare chested. "I must have left it in the cellar."

"It's alright," Jack told her. He reached over to where his t-shirt, from earlier, had been hanging over the fire to dry. "This one's okay now," he said as he put it on (much to Carrie's dismay - she'd quite enjoyed admiring his ripped torso).

"Do you think one of the ghosts locked you in?" Minnie asked them - hoping it wasn't.

"Ghosts can't turn keys in locks," Sophie reassured her. "They don't have hands."

"Oh, they most certainly can," Kaya retorted. "In the case of the…" she began to say but Wolf interrupted her.

"Did you encounter any paranormal activity down there?" he asked hopefully.

"Jimmy got possessed by the spirit of a monk," Carrie said. "He doubled over with the pain and that's when Lucy was injured."

"It looked more like trapped wind than a possession to me," Jack said. He looked as if he was about to deck Jimmy but Robert held him back.

"Well, there's no doubt that the door was locked by somebody," India said. "How do you explain that?" She looked at Wolf but he couldn't give

137

her an explanation.

"It can be a paranormal phenomenon - doors being locked and unlocked. In the Amityville Horror that happened a lot," Kaya said, finally able to finish what she had wanted to say.

"How many times have you seen that bloody movie?" Jack asked. "Don't you know the difference between fact and fiction?"

"This house is evil," Lucy said and shivered. "That's a fact. I can feel someone with us, watching us. It's as if they want to kill us."

"That's a bit melodramatic, old girl," Jack said.

"Then how do you explain the steps just breaking away like that?" Lucy replied. "Something locked the door on us and then sent us to our deaths."

"There'll be a rational explanation, you'll see, old girl," Jack reassured her. "A house can't hurt you - it's an inanimate object, just bricks and mortar."

"Most religions believe there is a place where the unconscious souls of the dead wait for their final judgement," Lancelot said. "Perhaps this house has become part of that cloud of consciousness - a place of limbo or purgatory."

"We need to leave," Minnie said anxiously. "We can't stay here all night; we'll be murdered, or worse - we'll all go mad."

"This house seems to be calling out to you more than anyone else," Kaya said to Minnie. "Perhaps it wants you to stay, like in the 'The Haunting' by Shirley Jackson."

"Don't be ghoulish," India told Kaya, "You're frightening Minnie."

"And stop quoting ghost stories," Jack told her. "We're not in one of your horror movies."

Kaya was angry at his rebuke. "No-one can deny that there is major spirit activity in this house. We've all witnessed it."

"I think we could all do with a stiff drink," Wolf said and pulled a bottle of whisky out of his bag, "Or there's plenty of chocolate."

He offered a glass to India who gladly took it. She wished she could deny that she had felt, seen or heard anything, but she had to admit that she'd been spooked just as much as everyone else. "I hate to admit it," she said, "But we did have some strange things happen to us when we went to the library,"

"You've been to the library?" Robert asked her in surprise, thinking that all this time she'd had been safely in the kitchen with Minnie, Lancelot and Sophie.

"With Sophie," India told them, and everyone immediately huddled around to hear what they had to say.

Chapter 25
~ * ~

"It was my fault really," Minnie admitted. "I wanted to use the loo and didn't want to go alone. We, the girls that is, not Lance obviously, went together, and on the way back one of the servants' bells started ringing, out there in the corridor." The memory of it sent shivers down her spine. "India thought it might be one of you ringing for help."

"We tried using the radio but no-one answered, all we could hear was crackling," India explained. "The bell just kept ringing so I wanted to go and see if anyone was in trouble."

"So you three weren't in the library?" Lancelot asked Robert, Wolf and Kaya.

"No, we were in the hall the whole time," Robert replied.

"So who was ringing the bell?" Lance asked.

They all looked at each other in alarm and then looked to India and Sophie for more information.

"We never found out who had been ringing the bell," India told them. "We went around the back, through the old orangery," she pointed to it on the map, "It looked the quickest route. When we got there we wished we'd gone via the hall after all because it was dark and spooky. The rain was deafening on the windows so we went as quickly as we could. It didn't look as if anyone had been in there in years. I think I was more scared we'd be cut to death by falling glass than of meeting a ghost though."

Sophie shuddered as she remembered the scene. "It was horrible in there. A flash of lightning illuminated the whole room for a moment and we saw..." she took a deep breath as she was still a little traumatised by it..."Scattered all over the window sills, and the floor, were hundreds of dead flies."

"'Amityville' all over again," Kaya interrupted, rather triumphantly and looked at Jack as if she was vindicated in her belief in the supernatural.

"It was certainly like something out of a horror film," Sophie had to admit. "The wind made it sound as if the undead were whispering all around us. I couldn't wait to get out of there."

"We found the library but we couldn't find the light switch so all we had were our torches," India explained.

"The library was so dark we could hardly see anything," Sophie said.

"We kept freaking out at every little noise and shadow. We thought someone was in there but we couldn't quite tell if it was human or…" she didn't like to say 'a ghost' in case it frightened Minnie.

"This house has some seriously chilling things in it," India had to admit. "There were paintings in that library which I can't believe anyone would want on their walls."

"You must be talking about the images of 'Lucifer' by Franz Von Stuck and of 'St Catherine of Siena Besieged by Demons'," Kaya said. "I quite like them myself. Images of death are not necessarily scary," she added. "They are representations of the human condition. We must all accept suffering and death as part of life. You only have to look at some of the Buddhist illustrations to know that."

"Well, all I can say is that someone in the Montgomery family must have been into the occult," Sophie said. "On the desk there were old copies of sinister books, including the 'Book of Soyga', and 'Deamonology' by King James I. Not your usual reading matter."

"On the desk?" Robert asked them. He was puzzled. "They weren't on the desk earlier when I was in there with Kaya."

"Well, someone put them there," India replied.

"Or something," Kaya said but everyone looked at her impatiently, wanting to hear from India what had happened next.

"The next thing we knew, there was the strangest sound coming from the room next door," India told them.

"Yes, it was really odd, we had no idea what it was at first - scared us half to death - I have to admit," Sophie added.

"It was a rhythmical sound like a click, click, click, click, click, click," India recalled. "As we opened the door another flash of lightening lit up the room and we could see it sitting on the piano…"

…Minnie and Carrie both gasped - thinking there must have been a terrifying ghoul sitting on the piano top.

…"A metronome was nodding slowly back and forth," India said. "Just constantly going back and forth…click, click, click."

"Oh my god, you must have been so scared. What did you do?" Lucy asked.

"Well," India replied, "I couldn't stand the sound any longer so I fastened it back, but I will admit that the whole scenario was creeping me out big time. I was expecting to see someone else in the room but it was empty."

"Were you filming all this?" Wolf asked hopefully.

"No I flipping well wasn't," India snapped and then wished she'd not said it in that way, so added in a kinder tone, "Sorry, I didn't think about filming any of it. I didn't even take the camera with me. We thought one of you was in danger or we'd never have left the kitchen in the first place. I wasn't going ghost hunting."

"But how did the metronome start going?" Minnie asked and shuddered. "If there wasn't anyone in the room it must have been a ghost."

"I think my presence in the house is creating even more psychokinetic activity than usual," Kaya said. "Some people just attract it more than others. When I was fifteen we had a series of poltergeist activities in our house. My mother said it was my electromagnetic energy which was setting off the spirit activity..."

...Wolf interrupted her again, asking India and Sophie, "Did you feel a spirit presence in the rooms?"

"Not a presence exactly," Sophie said. "I think it was just our imaginations running wild."

"I can feel them all about me, they are everywhere," Kaya interjected. "When you have the gift, as I have, you know when there is a spirit presence."

Lucy and Minnie looked around, hoping to god there weren't any in the kitchen.

"I'm not an expert," Sophie admitted. "I could sense a sinister force in the air - a seriously bad vibe - it gave me the heebie-jeebies and the hairs on the back of my neck were bristling, but the metronome wasn't the worst of it," she added.

"Oh god no, it wasn't!" India agreed. "That planchette! The one we saw earlier on the table - you remember Lucy? Well, someone's written on it - GET OUT OR DIE."

Minnie put her hand to her mouth to stop herself exclaiming in terror. "I knew it," she whispered, "They want us out of here - Isabelle and the others."

"This is amazing paranormal phenomena," Wolf said. "We must go and film the writing and investigate the library and those renovated rooms straight away. Charge up the batteries! I'll find the spares."

"Wait," India told him. "That's not all we found in the drawing rooms."

"Good god, what else happened?" Lucy asked.

141

"As we were about to go through the second room, to get to the hall, Sophie noticed a table that had previously had its back flush against the wall was now sticking out at an odd angle. Behind it were a disguised panel and a secret passageway."

"Fantastic stuff!" Wolf exclaimed, he felt so excited he could burst. "You have to come with me and show me all this," he said to India (really hoping she would).

"You didn't actually go down the passage did you?" Robert asked.

"That's when my courage returned," India explained. "I thought - a ghost wouldn't need to use a passageway, would it - not when they can walk through walls?"

"You should have waited for us to come with you, you could have fallen through the floor or something," Robert told them, thinking of the steps in the cellar.

"The lath and plaster walls were patchy in places, as were the floorboards, but we were careful," India said.

"It was dark and there were too many spiders for my liking," Sophie admitted. "But India wanted to keep going to see where it led. We went down some steps at one point and I was sure we could hear someone singing."

"You're mad, the both of you," Minnie squeaked, horrified by the whole idea.

"And where did it lead to?" Robert asked.

"It came out at the bottom of the servant's stairs, just out there in the corridor. We didn't get chance to tell anyone straight away because you all came back from the hall, then there was the business with the cellar…"

"Can't we just get out of here?" Minnie asked. "It's sending me out of my mind."

Robert went over to Minnie and gave her a hug to reassure her - much to Kaya's chagrin.

In her jealousy Kaya couldn't quite stop herself from saying: "In 'The Haunting' the house sent one of the paranormal investigators out of her mind. And she died trying to leave."

"Next you'll be saying aliens exist because you've watched 'Star Trek' too many times," Jack said, but then remembered about the Star Children in Little Eden and realised that perhaps he did believe in aliens, just not in way most people did.

"You can't deny what's been happening here though," Wolf said. "We've all witnessed so much, it's amazing. It's like all our Christmases have come at once. No wonder no-one stays after midnight. We've had orbs, noises, cold spots, doors locking, bells ringing, clocks striking, spirit writing, laughing, crying and singing as well as major poltergeist activity. It's incredible."

"I told you this is the most haunted house in the world," Kaya said gleefully.

"It's a humdinger alright," Jimmy grinned.

Jack looked at everyone in bewilderment. He could see that even Lancelot and Robert were starting to believe the house was haunted. "For Christ's sake," he said exasperated, "Can we come back into the real world? As India pointed out, ghosts don't need to open doors; and they can't hold pencils and can't turn keys to lock doors. If they do exist they are an incorporeal consciousness without hands or feet to write or walk with."

"I agree with Jack," Sophie said. "It's like every horror story ever written all rolled into one. It's almost too good to be true."

"Someone human locked that door, wrote on that paper and set that metronome off," Jack said, "And I have a pretty good idea who it was."

Sophie nodded her head in agreement - she had suddenly begun to see things more clearly.

Chapter 26
~ * ~

"You mean, you don't think this place is haunted after all?" Lucy asked Sophie.

"I knew it!" India said.

"Of course it's haunted," Kaya retorted.

"This place has a reputation amongst the best in the business - it's definitely haunted," Jimmy agreed.

"There might be rational explanations for some of the phenomena, but I've never seen anything like this before," Wolf added.

"Who stands to gain by making sure this place seems haunted?" Jack asked them.

They all looked at each other, unsure of who would go to such lengths.

"Ada and Arthur. Of course!" Robert replied. "Why didn't I think of that before?"

"The scamming...," India said but stopped short, not wanting to swear in front of Wolf. "I knew I didn't trust those two!"

"No!" Carrie protested. "They couldn't have faked all the things we've witnessed tonight."

"I don't believe it either," Kaya said emphatically.

"They set us up to expect this place to be haunted and then they disappeared," Jack said. "Where did they go and where are they now?"

Everyone looked at each other again. No-one knew where they were.

"I presumed they would be in bed at the Lodge House at this time of night," Lucy said.

"Do you think they are in the house with us?" Minnie asked, "That they've been watching us all this time?" She looked around at the ceiling and the walls thinking that the room might be bugged or that there might be hidden cameras. She didn't like the idea of being watched by the living but it was better than being watched by the dead! It wasn't long before her fear turned to anger and she was looking forward to giving Ada and her brother a piece of her mind when she found them. "If you can hear us, we're onto you, you lying bastards," Minnie called out loudly, in case they could hear her. "We know what you're up to and we're not happy about it!"

"Ada and Arthur are famous in the area for being real psychics," Kaya said, defending them. "Their great-grandmother knew Edgar Cayce and

Madame Blavatsky."

"I wouldn't exactly trust those two either, famous or not," Sophie said. "A great deal of New Age philosophy is based on their teachings, a lot of which is seriously flawed."

"This house really is haunted," Kaya protested. "They wouldn't have to make it up, they believe in the spirit world as much as I do."

"Do they?" Robert asked, suddenly remembering something he had seen at the Lodge. "They had a poster of Harry Houdini on the wall and..."

"...Harry Houdini was famous for believing all supernatural phenomena was fake, "Sophie added, finishing Robert's train of thought.

"Exactly," Robert continued. "Why would they admire him if they were true believers in the paranormal? It's more likely they know enough illusions to trick everyone who comes here. I bet that magician and his assistant in the photographs I saw were Ada and Arthur's parents."

"I still don't believe what we have witnessed here is fake," Wolf said, unwilling to give it up. "We've got orbs on camera and a spirit speaking to us on tape."

"We all felt those stones being thrown and all heard footsteps in the cellar," Carrie reminded them.

"All three of us saw the white ectoplasm and felt the cold on the stairs," Kaya said, looking at Robert, "And how do you explain the clocks chiming and the noises we heard in the hall?"

"The fact we all saw and heard the same things is what makes me suspicious," Sophie said. "Supernatural phenomena are registered with the psychic brain and not everyone's antenna is sensitive enough to pick-up the same frequencies. That's why it's so easy to dismiss what happens as someone's imagination. If everyone saw or heard every ghost, no-one would be arguing about whether the spirit world exists or not."

"She's got a point," Wolf had to admit.

"Think about it," Sophie said. "Lucy can smell spirit scents, like tobacco or perfume, but I can't. I might feel a spirit presence like an electrical charge through my aura, but India doesn't. Robert can sometimes hear spirit, but Jack doesn't. The fact that everything has been so clear to everyone makes it unlikely that it is really supernatural phenomena."

"Precisely," Robert said. "That's the problem with psychic experiences, there are too many variables for scientific tests to show consistent and conclusive results. Sophie's right, the goings on tonight have been too obvious to all of us."

"We need to go into the hall; I have an idea," Sophie told them.

They all, even Lance, who hopped along with Jack's help, headed upstairs to see what Sophie had in mind.

They turned on the lights and stood, looking up the grand staircase.

Robert showed Sophie the exact stair on which they had seen and felt everything. She knelt down and tapped on the wooden tread. She felt along one edge and then pushed down on it.

To everyone's astonishment the other end flipped up.

Robert took hold of it, and it slid aside.

There, inside the step, they found a mini face-fan, a small Kilner jar, with the lid open and a wire attached to it, and a board on a spring which wobbled back and forth - they were all linked up to a remote-controlled timer.

"The cold was created by the fan," Sophie surmised. "The timer could be turned on remotely at any time."

"What's the jar for?" India asked.

"I bet that had smoke in it!" Robert said and sniffed it to be sure. He was shocked that he had been duped so easily. "It just shows, when we are set up to believe or expect something, we forget to think it through rationally and just accept it at face value."

"What about the crying?" Kaya asked. "We all heard a woman crying in the distance."

"Didn't you say in the Lodge you'd seen a ventriloquist's dummy?" Sophie asked Robert.

He nodded.

"Ada or Arthur, one of them at least, can probably throw their voice," Sophie said. "Even if they were standing just behind one of these doors, they could have made it sound as it there was someone talking, laughing, singing or crying anywhere in this area."

"What about the face in the mirror?" Minnie asked. "How did they do that? Please tell me they did that, and it wasn't really a ghost."

"That's an old magician's trick if ever there was one," Sophie said. "I didn't look properly before. I admit I was scared myself at the time so didn't really give it a proper going over, but I'm sure, if we took the mirror apart, we'd find a sliding screen hidden inside."

"I'll go and check," Jack offered and he and Wolf went off to investigate.

"The clocks?" Robert asked Sophie. "Remote control again? Some kind of pre-recording?" He and India looked behind the faces of the clocks and each had a small microphone in them. "They had us good and proper," he said, exasperated and angry.

Jack and Wolf came back and confirmed that the mirror had been tampered with and showed them a photographic plate which slid behind the mirror-glass. The image was from the painting of Isabelle but had been overlaid by a three dimensional photograph of a skull and vampire making it look so hideous and macabre.

"But Jimmy was possessed in the cellar," Lucy said, her nose and cheek were still sore. "There must have been a real spirit down there surely? It felt as if there was something evil down there with us."

They all looked at Jimmy, who looked at Carrie, who looked at Wolf and, after a few moments, Carrie gave in to peer pressure, "Alright!" she admitted. "Sometimes Jimmy does his little 'act' for the camera. I know we shouldn't, but some places we go to film at, nothing happens, and we have to have something for the viewers. Besides, they have come to expect a possession, and we get letters if we don't have one in every episode now. Jimmy doesn't tell us when he's going to do it so that it looks more convincing."

Jimmy had to admit that his possession in the cellar had been a charade.

"How could you?" Lucy scolded him. "You knew how scared I was and you really hurt me."

"I didn't think you'd take it so seriously," Jimmy replied sheepishly.

"Well, I did!" Lucy cried. "You are a liar - a total and utter liar."

Jack got hold of Jimmy by the scruff of the neck and frog marched him into the first drawing room. He slammed the door behind them both and then rammed Jimmy violently up against the wall, pinning him to it by his neck. "One more word out of you and you'll be haunting this place for eternity," Jack told him. "You touch or hurt Lucy again - even go near her - and I'll kill you, you got that?"

Jimmy didn't reply so Jack pushed his head hard against the wall again and squeezed his throat as if to really strangle him. "You got that?" Jack repeated.

Jimmy nodded frantically, he felt as if he was about to pass out, or worse - die of asphyxiation.

Jack dragged him back into the hall and almost threw him onto one of window seats, discarding him like a piece of rubbish. "You're nothing but a faker and a liar," Jack told him.

"I'm not a liar," Jimmy protested pathetically. "I am a real psychic. It's just sometimes the viewers want what the viewers want. I might embellish the truth from time to time but that's show business."

Kaya wanted to slap him (and she wasn't the only one). "You give us all a bad name when you make stuff up," she said angrily. "You should be ashamed of yourself. I thought you and your team were professionals."

India's heart sank. She realised that Wolf might also be a fraud along with Jimmy and Carrie. "Do you know Jimmy fakes it?" she asked Wolf.

Wolf had to admit that he was aware of a bit of ham-acting now and again. "It's the magic of television," was his excuse. He could see that India was disappointed in him. "I didn't fake anything else here though," he told her. "I've been duped along with everyone else."

"Oh, well, that's okay then," India replied scathingly. "Not here, but everywhere else. How can anyone trust a word you say?"

"So you've never exaggerated, or lied, or cheated, in your whole life?" Wolf asked her.

India thought for a moment and remembered that she was, at times, willing to overlook the whole truth if it meant saving Little Eden. "Maybe, but a white lie for the greater good is different from systematic deception for your own ends. Lying to deliberately deceive is evil - that's how evil starts - one lie leads to another and another, until in the end, you don't know what's true and what's not anymore. I don't believe in the supernatural, but I thought you did. Now I realise you don't have any principles or scruples and you're no better than Jimmy Pratt!"

"Hey, don't lump me in with him!" Wolf complained.

"I can hear you," Jimmy said, clutching his sore throat and lying out on the window seat as if he was in pain.

Lancelot intervened, "I think we can all agree that we've been taken in by Ada and Arthur, as have many people before us, but pointing the finger isn't going to help us now. Let's just be thankful that Malinwick Manor is not haunted after all."

Chapter 27
~ * ~

"Hang on, what about the library bell and the metronome?" Kaya asked Sophie.

"I think Ada or Arthur rang the bell then went through the drawing rooms, set the metronome going and then escaped via the secret passageway," Sophie replied. "If they had fully pulled the door closed, we'd never have found it."

"I bet there are plenty of secret passageways around this house," Lucy said.

"They probably know their way around like rats," Jack suggested.

"And you think they were the ones singing?" India asked.

Lucy looked at Jack, and India realised it might have been Lucy they had heard when she was singing in the cellar to cheer herself up.

"Do you have that map of the house?" Jack asked Wolf.

He produced one from his pocket and they scanned it. "If that passageway goes from here, then down some steps and comes out there, it must go over the cellar/crypt just about here."

"We did hear footsteps over our heads," Jack said.

"We assumed it was a spirit," Carrie sighed.

"We heard the singing when we were near those missing floorboards, remember?" India said to Sophie.

Jack took a torch and headed back into the drawing room. They all followed him and watched as he shone the light into where the passageway began.

He squeezed through the opening.

Robert followed him into the darkness.

"What are you looking for?" Robert asked him as they made their way along.

"I've got a theory," Jack replied. "When we were in the cellar, several stones came hurtling through the air at us. They had to come from somewhere."

They went down the steps and there, at the bottom, they found the gap in the floor. Jack shone his torch into the space below. It was full of dust and dead woodlice, but just near the wall, there was a small hole, and next to it was a pile of tiny stones. Jack picked one up and aimed it through the opening - it flew through - and listening intently, he heard it hit the cellar floor down below. "There!" he exclaimed. "I bet one of those batty old buggers was in here, watching us, throwing these stones at us and making all sorts of spooky noises."

When the boys came back out into the drawing room, they explained to the others what they had found, and Jack showed them a handful of the projectiles.

Minnie was really angry now. "I'll give those two what for when we find them!" she exclaimed. "How dare they scare us half to death like that?"

"This is a nightmare!" Carrie moaned. "I know we sometimes ham things up for camera, but we don't usually go to these lengths to fake it. Van Ike isn't going to be pleased about this."

"The orbs were real," Wolf said. "We still have those."

"If you watch any film, you can see orbs," Sophie told him. "It's just that when the show isn't about ghosts, no-one notices what's going on behind the actors. On any TV programme you'll see them floating about if you look for them."

Jimmy felt deflated. "This was my shot at the big time. I thought we could go worldwide after this. This is un-fu*king-believable!"

"I'm going to find those two fakers," Jack said and headed for the front door.

"Leave it for now," Lancelot suggested. "It's dark, it's raining, and if they have been watching us, they'll already know we're on to them. It's over. We'll confront them in the morning. I think we should try to get some sleep, and hopefully tomorrow, we might be able to get back to the village somehow."

"I don't think I could sleep," India said. "I feel violated."

"I'm just so glad it wasn't ghosts after all," Minnie said.

"You don't think Ada and Arthur would try to really harm us, do you?" Lucy asked, remembering the shot gun she had seen at the Lodge House and wondering if they had tampered with the steps in the cellar.

"I doubt that," Robert reassured her. "There are too many of us to try to bump us all off!"

"Let's go upstairs and we can all bunk up in those renovated rooms," Jack suggested. "If we're altogether we'll be safe, and we might get some shut-eye if we try."

"There's not room for everyone upstairs," Lucy told him.

"Jimmy and I can sleep in the drawing room on the sofas," Wolf offered.

"I'll join you," Lance replied. "Save me trying to get up those stairs. It'll be light in a few hours. Everything seems better in daylight."

"Jack and I can sleep in the other drawing room," Robert said. "Let the ladies have the upstairs rooms."

Sophie and Minnie shared the Chinese room. Lucy and India took the double bed in the pink room, leaving the interconnecting doors open through the en-suite. Carrie and Kaya settled down in the yellow bedroom.

They all locked their outer doors just in case Ada and Arthur were still about.

None of them thought they would be able to sleep, but everyone, except for Sophie, was soon dead to the world.

Sophie had done far too much that day for her body and brain to cope with and the adrenalin had kicked in several hours ago. Now she was past the point of no return. Hyper-insomnia had her in its grip and there was nothing she could do about it. She felt as if she was plugged into an electrical socket, and whilst everyone else was snoozing away, she was wired. Lying there, wide awake, she tried to meditate to keep herself calm, but the house creaked and groaned in an unnerving way as the storm raged outside.

Her heart stopped when a terrifying and creepy sensation suddenly enveloped her. The room seemed to come alive as if the undead had entered it. She lay as still as she could and said the Lord's Prayer to keep her fears and evil at bay. She was glad of Humphreys' astral company but prayed that any other ghosts would leave her alone. She knew that it wasn't Ada or Arthur's doing. She knew a spirit presence when she felt one.

Suddenly, Minnie sat bolt upright in the bed beside her, staring, with a fixed gaze, at the wall in front of her.

"Minnie!" Sophie gasped and looked over at her friend, soon realising that Minnie was not awake. "Wake up! You're dreaming," she whispered.

Without responding, Minnie, with the same eerie hypnotic stare, rose slowly out of bed and walked towards the door.

Sophie wasn't sure if it was just an old wives' tale about not waking up sleep-walkers but she didn't like to try to if she didn't have to.

When Minnie began to turn the key in the lock, she thought she had better do something!

She jumped out of bed, slipped on her fluffy boots and tried to reach Minnie before she opened the door. "Minnie!" she whispered again,

"Minnie, its Sophie. You're dreaming, please wake up."

Minnie seemed to hear her and turned her face towards Sophie.

To Sophie's horror, Minnie didn't look like Minnie at all - she looked like the lady in the painting.

She looked like Isabelle!

"Sh*t," Sophie couldn't help exclaiming, then quickly put her hand over her mouth to stop herself from screaming. *Okay, breathe! Let's stay calm*, she said to herself. Minnie's face seemed to slide back to her own features - much to Sophie's relief. *Right, okay, think! What should we do? Is this Minnie or Isabelle standing in front of me?* She noticed that Minnie was wearing the ruby and diamond necklace and wondered when she had put it on. She was sure she hadn't been wearing it when they went to bed. *F*ck! Okay, this is really freaking me out now. Should I wake up the others?*

Before Sophie had time to do anything, Minnie had unlocked the door and was leaving the room.

Sophie realised she needed to follow Minnie immediately otherwise she'd be out of sight, and it could take hours to find her again - there were so many rooms in the mansion - plus she remembered Ada's warning about the dangerous floors and ceilings and feared Minnie might come to harm. She tried switching on the bedroom light and then the landing light but found that neither of them were working and she realised that the generator must have gone off. There was no time to search for the torch or a radio - Isabelle had taken Minnie halfway down the landing already.

Luckily, Humphrey was in hot pursuit, and he turned back regularly to make sure Sophie was following them both.

In the blue-black of night, Minnie walked, like a zombie, across the top of the main stairs and towards the staircase leading up into the north wing. The rain had ceased, creating an unnerving silence, and bright moonlight flooded through the lantern roof, throwing ghastly shadows against the walls and staircases, making Sophie catch her breath at every turn.

She shuddered as the eyes of the family portraits seemed to follow her every move and she nearly jumped out of her skin when she thought she saw a figure over by the window. A second glance made her realise it was just a branch moving behind the net curtains. She put her hand to her chest - her heart was beating so fast it was deafening. She really wanted to go and wake up the others, but she didn't know where Isabelle was taking Minnie and she didn't want to lose her to the vastness of the gloomy house.

As she followed Humphrey and Minnie up the next flight of stairs, Sophie started to become disorientated and, feeling a little dizzy, she held onto the balustrade to steady herself. She realised she could simultaneously see the house as it was right now in 2012 and also how it was when Isabelle had lived there in the early 1600's.

She was astrally time travelling and, in the dead of night, the sensation of switching time-frames was scary.

In the present day, most of the house was devoid of homely decoration, it was grim, dingy and morbid to say the least, but in the past, it was quite the opposite - there were coloured Turkish rugs on the floors, occasional tables adorned with vases of fresh flowers and many ornate mirrors which hung along the corridors reflecting the moonlight from up above. Instead of the unsettling family portraits, there were murals of idyllic gardens and Mediterranean landscapes, as well as some brightly coloured, finely-woven, tapestries, depicting biblical scenes. The house seemed full of love and life, joyfully and freshly decorated - in such stark contrast to the present day of disrepair and dilapidation. Sophie wished the cut-glass sconces, which were still there in the present day, had had their candles burning in them right now as she only had the moonlight to see by and walking alone through the cold, sombre hallways was freaking her out.

Sophie stopped; she was starting to feel a wave of exhaustion wash over her. She watched as Isabelle took Minnie up the next staircase. Minnie remained silent and transfixed, as she continued up and up until she reached the fourth floor attics.

Sophie struggled to keep up, *Why does she want to go up all the stairs?* Sophie thought to herself. *I don't think I'm going to make it back down, even if I can make it up there. Stupid body, why can't you just be normal and do what I want you to do? I need to help Minnie so we are pushing through this, we are doing this, we will be in bed for a month after this weekend, but we are here now, so we don't have any option but to keep going.* Humphrey seemed to know that she was struggling and came back to encourage her. He nudged her astral-self with his nose as if pushing her onward and upwards. Sophie forced her human-self, with military determination, to carry on ascending the stairs and to keep Minnie in her sights.

The walls up on the fourth floor were not so highly decorated as on the lower, and it was obvious that these rooms had been the servant's quarters. In the present, the walls were a revolting, yellowy-brown colour - the peeling paint looking like flaking skin. Sophie didn't want to go near them. Thick, fly-filled cobwebs criss-crossed the ceilings and broken floorboards revealed centuries of dust and thousands of dead cockroaches beneath.

Sophie shivered, it seemed chillier up here than down below, and she wrapped her cardigan around her, hoping Minnie wasn't too cold.

Along the grimy corridor, one of the doors was open, and glancing in, she could see that there were two empty, cast iron bedsteads and a fireplace covered in layers of fine white dust. Suddenly, a psychic vision showed her how it used to be - the twin beds were neatly made, covered with pretty patchwork quilts, and in the corner was an oak dressing table with an ebony comb and brush laid out upon a glass tray. Around a small mirror was a garland of fresh flowers and above that was a beautiful painting of Saint Anne. It must have been a maid's room, Sophie thought to herself. As the thought passed across her mind, she felt an uneasy sensation run through her, and she caught sight of a maid, hurrying along the passageway towards the stairs, arranging her hair under a white cotton cap, as if she was late for work. Sophie jumped sideways as the maid nearly ran right through her and disappeared into a wall where there was no longer a door.

Suddenly, Sophie felt a frisson of panic; due to the distraction of the ghostly maid, Minnie had disappeared from view and Humphrey had too!

Chapter 28
~ * ~

Terrified and alone in the chilled, eerie corridor, Sophie tried the last few doors. They were all locked and unless Minnie had suddenly become incorporeal, like the maid and able to pass through solid matter, there was nowhere else she could have gone.

"Isabelle! Minnie! Where are you?" Sophie called out.

Suddenly, she thought she saw someone skulking in the shadows and involuntarily she froze, rooted to the spot in terror. Her heart was racing and she hardly dared breathe or look again. After a few moments, which seemed like forever, no-one appeared, and it took all her courage to peer down the corridor again to see that there, hanging on the end wall, was a large, silvered mirror.

Sophie realised it had been her own reflection that had scared the crap out of her.

"Minnie?" Sophie cried out again, her voice trembling with fear. "Isabelle?"

Stay calm, for god's sake, Sophie told herself. Luckily Humphrey re-appeared, pootling through the mirror as if it wasn't even there. He seemed to want her to follow him through the looking-glass. *There must be a hidden doorway*, she thought, *Like in the drawing room.*

There was no other explanation for Minnie's sudden disappearance.

Reluctantly, she began to press on the mirror, feeling down its sides and trying not to touch the repulsive, flaking walls.

The moon, which was her only source of light, faded away from the dormers as the furious storm returned to attack the Manor with full force. A sudden crash of rain, like a banshee trying to smash through the windows, frightened the life out of her.

Now in total darkness, Sophie felt trapped. "Minnie? Isabelle?" she called out in despair. She didn't know how she was going to go forwards or backwards now. She wasn't even sure if she knew the way back to the bedrooms.

She tried to keep her composure, but she was scared - really scared.

She pushed against the mirror one more time and, to her utter relief, it yielded. Pulling it towards her, it opened like a door, and in the darkness beyond she caught a glimpse of Minnie's white pyjamas.

She knew she had to go in.

Sophie had no idea what lay beyond and hesitated. She was startled by a terrible creaking sound and she gasped with fear as a sudden gust of freezing wind hit her in the face. It whirled around and seemed to ransack the mysterious room beyond. Unsure what had happened, and terrified that Minnie was in danger, she took a deep breath and stepped through.

She gasped in horror as a sheet of lightening lit-up the space and she saw her friend standing precariously outside on a small balcony. The French windows were wide open to the fierce night air. The rain lashed down like sharp lances. Minnie was seemingly unaware of the tempest which whipped against her, drenching her with its wrath.

"Minnie!" Sophie screamed and ran towards her in panic. She managed to catch hold of her friend just as the crumbling stone balustrade and part of the balcony floor gave way, crashing down through the wild night air, shattering into pieces on the gravel below.

Sophie looked down in horror at the broken stones which could so easily have been Minnie's broken bones.

Trembling with shock, Sophie pulled them both back into the room and pushed the tall windows closed to keep out the vicious gale. The storm seemed enraged by being shut out and threw itself at the glass, flinging open one of the doors again, roaring into the room like a great beast.

Sophie tried to slam the windows shut again but the rain stung her eyes and the wind seemed intent on beating her down - she couldn't fight it. *Help me!* she called out to Mother Mary and, in that moment, she found a burst of superhuman strength, enough to snap shut the latch and keep the hideous force of Nature outside.

In the pitch dark, Sophie held Minnie close to her as they lay, exhausted, on the floor.

"Don't let Isabelle take you over," Sophie told her. "You're stronger than she is, tell her to go."

Whether it was nearly falling to her death which had awakened her or the wild weather, Minnie seemed to become aware of herself again. "What's happening to me?" she whispered, clinging to Sophie's hand.

"Isabelle is using your human body and your consciousness to manifest herself," Sophie explained. She was losing her ability to speak she was so exhausted. A wave of deep fatigue was washing over her and she was shivering with cold. Trying her best to say the words out loud, she told

Minnie; "You have to tell her to leave you alone - to get out of your aura."

The relentless storm still wanted in, rattling and shaking the windows with demonic ferocity. Sophie was sure it was only by the grace of god that the windows stayed shut, and she prayed to every angel, saint and buddha she could think of.

"Don't let Isabelle take you over completely," Sophie urged her friend.

Minnie seemed to understand. She had felt Isabelle's consciousness taking her over little by little all day long and was finally relieved that someone had noticed and would believe her.

"Get out of me!" Minnie shouted and, as she did so, she began to shake uncontrollably, all over.

"Push her out harder," Sophie told her. It came to her mind to say The Lord's Prayer, which she muttered under her breath, but every word was such an effort she could hardly get through it.

With every fibre of her being, Minnie yelled again, this time from her boots, "You won't have me! Get out of me you bitch!"

All of a sudden, the storm hit the windows with such ferocity that the windows burst open again and swung back so violently that the glass in one of them shattered with a loud snap.

Sophie wanted to get them out of there as quickly as possible.

"Give me the necklace," she said and unclasped it from around Minnie's neck. With the last drops of her energy she commanded, "In the name of the true source of all that is good, I command you, Isabelle de Lacy, to come into the necklace and leave Minnie alone."

With that, Sophie saw a hologram of Isabelle step out of Minnie's body and stand beside her. She shimmered in the darkness, dressed in her golden gown and wearing the stunning necklace which fell gracefully over her décolletage. She seemed to be reaching out to them both, desperate for their help; and Sophie realised that Isabelle wasn't an evil spirit. She meant them no harm; she was begging for their attention - for them to rescue her. Her spirit swirled into a spiral and her ectoplasm coiled like a spring, disappearing into the ruby. As Sophie took a deep breath, the spirit of Isabelle was safely embedded inside the jewels.

Sophie involuntarily sighed, which was always a signal that the energy work she was doing was finished, and put the necklace into her pocket for safe keeping.

Minnie could still feel the imprint of the necklace against her skin. She was disorientated and didn't know when she had put the necklace on, or why they were not in the bedroom. "Where are we?" she asked Sophie.

"The round tower," Sophie whispered and then she couldn't move or speak anymore.

A few moments later, the terrible rain abated, and the moon came out from behind the menacing clouds. Minnie could just about make out the whitewashed walls of the gloomy room, and in the dim light, she could see a small, alabaster altar, with a gilded arch above it, glinting amongst the shadows. She stood up and walked towards it. Inside the alcove was a painting of Mother Mary wearing a golden crown and holding out her hands as if to embrace her. Two ornate candle sticks, with half-burnt down honeycomb candles in them, and a plain silver chalice, stood on the altar. Everything was covered in cobwebs and dust. It had obviously not been touched in a very long time.

Minnie felt a shudder of evil run down her spine and a sudden urge to run rippled down her legs. She turned and helped Sophie to her feet. "Come on," she said. "We need to get out of here."

But before they could reach the doorway, the moon went behind the looming clouds again, suddenly plunging them back into darkness.

"Hold my hand," Minnie told Sophie. A few steps further on she felt Sophie's hand slip away from hers…

…Sophie disappeared.

Chapter 29
~ * ~

Sophie had completely vanished.

"Sophie!" Minnie called out blindly. She couldn't see anything - the chapel was as black as pitch.

"Sophie! Where are you?" she cried again, turning around and around, peering through the darkness, trying to see anything which might explain where Sophie had evaporated to.

Minnie felt a wave of sickening dread in the pit of her stomach. *What if Sophie has been taken into the ghost dimension? What if she's slipped into the past and can't get back? That's how I started to feel earlier, I wasn't sure where I was. What if there is such a thing as time travel?* Minnie tried to hold onto her sanity. *That's ridiculous*, she told herself. *Now think! Sophie was here then she wasn't. There has to be a logical explanation. At least I hope there is!*

If only Minnie had been able to see Humphrey's ghost, she would have seen that he was barking and wagging his tail trying to show her where Sophie had gone!

Minnie called out for her friend again and heard the faint whisper of Sophie's disembodied voice calling back.

She looked around again and realised the sound seemed to be coming from below.

"Down here!" Sophie called upwards. "I'm in the floor! Help! Can you see me?"

Feeling her way with her hands, Minnie carefully knelt down, and was shocked to find part of the floor was no longer there. Gingerly she put her hand down into the hole and felt something warm and fluffy moving about.

"That's my head!" Sophie told her.

"Can you put your arms up?" Minnie asked her. "I'll try and pull you up."

"It's a really tight hole," Sophie replied, trying to wiggle her arms free. "I can hardly move. I think you need to go and get help."

"I'll go as fast as I can," Minnie promised and hoped to god she could find the door. Suddenly, she heard something which caught her attention. *What's that noise? It sounds like voices. Please don't let it be ghosts*, she thought, *Please don't let it be ghosts. Please don't let it be ghosts.*

Listening again, her heart racing with dread, she realised that one of the distant voices sounded like Jack's.

The voices were coming from outside the house.

Minnie carefully retraced her steps towards the window. It was only drizzling with rain now, but the wind was still strong, and the water hit her in the eyes like sharp needles. Not daring to step onto what was left of the broken balcony she shouted into the night, "Jack? Jack is that you?"

"Minnie?" Jack yelled up to her. "What on earth? What are you doing up there? Where are you?"

"In the attic," Minnie shouted back as loudly as she could. "Jack come and help us; Sophie might be hurt. I can't get her out!"

"We're coming up," he replied. "Don't move! Keep away from the window."

Minnie crawled back to where she thought Sophie was. "They're coming for us," she told her friend.

It seemed like an age before they were rescued.

Finally, Minnie shielded her eyes as torch light shone brightly into her face - it was Robert, Lucy and India who were coming into the room, holding the map of the house and looking bewildered.

"Thank god you're here!" Minnie cried. "Quick! Sophie's trapped."

They flashed their torches about, not seeing any sign of Sophie.

"Down here!" Sophie yelled up when she heard them. "Robert! Down here!"

"Come and help me," he said to India and Lucy. "Help me lift her out."

But Sophie was stuck fast.

There wasn't room for her to raise her arms above her head and pulling her by the neck was quickly found not to be an option.

Lucy lay on the floor, reassuring her sister and telling her they would get her out as soon as they could, whilst Robert tried to pull up more of the floorboards hoping to make the hole bigger.

"We thought we'd never find you!" India told Minnie. "The boys heard an almighty crash. Jack and Wolf went outside to look and saw the balcony on the tower had fallen away. Wolf radioed to us that you were up here but there was no mention of how to get into the tower on this floor on the map."

Jack and Wolf arrived, both looking bedraggled from the rain and out of breath. "This must be some kind of secret chapel," Jack commented as he surveyed the room. "Where's Sophie?"

160

"Down there," Robert told him and pointed into the floor. "There was a trap door here but it's rotted through. I think Sophie's fallen down a priest hole. I can't make it any bigger."

"A what?" Minnie asked. The adrenalin was starting to wear off and the aftershock was starting to kick in - she couldn't stop shaking. India held her hand and tried to keep her calm.

"It's a hiding place for a Catholic priest," Jack explained. "From the 16th century onwards, it was illegal to be a practising Catholic so aristocratic families started building hiding-places for the priests in case soldiers came looking for them."

"There are quite a few priest holes around Little Eden," Robert told them. "There must be a way out of it though. If it isn't upwards, maybe it's downwards or out of the side? Sometimes they lead to a hidden passageway out of the house," he explained. "Try pressing the walls around you," he suggested to Sophie.

Sophie pushed on the walls but they didn't give.

"Try stamping on the floor," Jack said.

Sophie stamped as hard as she could and Jack was right - the floor beneath her gave way; having nothing to hold onto she disappeared out of sight again.

The last they heard of her was her screaming as she plummeted down what was essentially a slide which ran diagonally downwards about ten feet.

"Oh my god!" India exclaimed. "Where's she gone?"

"What's beneath here?" Jack asked Wolf. "Look on the map, maybe we can get to her from below?"

"It looks as if there are bedrooms below us," Wolf said. "Come on."

They all piled down the stairs as fast as they could.

Thinking they would need more help to search for poor Sophie, Robert radioed to Lance.

India tried to persuade Minnie to go back to the renovated bedrooms to dry off but she couldn't bear to leave Sophie until she knew she was found safe and sound.

The bedroom beneath was derelict, with faded wallpaper hanging off the walls where patches of black mould had taken root. The emptiness echoed with their footsteps and their voices as they called out for Sophie. Flashing their torches around the walls, the floor and the ceiling, they hoped to find another trap-door or secret-panel. The alcoves at either side of the small brick fireplace were filled with heavy Elizabethan oak dressers, decorated with twisted legs and linen-fold decoration. They were so heavy, they were immovable - in fact they seemed to be fastened to the walls.

The friends pushed, and knocked, and tapped on every inch of the cracked, crumbling room but it seemed impregnable.

"Sophie!" they all called out, then listened for her reply; there was nothing but silence.

Everyone could hear their own breathing and their own hearts beating, but there was no sound from Sophie.

"Sophie!!!" Lucy shouted in desperation.

Silence.

"Sophie where are you?" Jack called out.

Silence.

Lucy was starting to panic and felt as if she couldn't breathe.

Still, terrifying silence.

Robert's heart was beating ten to the dozen and he was starting to break out into a cold sweat.

They called and called and listened and listened but...

...Nothing.

"Listen," India said suddenly, "Shhh. Quiet!"

They all stood motionless, straining to hear.

A faint voice was calling for help!

Everyone put their ears to the walls.

Jimmy arrived with Carrie and Kaya and they were quickly recruited into searching.

"Over here!" Jack said. He could just make out Sophie's voice responding. "She's behind the fireplace!"

All of them pressed on the bricks, the carvings, the tiles, even the hearth, but nothing moved.

"How the hell do we get in?" Robert asked, exasperated.

Jack looked around for something to start smashing the back of the fireplace with but there was nothing to hand.

The room was awash with panic and fear.

Lucy was so afraid for her sister she could hardly stand it and Minnie was so tired, cold and traumatised she felt near to hysterics.

No-one knew what to do next.

"Let's stay calm and think this through," India said. "If a priest used to hide in that hole either Sophie has to go further down or there has to be a way in from here to let her out. There has to be. The priest had to get out somehow."

They kept pressing and pushing on everything, but nothing was shifting.

Robert put his face to the part of the wall where Sophie was trapped and shouted to her, "Can you hear me? Knock on the wall if you can hear me."

They waited but there was no knocking in reply.

They waited and listened and then very, very faintly they could hear poor Sophie calling for help again.

"I don't think she can hear us," Robert sighed. "She's just calling out at random."

"You've got to do something!" Lucy cried to Jack in despair. "Pull down the whole wall if you have to but get her out of there!"

Chapter 30
~ * ~

"I'm going down to those sheds to get some sledgehammers and smash through the wall," Jack said and, without hesitation, he told Jimmy and Wolf to come with him. "We'll try to get the generator working again whilst we're there."

Robert shone his torch at the big-light in the room and there was clearly no bulb in it. "In here it won't make much difference, but yes, we'll need some light once we've got Sophie out."

Minnie still refused to go back to her bedroom and get dry, even when India offered again to go with her. "I can't bear to think she's trapped in the wall all alone, she must be so frightened," Minnie said.

Robert couldn't bear to think of Sophie trapped and alone either, and relentlessly kept pushing at the walls and pulling at the dressers, calling out her name and reassuring her in case she could hear him after all. He felt a wave of utter panic run like quicksilver through his blood. He didn't want to alarm the others by saying it out loud, but he feared that Sophie might run out of oxygen if he didn't get her out of there soon. His greatest fear was that she would die in agony, walled up alive, slowly gasping for her last breath, and he wasn't there to save her.

They seemed to be waiting hours for Jack to return with the wrecking-gear and it was driving them all crazy, including the ghost of little Humphrey, who kept coming and going through the wall, wining and scratching at the side of the fireplace, trying to show them where Sophie was - but no-one else could see him, not even Kaya.

"If only we could ask someone who used to live here back then how to get the priest out," Lucy suggested.

"Maybe we can," Minnie replied. "I could ask Isabelle."

Robert spun round and shone his torch at Minnie, "You mean there are actually ghosts in the house? It's not just Ada and Arthur's pranks? You can talk to the spirit of Isabelle?" he asked her.

"I'm afraid so," Minnie admitted. "We seem to have some kind of connection. She's the one who led me up to the chapel in the first place. She'd possessed me, so Sophie said. Whatever happened, she got into my head whilst I was asleep. I don't want to let her back in - it was terrifying. I thought I was losing my mind." She shuddered with the fear of going insane. "But for Sophie's sake, I could try to ask her to help us. I've been seeing the house as it used to be when she lived here, on and off. If I could see through her eyes again, maybe I can see how you open the wall?"

"I don't want to put you in danger too," Lucy told Minnie, "But could you? Would you?"

"I'll try," Minnie agreed. She closed her eyes and reached out to Isabelle with her mind. "Isabelle," she called. "Please help me. If you know how to get into the priest hole, please show me. My friend is trapped in there. Please, show me."

They waited…

And waited…

And waited...

Minnie opened her eyes and shook her head. "I'm sorry, when I don't want her with me, she's here, and when I do, I can't seem to get hold of her."

"I'll try," Kaya offered but she didn't fare any better either.

"Sophie says it helps to call out a spirit's name three times," Lucy suggested.

Minnie tried again, "Isabelle, Isabelle, Isabelle," she cried out, just as Jack, Wolf and Jimmy rushed back into the room carrying sledgehammers and crowbars.

~ * ~

Inside the wall, the suffocating cavity felt like a coffin. Sophie tried not to panic but it took all her courage not to scream, cry or have a full-blown panic attack.

She had slid down the pitch-black tunnel and come to a standing stop in what felt like a brick-lined funnel. The space was so tight, she couldn't move her arms, or bend, or sit down. There was something uneven under her feet, but she wasn't sure what it was and, apart from an air brick through which she could feel a cold chill, there were no apertures or openings.

Sophie had lost all sense of direction and had no idea where she was.

She called out for help but couldn't hear anyone responding. She carefully listened for footsteps or the sounds of doors banging but she was beginning to feel claustrophobic in the deathly silence; and the terror of being walled up, never to be found again, began to creep into her mind.

What if they never find me? she couldn't help thinking. *How will they know where to look for me?* The story of 'The Black Cat' came to mind and she realised that this was what being buried alive must feel like.

She prayed to every light-being she could think of and said the St Hilda and St Katherine prayers, to calm her nerves, as well as the Lord's Prayer, over and over for good measure. She was thankful when she felt an inner peace enveloping her and her higher-self taking over. Part of her felt she should be crying with fright, but her spiritual-self was so tranquil from being connected to the divine consciousness, that the feeling of horror slipped away, leaving her bathed in a blanket of serenity.

After a while she began to fall asleep standing up. *I suppose it might be better to die here than carry on as I was, anyway*, she thought. *I will die of hyperthermia before I starve to death, hopefully. This is more peaceful than having to throw myself off a bridge or cut my wrists. I know I've prayed for death a million times, when the pain and exhaustion were just too much, but I've never had the nerve to actually commit suicide, maybe this is a way to force my hand and accept death as a sweet release.* Tears ran down her cheeks as she felt her heart breaking at the thought of leaving those she loved behind; then she realised that she would be reunited with Aunt Lilly and began to feel a wonderful aura of peace surrounding her. Gradually death didn't seem so sad or terrifying anymore. She knew in her heart that Heaven would be the end to all her pain and suffering.

Sophie was preparing to die.

As her mind emptied of all human troubles and fears, she sensed a spirit presence gliding around her in the ether. Focusing her second sight, the vision of a man began to materialise. He was reaching out his hand to her and seemed to want to communicate something important. As always (she never had conversations with any spirit who wasn't a true light being) she asked three times if it was safe to hear what this mysterious stranger wanted her to know.

She received an affirmative each time and agreed to listen.

The man had kind eyes and, as he became clearer in her mind, she saw that he was dressed in a red robe and was wearing a Biretta over his white hair. She was surprised to be greeted by a Cardinal - she wasn't religious - then she thought that maybe he had come to take her into Heaven. This is what he had to say…

…"You have come at last. I have been waiting for you," he told her softly. "With my last breath, I prayed to our Lady to send a warrior to save our sacred site from the grip of evil, and at last, here you are."

Sophie thought he might have the wrong person and was about to say as much when he carried on speaking, so she let him continue…

…"I am Father John. I died in this hiding place many years ago. When my time came to pass over to join our beloved Mother in Heaven, I found I was unable to do so. The Heavenly portal here is guarded by witches. Evil bars the way to Heaven for anyone who dies here at the Manor. All goodness has been swept away by the darkness."

Sophie felt a terrifying ripple of fear. What if she couldn't get across to Heaven either? She didn't want to die if it meant being stuck in limbo, walking the house as a ghost for eternity, or worse, stuck in this hell-hole forever.

"What happened to you? Why didn't someone let you out of here?" she asked him.

"No-one but Lady Isabelle knew of my whereabouts," Father John explained. "I came in secret that night to help her. She was so afraid, poor child, of being possessed by the Devil. She was tormented by evil. The witches led her into madness. My presence here had been betrayed. Isabelle begged me to hide, and so I did, but she never came to let me out."

"Why didn't she come for you?" Sophie asked but before she'd even finished asking she knew the answer and saw the events of that night play out like a movie in her mind…

Chapter 31
~ * ~

The images of what had happened that night, so many centuries ago, ran through Sophie's mind as clearly as if they were happening right there and then…

It was raining that night too and she could see Father John rowing a small skiff down a narrow, high-banked syke which used to feed into the lake. Cloaked from the wild night and immediate sight, he made his way silently, gliding upon the water, down into the shelter of the boat house. He seemed anxious as if he suspected someone had followed him and, looking around to be sure he was not observed, he lifted away one of the coracles which was leaning against the outer wall, to reveal a concealed panel into which he crawled. Confined, stuffy and damp, the underground tunnel was so low that Father John had to bend almost double in the pitch darkness.

Sophie could feel, as well as see, the past unfolding before her and her breathing became shallow, then it quickened, as if she too was scrabbling along the hot, airless rabbit hole.

The subterranean passage led into the old Abbey crypt and Father John stepped out onto the painted floor tiles. Brushing himself down and removing his hood, he was glad to be greeted by a lit candle that was waiting for him in the usual place.

Using the secret passageways throughout the house, he stealthily made his way to the hidden chapel in the tower and his clandestine rendezvous with Isabelle.

In the shadows he found Isabelle, dressed only in her night gown and satin slippers, kneeling before the white marble altar. She was shivering with cold but she wanted to feel the sharpness of the night air against her skin - it reminded her that she was still alive. He lit the candles on the altar and placed his cape around her shoulders. In the half-light, he gasped at the sight of her. Since he had last seen her she was even thinner, like a cat without fur, and he could tell that she had not slept in weeks. Her pale, drawn face had lost all its lustre and her outer beauty had breathed its last breath.

Taking the sacrament, in the hope that she could free herself from the witches' curse that had crept inside her mind and tortured her for years, Isabelle almost fainted to the floor.

Since sending Molly to her death, she had been haunted by Molly's vengeful, wandering spirit. Molly had psychically attacked Isabelle with spells, hexes and curses whilst she was alive, hooking into her auric-field like a blood-sucking louse drawing the life-chi out of her; now that she was dead, she continued to sow destructive and wicked energy throughout Isabelle's etheric body. Molly fed Isabelle's guilt and played with her darkest fears. Incessantly chattering damnable, poisonous words into Isabelle's mind, she had tried to undermine her mistress's faith in God and had nearly succeeded. Isabelle was so terrified that she had judged and condemned Molly without God's permission that there were no prayers left in the world that could shut Molly's wickedness out. The dark maid wove malevolence into Isabelle's dreams creating obscene and terrifying nightmares which stirred together into a stinking, putrefying soup of foulness until Isabelle was drowning in insanity.

Father John tried his best to rescue her but Isabelle felt abandoned by the Holy Spirit.

Her self-disgust grew like the storm-clouds which shut out the sun. Unable to reach the compassionate consciousness of Mother Mary, Isabelle believed she had been forsaken; the house had become so full of evil and fear there seemed no way to reach divine salvation ever again.

Sophie's heart was breaking at the utter loneliness and abandonment which Isabelle was feeling because she could feel it too. Having a chronic illness, for which there is no cure and no support, felt at times as if God had abandoned her. All the prayers in the world had never manifested a miracle cure. There were times when her faith in the Holy Spirit was tested to the absolute limit but she knew in her heart that God's love was not necessarily there to cure her but to help her face the terrible hand life had dealt her - oh but how she wished it would.

Suddenly, Sophie could hear the banging and clattering of footsteps on the stairs followed by the slow thumping march of military men coming down the corridor towards the chapel.

Isabelle and Father John froze as they listened to the sound of soldiers, shouting and threatening the servants, demanding to know where their mistress and her priest were hiding. One of the soldiers held a razor-sharp sword to the throat of a young house maid - piercing her skin with its tip, letting blood drip down her neck and over her dress. Fearing for her life, the maid reluctantly opened the secret door to the tower and the soldiers crowded through, eager to find their prey at illegal prayer.

To their dismay, the soldiers found only Isabelle, lying on the Persian rug, weak with cold and exhaustion unaware that she had lain herself deliberately over the trap-door. Two of the Queen's men dragged her, by her hair, out of the chapel and down the stairs. They pushed and tormented her, trying to force her to betray her priest but she would not give him up. When they reached the top of the main flight of stairs one of the men pushed her hard against the balustrade and she lost her footing.

Isabelle fell, crashing downwards, tumbling head over heels, until, halfway down, her neck snapped in two.

Isabelle lay in total stillness on the stair - her body contorted and deranged.

She was dead.

Sophie was chilled to the bone by the ghastly scene just as the other witnesses had been that terrible night. Overwhelmed with sadness and compassion for poor Isabelle she began to cry.

But Sophie's vision continued, whether she wanted it to or not, and she saw how the soldiers, unnerved by their fatal actions, conspired to hide Isabelle's body. One of the soldiers carried her, unceremoniously, over his shoulder, into the dark night and the pouring rain, down to the lake and casually threw her lifeless body into a cold, watery grave.

The servants were threatened with the same fate if they ever spoke about what they had seen. Terrified for their lives, they remained silent for the rest of their days, never confessing their ordeal to their master or even in the confessional.

Where was Roger? Sophie thought. *Why wasn't he there to help and protect his wife?* Her question set in motion the answer and she saw that Roger was far way, walking in the sunshine by the sea in Monaco, having left his wife in the care of a skeleton staff back home in England. *How could he abandon her like that?* Sophie thought indignantly. *Just because she was ill doesn't mean he should bugger off and leave her to suffer all alone.* She thought of her own suffering, the nights she cried herself to sleep, the isolation from the world that her condition forced upon her and wished that she had a partner who would care for her no matter what. Knowing that Roger, who had loved Isabelle so much, had chosen to live his life without her, and had left her to rot and to go insane in this dreadful house all alone, she remembered that 'for better or worse' was not a vow that many took seriously, and love wasn't always enough in the face of adversity. She thought of Tobi and felt her heart breaking.

Sophie wondered why none of the servants had come back to rescue Father John from the priest hole. Then a dreadful realisation came upon her, "No one can hear you from in here, can they?" Sophie asked him.

Father John shook his head. "Only Isabelle and Roger knew about this hiding place," he explained. "The servants fled the house at dawn, fearing the soldiers would return to murder them. I presume they thought I had made it back to the boathouse."

"Do you think I will die in here too?" Sophie asked him. She thought of how he must have prayed, day after day, that someone would come for him. How at the slightest noise his hopes would have been raised and how despair must have taken hold with each day that passed.

"You will not die here," Father John replied. "There is someone who loves you, someone who would tear- down this house to find you."

Sophie immediately thought of Lucy and her resolve strengthened. She knew that her sister would not desert her so was surprised when Father John added, "He is coming for you."

Sophie wasn't sure who he meant.

"When you are rescued," Father John told her, "You must free all the souls trapped here and help us all find our heavenly peace. You must take back the ring site from the servants of Satan."

"How can I do that?" Sophie asked him, thinking that if he hadn't managed it, in life or death, she couldn't see why she should fare much better. "I think you have an inflated idea about my abilities," she told him. In that moment it felt as if the whole universe was willing her on and she had the strangest feeling that the Pleiades had sent her to the manor for that very reason.

~ * ~

The wall in front of her unexpectedly opened and she found herself falling forwards and into Robert's arms.

Chapter 32

~ * ~

Robert had not needed to use a sledgehammer after all as, just in the nick of time, Minnie had had a flash of insight and Isabelle had shown her how to open the priest hole.

Minnie watched Isabelle put her hand up the chimney and release something.

"I have to put my hand up the chimney," Minnie told the others.

Jack looked at her with surprise and paused, just as he was about to smash into the chimney-breast with a crowbar.

"You wouldn't believe me if I told you how I know but I've got to try it at least," she told him.

"Go with it," Lucy encouraged her. "We've got nothing to lose."

Minnie knelt down and reached up the blackened chimney. Feeling along the front edge she found a thin, slate ledge sticking out. Ignoring the accumulation of soot, she patted her fingers along the shelf and found what felt like a metal pull-handle.

Then they all screamed with terror!

A pigeon suddenly flew down the chimney and into the room; its wings flapping over Minnie's head, frightening her almost to death. The crazed frenzy of the frightened bird sent them all running - protecting their faces with their arms. The more they panicked the more the pigeon did too and it wasn't until Jack managed to shoo it out of the door and onto the landing that they all calmed down.

"Oh my god," Lucy cried. "I swear I can't take much more of this house."

Minnie was reluctant to put her hand back up the chimney again but she knew she had to for Sophie's sake. Unable to see what she was doing, she fumbled about, pulling and twisting the handle, until, at last, she heard a sharp click and the dresser, in the right-hand-side alcove, snapped forwards about an inch from the wall.

"The dresser! Look! It's moved!" Lucy gasped.

They all huddled around for a closer look.

"It's on some kind of lever in the floor," Robert told them as he saw a curved, brass runner embedded in the floorboard. He thought it was going to take all his strength, and more, to pull the whole of the heavy piece of furniture further away but to his relief it glided forwards with ease. Looking into the gap, he was surprised to see Sophie falling towards him; he braced himself and caught her in his arms.

Covered in soot, dust and cobwebs, and shivering with shock, poor Sophie burst into tears as soon as she felt Robert holding her tightly.

"Are you alright?" he asked her.

"I'm okay," Sophie sobbed but she wasn't letting go of him for a while yet. She had never felt so glad to see him.

At that moment, Robert felt as if he never wanted to let her out of his sight again. He wiped away her tears, smudging the soot even more around her face; it didn't matter - to him she had never looked so precious. She was his beautiful Sophie.

Lucy came and hugged her sister from behind; then everyone else piled-in for a group-hug. The friends were laughing and crying with relief, especially Minnie who now felt the state of shock she'd been trapped in break like a damn and the flood gates opened.

"I'm okay," Sophie said again, nuzzling into Robert's shoulder and supporting herself against his chest, "But," she added, "I don't think Father John was so lucky."

"Who?" Wolf asked.

Sophie turned her head towards the hole and, shining their flashlights, they all looked inside. A pile of white bones was scattered on the floor and a human skull was wedged in the corner - staring at them with blank, empty eyes. A rosary of black-onyx beads lay over one of the skeleton's hands, its silver cross dangling from a broken bony finger.

Sophie shuddered. She realised that what she had felt beneath her feet had been the remains of poor Father John.

"Woah!" Wolf couldn't help exclaiming. "Who the hell is that?"

"He said his name was Father John..." Sophie began to explain but she had no energy left to think or speak with. Robert picked her up and as he carried her back down the stairs, to the renovated bedrooms, he whispered, so that no-one else could hear, "So the house is haunted after all?"

Sophie nodded. "I'm afraid so," she replied.

Robert laid Sophie on the bed and covered her with a quilt as well as several blankets in an attempt to warm her up. Her body felt like she had been hit by a bus and she sank into the soft mattress with relief. Her brain ached as much as her bones and she fell asleep immediately - unable to fight anymore.

Robert sat with her for a few moments and gently stroked her hair from her forehead. "Don't ever do that to me again," he whispered. "I thought I'd lost you. You nearly gave me a heart attack. What would I do without you?"

Chapter 33
~ * ~

The Haunted or Not team were eager to film the attic chapel and the priest hole but Wolf and Jimmy needed to change their clothes first, having been soaked through when they went to the sheds with Jack. They headed down to the drawing room and Jack went to change in the yellow bedroom.

Not realising he was being watched, Jack stripped off fully and started to root-about in his bag for some dry jeans and a top. Carrie, who had come to fetch her make-up bag, opened the door and gasped in delight as she saw the full masculine beauty of Jack's naked body.

Jack froze for a moment, sensing there was someone behind him, and out the corner of his eye he caught sight of her in the mirror. Jack smiled to himself and turned around, giving her a full frontal view saying, "I'm running out of dry clothes. I don't suppose you have one of those Haunted or Not t-shirts I could borrow do you?"

Carrie, not taking her eyes off him for a second, stared at him, wide eyed and pouting, "I think you look better as you are," she told him with a sexy smile.

"I know," Jack replied as he pulled on his jeans. He came close to her and she thought he was going to kiss her but, instead, he reached for some dry socks off the bed and asked again, "So, do you have a t-shirt I could wear?"

Carrie felt rejected and couldn't help herself from lashing out, "I bet you wouldn't say that if I was Lucy," she retorted.

Jack looked surprised and took a step back.

Before Carrie could say anything more, Robert entered the bedroom, also looking for clean clothes; his shirt was covered in soot and Sophie's tears. "Sorry," he said, "Did I interrupt something?"

"Not at all, old boy," Jack laughed.

Carrie quickly departed in a huff.

"You probably saved me," Jack told Robert. "She isn't exactly backwards in coming forwards."

"No, I suppose not," Robert agreed. "Although, I thought Carrie was having a thing with Jimmy," he admitted. "That's what India thought anyway. But I'm not the best judge of these things."

"No you're not," Jack smiled. "For example, I doubt you realise that Kaya is gagging to get into your pants."

"Yes, I had noticed, thank you," Robert replied as he began to undress. "She's nice enough, although she seems to have a chip on her shoulder about something."

Carrie returned and, without knocking, came in. She was surprised at how buff Robert looked too and thought, for a moment, that he might be a better catch than Jack but her pride was hurt now and she just threw a couple of new t-shirts at them and left without saying a word.

"I don't think she takes rejection very well," Jack smiled. "It's not my fault I'm irresistible to the ladies. This t-shirt's a bit on the small side," he added as he squeezed himself into it. The logo was stretched out across his pecs and the soft fabric clung tightly to his abs and bi-ceps. "Still, it'll have to do until my others dry. I've never had to change so many times in one day in my life, well, not unless..." he chuckled to himself, deciding not to finish his sentence out loud.

Robert realised he'd left his last, dry shirt in the kitchen so he also put on a t-shirt too. It wasn't quite as tight as Jack's but it certainly showed off every sinew and contour. Looking in the mirror he laughed. "I don't think the ladies will find us irresistible in these," he said (although, dear readers, I think some of us might disagree).

Jack shrugged. He remembered what Carrie had said about Lucy. He wondered about Lucy for a fleeting moment but dismissed, as he always did, any ideas of romantic or sexual intention towards her, before they took hold. He looked at the portrait of Isabelle and sighed. "Old Roger couldn't remain faithful to a woman as beautiful as that and he was supposed to love her. It just shows men are not made for fidelity. If I thought I could remain faithful, I might..." his voice trailed off; he was unwilling to take himself down that train of thought.

Robert had a flash back to when Sophie had fallen into his arms and how utterly relieved he had been that she was safe. But, just like Jack, he dismissed the feeling fluttering in his heart as brotherly love. "Perhaps Roger did love Isabelle but the witchcraft led him astray," Robert suggested.

"Oh come on, old boy," Jack laughed. "Get real. He was just a horny devil who couldn't keep his d**k in his pants."

"I suppose adultery is a kind of evil," Robert mused and felt ashamed of his behaviour with Shilty Cunningham over the years. "It seems like a game at the time but it can destroy whole families." He thought of his own father going to America with his new wife, leaving him and Collins to fend for themselves and how it had turned his mother into the worst version of herself. "Some people never recover from a broken heart or a betrayal of trust," he said sadly. "Perhaps deceiving the one you promised to love is one of the worst kinds of evil."

Suddenly, there was an almighty crash!

It came from the pink bedroom.

Rushing next door, they immediately saw that the portrait of Isabelle was lying on the rug in front of the bed.

"Bloody hell," Jack exclaimed. "That could have hit someone."

Sophie, Minnie, India and Lucy came running through the en-suite, afraid that someone had been hurt, and were astonished to find the painting lying face-down on the carpet.

The portrait wasn't smashed or damaged and, on examining the wall, Jack could find no sign of why it had fallen.

The hook was still firmly in the wall and, the string on the back, was in perfect condition too.

They looked at each other wondering what on earth had happened.

The highly ornate frame was heavy and Jack needed Robert's help to try to hang it back on the wall.

"Oh no," Minnie shuddered. She went pale and felt sick. "I think Isabelle wants back in. I can feel her - she's with me again."

"It's okay," Sophie reassured Minnie but her own heart went cold. She knew Isabelle's spirit was on the move again - she could feel her ghostly presence all around them.

Minnie was looking as grey as Sophie and had begun to shiver.

They both climbed onto the bed.

"Were you Isabelle's maid in a past life?" Sophie asked Minnie.

"Oh my god," Lucy said. "I've got goose-bumps you saying that."

"So have I," Minnie said. "I think I was a maid here. Did I do something terrible? I feel so guilty about something"…Minnie paused for a moment then she knew deep in her soul what she had done…"I betrayed Isabelle," she cried.

Sophie told Minnie, and the others, of the vision she had had in the priest hole and how a maid had given away Isabelle and Father John, under pain of death.

176

"Oh god," Minnie exclaimed. "I didn't mean to betray her, it's just…" Minnie put her hand to her throat…"I can feel the sharp steel of that soldier's blade right now." She was freaked out by the very real sensations she was feeling from something which had happened hundreds of years ago. "I thought he was going to cut my throat. I honestly didn't mean to hurt Isabelle. If I could go back and change what happened, I would."

"You did what you had to do at the time," Lucy reassured her.

"Hindsight's a great thing," India agreed. "You didn't know what would happen next."

"Two people died that night and you could have been killed too. It must have been terrifying," Sophie said.

Minnie thought she was going to throw up. "I feel as if I am responsible for Isabelle and Father John's deaths," she said. "That poor man - walled up alive. It doesn't bear thinking about. I was a coward."

"Do you think Isabelle is possessing Minnie to punish her?" Lucy asked Sophie.

"No, I don't think so," Sophie replied. "I can feel her spirit presence but it doesn't feel evil, just really, really sad. I think Isabelle is trying to possess Minnie so that we will help her and Father John pass over to the other side. Father John asked me to clear the darkness from this place and help the lost souls of the house go into Heaven as they should have done."

"Why is she possessing Minnie and not you then?" India asked, not at all sure she should be believing in such things although, as it was happening right in front of her eyes, she didn't have much choice anymore.

"I think the fact that she knew Minnie, and that Minnie still feels guilty for betraying her, makes it easier for Isabelle to get into Minnie's aura," Sophie explained. "Guilt makes us willing to help when we are given the chance to put things right."

Minnie agreed. "I do feel as if I want to help her. I need to help her."

"Where's Isabelle's spirit now?" Lucy asked Sophie, half expecting Isabelle to materialise at any moment.

Sophie fished in her pocket and laid Isabelle's necklace on the bedspread. "She was in this necklace," Sophie explained. "But I think she's back in Minnie now."

Chapter 34
~ * ~

Minnie began to shake uncontrollably and they gasped in horror when she lurched upwards from the waist; her arms flew outwards with her head dropping backwards as if she was being flayed alive.

"What's wrong with her?" Jack asked, astounded and anxious about what he was witnessing.

"Isabelle's spirit is running through her," Sophie explained.

"Oh my god," Lucy exclaimed. "It's like the 'Exorcist'."

A flash of lightning lit up the room and more than one of the friends saw Minnie's face change to the features of Isabelle.

The tremendous clap of thunder which followed made them all jump with fright.

"What do we do?" Jack asked. "What can I do?"

They all looked at Sophie who had to admit that what was happening was beyond her knowledge.

"Radio Jimmy," Lucy suggested. "He'll know what to do. He's been possessed before."

"He's admitted he fakes it," India said.

"Maybe not all the time," Lucy replied.

"Anything's worth a try," Robert said, fearing for Minnie's life. "Perhaps Kaya might know what to do if Jimmy doesn't?"

Jack called everyone on the walkie-talkie and, within minutes, the Haunted or Not team arrived - with their cameras still running in case there was something worth capturing on film.

Jimmy and Kaya gasped in shock as they saw Isabelle where Minnie should have been.

Once he realised that this was a real possession, Jimmy couldn't help smiling with excitement. "You are getting this on camera aren't you Wolf?" he asked. "Give me the EPV."

"I told you this house was haunted," Kaya couldn't help saying. "I told you it wasn't Ada and Arthur faking it. Now do you believe me?"

"Alright," Lucy said impatiently, "We believe you. It wasn't all just Ada and her brother. Now, do you know how to help Minnie?" She turned to Wolf and added, "And stop filming! This isn't going in one of your stupid shows."

Kaya, Carrie and not even Jimmy had any helpful advice to offer.

"Don't any of you know what to do?" Lucy begged them.

The storm raged against the windows and sheet lightning illuminated Minnie's terrible state again.

"I've seen trans-mediums shake like that and take on the appearance of the spirit who is using their aura," Kaya admitted. "Their face and their voice changes but it was under controlled conditions and done by a professional."

"I thought you were all experts in your field," India said, exasperated that no-one knew what to do.

"We are," Kaya replied defensively.

"Didn't they teach Possession 101 at your spook school?" India replied.

Kaya looked angrily at India but, as she didn't know what to do, she just seethed and kept quiet.

"For f**ks sake!" India exclaimed. "Somebody do something!"

Everyone started talking over each other and accusing each other of not knowing what to do or started making absurd suggestions whilst poor Minnie was still shaking no matter how Lucy and Sophie tried to hold onto her. She was getting weaker by the minute and looked as if she was going to pass out.

Suddenly, Sophie cried out over the din, "Shut up!!!!"

They all went quiet and looked at her.

Sophie took a deep breath and said, "If you will all just be quiet for a few minutes, I'll ask Father John what he recommends we do," she said calmly.

Closing her eyes, Sophie lay on the bed paying attention to the visions flashing through her mind and trying to stay focused on what Father John was trying to show and tell her. It was like downloading information from a divine computer-file.

They all waited patiently but the electrical display going on outside took them by surprise every-time and put them all on edge.

"Right," Sophie said as she opened her eyes. "This is what Father John is telling me...

"There is a witches curse on Isabelle and this house, the Abbey and the Fianna Stones. When the monks were forced to leave the Abbey by King Henry VIII, the dragon portal was left unguarded and local witches took over the lay lines in this area. Evil attracts evil so they were able to recruit more and more people over the centuries to join them, and when anyone died, they tried to recruit their spirits too. They would intercept the dying

179

spirit, hoping that anyone who had been mistreated, abused, disenfranchised or murdered would want revenge and join them. If a spirit refused to go with them into the dark side, they would bar their way into Heaven and trap them in limbo until they gave in."

India grabbed hold of Wolf's arm - she was sure there was someone tapping at the window but when she looked again there was nothing there.

"Over time, the witches became so powerful that the Heavenly portal here, which would normally open as a sky portal and send a divine ladder of consciousness down to the dragon portal, was overwhelmed by darkness," Sophie continued to explain.

"Like a Jacob's Ladder?" Robert asked.

"Yes," Sophie replied. "There are lots of souls trapped here, including Isabelle and Father John. They are hoping we can get rid of the witches so that they can pass over into the Heavenly portal."

"We have to find a way for the Light to prevail," Robert said. "We were sent here to do this. The trees told me."

Everyone looked at him as if he was slightly crazy and he felt he had to explain about his strange experience in the woods the previous morning.

"Why do we always get mixed up in these things, these days?" Lucy sighed.

"I'm afraid that since the dragon portal opened in Little Eden, we all seem to have become part of the huge spiritual upgrade of the planet and mankind," Sophie explained. "Wherever we go from now on, we will probably have been sent to clear a portal or open one or close one. The Earth is ascending and we have somehow been roped into helping. The Pleiades need to gain control of all the existing lay lines, dragon portals, sky and time portals if the Star Children are to build a new matrix of consciousness for themselves here on Earth and live as humans."

"I thought we came here to see how much the Manor was worth," India said.

"I don't think we can assume anything we do from now on is just about raising the money for Little Eden," Robert replied. "Each dragon portal is connected to another and so on and so on - like a huge energy grid around the planet. That's a lot of portals to upgrade."

Sophie's mind was fogging over and she was struggling to sync her thoughts and her words.

Suddenly, to everyone's amazement, Minnie began to speak - but not in her own voice. Her strange and creepy transformation made everyone gasp; and this, dear readers, is what Isabelle had to say through Minnie…

"I was happy, so happy, when I came to live here. I was so in love with Roger I couldn't eat or sleep. I just wanted to share the joy I felt with everyone around me." Isabelle looked directly at Robert and pointing her finger in accusation her tone changed. She cried out venomously, "You betrayed me!"

Robert was shocked at the viciousness in her voice.

"She thinks you're Roger," Lucy realised.

"Why would she think I'm Roger?" Robert asked.

"Perhaps because you look like him," Kaya suggested, recalling the portraits in the hall and how much Robert resembled some of his ancestors, "And you're a blood relative. Family karma can be very strong. What your ancestors did can be in your DNA, just as eye colour or height. Emotional karma can travel down the generations too."

"The sins of the father and all that," Jack said and turning to Robert he added, "Looks like you've not just inherited this Manor but a whole load of trouble to boot, old boy."

Chapter 35

~ * ~

Isabelle began to cry and it was difficult for her friends to watch poor Minnie sobbing when it wasn't even her own emotion she was feeling.

"I think you'd better reassure her," Lucy suggested to Robert. "Isabelle I mean."

"If she thinks you are Roger just go with it," Kaya agreed.

"Okay," Robert said reluctantly. He knelt down in front of Minnie and took her icy cold hands in his. "Izzy," he found himself saying - he was surprised that he had used an abbreviation of her name but weirdly it felt right to call her by it - "Izzy," he repeated. "Look at me darling. It's Roger. I'm here. I've come to help you pass over to the other side. I've come to take you to Heaven."

Isabelle's tears stopped and her eyes shone with radiant bliss. "I knew you'd come for me," she said, smiling at Robert. "You loved me not her, didn't you?"

Robert looked up at the others for guidance.

"Tell her you never loved Molly," Lucy urged him.

"I never loved Molly," Robert told Isabelle. "It was only ever you, my love, only you."

Isabelle was enveloped by a wave of sadness and her demeanour changed again to one of fear. She leaned in closer to Robert and put her finger to his lips, "Never say her name out loud," she warned him, then whispered into his ear, "They came for me. Whilst you were gone."

"It's alright my love, just tell me what happened," Robert told her kindly.

Minnie took such a deep breath that it looked as if her chest might explode and then Isabelle continued to speak; "That harpie was trying to kill me but you didn't believe me. No- one believed me. She got inside my head." Minnie put her hands to her head in total despair and the horrified look on her face made everyone shudder. "She put voices and words into my mind and I couldn't shut them out. Horrible, twisted faces I saw when I closed my eyes." She put her finger to her own lips as if she shouldn't be speaking out loud and whispered under her breath, "Witches and spells. She took you from me. When she died I thought it would stop but it did not. The haunting grew stronger, night by night, sending me into madness. You didn't see. You didn't care. You left me alone here with her and the Devil."

Robert could feel the abyss of madness that Isabelle had been drowning in and he actually felt guilty for not helping her as if it was his own fault not Rogers. He kissed her hand saying, "It's alright now, my love. I believe you now. We're going to take you into Heaven. You'll be free from her and all the spells."

Robert hoped he was saying the right things.

Minnie was all but gone - Isabelle seemed to have completely taken over Minnie's auric field.

"I still don't see how Molly could have made Isabelle run mad," India said.

"Haven't you ever felt someone thinking about you from a distance?" Wolf asked India. He had hoped that his lustful thoughts about her might have found their way into her energy field and were making her feel the same. "If I was to think really hard, right now, about someone they might be able to feel it."

India felt a sudden rush of dizziness, her skin began humming with desire, and she had to catch her breath. It was as if they were connected by an invisible electric current which surged whenever they thought about each other. She steadied herself against one of the bed posts and tried to regain her focus. In that moment she understood exactly how an invisible force, emanating from one person to another, could scramble all your senses and how you could fall under someone else's spell. She had been seduced simply by the force of his willpower. She looked at Wolf and they both knew what they were feeling.

He hoped to manifest the fantasy into a reality as soon as he could.

The sexual charge in the room was becoming so electrified that Robert had a sudden vision of Roger and Isabelle together three hundred years ago. He could feel the love they felt for each other and the uncontrollable passion too. As they made love to each other they seemed almost as one being and for a few moments he let the heady stream of love wash over him and he wished he could hold the blissful sensation forever. But the vision quickly began to transform and a sinister force crept through his blood and oozed, like black oil, between the couple as they lay together, entwined upon the bed. A repulsive, unclean and unnatural feeling took hold of Robert as he was enveloped by the jealousy, deceit and betrayal which had driven them apart. He watched in horror as Isabelle fell away from Roger's arms and down into the mattress as it opened up like a great aching chasm of treachery swallowing her with its satanic jaws. She fell faster and faster down into the darkness just as Molly rose up from the terrible void to join him.

Molly's face was stunningly beautiful but her hands were long and sharp and her snake-like arms rapidly multiplied until she had a thousand coiling limbs, all clawing at Roger with putrid lust. As she opened her mouth to kiss him her teeth were like razor-blades and like a vampire she began to devour him.

Robert recoiled, letting go of Minnie's hand, he quickly stepped away from the bed and nearly fell over the side table in his haste.

The others looked at him in astonishment.

He put his hand to his head as if it hurt him but he was really trying to stop the vision - to close the time portal to the horrific dimension he was witnessing before he was sucked into it himself.

"What is it? What's wrong?" Lucy asked him, alarmed that he might go the same way as Minnie.

Robert was relieved when he looked at Minnie again and the bed was intact and gradually he felt like himself again.

"Roger and Isabelle," Robert replied. "I saw them."

"It's such a tragic but romantic love story," Lucy sighed, "So full of sadness and regret."

"Roger was a cheating rat," India said. "One person was hanged and another went mad. There's nothing romantic about that."

"But, poor Roger was controlled by witchcraft and spells," Lucy defended him.

"Yeah, right," India replied, "Everyone who cheats and lies can just blame it on spells can they?" She looked directly at Jimmy as she said it.

"India's right, old girl," Jack said. "Men don't need spells to be unfaithful. A man who can stay faithful is a rare man." He wished again that he had it in him to stay faithful and commit to a lifelong love but he knew he couldn't do it. He looked at Lucy and sighed.

Suddenly, Minnie suddenly rose up again, as if convulsing, then slumped heavily back down into the bed with an agonising cry.

She had passed out.

Chapter 36
~ * ~

"We have to do something!" Lucy screamed.

An argument ensued again, everyone hurling accusations around such as, 'you shouldn't mess with things you don't understand', 'calling on spirit without protection is a dangerous business' and 'call yourself a ghost hunter? When you actually meet a real ghost you've no idea what to do'...

Sophie got up off the bed and went to look out of the window to get away from the din. The storm had subsided again. The first frisson of dawn made her feel nauseous. Sophie rarely saw the dawn. Even when she did, the transition from night to day always gave her an uneasy sensation and a slight wave of sickness. She wished she could enjoy, as some people do, the enticing freshness and rousing sense of newness the break of day brought with it. The first rose-gold rays of sun were lapping, like gentle waves, though pools of azure blue, caressing the scudding white-tipped, dark-grey clouds. Looking down across the lake, where the dark water quivered as it was kissed by the early morning light, she shuddered, knowing Isabelle's broken body lay abandoned beneath its glassy surface. She remembered too that the children of Lady Edith had lain, for nearly a hundred years, in the same silent, watery grave. In her reverie she saw a vision appearing in her mind's eye - the apparitions of the three young children rose up through the morning mist which hovered eerily over the lake and the fields. She watched as their innocent souls floated towards the manor house, their white, flowing night clothes fluorescing like fireflies in the half-light. The eldest, a girl of about seven, and her younger brother held the hands of their baby sister, who was barely two years old. Sophie stared at them as they mysteriously glided over the long grass, their own gaze transfixed - frozen in time.

The ghosts of the children came to rest upon the stone terrace beneath the window and they looked up at Sophie.

Sophie's heart went cold and skipped a beat. She realised that they could see her standing in the window.

"Sophie! Sophie!" Robert repeated but she hadn't heard him. He placed his hand gently on her shoulder and startled her out of her vision.

"Can you see them?" she asked him and nodded down to the dew-laden ground.

Robert didn't know who she meant and shook his head. "I don't see anyone," he admitted. He presumed she had meant Ada and Arthur.

Kaya came to stand next to him and also looked out. "I can see the apparitions of three children," she said. "They must be Lady Edith's - the ones she drowned."

Jimmy couldn't resist the call of the supernatural and rushed over to the other window, beckoning to Wolf and urging him to point the camera to where the spirit manifestations were; but nothing could be recorded on film.

Only those with second sight could see the haunting.

"Look!" Jimmy said. "Who is that?"

The spirit of their mother - their murderer - Lady Edith, smoothly skimmed her way from the north side of the house, where she had thrown herself from the round tower all those years ago, and joined her children. She too looked up at the window as if she was aware of Sophie's presence.

Sophie shuddered.

Lady Edith's face was half-shattered from her fatal fall. She looked ghoulish and horrific.

The ethereal family remained creepily still - just waiting.

"I see Lady Edith too," Kaya said.

"I'm not getting anything on camera," Wolf said, disappointed. "Not even an orb."

Sophie felt Father John's spirit standing next to her and took comfort in his presence. She didn't like seeing the dead. She loved to feel and see angels, true light beings, the saints and her spirit guides, including her aunt Lilly, because they brought ascended wisdom and complete compassion with them. She had to accept though that in the spirit world there is also fear, manipulation and evil just as in the human world.

To her horror, more phantom spirits of previous residents began to gather on the terrace. A gardener came - his spade in hand - and was joined by a young housemaid carrying a basket of apples. A housekeeper came out of the French doors, shaking a white cloth as if she had been dusting, followed a tall, smartly dressed footman, who was pushing a grand, old lady in a wicker wheelchair. Within minutes, at least fifty, long dead, family members, servants, visitors, monks and strangers were gathered like a flock of birds perching on the walls, steps and terrace as if waiting for help to come. Within the crowd, Sophie could see the poor lost souls were of all ages; from tiny babies to the elderly and were dressed in fashions from

186

throughout the ages. There was even one teenage girl who looked as if she had died since the millennium and Sophie couldn't help but wonder what she was doing there.

"Did a young woman die here not that long ago?" she asked Kaya.

Kaya nodded. "I can see her too," she replied. "That must be Abigail Fairlie. She was reported missing around twelve years ago - she is believed to have disappeared after a visit to the stones. Local police thought she'd run away from home, but Old Meg, from the pub, she told the coppers she was dead and that her body had been buried near the old chapel. Unfortunately, the Detective Inspector thinks all psychics are crack-pots and they never organised a dig or proper search to find her. She's never been found - dead or alive."

"She's had her throat cut and been sliced open," Jimmy said, "Look! Her heart is missing. This is outstanding! This really is the most haunted house in the world. We've hit the jackpot this time!"

"Poor girl," Sophie said and felt like crying. "Someone must try to find her body and give her a proper burial." She turned to Robert. "Can't you see any of the spirits?" she asked him.

Robert tried to focus his third-eye but although he felt an uneasy sensation, and his spine was tingling, all he saw were some shadowy movements within the misty morning air.

"If we could find her body we could put it in the show," Jimmy grinned with delight. "I'm going to track down her grave," and without waiting he went to the door.

"What, right now?" Wolf asked him.

"Her spirit is awake," Jimmy replied. "What better time to communicate with her and find her body? She can show me where she's buried. Imagine the publicity?!"

Carrie liked the idea and, in an instant, could see the many opportunities for a show.

"I think we have more pressing matters to hand," Lucy called out, "Minnie, for example!"

"Oh, I'd forgotten about her," Jimmy admitted. "She'll snap out of it eventually," he said flippantly.

"No-one is digging up corpses on my land just to get themselves on television," Robert said emphatically.

Carrie sighed, "We do need the landowner's permission to dig up anything," she told Jimmy.

"And you won't be getting any such permission from me," Robert told them. He could hardly believe they would contemplate such a thing. He had already made up his mind that, once all this was over, he would see to it that poor Abigale was found and returned to her family for burial in a private and respectful manner.

"Excuse me!" Lucy said again. "Can we concentrate on the living? What are we going to do about Minnie?"

As no-one seemed to have any idea what to do for the best, Sophie asked Father John again for his advice.

Father John, wanting to help, suggested Sophie take Minnie to the Fianna Stones so that hopefully Isabelle, and all the trapped souls, would be able to pass over...perhaps.

Not too keen on the 'suck it and see' plan, Sophie was reluctant, although she did have some experience of dealing with dragon portals and the dark side, so with no other proposal on the table she agreed.

"We have to go to the stones and ask for help," she explained to the others. "The only thing is, I can't walk that far and neither can Minnie - or Lancelot for that matter - so how are we going to get there and back?"

Jack radioed Lancelot who had been in the kitchen all this time, wondering what had happened to everyone. Jack asked him if he thought he could walk to the stone circle and back.

"Go without me," Lancelot called over the walkie-talkie.

"I don't know why but I have a really strong feeling that you're needed," Sophie shouted down the radio.

"The cart!" Jack said. "There were other carts in those sheds. We could push you three there."

"Good idea," Robert said. He looked out the window again. "Let's go before it starts to rain again." He looked at Minnie lying unconscious on the bed, "And before anything worse happens to poor Minnie."

Chapter 37
~ * ~

Soon, they were all assembled on the driveway. In the fresh, damp morning air they all felt a sense of relief that dawn had broken and realised how stuffy and oppressive the energy inside the house really was.

The skyscape was a dramatic scene of heavy, gold-tinged storm clouds, billowing out into turquoise rivers of light. The sun was almost too brilliant when it came out from behind them, its rays illuminating the patchwork greens of the park as if each leaf and blade of grass was made from precious jade and peridot crystals.

The Haunted or Not team had their equipment at the ready and when Robert and Jack returned with a hand-cart Lucy filled it with cushions, quilts and blankets upon which Minnie and Sophie were carefully laid. They had also found a large sack barrow and, as Robert tipped it backwards, Lance stood on it ready to be pushed along.

As the motley crew headed towards the little bridge over the Ha-Ha, which led towards the Fianna Stones, a red squirrel hopped along the top of the low stone wall, stopping for a moment, transfixed, as if it could see the ghosts which were following the friends in silent procession.

Sophie, Jimmy and Kaya could see the mass of spirits, who were floating, silently and eerily after them, but the camera still didn't pick up their energy signature - much to Wolf's dismay.

"Still no sign of Ada and her brother," Lancelot remarked, as he looked over towards the Lodge.

"I'd almost forgotten about that odd couple," Robert said, trying his best to steer the sack barrow which seemed to have a mind of its own!

As they made their way across the field, the sun came and went, flowing in and out from behind the sumptuous clouds; one minute plunging them into a grey, misty enclave, the next illuminating the rain drops, puddles and dew which twinkled like stars scattered across the landscape. Moment to moment it was warm then chilly and rain threatened to pour down on them at any time.

Lucy shuddered. "We should have brought some umbrellas," she said. "I hope this rain keeps off 'til we get back."

"Keep to the path," Kaya told them. "The bogs might look small but they are deep and can be treacherous."

Everyone kept a look out, afraid of sinking into the ground at any moment. Some of the larger boggy areas, dotted here and there, shone like black-onyx amongst the bright green-white thistles and willowy fools' parsley.

"Look!" India said, pointing up at the tumultuous sky, "Bats!"

They all looked up to see the tiny, winged creatures flitting and swooping over the copse which hid the old chapel. The pale moon was still visible and the bats were making the most of the lingering darkness amongst the trees.

Noblet Wood flanked the north and west sides and they couldn't see either Hellifield Road or Gobin Lane from the manor park. As they approached the outer stones, the surrounding forests created an enclave which seemed to wrap around them like a tenebrous blanket; they felt as if they were entering another dimension - cut off from the world and even from the rest of the Manor.

The grass, amongst the stones, was flattened, not only by the rain but by the solstice worshippers who had danced and prayed there the day before. The grass was quite different in the very central circle - it was low growing (fairy-grass as Minnie had always called it) and tiny mushrooms formed rings of varying sizes, some of which had been stomped on and destroyed (much to Lucy's dismay).

They were all shocked to find more desecration of the sacred site in the form of empty beer cans and bottles, crisp packets and cigarette stubs, plastic bags, condoms, syringes and chocolate wrappers, which were strewn all around. Wilted garlands of flowers, corn dollies and wooden crosses lay abandoned; even a dead cat, which had been gutted - its entrails splashed across one of the fallen stones.

"How awful," Lucy cringed and looked away. The disrespect she was witnessing almost brought to tears to her eyes as did her compassion for the poor cat. It felt to her that the stones should be alive, singing, humming, calling out to her with joy and welcome. Instead, they seemed to mark the graves of evil souls and any divine energy that had once lived there was now dead to the world.

Sophie was overwhelmed by the heavy atmosphere of aching sadness and joined her sister in wanting to cry - she felt the sickening, gut-wrenching grief that had grown and congealed over thousands of years and was now encrusted, like the lichen, into the stones.

"How could people, who are supposed to revere this place, leave their litter behind like this?" India asked aghast.

"I suppose you could say it's symbolic," Sophie replied, viewing the stones from amongst the pillows and blankets in the hand-cart. "The wishes and spells, thoughts and energy signatures people leave behind here might be invisible but they are here, just like all this rubbish. They clog up the dragon portal and layer by layer they cover over the pure source energy until no-one can see or feel the compassionate well-spring anymore. A wish, a spell - they might as well be an empty bag of crisps or a discarded condom."

Lucy shivered again. "It does feel like that," she agreed. "It feels as if the divine love that was once here has been lost under mountains of invisible landfill."

Robert and India began to clear some of the physical rubbish and put it in a pile near one of the stones, being very careful about what they picked up. "I'm going to ban these celebrations from now on," Robert muttered. "Spirituality seems to have become a fashionable badge worn by anyone who can dress the part or do yoga."

"It would seem so," India agreed.

Robert was so indignant he couldn't help but add, "Anyone who actually feels the divine energy within them is so in awe of it, so blessed by it and so enamoured with it that they just want to celebrate its purity and never defile it. These people have obviously never felt the true Holy Spirit or they wouldn't, they couldn't, treat this place with such contempt. I'm going to put an electric fence around it. If people can't respect it, I will have to protect it."

As Robert continued to chunter, Sophie asked everyone to stand in pairs, in front of a stone, and make a circle. Then, she asked Jack to carry the unconscious Minnie over to the central stone which made a low, natural altar.

Lucy put some blankets down for Minnie and placed a pillow beneath her head then covered her with a quilt.

Sophie was too exhausted to get out of the cart and she lay there, hoping they wouldn't be out too long. She was chilled to the core - she rarely knew what it felt like to feel warm.

The Haunted or Not team set up their cameras hoping to film the exorcism of Minnie but to their dismay, the batteries, which had been newly charged, were already drained.

"Damn it!" Wolf exclaimed.

"What a waste of a good exorcism," Carrie moaned. "I think we should go back. We're wasting our time if we can't get anything on camera."

"I'm going to conduct the exorcism myself," Jimmy announced. "Even if we can't film it, we can write about it on the blog."

"That's true," Carrie agreed. "We could use some still images. My phone has some charge." The idea they would get some publicity out of it cheered her up - for a while at least.

In the delicate light of the dawn, they all stood in silence. A translucent, white haze was hovering around them and even India and Jack felt almost ethereal - lost in the mists of time. Sometimes, the fog swallowed up the outer stones and the space they were in became smaller, more sombre and quietly ominous.

Not sure what she was supposed to do, Sophie closed her eyes and went into deep meditation. Rising up from her heart chakra, her spiritual-self shimmered and shone as a slender, tall, white Elven queen. She bi-located and joined Father John and all the lost spirits upon the astral plane...

And this dear reader is what happened next...

The spirit of Father John handed Sophie his rosary. It was identical to the real one they had found with his skeleton. She knew it was a key which opened the portal to Heaven and would normally be triggered by saying the Lord's Prayer; however, when she tried it, just as Father John had warned her it wouldn't, the Heavenly portal did not open. Instead of a bright-white light, astral clouds of swirling shadows came over the stones (as did physical storm clouds - shutting out the sun and plunging them all back into night).

Everyone was aware of the sudden darkness and the drop in temperature. An ill-wind rustled through the trees and the dawn chorus fell silent. Apart from the sound of the wicked-breeze rippling like an ocean through the trees, a deadly hush fell upon the stones and everyone felt the breath of evil whisper its way around them.

The lost souls of the house looked on as their last hope of salvation faded away.

Instead of the Lord's Prayer summoning the angels, it had done the opposite.

It had summoned the Evil instead.

Chapter 38
~ * ~

Jimmy proudly positioned himself in front of the altar stone and stood, like a patronising priest about to give a blessing, over Minnie's body.

He was totally unaware that Sophie had been given a key to Heaven already and that it had not worked. He couldn't see Sophie's astral, queen-like spirit or the ghostly apparition of Father John. He called on the spirit realm; unfortunately, he wasn't wise enough to be concerned about who those spirits were.

Without consulting anyone else, he began his exorcist theatrics in earnest and, closing his eyes, he summoned the great and powerful spirits. His call was answered when, throwing his head back, his eyes rolling and his spine tingling, he began speaking in tongues. He rambled and gestured, convulsed and raved like a man possessed.

Sophie's spirit tried to attract his attention but he seemed blind to her astral presence. He was so engrossed in his shamanic antics it never occurred to him that he was tapping into and harnessing the Evil Spirit rather than the Holy Spirit - he was ignorant of the difference.

The ground began to vibrate and Jimmy, Kaya, Wolf and Robert all felt a fizzing sensation rising up their legs as the extra electromagnetic earth energy triggered their Vagus nerve. They looked down and saw that beneath the stone circle a huge, blazing dragon's eye had appeared in the ground and as it blinked, the white of its eye and flame red of its iris were revealed - the dragon had awoken.

India felt uneasy and Lucy could smell the foul odour of decomposition and decay. The fresh scent of the dew was replaced by a sickening, putrid stench, so offensive that she almost gagged, "What the hell is that smell?" she said out loud, "It smells like rotting corpses."

The rancid emanation was created by the release of thousands of years of human fear.

"It's the boggarts," Kaya said. "I can see them. They're surrounding us."

Pulling themselves out of the dragon's eye, up through the soil, and creeping through the long grass, were hundreds of slimy, stinking boggarts.

Wolf and Robert could also see the boggarts and were becoming alarmed; they multiplied in number so rapidly that there was hardly a piece of ground left on which to stand which didn't have a revolting boggart squatting upon it.

Robert shouted to the others, "Be careful, if you let them near enough to you, they'll eat your energy field and steal your soul. Get onto one of the stones. Get off the grass and call on Mother Mary for protection. Do it!" He commanded them. "Do it now!"

As Robert's words reached them, they all felt the strangest sensation - a sinking feeling - as if the ground had transformed into a bog and was sucking them down. Wolf grabbed hold of India and lifted her swiftly onto a stone, then clambered up next to her. Jack assisted Lucy onto the nearest one with him and Robert helped Kaya join him on another. Lancelot clambered up onto a low stone with Carrie and everyone, except for Jimmy, managed to get their feet off the quaking ground.

Jimmy, entranced by his magical shenanigans, didn't hear Robert's warning and being totally unaware of the mayhem he was creating, he continued to chant and stamp the floor in a bizarre, contorted dance.

In desperation, Sophie called on the angels but they couldn't reach her. They were trapped behind the heavenly gates. They needed to anchor into the dragon lines, to build the bridge to reach human consciousness, but the dragon consciousness was under the control of the dark side - no divine energy could flow through the lay lines or the portal.

All she could see were the slithering boggarts who were now wrapping their glutinous bodies around the stones to strangle and smother any light which might try to escape from inside them.

A multitude squatted like toads upon the dragon's eye as if to blind it to Sophie's presence.

As Jimmy continued to raise the Evil Spirit, it empowered the boggarts who began to devour each other. Instead of disappearing they threw up undigested gloop which then gave birth to even more boggarts. They multiplied exponentially around his feet and, to Sophie's horror, they began to feast on him.

Before she could do anything, Jimmy's aura was ravaged by the boggarts, who guzzled his energy field as if it was their favourite meal; they devoured his etheric body within seconds; the consciousness of Jimmy Pratt was no more and his human body became an empty vessel.

"We have to stop them!" Sophie cried to Father John but he had no power over such swathes of demonic energy.

He had pinned his hopes on Sophie.

Sophie felt all alone - completely out of her depth.

She feared for the souls of all her friends and for her own.

Now that the boggarts had removed any shred of Jimmy's soul's consciousness, he was ripe for true possession and, as if on cue, from one of the tallest stones materialized the hologram of a white wizard.

Sophie breathed a sigh of relief - Merlin had come to help them.

The wizard didn't hesitate; he walked straight into Jimmy's open body. He hooked himself into, what was left of, Jimmy's heart chakra and as his white cloak swished around, it created a new auric field for Jimmy - one that was not his own but that of the wizard.

Kaya, who had also seen the transformation of Jimmy, seized her opportunity to communicate with the wizard, recognising him as an ancient druid. She projected her astral-self from her human body so that she could speak with him and as she did so Sophie saw her appear as a white witch.

"Who are you?" Kaya asked the druid wizard.

As he spoke, Jimmy's eyes lit up with red flames coiling and snaking around his pupils, like serpents in a pit, "I am the Master Druid. I am Merlin, I am Loki, I am Izanagi - I am the ten wizards of the world," he replied.

Kaya assumed that the snake eyes were symbolic of the creation serpent and felt completely in awe of him. "Master, I am here to help you," she said, feeling exhilarated by such close contact with an Ascended Master.

The Master smiled. His voice was honeyed, yet commanding, and as he raised his wooden staff he declared that all the lost souls would find solace and welcome with him in the realms of the dead. He claimed that they did not need the heavenly portal, which was corrupt Atlantean energy, and that they would receive safe passage to the other worlds through the stones instead. "The passage to the Elemental Kingdom is your salvation," he told them.

Kaya's body was humming and rippling with kundalini energy and she assumed it was the divine energy rising through her and she let it flow.

Sophie was much more wary. The wizard's features were that of Merlin but when Sophie asked her guides if he was a true light being, to her surprise, the third time she received a resounding NO! She was horrified when she realised that the Master's white cloak was merely glamour to fool the psychic eye into thinking that the Holy Spirit was present.

She tried to catch Kaya's attention but Kaya wanted to believe in the Master and was blinded, by her own pride, to his true dark side.

Sophie felt she had to intervene. "Stop!" she shouted. "You are not the divine, holy Merlin."

The Master laughed, a cruel, scathing, patronising laugh. "Those who believe in me and call me Merlin would beg to differ," he replied and with a flick of his staff he sent boggarts to climb up the side of the cart, and the altar stone, to feed on Sophie's and Minnie's auric fields.

Sophie's spirit watched in horror as the syrupy, jelly-like bodies of the boggarts crawled and clawed their way towards them both.

Chapter 39
~ * ~

"Alright!" Sophie said to the Master, trying not to show any fear. "What is it that you want? Perhaps we can do a deal?"

The Master smiled and dissolved the clinging boggarts from the cart, and the altar, just before they reached the top. They ran back down into the earth like sticky sap runs down a tree. The others squatted impatiently around the stones just waiting for the order to devour the rest of the friends.

"This dragon portal and the dragon lines from coast to coast belong to me," the Master told her.

"I think you are meant to be a guardian not an owner," Sophie replied.

The Master laughed as if she was a poor, stupid, innocent child. "Fear comes so naturally to humans. They leave their sacred sites unguarded and they relish evil. In fact," he paused for a moment as if delighted by the idea, "Humans love fear. They seek it out. They feed on it. They spread it like a virus between themselves until they are consumed by it." He laughed again and licked his bony finger as if it had been dipped in the sweetest sugar. "Fear is delicious. Fear will devour itself a thousand times over and never be dissatisfied with itself."

The boggarts' hunger was ignited by the Master's appetite and they began to chatter, gnawing at their own slimy flesh as if their hunger was eternally insatiable until they were just jellified mounds, oozing over the grass, which regenerated back into their toad-like-selves again.

Sophie cringed at the disgusting sight. She despised and loathed the wizard to such an extent that it began to counteract any fear she might have felt. "I suppose you'd like us to leave?" she asked politely.

The Master looked at her with suspicion. He didn't like her calm composure. Most spirits cowered in his presence or prostrated themselves in awe of him but this female spirit, whom he couldn't quite decipher, seemed to lack the usual reverence he inspired. He wasn't sure if she was elemental, angelic, galactic…where had she come from? he wondered.

"Oh no, you are all welcome here," he replied, seeing everyone in human form and the spirits of the dead as potential recruits, especially Sophie. "You seem to be different from the rest. You have great power of your own. You are special," he told her. "You could do great and wonderful things with me as your guide."

Before Sophie could reply, Kaya's spirit piped up, "Will you be my guide?" she asked him.

"Kaya!" Sophie called out. "Don't even think about it. He's not a true light being."

"How would you know," Kaya retorted. She was jealous of Sophie's higher-self who looked so regal. "Look how he works through Jimmy. He could work through me just the same and then I could do anything."

"He's just eaten Jimmy's soul!" Sophie exclaimed, aghast that Kaya would even contemplate such a fate.

"Merlin is the ultimate healer and worker of magics," Kaya replied. "You are afraid of him because you've been tricked by Christianity. The Horned God is the first and true God."

The Master smiled at Kaya. "Ah, I see we have a true believer." He held out his hand and took Kaya's in his. "You are a great sage, a priestess, a powerful witch. If I worked through you, my dear, you could bend the world to your will. I can give you the key to draw upon the consciousness of millions of humans and their spirits who have pledged allegiance to the Elemental Gods. That power can be yours."

"That's not real power," Sophie tried to explain. "Kaya, listen to me! I know about this. You'd be borrowing power from the dark side, stealing power like a vampire from others. You'd have to give up your path to enlightenment - fear would own you."

Kaya wasn't going to listen to Sophie. "To give up one's soul to the higher power is enlightenment," she replied. This was what she had been waiting for all her life - the chance to really commune with the otherworld, to be part of the spirit realms and to channel the power of the universe. "I would use it for good," she explained, "For helping people - for healing."

"But you can't control such power," Sophie tried to tell her. "It will overpower you. It will end up controlling you!"

"You may be overwhelmed by it," Kaya scoffed, "But I am a professional." She looked around at the Fianna Stones and added, "This is my birth-right. I know I was born to be a ring-site guardian, here at the centre of the British Isles, to guard one of the most powerful dragon portals in the world."

"Oh, good grief," Sophie exclaimed and rolled her eyes in despair. She knew nothing would convince Kaya to give up the chance of wielding such power.

The Master kissed Kaya's hand and she felt a rush of excitement that filled her with such bliss, she knew that Sophie was wrong. But, as soon as the glorious sensation had reached her crown chakra it faded and, looking over to her human body which was sitting with Robert on one of the stones, she watched in horror as dozens of vile boggarts gobbled up her aura and began to feast on her soul. It all happened so quickly there wasn't time to go back; within seconds, Kaya's consciousness was devoured and her human body crumpled like a rag-doll into Robert's arms.

Robert had been unable to stop the boggarts - it had happened so fast. Afraid they would take him next, he called out to King Arthur and, to his relief, his white-knight astral armour was strong enough to keep the boggarts at bay. They smashed into him like road-kill, sliding off him back into the dragon portal.

It was too late to save Kaya. "She's unconscious like Minnie," Robert called out. "What the hell is going on?"

Sophie felt sorry for Kaya but there was nothing she could do.

Sophie's human body, still lying in the hand cart, stirred for a moment but she didn't want to break the vision by speaking and just hoped everyone would be protected enough until she was able to tell them, in person, what was going on.

Suddenly, the sky began to grow darker still as the gathering of terrible storm clouds closed in on them and a violent gust of wind ripped, like a tsunami, through the trees.

Lucy shuddered and held tightly to Jack's hand. "What's happening?" she whispered. "I can't see anything astrally but look…" she pointed to the sky and shuddered as hundreds of jet-black crows swooped overhead, calling to each other as if summoning the evil spirits. They perched and cawed from the trees, sending chills through everyone.

In the astral realms, the crows were not birds but witches.

Sophie gasped in horror as she realised a sky portal had opened but not a heavenly one; out of its swirling sphere flew hundreds, if not thousands, of witches. She was surprised to see that they looked just as folklore would have them look - dressed in flowing, black cloaks, wearing pointy, black hats and riding on long broomsticks. She realised that the black attire, once used to cloak them from evil, had now become symbolic of the dark side and that the pointy hats protected their activated upper crown chakras, through which they could communicate telepathically with each other, humans and the spirit world. Their brooms showed their ability to clear away energy, only something had gone wrong along the way. Where once their brooms had swept away fear from people and places, now they were used to whip up dust-clouds of evil. She realised that beneath their cloaks they should be glowing-white like angels not shimmering black like the wings of the ebony crows.

Carrie shuddered. The clouds were now blocking the sun so completely that the temperature had dropped even further. She moved closer to Lance, feeling the need for some protection. She knew that the crows were a sign of something ominous in the air and, although she couldn't see the witches, she could sense a sinister presence was swarming around them.

Lancelot was also unnerved by such a large murder of crows. Their calls seemed to pierce his heart. He called to King Arthur for help. As he said the words, he became aware of himself transforming into a white knight and felt the heavy sensation of his etheric armour. He imagined placing a psychic shield around himself and Carrie, hoping that it would work.

The witches circled and flew in flocks around the stones, as did the crows, calling in such wicked, screeching tones that Lucy put her hands over her ears to block them out.

Robert watched in horror as one of the witches suddenly plummeted down from the sky like an arrow and pierced Kaya's empty etheric body.

Sophie realised who it was…

…Molly Liptrop's consciousness had taken possession of Kaya's body and was human again for the first time in over three hundred years.

Kaya's human body shuddered and shook in Robert's arms. When her eyes involuntarily opened they were vacant and lifeless and her face changed to take on Molly's features.

Robert gasped and let go of her - he could feel the evil rising from her now and, although he had never seen a picture of Molly, the part of him that was connected to Roger knew exactly who she was.

Sophie's courage rose like a lion within her as she prayed to St Margaret and the idea came to her that whilst the dragon portal was off limits here, Little Eden dragon portal was not. She called to Aunt Lilly and Alienor to send the Holy Spirit from Little Eden, not through the dragon lines but through the trees.

Just as they had for Robert, the tree spirits rustled into life amongst the dark undergrowth of Noblet Wood.

Every tree in the world, being inextricably linked to every other, could be harnessed and the call to arms from Little Eden was soon heard throughout

200

The Forest of Bowland. Faces appeared in the bark; they nodded and winked to each other as they began weaving a web of silver thread between their branches creating a, delicate but infinitely strong, bubble of shimmering light which floated over to Sophie's astral and human bodies. The protective shield encased them in an impenetrable force-field. Cloaked from the dark side, the extra power and comfort it gave her made her more determined than ever to out-wit this satanic force which had taken possession of the ring-site for far too long.

"How dare you take advantage of these women," she scolded the Master.

The Master laughed. "They are not all women," was his reply, "And I do not need to force them to join me. Revenge for the wrongs done to them in their lifetimes makes them willing participants."

"You are the Devil," Sophie accused him.

"No, my dear, I am not the Devil," he replied. His eyes narrowed and, for a moment the snakes inside them shot out, hissing venomously only an inch from her face. "You would not still be here if I were the Devil himself."

Sophie recoiled but stood firm and met his terrifying gaze with her own. She saw in his terrible eyes an army of dark witches stretching back over millennia.

"I am the accumulation of millions of years of human fear," he told her. "Through their worship of wickedness they gave me life and form. They made me guardian of their cloud of consciousness and grounding their spells and worship into these stones, the lay lines and the portals have become mine. The more who join our wrathful community, the more power we have. The more powerful we are, the more attractive we are and so it goes." He smiled as if chuckling inwardly at a private joke, "Everyone loves a wizard," he said.

Robert realised that the trees had sent their support to Sophie and he couldn't help but look over towards Noblet Wood.

The Master wondered what Robert was so interested in, over in the forest, and he tried to see what Robert could see. He couldn't fully penetrate the cloaking but was able to glimpse the edges of the leaves twinkling with fairy dust. Realising that he wasn't going to be able to take advantage of Sophie as easily as he had hoped, he looked over to Lucy with a wicked smirk.

Sophie saw him glance at her sister and her heart went cold.

It was actually the best thing the Master could have done.

If he dared endanger her sister, Sophie was going to take him down!

Chapter 40
~ * ~

L ucy didn't need her sister's help.

As the Master sent the slithering boggarts to attack her, Lucy and India were transformed into astral white witches, with Aunt Lilly and Alienor standing with them, ready to defend the Light at any cost.

Lucy's human-self had no idea that shining out of her eyes was a white light so dazzling and intense that the Master, boggarts and witches were blinded by it for a few moments.

When they could see again, they realised that the stones were encircled by hundreds of white witches who had flown out of the trees.

The Master had underestimated the power the friends could channel.

The white witches' broomsticks gave out sparks of diamond-light and as the black witches dived downwards from the stormy sky to attack, they were burnt to ashes in mid-air. The grasping boggarts were easily swept away, disappearing into nothingness in an instant.

The Master had never seen such Light!

This was new matrix energy.

Suddenly Kaya, awakened from her fainting fit, jumped off her stone and ran towards the altar.

Without warning, she violently ripped Isabelle's necklace from around Minnie's neck.

Robert ran after her and grabbed hold of her wrist, trying to wrestle the jewels from her hand but she seemed determined to keep them.

Sophie wondered why Molly wanted it so badly. As she asked the question in her mind, before she had even finished the sentence, the answer came to her - the necklace held a key.

The ruby at its heart was encoded with Latin letters which were laid out as thorns on the stem of a rose; they shimmered up and out of the crystal hovering in front of Sophie and the altar. Why are codes always in jewels, she thought to herself. We've been here before. Within the code she saw a vision of its origin which read like a pop-up story book in her mind's eye…

She saw how the code had been placed into the ruby by Pope Julius III and sent as a gift to Queen Mary I of England. Seeing the chapel at Hampton Court, Sophie watched the exchange between Queen Mary and her religious advisor as he presented her with the stunning necklace. The precious jewel was worth more to her than just its worldly value. The coded key could be placed in the Malinwick dragon portal as an attempt to ward off the growing number of Protestants who were battling for control of the collective consciousness and of the ring-sites all over the British Isles. The Queen had gifted the key to Roger's three-times-great-grandmother so that it might remain at Malinwick Manor in perpetuity.

From that time on, the Master had been empowering himself by using the key to draw on millions of Catholic souls, as well as any souls he could get to join his vengeful army. Over fifty years passed until Isabelle inherited the necklace and, under the guidance of a truly compassionate Catholic, Father John, Isabelle had sworn to take the code from the dragon portal and the necklace and take it into Heaven when she died.

The Master knew that if the code entered the heavenly realms it would be destroyed and all the power it contained to bewitch, confuse and brainwash others would be lost forever. He had sent Molly to take the code from Isabelle but his plan had been foiled when she had been hanged for witchcraft.

The Master had subsequently attempted to undermine Isabelle's faith in the pure light of Mother Mary hoping she would give him the key. He used Molly and other witches to send her into madness, he even sent soldiers to murder her, but when Isabelle died, falling to her death on the stair, her soul was still not as willing to join him as he had hoped. Isabelle had spent years praying to forgive Roger, Molly and herself and as her soul left her human body she found herself able and willing to forgive the soldiers who had taken her life. Her soul was not interested in vengeance or in drowning in self-pity; instead, she was ready to go straight into Heaven and take the key with her.

As a last ditch attempt to get the code, the Master had barred the entrance to the heavenly portal, hoping that, over time, stuck in limbo, Isabelle would finally give in to her own dark side.

Sophie admired Isabelle for her steadfastness and determination. She knew how much easier it was to give into hate and revenge than it was to forgive and let go. If Isabelle had stood up to the Master all this time, in life and in spirit, so could she.

Robert finally wrested the necklace from Kaya. As she clawed at him like a wild cat, he continued to restrain her as best he could but she kicked and screamed so vehemently that Jack had to come and help him.

With two white-knights standing between him and the code, his dark witches burnt by the light and his boggarts dissolved, the Master needed re-enforcements.

He summoned the ancient wizards of the land.

Chapter 41
~ * ~

The stones began to hum with energy and those with psychic sight saw that they were no longer solid but had transformed into translucent crystals; from each one appeared a druid.

Dressed in long, grey, flowing robes, and carrying staffs made of hazel wood, each druid stood before their stone and bowed to the Master.

He commanded them to infuse Molly with all the power they could summon and, drawing on every spirit, in a human body or in the ether, who had ever pledged allegiance to the horned gods, they pointed their staffs towards Kaya.

Black light, as powerful as a bolt of lightning, struck Kaya through the heart.

With the extraordinary level of chi running through her, Kaya was able to break free of Robert's and Jack's restraints and she knocked them both to the ground.

As Robert hit his head on the corner of the altar stone a few drops of his blood fell upon Minnie's outstretched hand. His blood seemed to have magical powers, releasing the spirit Isabelle.

Isabelle rose, as a spectre, from Minnie's heart chakra and hovered above her body.

Released from Isabelle's consciousness, Minnie awoke to feel a sharp pain in her neck where Kaya had ripped off the necklace.

She sat up with a jolt.

Trying to get her bearings, wondering at first what on earth she was doing amongst the stones, Minnie wondered if she was dreaming. Then she saw Robert was injured and everyone was there; she realised this was really happening to her.

Kaya had hold of the necklace again.

Minnie felt Isabelle willing her on to take it back.

Although Kaya had almost super-human power, Minnie had skills that could take a giant down in one move.

Minnie flipped herself up and off the altar stone, landing on the grass in a squat. Spinning around, she took Kaya's knees from under her with sharp kick. Before Kaya knew what was happening, Minnie had rolled her over onto the grass and swiftly pulled her arm behind her back, forcing it up towards her shoulder whilst holding her face down in the mud.

Jack pulled Robert to his feet and then helped Minnie to restrain Kaya.

Wolf, who had been sitting on his stone with India all this time, was in shock and awe. He had had psychic visions in the past but nothing compared to this. The clarity, the speed, the complexity of what was happening had him almost paralysed with disbelief. He felt as if he had no clue what to do and wasn't sure if he should even do anything - that is up until now. He felt a sudden, strange tug inside his heart and a flash of a long-lost memory shot across his mind. He knew these druids of old and he recalled how the first ones had grounded divine consciousness into human bodies, becoming leaders, shamans, gurus and saints to help souls release themselves from the wheel of karma. Sadly, as time passed, the very karma they had come to dissolve had taken them into its sticky web. They began to fight amongst themselves for supremacy over the dragon portals, breaking into religious sects; creating false clouds of consciousness into which human souls were initiated and bound, rather than being set free.

Wolf had the strangest feeling that he knew how to summon the last remaining true druids. He wasn't sure how he knew but, as soon as he had the thought in his head, he saw, arising from the overflowing sykes, the re-assembled, walking skeletons of the ancestors.

At first, he wasn't sure if he had summoned more evil by mistake but as the lumbering skeletons approached the stones, the druids began to cower. The ancestors easily took their staffs from them, snapping them in two and throwing them to the ground. Then they wrapped their bony fingers around the druid's necks, popping their heads like corks and sending thousands of tiny serpents flying through the air, which were then burnt to a cinder by the white witches' brooms.

In desperation, the Master forced Jimmy's body to take the necklace from Minnie. He really shouldn't have tried as he found himself doubled over in agony when Minnie kicked him in his own crown jewels and then kneed him in the face - even the Master was subject to the frailty of the physical human body.

Lucy and Carrie rushed over to see if Jimmy was alright. Then, abruptly, they were all distracted, even Jimmy, as the clouds above them suddenly parted in, what appeared to be, a perfect circle.

A sphere of bright-blue sky was etched out of the storm-clouds by the sun.

In the astral realms, the portal revealed a flying saucer, hovering overhead. A beam of white light cascaded downwards, into the centre of the stone circle, grounding into the dragon portal, and Sophie realised that the Pleiades had arrived.

As the base of the etheric spaceship opened, five, tall, blue, glowing beings beamed down to the altar stone.

Their presence seemed to stop time - as if they had pressed pause on the earthly computer game.

The towering light beings were the ones Sophie knew well and she realised that they had come for the key. Now that Minnie had the real necklace in her possession, Sophie could remove the etheric key from the ruby. She handed it to the galactic guides, glad to get it off her hands. She was surprised when they then asked her for two more keys.

She had to tell them that she didn't have any more - at least not that she knew of.

Sophie suddenly remembered what Lancelot had experienced on Pendle Hill and understood that the strange V shaped formation of silver balls was also a key of consciousness.

Before she even needed to ask him for it, the code floated out of Lancelot's crown chakra and into the hands of the Pleiades beings.

"But the third key?" Sophie asked, "Who has the third key?"

Astonished, she saw Wolf's astral-self project from his human body as a sandy-coloured wolf. It ran towards the altar carrying a human skull in its open jaws. Just as he was about to present the skull to Sophie, several of the skeletal ancestors attempted to stop him.

Flesh formed on their bones and teeth returned to their mouths; eyes developed in their sockets and brains returned to their skulls. Their consciousness, ancient as it was, was restored, and they were able to communicate with the other spirits there.

The leader, wearing the pelt and head of a wolf, took the skull from Wolf's mouth and, to Sophie's dismay, he refused to relinquish it.

The Pleiades, a race of beings new to planet Earth, were not necessarily welcomed by all. The first humans did not trust the new guardians to look after the Earth any more than they had been able to. The corruption and karmic bonds they had suffered had left them territorial and bitter.

The Pleiades and Sophie understood the reticence of the ancestors to participate in another 'experiment.' Was it really a good idea to create a new matrix of consciousness, which was to be anchored within the dragon portals and lay lines, allowing the galactics to incarnate into human bodies as Star Children.

What had gone wrong the first time may well happen again.

Sophie tried to help by playing the diplomat between the Pleiades Council and the ancestors but it was no use.

The ancestors saw Sophie as a galactic too - with no business here on Earth.

Chapter 42
~ * ~

It was Wolf who became the go-between.

He was one of them. His soul was as old as human-life itself.

Wolf was able to convince the ancestors that the Pleiades came in peace and that their matrix was going to be the future with or without their help.

"Better to be working with them to protect the planet and human souls than to work against them and create trouble, fear and war," he told them. "Our time is over," he explained, "We must accept that the guardians of the Earth will always change. Once it was our planet, our home, but nothing stays the same. We know this. We must accept this. For us, and now for the Atlanteans, it is Armageddon - the end-times - and we can embrace the Star Children or we can reject them but we can never stop them coming. It is written. It is inevitable."

Putting it to a vote, the ancestors reluctantly agreed to pass their precious key to the Pleiades.

As Sophie handed over the human skull to the galactic beings, the V shaped key, the skull and the ruby merged together and spun like a Catherine wheel, sparks flying all around, until from the three keys created one new key that looked like a glowing micro-chip.

Sophie threw it into the dragon portal and it exploded like a million fireworks.

Now that the dragon portal was under the jurisdiction of the Light once more, Sophie was able to summon the true Merlin who had been buried beneath the false codes and spells for so long…

Merlin, Merlin, Merlin
Wizard of all wizards
Healer of all healers
Come, with your holy staff
Made of the tree of life
Bound with crystals and with gold
Heal my sickness, my hurt, my pain
Come, my supreme and unfailing friend
Through the holy waters and the sacred flame
Weave your white and holy magic
Through space and in time
By your hands I am healed

The Pleiades guides, their new key in place, unfroze time and bid the friends farewell; as they ascended away into the clouds, the true Merlin consciousness arose in their place from within the dragon's eye.

Immediately, the compassionate Merlin bound the consciousness of the Master and of Molly with threads of silver light emanating from his staff and drew them like poison out of Jimmy and Kaya's bodies. Both of the human bodies went limp and, like zombies, they just stared into space as if empty of life. They needed no more restraint.

Merlin knew he had to act quickly before the Master and Molly could draw on more evil energy to empower themselves and break free from his binding spell. He threw them, like a ball from a Lacrosse net, into their dark sky portal and sealed it behind them with a flaming, golden cross.

"Won't they just return when someone summons them?" Sophie asked Merlin.

Merlin smiled, his eyes shining with joy as happy wrinkles formed around them. "You must learn to accept that Earth is a hell dimension, my dear Sophie," he said. "If I had the power to stop the darkness, do you not think I would have done it by now? Do you not think the angels and the buddhas would have taken back the ring sites long before the Pleiades came?"

Sophie had to agree that the darkness seemed a formidable and everlasting power on Earth, although she didn't like the idea of accepting it.

Merlin smiled again. "How does anyone decide what is evil?" he replied. "Do the law makers of each land agree what is punishable and what is not? Of course they do not. In one land you may kill another, over the mountains you may not. On one side of the river you may own your wife and daughters like cattle but on the other side of the river you may not. How do we judge the karma which binds humans to evil thoughts and deeds? You give me an impossible task."

"Then what is the answer?" Sophie asked him.

"For each soul to strive for a life of compassion and community so that they may free their souls from the wheel of karma and to be released from this hell dimension forever," Merlin replied.

Sophie laughed. "Now it's you who are giving us the impossible task!" she replied.

Merlin chuckled. "Perhaps," was his reply.

Turning to the ancestors, he told them to return to their own matrix or to embrace the new one when it was completed. He asked for their help but they didn't want anything to do with the future of mankind and left forever through the stones. Before stepping into the largest stone, the leader turned to Wolf and asked him to join them. Wolf felt a deep sadness rising in his heart. The ancestors, who refused to embrace the coming of the new age, would remain in their cloud of consciousness, as if archived in a library, and their spirits would not exist in the new matrix. He knew he had to ascend and merge his energy field with the galactic consciousness if he wanted to be part of the future. He had to accept the new key. But the new world demanded he relinquish all previous karma, creating the ultimate break from his soul family; the sensation was heart breaking and gut wrenching. It felt as if he was being asked to choose between all that was familiar and dear to him and an unknown world with no plan, no guarantees and no home. He had to let go of all he had ever learnt or come to love. His identity was built on the karma of his soul-family which they had woven over millennia, and without it, who would he be?

Wolf made the, almost unbearable, decision not to go with them but to take his chances in the new matrix - with the Star Children.

As the stones closed, Lucy felt the air around her begin to lift. The murder of crows suddenly squawked loudly and flew away as if frightened by an invisible force. Lucy smiled to herself. She knew the angels had triumphed over evil.

Through the circle in the sky appeared the swirling light of the heavenly portal and shafts of sunlight poured down towards the ground.

The time had come to release the poor, trapped spirits of the house. They gathered at the base of the heavenly ladder and, slowly, each one began to ascend towards the pearly gates.

Lady Edith, taking the hands of her children, floated upwards towards the Light and, as she did so, her face was healed - she looked as she had done before she fell from the tower. The family were followed by little Humphrey who was wagging his tail in delight. Sophie felt sad to say goodbye to him whilst at the same time she was elated to see them all united in bliss.

When all the souls were safely through the glistening portal, Isabelle thanked the Little Eden friends for their help and Sophie thanked Isabelle for holding onto her faith and the Light in the face of such terrible odds. "I hope Roger is waiting for you," Sophie told her.

She was surprised, however, by Isabelle's reply.

"I hope he is not," Isabelle said. "He betrayed my trust and he abandoned our love. I have forgiven him but it took me centuries of prayer to do so. In my next life I want to be with a man who is loyal and courageous." She looked at Minnie and smiled. "Or perhaps I shall be with a woman instead."

Sophie was about to say goodbye to Father John when she became aware that there was one more soul still to leave - it was Abigale Fairlie.

She wanted to show Sophie where to find her body.

Chapter 43

~ * ~

To Sophie's absolute horror, she witnessed Abigale's terrible murder as a hideous vision in her mind's eye.

Hardly wanting to look, she saw how, having come to Lodge House for a tarot reading with Ada Mould, Abigale had found herself in the wrong place at the wrong time.

Ada and Arthur had been contemplating carrying out a human sacrifice for years but had never dared to see it through until poor, vulnerable Abigale came into their home. During the reading, Ada ascertained that Abigale had no family and few friends who would miss her. Abigale was young, petite and thin, lacking the physical strength to fight back, and her mind was weakened due to years of gas-lighting, neglect and abuse. Ada and Arthur easily overpowered her; the next night, under the first full moon of the new millennium, she was laid upon the altar stone as a monstrous satanic rite was performed and she became their unholy sacrifice to the Master.

Sophie wanted the vision to stop; it was unbearable to witness such a horrifying scene of mutilation and death.

Ada and Arthur had buried Abigale's bleeding body below a black elder tree in the graveyard of the old chapel. Beneath the tree was an ancient tomb, its sandstone engravings worn away by the wind and rain long ago. No-one had thought to look inside an existing sepulchre and poor Abigale had been lying amongst strangers, alone for over a decade, waiting to be found.

Sophie promised Abigale's spirit that they would rescue her body as soon as they could and urged her to ascend the heavenly ladder and find peace at last.

Father John, who had been waiting until the last soul was safe, was about to depart when he realised that Sophie, seeing the souls released from torment, wished she could join them. Before he left her, Father John kissed her forehead and held her hands in his saying, "I know you long to be free from your earthly pain but it is not your time, not yet."

Sophie sighed. "It never is," she replied sadly.

"When it is," Father John said, "We shall all be waiting for you in Heaven."

Sophie took comfort in his words and woefully watched him leave, glad

211

for him, but sorry for herself left behind.

Knowing that the sacred site was secure, the white witches also took their leave and flew away into the woods, where the tree spirits also whispered their goodbyes.

When all were safely home, Merlin looked at Robert and bowed his head. "I leave this portal in your capable hands," he told him.

Then smiling at Sophie, he winked and added, "There is much left to do, you will be needed again soon," and with that he closed the shimmering heavenly portal. Bidding all of them farewell, he disappeared into the dragon's eye, which blinked one more time, before it was sealed with a burnished cross and all was quiet.

Sophie's human-self, still lying in the cart, opened her eyes - her job was done. The portals were closed, the spirits were where they should be and all was right with the world again or so she thought...

Suddenly, storm clouds enveloped the sky again and Lucy shuddered. The temperature dropped.

"Let's get out of here," Lucy suggested, sensing trouble not far away.

But, before anyone could move, as if out of nowhere, Ada and Arthur appeared from behind some of the outer stones, brandishing their shotguns.

Everyone gasped in shock and fright when the old couple aimed their guns at Robert and Jack.

"Woah," Jack said. "Now just be careful with those, we don't want any trouble." He pushed Lucy and Minnie behind him and the altar stone, trying to shield them.

"Stay where you is," Arthur growled.

Robert feared someone may get hurt by accident.

Sophie's heart went cold; she now knew what Ada and Arthur were capable of and didn't think, for a minute, that if someone was shot or killed that it would be by accident.

Half hidden by the altar, and by the others, she climbed out of the cart and attracted Minnie's attention. "They're dangerous," she whispered to her friend. "Seriously, they're not playing around."

"What do they want?" Minnie whispered back but Arthur answered her question before Sophie could...

"Give us tha necklace," Arthur ordered Robert. "I knows yous has it."

Robert, whose head was still bleeding, making him feel slightly woozy, thought it best just to hand over the jewels rather than play the hero and

212

risk anyone's life. He stepped forwards as if to bring it to them but Arthur, unsure what he or the others might do, told him to stay where he was. "Everyone put your hands in t' air where I can sees 'em," he shouted and motioned, with his gun, to India and Wolf, who were over by one of the further away stones, to join the group.

Ada motioned with her gun for Lancelot, who was standing to the side of them, to also go towards the altar but Lance explained that he couldn't walk unaided, due to his ankle, and he told them, "You can't get away with this. You can't shoot us all."

"We doesn't needs to shoot yous all," Arthur replied. "Just 'im." He pointed both barrels at Robert again. "We won't lets yous sell our home," he snarled. "This is our place."

Everyone thought he really might shoot Robert - he seemed crazy enough to not understand the consequences.

"Throw tha necklace o'er," he commanded Robert again.

"There's no key in it anymore," Sophie shouted out. "The key has gone from the ruby."

Ada looked surprised and then angry. She aimed the barrel of her gun at Sophie. "You'll not take tha stones. We is ring-site guardians. We has rights."

"The Master has gone," Sophie told them, her voice quaking with fear. "There's nothing you can do here anymore. Killing Robert won't bring him back."

Arthur decided not to believe her and barked again, "Throw tha necklace o'er."

Robert hurled the necklace through the air but it landed short of where Ada and Arthur were standing and disappeared into the long, wet grass, then sank into a dark bog, disappearing from sight.

Unseen, Minnie had taken the opportunity of the distraction to crawl away from the group and, like a Commando, she ran between the stones then stealthily crouched around the back of the one nearest to Ada and Arthur.

As Ada tentatively came forwards to try to retrieve the necklace, her gun pointing downwards as she bent down to pick it up, Minnie launched herself from her hiding place and threw her whole body onto Ada's back, flattening her to floor.

As Ada's gun fell it fired with an almighty bang!

In the ensuing panic, Arthur also fired his gun, but luckily, Lancelot had thrust the sack barrow at him sending him down to the ground and the bullet went shooting into the air as Arthur lost his footing.

Jack ran forwards and tackled Arthur, taking away his gun. Opening it, he took out the other shells and threw them as far away as he could. He then whipped off his belt and tied Arthur's hands behind his back.

Robert did the same to Ada and took possession of her shotgun.

In the chaos, with everyone screaming, it wasn't clear if anyone was hurt. Then, when everyone else had stopped shrieking and Jimmy continued to wail, they realised he'd been shot in the arm by Ada's bullet.

Lucy grabbed the pillow from the altar, pulled off the cover, and quickly wrapped it around Jimmy's arm, putting pressure on the wound.

Jack looked around to check that everyone else was okay but, to his dismay, and to everyone else's horror, Kaya was lying, motionless and silent on the ground.

Chapter 44
~ * ~

India checked Kaya for a pulse.
She was dead.

Chapter 45

~ * ~

India looked up at the others and shook her head.

She was too shocked to speak.

Jack told everyone to stay exactly where they were. "Don't touch anything," he warned them. "This is a crime scene now."

Everyone was too stunned to move anyway.

They just stared at Kaya, aghast - not really taking it in.

Then, Carrie realised what had happened and started screaming again. Her next realisation was that someone had been murdered on her watch - what was Van Ike going to say? Her Health and Safety hadn't really been up to snuff after all.

Jack double checked that Kaya was dead, then said, "We'd better get back to the house," "We'll lock these two up idiots somewhere (meaning Ada and Arthur of course) and then I'll go and get help - somehow."

Lucy couldn't bear to leave poor Kaya exposed and alone. "We can't leave her here," she told Jack.

"We mustn't touch anything, especially not the body," Jack explained.

"But, can't I at least put a blanket over her?" Lucy begged him.

Jack didn't think it was a good idea, from an official point of view, but he didn't like the idea of leaving her open to the elements either so he agreed.

The walk back to Manor, with Ada and Arthur tied up, was a quiet, grim and pensive one. Apart from Carrie, who was still visibly upset, everyone else felt numb.

In deathly silence they made their way back through the wet grass to the bridge then, just as they were halfway over, they were all startled by a rustling in the trees. Out of the undergrowth appeared a majestic stag, whose coat looked like burnished-amber in the bright sunlight and whose antlers rose like a crown from his noble head.

He stared directly at them, unflinching, unafraid.

Robert felt the stare burning into his chest and his heart began to race. He felt as if the stag was charging him with a solemn oath to protect the land and the sacred site from now on as a great and good king should.

As they reached the house, huge, fat rain drops began to fall like saucers out of the sky and they were glad to make it into the hall just in time to avoid the next downpour.

Jack looked at Ada and Arthur with a mixture of dismay, disdain and disbelief. "Take them into the kitchen," he told Robert and Wolf. "Lock them in that pantry."

"Where are you going?" Robert asked him.

"I'm going to try to get to the pub over the fields," Jack explained.

"No!" Lucy said, "It's too dangerous. The bogs!"

"Someone has to go and get the Police," Jack replied and reluctantly added, "And an ambulance for this idiot," (meaning Jimmy).

"There's no rush," Robert said. "It's only a flesh wound by the looks of it. At least wait for another break in the rain or at least let's find some waterproofs and I'll come with you. You shouldn't go alone."

India, who was still standing in the stone porch, looked down towards the windswept silver-black lake and an idea flashed into her mind. Taking hold of Wolf's arm, she pulled him back and pointed down to the boathouse. "We could go and see if there's a canoe in the boathouse and row back to the village to fetch help."

Wolf thought it a great idea. "I'll go with you," he offered.

India didn't want Jack or Robert to go instead so she whispered to Minnie, "Tell the others that Wolf and I have gone to the boathouse and we'll be back in a while."

Minnie looked surprised. "What for?" she asked, then realising what India was thinking, "I'll tell them," she replied.

Down in the kitchen, Wolf opened one of the pantry doors and pushed Ada and Arthur inside. He was just going to leave them there when Robert felt they should at least be given some chairs to sit on.

"You'd give a bloody Nazi an armchair," Jack mumbled. "Do you want to give them a cup of tea and a slice of cake as well?"

Lucy overheard, "Oh, do you think we should?" she asked.

"I was being sarcastic," Jack laughed as he slammed and locked the door.

"We don't know what has happened to them to make them act like that," Robert said. "I feel partially responsible. I was going to take their home from them. I still am. I suppose losing your home sends everyone a little crazy. We know what that's like - the threat of losing Little Eden is frightening us all. I have considered shooting Collins a dozen times - I can't lie."

"The difference is you won't actually do it," Jack replied.

"Maybe the step from thinking it to doing it isn't very wide," Robert said.

Everyone was still in shock and the reality of what had just happened hadn't fully sunk in.

Lucy boiled the kettle and using the second bottle of whisky from Wolf's bag she sterilised some cloths to clean Jimmy's wound. He winced; grabbing the bottle from her he quickly drank a few big gulps as if he was having a major operation.

A few minutes later, now a bit tipsy and slightly delirious, Jimmy kept pawing at Lucy, "You love me, don't you babe?" he kept asking her pathetically.

Lucy felt sorry for him; part of her did still love him, she couldn't deny that.

"I want you back," Jimmy whispered. "You want me don't you babe?"

"This isn't the time or place," Lucy replied, reluctant to talk about it with the others present, afraid that they might hear.

"But it is," Jimmy told her. "Death makes you feel alive - puts things in perspective. Makes you see what's really important. I've had a lucky escape. That could have been me lying dead on the ground. I could be dead right now."

Lucy was falling under his spell again and Sophie could see it. She thought it best to distract her sister until she could tell her how Jimmy was no longer Jimmy, that his soul had left his body leaving, at best, an empty shell. A man without a soul would be dangerous to say the least, as any spirit wanting to possess his human body could jump in and out of him at any time.

"Where are Wolf and India," Robert suddenly asked, realising that they were not there.

Minnie explained that they had gone to the Boathouse; she had to stop both Robert and Jack going to help them.

"Oh, I see!" Jack smiled, when he realised why Minnie told him to leave them alone for a while. "Good for India."

It took Robert a moment longer to understand but when Lancelot raised his eyebrow in a certain way he got the message. "Oh," he exclaimed. "I wouldn't have thought Wolf was India's type."

"Being so close to death can make us all want to feel alive," Jack said as he helped himself to a glass of whisky. He offered a shot to everyone else, especially Carrie who was the only one who seemed to be dramatically affected by Kaya's death.

"What the hell happened at the stones?" Carrie asked Sophie. "Not that I really want to know but I can't help thinking it's my fault or at least others will think it is. When we get out of here, I'm quitting. I'm going to do QVC or a cookery show, something where there are no ghosts and no lunatics on the loose."

"No-one blames you," Lancelot told Carrie. "It's no-one's fault except those two in there. They are to blame. Or at least their karma and dark witchcraft is to blame."

"I'd like to know more about what happened," Minnie admitted. "I mean how did you get me to the stones? Why did you take me there?"

Sophie explained, the best she could, but it all sounded rather farfetched.

"I'm so glad Isabelle went to Heaven at last," Minnie said. "I feel as if a weight has lifted and all my guilt about betraying her in that past-life has gone. In fact, I'm starting to wonder if I ever felt those strange feelings at all. It's as if it never happened now. I'm glad it's all over. Although poor Kaya and her family, it's not over for them is it?"

"She didn't deserve to die like that," Lancelot said. "She was so young and full of life."

"I wouldn't worry too much about her," Sophie replied. "Her soul was sucked out of her before she was shot. If she was here with us now it would not be the Kaya you knew standing in this kitchen."

Minnie shuddered at the idea.

"What has happened to her soul?" Lucy asked, thinking it sounded horrific having your soul ripped out of you whilst you were still alive.

"The Master will have put it in a time-fold." Sophie explained. "He'll be able to use it to empower himself when he needs to. In another lifetime, someone from Kaya's soul family may go and retrieve it."

"Is that what they mean by soul-retrieval?" Lucy asked.

Sophie nodded. "Yes, if you can locate the dimension in which the soul is being stored and break all the spells that keep it there, it is possible to find a lost or stolen soul."

"I've just realised," Lancelot said, "That's what it meant in Mr T's notes about boggarts eating children. They eat people's souls - they steal souls - and I presume children are easy prey, so in myths and legends the story becomes that they 'eat' children."

"I guess so," Sophie agreed. "Talking of children, or teenagers at least, being taken, there was a girl killed here a few years ago called Abigale and, before she passed over, she showed me where her body is buried. I wasn't going to tell you all until later, but I suppose it doesn't matter when you hear it. Ada and Arthur murdered her and buried her body in the graveyard of the old chapel."

"Bloody hell," Jack exclaimed. "You still feeling sorry for them?" he asked Robert. He could just shoot the two old coots there and then and bury them where they had put Abigale. "It's more important than ever that we get those two evil bastards to the Police as soon as possible," he said.

They all looked at the pantry door and felt repulsed as well as a little scared.

"The evil in this house wasn't the ghosts after all," Lucy said. "It was the living."

Chapter 46
~ * ~

India and Wolf ran down the grassy bank, getting soaked as they went. Dramatic grey and white clouds scudded across the sky, painting the hills with rolling shadows as they hurried by. Patches of bright-blue sky were a welcome sight and to their great relief, the shower soon ceased. The sun came out above them but, over in the distance, heavy funnels of rain were still lining up to head their way.

The lake, which now reflected the blue of the summer sky, shone like a giant sapphire, surrounded by bright, twinkling, green grass which, as they approached, they could see was waterlogged and treacherous, boggy and spongy beneath their feet. They picked their way carefully towards the boathouse.

Abruptly, rain came thundering over from the southwest and a roar of glistening rain drops hit the lake like millions of tiny arrow heads, bouncing back up and then landing again creating millions of rippling circles across the water and tiny rainbows which floated over the pond.

They quickened their pace, slipping and sliding in places, until they finally reached the back of the old brick boathouse.

Long, yellow grass grew up the sides of the rough, red walls as well as in front of a shabby, wooden door that obviously hadn't been opened in a long time. Fortunately, it wasn't locked but the wrought-iron latch had rusted solid. Wolf gave it a good shove and bruised his hand in the process (he didn't let on to India that it hurt though) and opening the door he secretly sucked at sore his finger.

The crashing rain on the roof made the boathouse seem like a sheltering cave - a sanctuary from the wildness of Mother Nature outside. It was more spacious on the inside than it had looked from the outside and the smell of damp stone and wet wood wasn't unpleasant. A couple of varnished rowing boats and a long punt bobbed gently by the sides of two small pontoons which stretched the length of the shelter and went along three sides. Paddles and ropes hung around the back wall and some old canoes lay on rotting wooden racks. The oak beamed roof was leaking in places where the slate tiles had shifted in the wind and never been repaired; overall though, India quite liked it.

"There's something romantic about boathouses, don't you think," India said. "It makes me think of sunny days, messing about in boats. I expect to see Ratty or Moley from 'Wind in the Willows' go floating by."

Wolf grinned. "I've never been in a boathouse before," he told her."

"We have a lovely one by the canal in Little Eden," India told him. "I used to go there as a child. Locals and tourists can hire punts in the summer to float up and down the canal."

"I'd love to visit your Little Eden one day," Wolf told her. "It sounds idyllic."

"It is," India replied, "Although lately there's been trouble. It's under threat of sale and demolition and this year we lost a child; he died unexpectedly." She shivered for a moment recalling little Joshua and also now Kaya.

Unexpectedly, something shot out of the eves and skimmed the top of their heads, letting out a harsh, piercing scream.

Then another swooped down.

Then another.

A flock of shadowy, crescent shaped swifts were darting and rushing through the air as if to scare away the intruders.

India, startled by their sudden flight, grabbed hold of Wolf's arm and within a few seconds the birds faded from her mind as the electrical charge between them instantly aroused her and she felt a rush of overwhelming excitement and anticipation.

"Are you okay?" Wolf asked her. He could also feel the frisson between them and didn't want to lose the feeling just yet. He let it rise and ripple through his body making him lightheaded. "Let's sit down for a few minutes. We've all had a shock."

"We should try to get one of these boats back as soon as we can," India replied.

"I'm sorry to say it, but Kaya isn't going anywhere in a hurry," Wolf told her. "A few more minutes won't do any harm now."

He helped her sit down on the pontoon and handed her his hip flask.

India, also not wanting to leave him just yet, took a sip. The warmth of the whisky radiated through her chest.

Wolf then took a spliff out of his pocket and lit it. Taking a drag he offered it to her.

India shook her head.

"Don't you smoke?" he asked her.

"No," she replied, "And I don't do drugs."

Wolf smiled. "Is Little Eden some kind of monastery?"

India laughed. "No, but I suppose we - those of us who live there - try to be healthy and kind to ourselves and to others."

Wolf offered her the joint again and he could see that she was tempted. "It'll calm your nerves," he told her. "I've never seen anyone killed before. I know I need to calm down."

"I told you, I don't smoke," India replied.

"You don't have to," Wolf said. "I'll give you a blow back."

"A what?" India asked.

Wolf laughed.

"Kiss me," he told her.

India was taken by surprise and didn't know what to say. As she hesitated Wolf took his opportunity and kissed her.

A long, deep, passionate kiss.

India felt dizzy as he pulled away but not as dizzy as she was about to feel.

Wolf took another drag and, holding the smoke in his mouth, he kissed her again letting the smoke pass between her lips.

It was a slow, disorientating, fuzzy sensation that India felt floating through her and she reeled backwards as Wolf held her close to him.

"That's a blow back," he said.

"Wow," India replied.

"Feels good, eh?" he asked her and before she could reply he kissed her again.

India began to feel as if she was ascending on a cloud and laid her head against his shoulder.

"You've forgiven me then?" he asked her, "For sometimes embellishing the truth."

India nodded.

"Something has happened to me," he confided to her. "I know you don't believe in ghosts but…" he paused for a moment, unsure whether to tell her or not…"What happened at the stones - I can't even begin to describe to you and you wouldn't believe me if I did."

"I might," India murmured.

"I doubt it," Wolf replied. "I wouldn't if someone told me."

"No, you're right," she replied. "Don't tell me. I don't want to know."

223

India looked up at him and kissed him. He let his whole body release into hers and desperately wanted to make love to her right there and then, despite knowing that this was not the right time and place; it took every ounce of self-control to stop himself.

"The reason I don't believe in the spirit world," India confessed, "Is because it scares me. The less I know, the less scared I am, I suppose. Sounds crazy, I know."

"It's not crazy," Wolf smiled. "Opening up your psychic mind isn't always a good idea. If you are not born with it switched into hyper-drive, it's best left well alone."

They let the waves of euphoria wash over them for a few minutes, just watching the water lapping at the pontoons and the mesmerising rain splashing up from the water.

"I think I've had an epiphany," Wolf said. "Have you ever had a moment when your whole life flashes before you and you know you came here for something better? I realise I have to be a better man - honest and true. I have to make a difference in the world - you know - leave it a better place than I found it."

India smiled. She was enjoying the heady sensation from the marijuana. "I know what you mean," she replied. "I know exactly what you mean."

Wolf contemplated his experience at the stones and wondered where his destiny would lead him.

Kaya's death suddenly sank into India's mind. Until that moment it was as if she hadn't registered it emotionally. It had been hovering somewhere above her consciousness and the penny dropped so suddenly that she gasped. "Oh my god," she suddenly said. "Kaya's dead."

"You only just realised that?" Wolf asked her.

"I didn't feel it before, I saw it but...oh my god," India replied. She stood up, a little wobbly and dizzy at first before regaining her composure. "We've got to get to the village. Tell the police," she exclaimed. "Now!"

"Okay, Okay," Wolf said, putting away his flask and getting to his feet. He threw the cigarette butt onto the deck and stubbed it out with his foot.

"If you're going to be a better man," India said, "You can pick that up for starters."

Wolf laughed and put the butt in his pocket. "You're right. Respect for others and for the environment."

"The Golden Rule," India told him, "In everything, do unto others what you would have them do unto you."

Wolf smiled to himself. He knew India was going to help him become the man he felt he now wanted to be.

Looking around, they found a Cockle MKII in one of the racks which had 'Property of MOD' stamped on the side. It was the most lightweight boat there and still watertight. Finding some thick, strong rope, they manoeuvred it out of the door and dragged it slowly up the grassy bank.

India was thankful that the rain had ceased for a few minutes and, with her pulling and Wolf pushing, they finally reached the gravel drive. Out of breath, they sat on some of the old Abbey foundations for a few moments. Now that the effects of the hash were wearing off, India was embarrassed about their intimacy in the boathouse and she was a little afraid that Wolf had just used her. As she stood up to go to tell the others that they had found a boat, Wolf pulled her back and, to her relief, he kissed her again.

Wondering why they had been so long, Robert and Jack appeared at the front door, looking for them both.

"You've found one then?" Robert asked. "Good show!"

Jack, Robert and Wolf carried the canoe, above their heads, down the drive. The upturned boat sheltered them from the dripping avenue of trees and, by the time they passed the Lodge House, they were getting a bit too hot. The mid-summer sun, now that it was finally out for a while, was a shock to the system. They kept marching on, in line, until they reached the point where the ford crossed the Manor Raike. Now, however, the water stretched as far as the eye could see and the land was flooded all the way to Boggart Village, beyond Hellifield Road.

Jack and Robert offered to go but India wanted the adventure and Wolf wanted India to stay with him so they insisted on going themselves. "As long as the rain keeps off we should be fine," India reassured the boys. "Besides, I haven't rowed since University. It'll be fun and god knows I need something to take my mind off things after the last two days. We'll flag down the first person we see and send you back some help."

Chapter 47
~ * ~

As Jack and Robert headed back towards the main house, Jack suddenly went off the path, into the long grass, heading into the trees.

"Where are you going?" Robert asked him.

"I'm going to find that old chapel," Jack explained. "I'm going to find Abigale."

Robert didn't really want to join him. The undergrowth was dense and he was sick of getting wet but he felt as if he didn't really have a choice. He couldn't let Jack go alone.

Jack picked up a fallen branch to use as a baton to bash away some of the nettles and forge a path through the copse.

"For goodness sakes," Robert said as he followed after him. He could feel his trousers getting soaked and clinging to his legs again, whilst big drops of water from the canopy above kept hitting him on the head. "I'm not sure we need to find the poor girl right now," he muttered.

"I want the Police to take it seriously this time," Jack replied. "They'll not believe that Sophie was told by Abigale's ghost where to find her body. I can't blame them. There was a time I'd not have believed it either. Before I tell them where to look, I want to know for sure that she's there."

"So, you are coming round to the fact that the spirit world does exist then," Robert smiled. He suddenly called out in pain. Jack had let a low growing branch flap back behind him and it had hit Robert squarely in the face.

"I think I have to, old boy," Jack replied, unconcerned by the undergrowth. "I seem to have been put in these situations too many times now to explain it away. I saw what happened to Minnie with my own eyes. We all did. I'm not saying I believe all that mumbo-jumbo rubbish, a lot of it is highly suspect if you ask me, but I'll admit Sophie can speak to spirits - I don't know how - but she can and that's good enough for me."

As they came upon the mysterious chapel it was not at all as they had imagined. Instead of being a graceful Gothic style church, it was merely a turriform - one square tower with a small east chancel attached to it. What was striking about it was its plainness. The blank stone walls of the one story extension had one very small window in each side, giving it an austere and impenetrable aspect. The grey tower had a double-arched opening to the belfry and it felt as if the steeple was missing, even though there had never actually been one. The cemetery surrounding it was overgrown, undulating and full of rabbit warrens. "Mr T says there are graves here dating back to Saxon times," Robert said, "And that the nave is likely 9th Century; it very well could be the first stone church built in England."

"It looks as if it's about to fall down," Jack mused, "Like everything else around here."

Robert fought his way through nettles and brambles to see if the heavy oak door was unlocked. It was but had warped over the years and Jack had to help him force it open. Even with both of them putting their full weight behind it, they only managed to open it just enough to squeeze through. The interior was just as modest as the exterior with a dry, earth floor and no embellishments of any kind other than a crucifix hanging from the roof of the tower. It smelt rotten and the air inside was chilling. Robert sighed as he looked up at the collapsed wooden floors above which gave him a view of the ancient bell at the top of the tower. "It'd cost a pretty penny if we wanted to restore this place," he said, kicking some of the decaying floor boards which had smashed to the ground long ago.

"Some things are not worth preserving," Jack replied. "This place hasn't seen the Holy Spirit in a very long time - if ever."

"It's odd to think that the keys of consciousness the Pleiades wanted were all used right here," he mused. "Pagan, Catholic, Protestant - all merging their beliefs into sects and cults to suit their own needs - all their prayers and beliefs, interpretations of history and the teachings of the elders becoming jumbled and corrupted, generation after generation. The ancestors turn into druids who turn into monks, who turn into vicars."

"Until it all becomes gobbledygook," Jack agreed. "I wonder what the Star Children will want their spiritual leaders to look like?" He laughed. "Jedi or Storm Troopers no doubt!"

"Time for a fresh start," Robert said decidedly. "There's no point in keeping history alive if the present doesn't embrace the future as well. I hope to god that the Star Children can build a society in which religions, cultures and societies are all-inclusive without creating divisions with dogma and doctrine."

"Unlikely," Jack replied. "Human nature likes to divide and conquer. You can't change that in a hurry - if ever."

Robert wanted to hope for the best version of the future. "Any place, including Little Eden, is only worth fighting for if the people who live there open their hearts and minds. You're right, its human nature which needs an upgrade and maybe the Star Children are that upgrade?"

"Sounds like you're giving a sermon!" Jack teased him. "There's no-one here to hear you though."

Robert smiled sadly. "We only ever hear what we are ready or willing to hear anyway," he said.

"Do you think this place and the rest of the Manor, is worth keeping?" Jack asked him.

"I still don't know," Robert replied. "What happened at the stones has made me re-think about selling it. If the portal is that important, it needs to be guarded by someone - a true light worker - someone we can trust."

"Easier said than done, old boy," Jack replied. "None of us would want to come and live up here that's for sure. India won't be pleased if you don't sell it - she's hoping for some money for Little Eden."

"I'm hoping that Roger will allow us to keep the necklace," Robert said. "At least we could sell that."

"If you ever find it again," Jack told him. "I think the bogs might have claimed it, old boy. Come on, let's find Abigale and get back."

They scanned the gloomy graveyard and tried to work out where the tomb, which Sophie had described, would be.

"Do you know your trees?" Robert asked Jack. "She said it was beneath a black elder tree."

Jack shrugged. "Afraid not, old boy," he replied.

They slashed at the tall grass, uncovering hidden gravestones ravaged by the elements; choked with nettles and holly. They trampled and flattened the long, wet grass around the church and then explored the dark, dank thicket to the east side.

"Here!" Robert called out. "I think this must be it."

An oblong, sandstone sepulchre, standing about four foot high, was barely visible beneath the black, pointed leaves and the pink-white clusters of flowers of the spreading elder. Any inscriptions had been eroded away by the wind and the rain and it was almost buried in the strangling, spiky sedge.

The heavy, stone lid was brittle and rough and, as they each took an end, the edges flaked away and crumbled beneath their hands. When it slid aside far too easily, they knew they must be at the right spot.

Hardly daring to look inside, they gagged as a malodour of decay filled their nostrils and, to their dismay, a decomposed body lay on top of an old, grey, lead coffin. The skeleton still had some rags of clothing hanging from its bones and something shiny caught Jack's eye. As he reached in to touch it, he realised it was a silver necklace cast into the letter A.

They knew it had to be poor Abigale.

"We'll re-bury her properly when this is over," Robert sighed, "And I think we should gather up some of the ancestor's bones, after the flood subsides, and re-bury those in the barrows too."

Jack concurred.

They both felt pensive, pondering on life and death, as they walked back; as they approached the house Robert looked out, across the field, towards the stones and thought about Kaya still lying out there.

"You go in," Robert said, "I just want to stay out here for a while and think."

Chapter 48
~ * ~

R obert felt the ripples of spirit manifesting around him as he gazed across to the Fianna Stones. The ethereal holograms of King Arthur and Merlin, their eyes shining with blue, new matrix light, stood at the altar stone and they raised their right hands in greeting to him. In that moment he had no doubts that the manor grounds must remain under his and their protection from now on. Mother Mary shimmered into being, hovering like an angel above the dragon portal and there she would remain, invisible to the naked eye, waiting to welcome anyone who came there seeking guidance, comfort or enlightenment.

As Robert's heart and mind made the connection with her divine consciousness, his senses overflowed with such love it was almost more than a human body could stand; he fell to his knees in gratitude and awe.

Then, to his surprise, Dr G materialised, like a golden sunbeam, and joined the holy spirits amongst the stones. Robert understood the message he was being given. He must give the property into the guardianship of Dr G who would set up a second World Peace Centre. Here, the monks would anchor the new matrix consciousness of pure compassion, protecting the dragon portal and helping the new matrix vibration flow through the lay lines, far and wide across the British Isles.

The blissful stillness of his meditation filled him with such inner peace he wished the whole world could feel as he did in that moment. All too soon the vision faded and he was awakened from his reverie by the low, reverberating sound of a helicopter circling overhead.

The others had also heard the approach of the rescue helicopter and came up from the kitchen to the front porch to watch it appearing through the storm clouds over to the East.

It landed on a flat area of grass not far from the lake.

Jack went down the slope to greet the Police officers and paramedics. He took a while explaining the situation to them before they all came trooping up to the driveway, carrying a stretcher and their medical bags.

The Sergeant sent one of his officers to the stones to find Kaya's body and secure the crime scene whilst he was taken down to the kitchen to arrest Ada and Arthur, who were still locked up in the pantry. They were cautioned, handcuffed and led back upstairs. As they were steered through the front doors everyone gave them a wide birth but Ada stared at the friends and growled, "We'd still have our home and the stones if it wasn't for your meddling."

No-one replied, they just stared at her, incredulous at her total lack of remorse."

The old couple were escorted down towards the lake; needing a little extra persuasion at times.

It was decided that Jimmy should be flown to the nearest hospital for medical attention but that he didn't need to be placed on the stretcher - although he would have quite liked the attention if he had been.

Carrie, who also wanted to leave immediately, insisted that she went with Jimmy. For a moment Lucy felt a pang of envy and wanted to accompany him. Then suddenly, as she looked at him walking away his demeanour shifted and, instead of the Jimmy she knew, she saw a slimy, toad-like boggart in his place.

She gasped and shuddered with horror as she saw Ada and Arthur shape-shift into boggarts too.

She turned to look at her sister and Sophie guessed what she had just realised. "I'm sorry," Sophie said, "But Jimmy's soul has gone just like Kaya's has and I suspect Ada and her brother lost their souls to the dark Master a very long time ago."

Lucy felt too shocked to cry.

"They're going to send a boat to take us to The Boggarts Nest," Jack explained, "I've agreed to vouch for us all but, for now, we'll have to stay there until our full statements are taken."

"So it's all over?" Minnie asked. "We can go home?"

Jack put his arm around her. "It's all over now," he reassured her.

"Look!" Sophie said suddenly. She pointed towards the stones and, in the bright-blue, summer sky was a triple rainbow, as luminous and as resplendent as it could be. The pot of gold at each end was hidden amongst the trees and its glistening arcs seemed to frame the sacred site with a magical glow.

"Wow!" Lucy said. "I've never seen a triple rainbow before."

Everyone drank in the awe-inspiring moment - none of them had seen such an enchanting sight before either.

"It has to be a sign," Lucy said.

Jack was about to say that it was just a rainbow, then even he paused a moment and felt that perhaps, just this once, the trick of the light wasn't just any ordinary event but could, after all, be Heaven sent.

"I think it's a sign," Minnie said. "I think it's Father John and Isabelle telling us they are at peace."

"I'd like to think that too," Lancelot said.

As they walked, under the avenue of beeches, to meet the boat down at the ford, Jack helped Lancelot hobble along and Robert helped Sophie by taking her arm. Out of earshot of the others he told her of his plans to give the Manor to Dr G and asked for her opinion.

Sophie smiled. She thought it a fine idea. "This place makes me think of a prayer Dr G taught me," she said, "Or at least it would do if the dark side hadn't made it so oppressive and gloomy around here."

"Which prayer?" Robert asked her.

This, dear readers, is the prayer that Sophie recited out to the hills and through the woods:

> *Come, Joy Bringer Fairies bring joy into my heart,*
> *For you love with those who love with you.*
> *Singing and dancing high upon the mountain sides,*
> *I find the Holy Spirit there, who fills my heart with bliss and unending joy.*
> *Skipping and running amongst the trees and by the pebbled brooks,*
> *Great Beings of Light whom we adore,*
> *Hold our hands as we explore,*
> *Help us know great joy once more.*

As Sophie said the prayer out loud it seemed to invoke a warm breeze which went rippling through the trees and the rain drops glistened brighter in the sunshine than ever before. The whole park shimmered and shone with twinkling light, as if awakened from a terrible dream.

Everyone felt the oppressiveness lift and, for the first time that weekend, they felt their usual selves again.

The last time Lucy had walked the avenue she had felt as if she was being watched by evil spirits but now a tingle of excitement shivered through her - a familiar and welcome frisson she often felt in the woods in Little Eden - she called it her 'fairy shiver'. The invisible eyes looking out from the undergrowth now felt like good sprites and friendly fairies who were tinkering and bibbling amongst the wild flowers. A little wren pottered about on the gravel just ahead, looking for yummy insects and Lucy paused for a moment to listen to a woodpecker tapping in the trees.

The boggarts had gone.

The good fairies had returned to Malinwick Manor.

They all paused to watch some chaffinches, their blue and red feathers bobbing about in the bushes, and as Sophie glanced in the direction of the old chapel, her third-eye caught sight of some white witches, gathering nettles, elderflowers and pink purslane. One of them reminded her of Hector Livewell and she smiled to herself, imagining that in many past-lives he would have gathered his remedies from the woodlands and the hedgerows rather than buying them from a laboratory. She felt a little sorry that the ancient knowledge had been supressed and so much of it lost in translation but was glad that at least herbalists and healers were now safe from accusations of witchcraft.

Just as they reached the Lodge House, they could see an orange, inflatable rescue boat waiting for them up at the ford. As they climbed in, Sophie took one last look at the woods and thanked the Elementals for all their help. To her delight she saw the white witches, the tree spirits and the fairies waving them all goodbye.

Chapter 49
~ * ~

The boat trip back to civilisation was somewhat eerie, yet peaceful. The strangeness of the world being under water felt like drifting through Armageddon and, for a while, they felt as if they could be the only survivors left on Earth.

As they navigated onto what had been Hellifield Road, one or two people paddled by in canoes and they could occasionally see the flashing lights of the Rescue Services in the distance. Other than that, the whole area was deserted and still. As they floated by the second storey windows of stone houses, they all felt deeply sorry for those who had lost everything in the floods and thanked their lucky stars that they had been spared.

When the friends reached the edge of Boggart village the water was still several feet deep but as the road rose uphill they were able to walk the last few hundred yards to The Boggarts Nest.

They were glad to find India and Wolf waiting for them - sitting in the sunshine in the beer garden.

"I'm glad they got to you," India told them as she kissed them all. "But isn't this terrible?"

The pub was crowded with people fleeing the floods, many were left with only the clothes they stood up in. "I've asked if there is anything we can do to help," India explained as they all sat down at the slightly damp, wooden picnic table, "But I'm told that until the water subsides there is little anyone can do. Then the clean-up begins. Everyone has been working around the clock to get people out but they've told everyone to stay here, where it's safe, for now."

Lucy could feel the heartbreak of the locals. "I wish there was something we could do but perhaps kindness is all we can give any of them right now," she said sadly.

The barman spotted them and he came over with a round of drinks.

"So, yous made it through tha night then?" he asked. "These drinks are on't house."

They thanked him and ordered some food as well. They were starving hungry. "I've not got much 'cept sandwiches," he explained. "It's like feeding the five thousand 'ere at moment. Still, mustn't grumble, I'm one of tha lucky ones, we got to stay positive and just get on wi' it."

After taking their order he added, laughing, "By the way, some of locals ain't best pleased with yous lot."

"Why not?" Minnie asked.

Jack guessed why. "No-one won the bet on how long we would stay at the Manor did they?" he asked.

"Not a one," the barman replied with a grin, then he remembered about Kaya and his face became serious for a moment. "We was sorry to hear about your friend," he told them. "Bad business. Who'd a' thought Ada and her brother 'ad it in 'em to shoot someone."

"It was an accident," Robert explained, "Sort of."

"I think you'll find they've done more than just shoot Kaya," Jack said but then thought better of saying anymore and added, "Perhaps we should wait for the authorities to tell you." He nodded towards some Police officers who were taking the opportunity of a respite from their endless ordeal at a table nearby. "Buy them some drinks on us," he said.

"You'll not 'ave heard but we lost old Meg an all," the barman told them. "Died last night in't floods. Drowned."

"Oh, I am sorry," Robert replied but couldn't help wondering if it wasn't a coincidence.

The barman seemed to think that something supernatural was afoot too. "I takes it yous took back the stones just as she said you would?" he asked Robert.

Robert had a sneaky feeling that the barman might know more about the astral world than he let on. As he thought about it for a moment, his second-sight showed him the barman dressed in shining, silver armour with the golden cross - the mark of King Arthur - engraved on his chest. Robert nodded. "Yes, the Fianna Stones and the Manor will be in good hands from now on."

The barman nodded. He understood.

Robert felt sure the barman would help protect the stones until he could arrange for the Buddhist monks to come and guard the dragon portal. He suddenly felt a strong sensation of completion and a job well done.

"Here's to another dragon portal taken into the new matrix," Robert said, raising his beer to the others.

They all clinked glasses, "To the Pleaides, the Star Children and the future," they all said.

"I can't say this was much fun," Lucy said sadly. "Our road trip turned into a bit of a nightmare to say the least, didn't it? I'll be glad to get home to Little Eden."

"Sorry, old girl," Jack told her. "Next time we all go somewhere, we'll have to make sure there isn't a dragon portal nearby!"

They all laughed, except for Sophie who knew in her heart that this wasn't the last time they'd be asked to help with the ascension of the planet and of mankind but she prayed that the next time wouldn't be too soon!

Amongst the locals Robert noticed old Trevor, his son and grandson over by the snug door; they'd come outside to get a welcome bit of sunshine. Robert raised a glass to them in greeting. The three of them wandered over to the table, pints in hand, and they couldn't help themselves from asking, "So, cum on, tells us," old toothless Trevor said, "Is Malinwick Manor haunted or not?"

Everyone looked at Sophie for the answer.

Sophie smiled, saying, "Not anymore it's not."

Chapter 50
~ * ~

It was all timing,
and it is time to rejoice in celebration
The Master raises a jewelled cup over the land she loves
but does not own
it is yours again
and belongs to no-one

Rejoice in Celebration, Andrea Perry, Rise, Vocamus Press

Dear Readers,

Thank you for reading Little Eden Books 1 and 2 and now 3! I hope you enjoyed them and that you are wondering what will happen next in book 4.

Your support of me and my writing means the world to me. As you may know I have suffered with Myalgic Encephalomyelitis for nearly 30 years and am trying to help raise awareness of this misunderstood post-viral illness. I also have Fibromyalgia and Osteo-Arthritis as well as suffering with migraines, all of which make writing a long and often very painful process but hanging out in Little Eden, with the friends, keeps me going and I love to write when I can.

I am self-published as I cannot meet deadlines or do promotional activity so I rely on you, dear reader, to spread the word, leave on-line reviews and tell your friends about Little Eden as much as you can. Please consider taking a few moments to leave a review on Amazon (if you are reading on Kindle it will ask you to leave a review and on Kindle-Unlimited you'll need to make sure your e-reader goes all the way to 100% read for me to get paid and to leave a review) Reviews help other readers find Little Eden books and they mean so much to me too so if you are on Goodreads I'd really appreciate it if you'd add my novels to your to-read or read lists and leave reviews where you can.

If you would like to know more about ME please visit my blog where you'll find links to various sites.

Please feel free to join me on social media and don't forget to come and visit the little Etsy shop where you can buy hand-made healing & spiritual jewellery connected to the novels. You can walk through Little Eden in pictures on Pinterest and listen to the soundtracks on my blog as well as find more about the scrumptious bakes.

If you try any of the recipes from books 1 & 2 I'd love to see your bakes or read your comments on the Little Eden Dear Readers Facebook page where you can meet other readers and see all the latest news from Little Eden.

All my links can be found at https://linktr.ee/ktkingbooks

Lots of Love KT x

Dear Book Club readers,

I'm thrilled you're going to be reading Little Eden book 3, Haunted or Not, in your book club. Please get in touch and let me know where you are and a bit about yourselves. I love to hear from my dear readers! Connect with me via my link tree…https://linktr.ee/ktkingbooks.

I hope you enjoy the third instalment of Little Eden and that you'll look out for book 4 coming soon!

Love KT xx

Here are some question suggestions to get you started…

❖ How did the book make you feel - did you feel scared? If so what were you afraid of?

❖ Did you like that the story is set outside of Little Eden this time?

❖ Which characters did you identify with the most this time?

❖ Which parts of the story stood out to you and why?

❖ Did you believe in the supernatural elements or did you think they were fake?

❖ Did you know that KT used to work as a healer, psychic and astrologer before becoming a writer? Have you ever had a psychic or supernatural experience of your own?

❖ Have you read any gothic horror books before? Did you pick up the references to gothic horror novels, authors and films throughout the book? If so, which ones? How did this one differ from others you have read?

❖ Would you read the next book in the series?

❖ What would you say in your on-line review and why?

I'd like to say a big thank you to Andrea Perry for sharing her wonderful poetry with us again and to Louise, Sue and my dad for me helping with this novel xx

Printed in Great Britain
by Amazon